Willful Blindness

Lydia Langston Bouzaid

authorHOUSE®

AuthorHouse™
1663 Liberty Drive
Bloomington, IN 47403
www.authorhouse.com
Phone: 833-262-8899

Published by AuthorHouse 01/18/2023

ISBN: 978-1-6655-7999-5 (sc)
ISBN: 978-1-6655-7997-1 (hc)
ISBN: 978-1-6655-7998-8 (e)

Library of Congress Control Number: 2023900421

Print information available on the last page.

Any people depicted in stock imagery provided by Getty Images are models, and such images are being used for illustrative purposes only. Certain stock imagery © Getty Images.

This book is printed on acid-free paper.

Contents

Section 1

Chapter 1 End of a Marriage 1
Chapter 2 Sailing to Ireland 6
Chapter 3 Sad News 15
Chapter 4 Back in the USA 22
Chapter 5 Reading the Will 29
Chapter 6 Number Eleven Grosvenor Square 37
Chapter 7 Meeting Westminster 43
Chapter 8 Number Eleven—July 1992 48
Chapter 9 A New Home in London 55
Chapter 10 The Bombing 61
Chapter 11 Stolen Goods 69
Chapter 12 First Time to Scotland 74

Section 2

Chapter 13 Getting to Know Him 85
Chapter 14 Meeting Princess Rima—September 1992 91
Chapter 15 Life in London—October 1992 97
Chapter 16 Walking with the Prince 101
Chapter 17 The Westminsters' Dinner Dance 110
Chapter 18 Drama in the Highlands 116
Chapter 19 A Visit to the Village 126
Chapter 20 Show Down with a Prince 133
Chapter 21 Henry to Scotland 141

Section 3

Chapter 22 A Date with Destiny 151
Chapter 23 Highlands Paradise—January 1, 1995 159
Chapter 24 Rima Returns to Scotland 171
Chapter 25 Acknowledgment of a Marriage—Spring 1993 ... 179
Chapter 26 Three Days of Mayhem 183
Chapter 27 Aratex 194
Chapter 28 Sophia's Will 202

Section 4

Chapter 29 Arabia 215
Chapter 30 Abdullah's Home 228
Chapter 31 The Wedding 234
Chapter 32 Artifacts on Tour 242
Chapter 33 The Desert 246
Chapter 34 The Royal Court 253
Chapter 35 The Arabian Season 264
Chapter 36 Two Years On 270
Chapter 37 Date Night 278
Chapter 38 State Visits, 1996 and 1997 281
Chapter 39 And Then They Called Her a Whore 288
Chapter 40 Separation 297
Chapter 41 The King Comes to Scotland 303
Chapter 42 Divorce, 1998 308

Section 1

Chapter 1

End of a Marriage

*I*t was the summer of 1992 when Sophia Lawrence realized her marriage was over. She just didn't know *how* it would end. If she had ever stopped to be honest with herself, she would have realized that the union had been flawed from the start, that it had been built upon a shoddy foundation, and this inconvenient truth had plagued her for seven years.

Sophia and Edward had married suddenly in 1985 following a friend's funeral, when Sophia had felt vulnerable. She had been so overcome with heartbreak, and it had all happened so quickly, that now, ten years on, she often found herself wondering why she had married Edward to begin with.

There were, of course, the obvious practical benefits to their marriage. Edward Lawrence was, on paper if not in practice, the total package. He was a high-powered Boston lawyer descended from a long line of British aristocrats. He was handsome if boorish, intelligent if at times closed-minded, and incredibly well-mannered save for when he'd had too much to drink.

His connections, both the professional ones and those stemming from his illustrious bloodline, were nothing to scoff at either. Since her marriage to Edward, Sophia's extended family now consisted of her husband's twin brother Henry and his wife Janet and her mother-in-law, Lady Barbara Lawrence, the last daughter of the Duke of Devon.

Edward had for the most part lived up to the promises of his station, and by the summer of 1992, the Lawrences appeared to have everything one could dream of—two homes, a lovely yacht, and an enviable position in society.

They split their time between a penthouse in Cambridge, Massachusetts, filled with art and antiques that boasted stunning views of Boston Harbor and beyond, and a lovely yet modest antique farmhouse in Newport where they spent their weekends. Set on the famed Ocean Drive with a sweeping view of the Atlantic, this house was always full of young friends and guests. On such nights their home became a salon for minor society soirees that saw the mixing of former CIA agents, well-heeled scions of rich and famous families, and sailors of all kinds. The conversations around the dinner table were some of the most interesting and engaging to be found anywhere.

Saturday nights were reserved for club functions—the yacht club, the beach club, the shooting club. When not at a club, they could be found attending a variety of parties, from charity balls to waltz evenings. Sadly, these functions always included many of the same slightly boring people, endless gossip, and high volumes of alcohol consumption. These soirees also always culminated with more drinking and dancing at the local nightclub, the Sky Bar. The last song was also the same every time. Louis Armstrong's "What a Wonderful World" floated gently in one ear and out the other of a well-dressed and stumbling crowd of people too self-centered and too inebriated to grasp its meaning, let alone the irony of the whole scene.

The truth was that despite appearances, a wonderful world it was not.

After ten years, life with Edward had become routine as well—and not in a comfortable way. After a week of work, Edward would arrive in Newport in the early afternoon. His first stop would be his men's drinking club, where he would reconvene with his compatriots and drinking buddies. Then after a few sodden hours he would arrive at the house, friends in tow, demanding that an elegant dinner be served for him and his guests and generally expecting his every whim be catered to.

Dutifully, even if angry at being relegated to simply a cook, Sophia would prepare an exquisite gourmet dinner for ten to twenty people who would arrive around eight, loud, careless, and wreaking of alcohol.

This treatment of her, as little more than an adornment for Edward's social aspirations, was not limited to mealtimes either. Her fundraising and consulting projects were often and effectively belittled. "Just write a larger check, Sophia. And stop talking about it," her husband commonly remarked. There were often embarrassing remarks made at the dinner table—disparaging comments about her education, how neither William and Mary nor Boston College was in the Ivy League. Even her upbringing was called into question; apparently, California was not an acceptable place to live, not for anyone serious anyway.

While it was his general disregard that wore her down over time, there were stand-out moments of extreme cruelty. When, for example, she had been diagnosed with DCIS, a mild form of breast cancer, his answer had been that she should have both breasts removed. "After all," he had said, "a woman over thirty doesn't need tits."

While the statement itself was hurtful, his uttering it in front of twenty pale-faced dinner guests was, in Sophia's mind, simply humiliating.

Edward, the pompous Harvard-trained lawyer, was a partner in the most prestigious law firm in New England. "How proud you must be," people often crowed.

But as was always the case with Edward, the reality was far less glamorous. Alcohol and work were her husband's twin vices. Taken in tandem, this meant that he was never home on weekdays and often was out late with clients on weeknights. Sophia suspected that these clients were often women. When, early on in their marriage, she had prodded him on this subject, he had simply said that he preferred to stay in Cambridge. "Closer to my office," he had grunted, and that was the last they had spoken of it.

When they were together, the pair fought constantly. As a result of the fighting and to avoid it, she spent most of her weekdays in their home in Rhode Island, alone without Edward.

Now, at the age of thirty-one, Sophia was a waif-like woman, with the body of a ballerina. Her naturally wavy dirty-blond hair was always cut to show off her slightly patrician features and her vivid blue eyes. Most men found Sophia sexy, yet her sex life could most kindly be described as quirky. It consisted of hookups in their Cambridge apartment when Edward requested, accompanied by a lot of wine. These evenings routinely became painfully masochistic.

Intellectually, Sophia had always known the harsh realities of her marriage, yet she had never emotionally come to grips with the facts. It was her nature to be optimistic, so she had pushed through the hurtful comments, the judgments, the little criticisms, and all the other hardships to build a life for both of them.

There was, of course, an answer to the nagging question of why she had married Edward in the first place. It was an answer as deeply true as it was impractical. The truth was not so much that the wrong man had proposed to her, but that the right man hadn't.

She had told herself for years that it hardly mattered anymore. She was afraid of the stigma of being a divorced woman and petrified of the emotional toll that negotiating a divorce would entail. She had no interest in watching the sordid details of her and Edward's life play out in the small town of Newport or the hallowed halls of Boston society. She had watched the social diminution of other women who had gotten divorced in their circle, and it had been harsh. So while her marriage was at times a misery, it did provide two benefits that at this point in her life Sophia was unwilling to change: money and social standing.

It was early fall 1991, while driving home to Newport from Cambridge after a particularly violent midweek hookup, that for the first time in almost a decade Sophia consciously thought about changing her marital status. Still in pain from the sex toys Edward had used in her body the previous night, Sophia realized she was an abused woman. All the signs were there, including the bruises and the physical scars. For years she had swept them all under the rug, treated them like water under a bridge. She had told no one and stayed.

But the mind-numbing fear of what the future might hold, especially the economics of that future, kept her from acting on these thoughts.

The only thing that Edward and Sophia had in common was their mutual love of sailing. In the fall of 1991, at their home in Newport, she and Edward read the notification of a cruise celebrating the 150th anniversary of the Royal Irish Cruising Club.

Looking on as he read, Sophia commented, "That cruise would be fun! Afterward, we could fly back to cruise in Scotland and visit Barbara. It's a place we have always talked about sailing, our boat is perfect, and your mother would love having us spend more time in the UK."

"How would we get the boat there?" the ever-pragmatic lawyer asked. "I can't take that much time off from work."

"We could ship it on a freighter, or my workload is pretty light right now," Sophia said, letting the suggestion hang in the air. "I have the time, and I would love to do another ocean passage."

"That could work," Edward mused. "But ... what work does the boat need? I don't want to spend too much money."

Sophia sighed. This was expected. Even though they were by no means poor, Edward was always tight with his money.

"It will be fine, Edward. We can do a lot of the work ourselves over the winter."

Edward realized that Sophia was perfectly capable of taking the vessel across the ocean, having sailed around the world during her college gap years. She had raced her own boat in the Bermuda Race in her late twenties and presently sailed with a high-performance racing team, often traveling around the world without Edward. Therefore, without a lot of persuading, the decision was quickly made.

Chapter 2

Sailing to Ireland

Sophia's Log, June 1, 1992

We e sailed with the tide slightly after 9:00 p.m., destination Kinsale, Ireland. At our average rate of speed between 8 and 10 knots, I expect our 2,000-mile trip to take around fourteen days, weather-dependent. Our weatherman predicts calm conditions for the first week. And since we will be speaking to him daily, we will know if any gales are heading our way.

I am not up for a wild wet ride, so here's to a mild weather passage. A friend of mine once said that sailing across the ocean was tedium upon boredom interspersed with moments of sheer terror. I want boredom for this trip. I expect this to be my voyage of self-discovery.

First night out, and I have the first watch tonight: 10:00 p.m. to 2:00 a.m. We have a rotating watch system that puts teams of two on deck for the night watches 6:00 p.m. to 6:00 a.m., then a single person on deck for six hours each from 6:00 a.m. until 6:00 p.m.

Brenton light is fading into the distance as my first watch ends. Eight hours of sleep before I am back on deck. All is calm. The stars are bright.

June 2, 1992, Day 2—Cape Cod Bay headed toward Nova Scotia.

We sailed through the Cape Cod Canal at daybreak. We were supposed to motor through the canal, because the wind was behind us, so we sailed with the engine in neutral. Presently heading east-northeast along the great circle route, the shortest distance, to our destination. The breeze is a warm southerly as we head toward the Grand Banks.

A pod of gray whales joined us this afternoon. Hopefully, I got a good photo of the tail as they dove in front of us.

We are settling into a rhythm. Everyone is doing well at their daily cooking chores. We set the schedule up so the off-watch crew can make the meal. The meals' ingredients are all stowed in reverse order with instructions in the ship's notebook. So far, so good.

I awoke startled for my 4:00 a.m. watch. My old dream about Sean O'Neil has returned. It played like an endless loop in my mind for eight hours, so I don't feel very rested.

This is the dream I usually have when my life is crazy, or when I am depressed or sad. I have had it since I was seventeen. I can always see him clearly, a tall, handsome, black-haired Irishman with dark eyes. While I have known him since I was ten years old, I have not seen him for at least a decade. Today my childhood in California seems like a world away. However, the dream served to remind me that I have some serious thinking and decisions to make over the next couple of weeks. I promised myself I would begin enacting my reinvention plan when I land in Ireland.

On watch, during the day, everyone tried their hand at fishing, but only once did they catch anything—a large tuna that provided dinner and sushi for all on board. We even had soy sauce and wasabi on board, and I even knew where to find it.

Day 4—On watch heading toward Sable Island

Noon to 6:00 p.m. watch, coming up onto the Sable Bank, about fifteen miles to the south of the notorious shifting sands of Sable Island. We are approximately sixty miles from Halifax, Nova Scotia. Winds are light, seas are confused, and the fog is heavy. We received our first daily weather report this morning on the SSB. Bill Wren says the fog should lift by late afternoon. No news or word from home. Bill called Edward, but he didn't answer, so he left a message.

A pod of dolphins is following us, playing in our wake. They are so joyful. They always look like they are smiling. That must be why they are so comforting to have around.

But… my mind is not on the dolphins; it's on the damn dream.

The pea-soup fog finally broke around sunset. After my watch, I stayed on deck, watching the stars rise as the Sable Island lighthouse faded behind us into the night. We will not see another lighthouse until we reach the coast of Ireland, about ten days away. I hope all we will see for the next ten days are blue skies and indigo seas.

Day 5—Off the South Coast of Newfoundland in the Labrador Sea

It is time to worry about sighting icebergs, especially at night! Bill says we are well below the last known berg position. He is now checking in twice a day. The wind is about 15 knots, reaching along our course with the boat speed around 10 knots. Still no word from home. I would have thought Edward would have checked in at least once.

We keep trying to catch another fish, but after that first tuna, they have been elusive. Davy, the engineer, is extremely frustrated, so the crew attached a can of tuna to the line yesterday. He took it in good stride when he pulled up the can.

Today was my first day cooking. On the menu: mushroom soup made with dried mushrooms and long-life milk for lunch, then a round of bread baking and beef stew for dinner. I made the soup in our pressure cooker. I have a love-hate relationship with this machine. I love the results but hate removing the lid after it has been under pressure. Bread was from a bread mix and baked in the oven. The entire crew has quickly gotten very good at making our daily bread. It is the end of the day, and I have climbed into my bunk, ready for six hours of sleep.

Cooking sideways is never easy.

Day 6—Cape Race, Newfoundland, North Atlantic

We still have clear skies and a moderate 15-knot breeze. Bill says it will last for days. Still watching for icebergs—none so far. I have the 6:00 p.m. till 10:00 p.m. watch tonight, which gave me a brilliant view of the northern lights. They look like fireworks in the sky.

Damn, last night I dreamed about Sean again. I was back at my mother's funeral, and he was standing in the back of the church. He looked like a sea captain pacing the bridge of a ship. Sometimes I wonder if that image is really a mirage. We never spoke.

Day 7—South of Greenland

Today was the saddest day I have ever spent on the ocean. Around dawn, we came across a pod, maybe thirty sperm whales slowly making their way northeast.

At first, we were amazed and a little frightened that they let us sail so very close without diving. Then, as we sailed in among them, we discovered why.

A small group of four whales was trying to swim, sometimes dive, but were completely entangled in ghost gear. Old fishing lines and ropes were wrapped around the bodies of the two large whales in the center, while the two outer whales were connected by a rope around their dorsal fins.

We followed them for over three hours, trying to discern a way to release them. They wouldn't let us come close enough to touch the line. Our inflatable dinghy and outboard engine was stowed below, so we had no way to get close enough to help free them from the line. The crew discussed swimming, but without wet suits and the proper flotation gear, the water temperature would not have allowed us enough time to free the lines. The two outer calves were almost as large as our boat, and one flick of their tail would have rendered a swimmer unconscious. I vetoed the swimming idea quickly.

Sometimes one of the big center calves would start to sink into the water, and the outer ones would float it up. Then they would try to dive, pulling the others down with them and getting them all more tangled in the process.

We knew that our lack of ability to cut the lines had doomed the whales to eventual death—that in the end they would run out of energy, being unable to eat, and finally, maybe months from now, would drown. Just thinking about it made me cry.

Slowly, over about an hour's time, the rest of the pod turned their injured mates so they were all heading off to the north and away from us. Their plaintive cries echoed across the water for hours. Simply heartbreaking.

No news from home today. I wonder why Edward has not called Bill even once since we left Newport. It has been an entire week.

Day 8 —North Atlantic

A little cold and dreary today. Nothing significant to report. I guess Edward is too busy with his female clients to call and check in. And what does that tell you, Sophia?

Day 9—Life at Sea

Today the wind and seas kicked in—20 knots on the beam and ten-foot waves. Everyone needed to hand-steer; the seas were a bit much for Auto von Helm. It was exhilarating. We are surfing down waves at 12 knots and are still on course for Ireland. Bill says this system will die out soon, but we may have even bigger weather coming in a few days. He has left several messages for Edward but has no word from home yet.

I have managed to break my glasses. They are marginally held together with duct tape. Looks pretty goofy and not great for my consistently poor vision.

Day 10—Eastern North Atlantic

Last night the dream returned. Only this time, we were in Ireland. I felt as if some unexplainable force had been pulling me toward him again. It was a silly dream, really. He had become a duke with a big run-down house. We married, and I became a duchess. Basically, this version was a princess story straight from the pages of a Danielle Steel novel. Maybe it was because I just finished reading Five Days in Paris. *This dream really has become an obsession.*

Bill is predicting a big gale within twelve hours. Time to shorten sail and get ready for forty-eight hours of a rough ride.

Still no news from home.

Day 11—The Gale

Tonight was the first time at sea I truly believed I would die, and I honestly feel in hindsight that death was closer than any of us realized.

We were three days out from Ireland, I was on the mid-watch—midnight to four—and my little yacht was crawling and crashing upwind in the predicted force 8 gale. I was tethered to the boat, wearing a full flotation suit, when I heard and felt a loud rumble over the noise of the wind. Looking forward, I saw a flash of something silver, but it was gone too quickly for me to see what it was.

Yelling for all hands, I crash-tacked the boat. Everyone raced on deck just in time to see a white shipping container, semi-submerged, sliding down along our port side. The logo on the side was clear: Aratex Shipping.

The rumble I heard could only have come from the propeller of a ship rotating out of the water. It couldn't have been ours because our engine was off, and the fact that I could hear it over the screaming wind meant it was far too close. If any container ship was close enough for me to hear it, a collision was imminent.

I continued to focus on the now difficult job of steering the yacht safely through the waves. The rest of the evening, we all stayed up to keep a lookout at the mast, dressed in full flotation suits and life vests.

As the wind abated and other crew took the helm, I finally had time to think about the container. That container could have sunk us. It was floating high in the water, so it had yet to fill with water. It must have only recently fallen from the ship that was carrying it. Considering the proximity of the container, coupled with that awful rumble, we had very narrowly avoided catastrophe.

Now it is the next day. With everyone's emotions running high, the gale has abated, and the sun finally has broken through a blanket of gray clouds. Time to get to shore.

Day 12—After the Gale

Thankfully, today was slightly less eventful. The seas are still a little bumpy, but the wind has died down. Davy, our engineer, did essential engine maintenance, oil filters, and such. Joan cleaned the dirty bilges, and I unplugged the heads.

Today was also the smelliest and spookiest day I've ever had on the ocean. As the seas continued to calm down, we came across the foulest smell. That smell turned into an oil slick full of dead fish. They were everywhere, and the sharks, of which we saw about a dozen, were having a field day. It was a full-blown feeding frenzy. There was no place for us to go without hitting more trash—all piles of line, plastics, and ships' garbage.

By the end of the day, we came upon a dirty white factory-fishing ship flying a foreign flag no one recognized. And oh my God, the smell. Hard to believe anyone could stay on that ship with the stench, let alone eat anything that it was carrying.

We left the stinking fishing ship and its trail of fish guts behind around midnight. All through the night, we kept seeing smaller vessels on the radar. I assume they were the fishing boats returning to the factory with their catch. Davy had his hands full with the radar that night.

Day 13—Eastern North Atlantic, two days from Ireland

I have been thinking a lot about my father. He would have loved this trip. And oh, how proud he would have been of me. It is hard to believe he has been gone for only a year.

Day 14

My journal is almost empty. It can best be described as a disjointed jumble of words. Yet all my dreams have led me to question, yet again, why I ever married Edward. Why couldn't it have been Sean? Shouldn't it have been Sean? He's the one I've been dreaming of every night for God only knows how long, not the one who still hasn't even bothered to call.

Day 15—Approaching Ireland

The stars of the Milky Way are lighting up the North Atlantic as we approach the coast of Ireland. First, we smelled a tiny whiff: the faint smell of pine trees and peat fires from homes on shore mixed with the sea salt. The smell would fade away, and then, with another puff, it would return. There are still no lights in view, just a hint of change in the air.

Tonight was the final night of this trip across the pond. At first, I could see Fastnet Rocks behind me, marking the approaches to the Irish coast, and finally, I could make out a faint glimmer of lights on the shore. It's a little strange that I have not heard from Edward at all. I would have thought he would call Bill. I'll check in tomorrow. We will arrive at the harbor entrance shortly, so this is the end of my journal.

Sophia and her crew entered the harbor at Kinsale around 11:00 p.m. She had called the customs officials around six to tell them of her boat's arrival yet thought they would have to wait until morning to clear customs. As Sophia guided the little yacht toward the town dock, she realized that there was a large 180-foot navy-blue sloop docked in her space.

"That's odd," she said to her crew. "I booked this berth months ago and confirmed our arrival earlier today. Now there is someone else in it. It looks like *Andromeda La Dea*—can anyone read the name to check?"

"Yes, it is *Andromeda*," replied her navigator.

"Strange," she said. "I am going to make another pass, and we can tie up alongside them for tonight."

Swinging the little vessel around as the crew finished getting the lines and fenders ready, she noticed that two men had driven up to the quay and were presently boarding the mega-yacht to take her lines.

"Great!" she exclaimed. "We even get to clear customs tonight."

Laughing, the crew slowly docked the little Swan next to the bigger vessel. Of course, as anticipated, the noise woke up the crew and the one owner who was aboard.

The other owner, a billionaire venture capitalist, was not on board; however, his wife, noted romance author Katherine Grey, was. She was initially furious at the noise, but when her captain mentioned that her own ship had requested only mooring space, not dockage, and that the town had mentioned there might be a boat rafting alongside, she calmed down.

Katherine's curiosity was piqued when she heard that this was landfall from the USA, so she invited everyone aboard Sophia's yacht to adjourn to the larger vessel. As if the invitation for food and drink alone were not enough, it was accompanied by a potentially more tempting luxury: the opportunity for a long, hot shower.

Everyone stayed up until the wee hours of the morning, sipping champagne, eating sandwiches, and telling stories of their adventure. It was the early hours of the morning before Sophia wrote in her journal.

As Sophia went to sleep that night, she thought, *I bet this story ends up in one of her books.* She could never imagine that her real life was about to take a turn that in her wildest dreams, even Katherine could never have done justice to.

Chapter 3

Sad News

*S*ophia was dressed casually in stretch jeans, a beige cotton cable-knit sweater, and boat shoes. Her curly reddish-blond hair was loose and flowing in the wind while she read the international paper, catching up on the news of the world.

The crew was sleeping below while Sophia was relaxing on deck with a cup of coffee, her first with real milk in weeks. She'd had only a couple of hours of sleep and was slightly hungover from last night's champagne on *Andromeda*.

Looking up, she watched two uniformed men crossing over the inside yacht, heading toward her vessel. "Mrs. Lawrence, welcome to Ireland." The officer looked exceedingly uncomfortable while the second man held back, as if waiting for instructions.

"It's good to be here," she said. "Are you from customs? I thought we sorted everything last night. Do you need more paperwork or to see our passports again?"

"No, ma'am," he replied. "We're from the police department, not customs. Is there a place we could speak privately?"

Wondering why these men were here if they were not from customs, she replied, "Please come on board," and motioned to the cockpit as a place to sit.

One of her crew members, Joan, came on deck and offered everyone coffee.

Finally, Sophia asked, "Is there a problem?"

After a long pause one of the officers spoke. "We're sorry to be here, Mrs. Lawrence, but we need to inform you that your husband was killed in an auto accident in the United States. The authorities and your in-laws wanted you to know. They've been waiting for your arrival."

Sophia gazed at the officer as she ran her hands through her hair and then shook her head in denial. "I don't understand. What are you talking about?"

"Your husband, Edward Lawrence," the man said, nervously stumbling over his words. "He was in an auto accident in Massachusetts. From what we've been told, he slid off the road at high speed, hitting a copse of trees. He died instantly. He didn't suffer at all."

Staring at the officer, as if trying to comprehend what he was saying, Sophia held her hands in front of her face, almost as if in prayer.

The policeman continued, "It happened on June 3."

The mention of the date made her turn her head sideways. "You mean twelve days ago?" She thought back—where had they been twelve days ago? She had been about sixty miles from Halifax, chatting daily with her weather forecaster on the single sideband. Again, she shook her head. "I'm sorry, I don't understand."

Slowly, hat in hand, the policeman explained again. "Your husband was killed in a car accident twelve days ago. Your brother-in-law, Dr. Henry Lawrence, is waiting for you to call."

Finally, what the men were saying began to sink in. She waved her hands in front of her face as if to bat away something, and then the tears began to stream down her cheeks. "Edward is dead?"

The policeman, looking down, unable to meet Sophia's gaze, asked, "Do you wish to make the overseas call from our station?"

Nodding yes, as if in a trance, Sophia walked across Main Street to the police station, where they provided her a phone line to the US.

Sophia called Henry's number at the Mayo Clinic, and his secretary answered. When Sophia asked for Henry Lawrence, the assistant said, "He is in a meeting now and can't be disturbed. Maybe I help you?"

"This is his sister-in-law calling from Ireland. He can get out of his damn meeting to talk to me!" Sophia sobbed into the phone.

"Right, I'll see what I can do," his secretary replied, startled.

Sophia waited on hold for what felt like ages before Henry finally came on the other end of the line.

"Sophia, I—"

"What happened?" she interrupted with a hiccup, attempting to collect herself.

"Oh, Sophia, I'm glad you finally called." His voice sounded clipped, as if she had irritated him. "You should have called sooner."

Sobbing, Sophia wailed, "Henry, we only arrived in Ireland last night. How could I have called sooner? The police just told me Edward died two weeks ago. Is that true? Henry, two weeks ago, I was only sixty miles from Halifax. Why didn't you have me notified via the SSB—tell me what happened?" By now, she was hysterical.

With a slightly kinder voice, Henry said, "I am sorry, Sophia. Edward was on his way back to Cambridge from Newport. He must have been drunk, and he drove off the road. He was killed instantly, so thankfully, he did not suffer. And given his state of intoxication, we're all very grateful no one else was hurt or involved. That would have been a mess. Since we couldn't get a hold of you, we had the funeral last week in Cambridge."

Sophia was having trouble breathing. In almost a whisper she said, "What do you mean, you couldn't get hold of me? I spoke to our weatherman ever day! And the fax I sent to both you and your wife gave you all the details to get a hold of us."

"Yes, Sophia, you might have, but we couldn't find the fax, so we honestly didn't know how to reach you. Edward was in Newport when he heard that our stepmother Barbara had had a stroke and died. Once the accident happened, we were pressed for time because we needed to also have a funeral in England. It's been hectic, and my wife and I have had our hands full organizing everything since you were somewhere out in the ocean. We just got home ourselves.

You have a mess to clean up when you finally get home. There are bills to pay, the will to sort out."

And then the full impact of what he had said hit her. "Wait, Henry, did I hear you correctly? Barbara's dead? You're telling me that Barbara died, and Edward got so drunk that he had a car accident and killed himself?"

Curtly, Henry remarked, "I am going to London next week. I have to go back to my meeting, Sophia. Call when you land if you need anything."

Sophia was blowing her nose and wiping her face, trying to calm down. But she couldn't understand what Henry was saying. "Wait, Henry, am I missing something here? Why do you need to go back to England if the funeral was last week?"

"There is still some paperwork to finish before they can adjudicate Barbara's will. Even though you are the heir to Edward's estate, given that the deaths were only hours apart, it's not clear what Edward will inherit. As usual, I'll take care of everything overseas."

Sadness was rapidly being replaced by fury. Quickly trying to regain her composure and her ability to think, she asked Henry for the contact details for Barbara's solicitor.

Henry was slow to respond yet eventually provided her the details. "The reading of Barbara's will is this Friday in London."

By now, Sophia had stopped crying and was looking at a calendar on the wall of the police station. She was quickly formulating a plan, and given the outright disdain Henry was displaying, she realized there would be no room for histrionics. "I will see you in London on Friday, Henry. I have to go now."

Worry marred Sophia's features as she walked the short distance back to the boat. She told the crew her sad news and started preparing to head back to the States. Her crew agreed to find a marina where they could store the vessel long-term since Sophia now had no idea of her schedule.

The entrance to Kinsail is an old Roman fortification overlooking the harbor. She had several hours to wait before her cab to the airport in Cork, so she decided to go for a walk to the entrance of the harbor. It had been less than twenty-four hours since she and her crew had rounded this point of land. Then they had been basking in the glow of the accomplishment of sailing across the Atlantic. Now at the age of thirty-one, she was sitting on the edge of an ancient embankment, thinking about her future.

Her mind wandered off, thinking about the battles that had been fought for this little town and then back to Henry. *I guess,* she thought, *I have a battle on my hands both in the USA and in England.* For her entire life, especially after years of adversity with Edward, Sophia had practiced burying her emotions and soldiering on in the face of crisis. Knowing this, Sophia promised herself that she would face the upcoming months and weeks with thoughtful dignity, no matter what happened.

She was immensely saddened at the death of her mother-in-law, knowing she would miss her as much as she did her own mother. She thought back lovingly to their last conversation, when they had been planning a girls' getaway to Paris.

When she thought about Edward, she felt almost no emotion at all. It was as if a void had been created in her mind. When she thought about Henry, though, her anger overflowed. His cold, calculating manner had frightened her, and she wondered what he knew that she did not. She felt threatened and vulnerable.

Her friend and crew member Joan found her still sitting by the Fort several hours later, and the two women walked back to the boat for a light supper before she headed to the airport.

She slept fitfully on the six-hour flight across the Atlantic. As the plane landed, the advice she gave herself was to listen to her legal counsel and think clearly. Because she had nothing else to do—no service, no funeral to plan—she decided the best method for coping with the grief she felt was to make a plan for her future.

Wearing jeans and a white oxford shirt, with a sweater around her neck, Sophia looked like a preppy Ivy League student as she entered her apartment in Cambridge. It was precisely as it had been left, save for the accumulated pile of mail, mostly junk, that sat on the kitchen counter. Her clothing still hung in the closet, as did

Edward's. The space was neat and clean. It was a time capsule of a life now gone.

As she was changing her clothing, she could not help but remember that she had not always liked or enjoyed her life in their Cambridge apartment.

Finally, after one more cup of coffee she did not need, she went across the river to her attorney's office. There were no surprises in Edward's will. Everything had been jointly owned and was now hers to do with as she pleased.

The next topic her lawyer raised was something she had not yet thought about. "You know, Sophia, that because Barbara died before Edward, you will receive his portion of the estate. Additionally, I have it on excellent authority, even though I'm not supposed to divulge the contents, that you are individually named with several bequests.

"I do find the letter we received from Henry's attorney last week strange. It stated that you would be relinquishing any claim you have to Edward's estate in England. When I called, his lawyers implied that you had discussed this with Henry and agreed. Since you were not available, I didn't understand how you would have decided this. They even asked me to sign with your power of attorney. I declined on your behalf."

Looking pensive, she said, "This is bizarre considering Henry made no attempt to contact me."

"To be fair, Sophia, you were incommunicado."

"No, I was not!" she snapped. "I spoke to someone from the weather routing service every day. Henry and Janet both had his phone number. Twelve days is a long time. What do you think Henry is up to? I won't be relinquishing anything."

"Good. I am not certain that the UK lawyer has been as forthcoming with Henry about the division of property. The final reading of Barbara's will is scheduled for this Friday."

"Yes, Henry let that slip out in our conversation yesterday. After some loud tears on my part, he also finally gave me the contact details for the lawyer on the phone. I have spoken to Sir Joshua Reynolds, who told me the date and time of the reading and admonished me not to be late. I wonder why Henry thought I didn't need to be there. I am leaving for London tomorrow night. Do I need to hire an English lawyer?"

"I would say yes," he replied. "I can recommend David Grosvenor and will arrange a meeting for you immediately. My advice would be to have him with you on Friday."

"I want someone who is very good," Sophia said. "Barbara's lawyers are Reynolds and Winston, members of the Magic Circle."

"You will be just fine with David Grosvenor. Just to make certain, let's call Reynolds and Winston now. I think Sir Joshua will be available. We should confirm that you will be attending."

The operator at Reynolds and Winston quickly put the call through to Sir Joshua Reynolds. "Good afternoon, Paul," Sir Joshua said. "Have you spoken to Sophia yet?"

"Yes, sir," he replied. "She is with me right now. We're just confirming the time and place again. I also have a professional question for you. Should Sophia have her English solicitor in attendance?"

The older gentleman sighed. "Of course, if you believe it is necessary."

"The reason I am asking is that Dr. Lawrence is requesting that Sophia relinquish any claim she may have on the estate. Obviously, we find that a little odd, so I have advised her to hire David Grosvenor as separate counsel."

Hearing the name, Sir Joshua let out a throaty laugh. "Yes, I know young David and most of his family. If it is David, please include him. Tell him I suggest he sit in the gallery."

Chapter 4

Back in the USA

*U*pon returning to the apartment in Cambridge, Sophia realized it had never truly been her home. Making a mental note to put it up for sale, she finished some organizing, emptied the refrigerator and garbage, checked the mail, paid the unpaid bills, and collected some of her clothing to prepare to drive to Newport. Walking out of the lobby of the building, she casually mentioned to the live-in manager that their penthouses—they owned two combined into one—would soon be up for sale. The building was a cooperative apartment, so the manager would be part of any sales team for the unit. She mentioned an asking price, and his immediate response was that it was far too high.

She smiled at him. "My asking price is firm." She knew that her neighbor in the opposite penthouse wanted to own the entire floor and that he could pay that price at the drop of a hat.

As Sophia drove to Rhode Island, she called her friend Douglas Winthrop, a prominent investment manager in New York. After explaining her news, including the possible inheritance from her mother-in-law, she finally said, "I want to sit down with you and make certain you will manage everything. Are you free tomorrow?"

"I am. I can drive to Rhode Island if you like."

"Thank you," she replied. "I'm taking the evening flight back to London from JFK tomorrow."

"Sophia, you just got home."

"I know, I know. I'm taking the Concorde. I'll be in London by Thursday morning. That gives me a day to meet my new lawyer and prepare for battle. Believe me, Doug, I have a feeling that's exactly what this is going to be."

She hung up, thinking about what to expect in London. Given the information from her lawyer, she realized that her trip to the UK might take a month or two. Her thoughts on her way home to Newport alternated between wondering what she would find in the pile of mail there and worrying about what to pack. She decided about halfway home that figuring out what to pack would be easier than worrying about things she could not control, and she focused on that for the rest of the drive.

Sophia loved clothing and jewelry. Her closets were full of beautiful cocktail dresses and stylish designer work outfits. Every outfit was stored in an individual clothing bag with detailed descriptions of which accessories and jewelry to wear with each outfit. As night fell, she had packed two suitcases with a well-thought-out work wardrobe and booked herself a one-way first-class flight from New York to London.

She laughed when the manager of the Cambridge co-op called to inform her that two parties were interested in the unit. Both were willing to pay over her asking price. Typical of Sophia, she immediately responded. "Fine, the first person with an offer of over five for both of them with a nonrefundable deposit wins."

He called her back in twenty minutes, with a final offer of five and a half. Resisting the urge to gloat, she gave the manager Doug's address in New York for all further communications.

That evening, she sat on her porch in Newport looking over the ocean, vacillating between gazing out over the water, wondering what her life would be like in the future, and writing to-do lists. Intellectually, she wanted to look forward.

Her mail contained a myriad of condolence letters, all of which mentioned what a warm and loving husband Edward had been. The juxtaposition between the heartfelt sympathy and the reality of her marriage to Edward made her feel uncertain of her future. Finally deciding that the obligatory responses to the cards could wait—after all, some were now two weeks old anyway—she went to sleep.

The following bright summer day, a limousine dropped her at the airport for her flight to New York. Doug and Sophia had been friends for decades. For years, she had sailed and raced with him worldwide, and he had supported many of her charities. Sophia confidently walked into Doug's plush office high atop the Chrysler Building wearing a fitted navy-blue power suit with three-inch nude heels. Over coffee, she outlined her ideas for the liquidation of the apartment and asked Doug if he would negotiate the separation from the legal practice with Edward's partners. Doug agreed to handle everything and walked her through the paperwork for new accounts. She authorized a power of attorney and was finally starting to feel a little more in control of her life.

Philosophically, she told Doug, "It will be fine. I have a lovely art collection, a lovely home, and good friends. I'm thirty-one, single, and financially independent. I can rebuild my life." Still, the emotional toll showed on her face. Her eyes were red, and she could not talk about Barbara without crying.

Doug was a tall, dark-haired (if slightly balding) man about ten years older than Sophia. She and Doug had been like brother and sister for many years, and he was worried about her. "Please, Sophia, keep me informed. If there is anything I can do to help, all you need to do is call. I know it is a little soon to plan fun adventures, but our next regatta is in Palma in August. I hope you will be joining us, or do I need to find a new navigator? Your friend Juan will be there."

Desperately trying to put on a brave face, she replied, "I will be there with bells on."

The first-class seats on the Concorde were beds, yet her mind was so filled with anticipation and worry about Henry and Janet that she could not sleep. The only contact she'd had with either of them since her call with Henry on Monday had been a terse note from Janet telling her they would be staying at the Berkley.

As the surgeon for most of the royal families in the Middle East, Dr. Henry Lawrence had acquired a stature in the medical world that set him apart from his peers, which he wore like a badge of honor, never letting anyone forget how important he was. On the surface Henry exuded a charming social persona. But she had heard his nasty side remarks about some of her friends, similar to those that Edward, his identical twin, used to make.

Their mother had been a founding member of the United Nations. Their father, David Lawrence, had been a famous World War II correspondent from London. Barbara Devon Lawrence had been the boys' stepmother. Because of their well-traveled and slightly aristocratic upbringing, both twins had a slightly pompous air about them.

Janet had been born in Montreal, the only child of a minor timber baron. She had enjoyed a privileged childhood, growing up with doting parents, immense amounts of travel, and exemplary private schools. Her father's small accumulated fortune had dwindled with bad business decisions, so her inheritance, often discussed, was relatively small. Janet had become a typical well-heeled midwestern housewife. She was a board member of the Rochester Museum of Modern Art, a division of the Museum of Modern Art in New York. A fine arts graduate of Concordia University, she was well versed in art history and knew many art galleries and dealers worldwide.

At heart, however, Janet was a snob with a mean streak. She continually looked down at Sophia over her patrician nose, with a glare that said, "You are a nobody."

Gossip was her intellectual fuel. Always current with who was in and out in Rochester and New York City society, she had an open adulation for the high-fashion, high-spending wives and doyens of New York that made Sophia shake her head in amazement. On Henry and Janet's annual visits to Newport, Sophia was routinely handed a list of who's who and badgered for introductions. Sophia hated gossip of any kind and found this behavior offensive.

While Henry's attitude toward Sophia never could have been described as warm, he had always at least been cordial, so his recent open hostility was strange to say the least. They were a well-off couple, and his requests to her attorney had frightened Sophia, making her wary of their upcoming meeting. Realistically, Sophia understood that while they had been related by marriage for seven years, there was no strong bond between the families.

Then she pondered what she actually knew about Barbara's estate. To the best of her knowledge, Barbara owned a home in London and a small cottage in Scotland, as well as a stunning art collection. Sophia had no knowledge of, and had never thought to ask her mother-in-law about, her finances. Sophia had always loved staying at the flat in the Royal Borough of Kensington, though "flat" was a misnomer. It was two three-story townhouses merged into one spectacular home. Filled with stunning eighteenth- and nineteenth-century art, the house also showcased treasures from Barbara's travels around the world.

Sophia had been to the little cottage in Scotland only once and did not remember much about the area. It was located in the tiny village of Carrick, which was maybe one or two streets wide and boasted a population of around one hundred. She remembered a small four-bedroom dower house set between two large estates.

Finally, feeling worn out yet unable to sleep, Sophia began reading her latest romance novel. She finished the book as the plane touched down at Heathrow an hour early.

Her driver was waiting to take her to the Connaught, an exclusive luxury hotel near Hyde Park Corner and Buckingham Palace. Knowing that Henry and Janet were staying at the Berkley in Kensington, Sophia hoped the Connaught, located in the Mayfair district of London, would give her some anonymity. As she exited the cab, a uniformed doorman opened her door. Asking her name, he offered her tea while her room, the Princess Suite, was finished being prepared.

Her suite was elegant. Consisting of three spacious rooms with a balcony overlooking the square, it was pale beige and green with subtle adornments on the walls. The living suite had a sofa and two chairs. In one corner was a small desk, including a printer, and on the wall was an old French provincial commode repurposed into a small bar and coffee station. On a table was a stunning bouquet of fresh flowers with a note that read "Welcome to the law office of Sir Joshua Reynolds." Soon after she was escorted to her room, a maid arrived to unpack her bags and ask what she wanted for breakfast service.

After a quick shower in the luxury bathroom containing both a shower and a spa tub, Sophia dressed in a bespoke fitted navy-blue dress, patterned after one Barbara had shown her from House of Worth, for her midday meeting.

Then she went down to the Savoy Grill for a light lunch with David Grosvenor, her new attorney. He seemed young to Sophia, maybe only a couple of years older than herself. He was slightly built, about the same height as Sophia, and his light brown hair was trimmed to perfection. His aviator glasses showed off his deep brown eyes. Despite his youthful age, he had an air of confidence about him that put her at ease. He explained the process of reading the entire will and that there would be a gallery of people who were all stakeholders in the document.

Sophia was curious about this, and he explained that the servants and other employees from the estates were all included. Sophia paused. "There were only three employees at each house," she said, "so that is six people—twelve if you count their spouses."

David smiled and said, "Not to worry, Sophia. It will be a small gallery."

It was a bright summer afternoon, and the sun was still high in the sky, so as a personal treat to keep herself from being overwhelmed, she spent the rest of the afternoon walking from the exclusive Mayfair district in the city of Westminster to Kensington, past Buckingham Palace. A left-hand turn at the hotel took her past the Italian embassy and the grand eighteenth-century houses in Mayfair, each sitting on an entire city block, then past Wellington Arch, designed to commemorate Britons' victory in the Napoleonic Wars. She marveled at the feeling of history and how wonderful London was. Finally, she headed past the Berkeley toward her favorite department store, the iconic Harrods, to window-shop. From Harrods, ambling the cobblestone backstreets brought her to Barbara's flat in Kensington. She considered knocking on the door, but not knowing who was there, she decided to wait.

Crossing the street to the private gardens filled with summer flowers in the center of Queens' crescent, she sat on a marble bench and looked at the houses while pondering her future. Slowly, she was formulating a new plan. *I love this city*, she thought. *Maybe I could find a cute little flat and reinvent myself here. The boat could stay in the South Coast. That would be a great way to start a new single life.*

The house next door, was an exact replica of Barbara's. Sophia vaguely remembered that it was owned by an Arabian prince. Finally, becoming tired, she walked to Kensington Gardens, past the Serpentine, before heading back toward Marble Arch, the formal entrance to Buckingham Palace, and finally her hotel.

By the time she arrived at her hotel, she was exhausted. Tomorrow would be a busy day. After a light dinner of Dover sole and one glass of crisp French white wine, she went to sleep dreaming about reinventing herself in London. Yes, this could be the new life she had been looking for.

Chapter 5

Reading the Will

*T*he following morning, Sophia's wake-up call came promptly at
eight. Five minutes later, the maid arrived with her breakfast, a
pot of strong coffee, and a pot of steamy foamed Irish cream. After
setting out Sophia's breakfast, the woman asked, "What can I get
from your closet and lay out for you to wear today, madam?" Then
she added, "After your shower."

This type of service was in a league that Sophia was totally
unaccustomed to, but she told the maid what she wanted to wear
and went to take her shower. Once she was dressed a driver was
waiting for her in the lobby.

Located in the Mayfair district of London, the prestigious law
firm of Reynolds and Winston was housed in a massive eighteenth-
century Grade I listed building. It looked more like a church than
an office building. Sophia arrived fifteen minutes early, dressed
in a navy-blue suit and court shoes. To remind everyone what her
relationship was with the family, she was wearing both her wedding
ring and, more importantly, her engagement ring, which had been
given to Edward by Barbara.

A uniformed doorman escorted her into the large meeting
hall that formed the center of the building. The three-story room
had mahogany paneling and a vaulted rotunda ceiling. The first
floor walls were almost entirely bookshelves, and a massive square

mahogany table set with eight straight-backed Georgian chairs covered in dark green velvet filled the center of the room. The second floor was the gallery, where bench seats for visitors were gently illuminated by massive stained-glass windows depicting the coronation of King Henry VIII. The vaulted ceiling was painted with different scenes from London's history, from the Tudors through Queen Elizabeth II's coronation.

Sir Joshua Reynolds was a portly man with steely blue eyes. He was impeccably dressed in a dark gray English-style three-piece suit. He welcomed Sophia warmly and signaled to his staff, who promptly provided her with water, a notepad, and a fountain pen. They motioned for her to sit alone on one side of the table, in a center seat facing the gallery.

As the time for the reading approached, she watched the upper gallery fill up with dozens of individuals. Some appeared comfortable in their finery while others looked a bit stilted, as if they had hurried to find their Sunday best for the trip to London. Her lawyer, David Grosvenor, who was dressed in an impeccable pin-striped suit, nodded and smiled at her as he took his seat in the front row of the gallery.

Henry and Janet arrived with their solicitor, an older gray-haired gentleman dressed in a blue pin-striped suit. Henry was wearing a navy blazer and khaki sport pants—a bit too casual, thought Sophia. Janet wore a flouncy summer dress that would have been more appropriate at a garden party than at the reading of a will. Their legal counsel sat between them, and the trio faced Sophia. A team of three lawyers had piles of folders set up to her left side, and to her right, Joshua Reynolds sat alone.

"Good morning, ladies and gentlemen," Sir Joshua Reynolds began, nodding to those assembled at the table and to the gallery. "We are here today to perform the reading of the last will and testament of Dame Barbara Devon Lawrence. Her will is long and filled with detailed instructions, so please refrain from any comments until the document has been read in its entirety."

With that, he began reading aloud. "I, Barbara Devon Lawrence, being of sound mind and body, do hereby bequeath all my worldly possessions in accordance with the terms and conditions laid out in this document.

"First, I would like to list the gifts set forth to various individuals who have worked for me, and with me, over the long years of my life. You have been the backbone of my existence and in many ways made me what I am today."

As the lawyer began to read the appendix outlining each gift, Henry promptly interrupted, ignoring Sir Joshua's earlier request. "Can't we just summarize these little things and get on with it?"

Sir Joshua shook his head. "No, sir, we cannot," he said brusquely. "In *this* country, it is customary to read the entire document aloud. As you may have noticed, while I sat you, your wife, and Mrs. Sophia Lawrence at this table, there is a full gallery behind you. It is their legal right to listen and hear the entire document as well! Especially as it pertains to them!"

Henry sneered at the man before nodding begrudgingly for him to continue. Sophia had to suppress a smile at her brother-in-law's annoyance.

"I hereby bequeath cash gifts of 20,000 pounds each to my entire personal staff, both past and present, at all my houses in London and Scotland. Other bequests are to the Victoria and Albert Museum, the Royal Marsden Hospital, the National Trust, and the Heritage Trust of Scotland, each in the amount of two million pounds."

At the mention of the words "both past and present," Henry, Janet, and Sophia looked quizzically at the lawyer. Sophia glanced at the gallery and finally realized that there were many individuals she had never met.

The list was long, and by the time it had been read, millions of pounds in gifts had been dispersed. A visibly irritated Henry was muttering to himself. Sophia was just curious.

The attorney turned toward the table and said, "As you may or may not know, Barbara owned many properties that she inherited from her father, the Duke of Devon. This is the portion of the will that I advise you to listen to carefully and hold your questions.

"I love my two stepsons, Henry and Edward. I also dearly love my daughter-in-law Sophia as if she were my own daughter. Therefore, the balance of the division of my personal property is in line with my view of my stepchildren. I hereby leave my family home at Number Eleven Grosvenor Square and the manor house and castle at Carrick as well as the artwork, but not the furnishings and personal possessions, equally one-third each, to Henry Lawrence and thence to his heirs, Edward Lawrence and thence to his heirs, and Sophia Lawrence and thence to her heirs. If either of my stepsons shall predecease me, their shares of this estate shall pass to their heirs, except in the event Edward shall predecease me; then Sophia Lawrence shall be entitled to his share of the estate."

Sophia turned toward Sir Joshua her face clearly asking the unspoken question, Did I hear that correctly? The twinkle in his eyes told her she had. *Ouch*, Sophia thought. *That takes care of one issue.*

Henry opened his mouth as if to speak and then hesitated, as if he'd thought better of it. Then changing his mind, he said, "That's not fair. They were about to get divorced! Edward told me that. Why, they barely even lived together!"

Sophia was so stunned at his red-faced outburst that she gaped at Henry but had no comment, which was just as well because Sir Joshua certainly did have one.

"Henry, one more outburst, and I will find that you are trying to contest this will. And as you will find out, if you do, there are grave consequences built into this document!" Sir Joshua snapped.

Henry said nothing, but just glared at Sophia and Sir Joshua as the old man read on with a slight note of defiance in his voice.

"The balance of my estate is held in the Devon Realty Trust. I again authorize these assets to be split into three equal portions, with the same stipulations as provided above." The solicitor droned on for thirty minutes, describing the property. However, Sophia was so dazed that she barely heard a word he was saying.

"The cottage at Carrick Castle and my flat located at Number Three Queens' Gate in Kensington, including art, jewelry, furnishings, and other personal possessions in these dwellings and their associated outer buildings, are left solely to Sophia Lawrence. At my home in London, Sophia will find all the documents for the personal possessions, land, stock, et cetera that have been separated as her share of my estate."

Sophia closed her eyes, trying to keep her face from showing any emotion. She was shocked. This morning she had believed that her presence here would be strictly as Edward's widow, not as a principal of the will itself. Her head was spinning.

"Mrs. Lawrence?" Sir Joshua inquired. "Is everything all right?"

"Yes, sorry, fine. Continue," she managed with a mouth gone suddenly dry.

This couldn't be real, she thought, but one look across the table at Henry pulled her back to reality. Henry's face was a darker shade of red than before, and he was squirming in his seat. In contrast to her husband, Janet was as white as a ghost. *This*, thought Sophia, *will be one hell of a battle.*

"The balance of personal property, including furniture located at both Number Eleven Grosvenor Square and Carrick Castle, is the sole possession of Sophia Lawrence except for mementos that reflect each individual stepson's childhood.

"The artwork located at Number Eleven Grosvenor Square and Carrick Castle will be split equally between the three parties. The five exceptions to this division are as follows:

"The two massive marine oil paintings by Turner located in Castle Carrick, the two Gainsborough paintings also at Castle Carrick, and the Sisley, which currently hangs over the fireplace in the library of Number Eleven Grosvenor Square, shall become the exclusive property of Sophia Lawrence."

Sophia, realizing that these five paintings alone were worth a small fortune, gasped aloud.

"The sole executor of my estate shall be Sophia Lawrence, who I trust will be scrupulously fair in overseeing the distribution of my assets and ensuring that both of my stepsons receive their allotted benefit from this will.

"Lest anyone named in this will feel that it can or should be contested, I have attached three medical warrants of fitness dated this week. This will attest to my mental and physical fitness to ensure that no one can dispute the contents herein. Furthermore, I affirm that to the best of my knowledge, none of the principals named had any knowledge of the additional properties listed herein.

"While I hope that no one is disappointed, all of you must remember that it is within my power to leave my possessions to anyone I wish. If this will seems biased toward Sophia, understand that it was my wish to make sure she is taken care of no matter what the future holds.

"If this will is contested in any way, then under the terms of this document, the will is broken. The party who by any means breaks the intent of this document shall immediately forfeit their rights, and their share of the estate is to immediately revert equally to the other parties.

Sophia touched her head as if she had a headache, reminding herself not to show any outward signs of fear. *Be calm, Sophia. That's what Barbara would have wanted.*

The attorney continued. "You must each sign your acceptance of the will today. If you do not acknowledge your agreement via signatures by midnight tonight, then your share of any sales' proceeds will be donated equally to the charities named in Appendix A."

When Sir Joshua Reynolds was finished, everyone in the room was silent. "Are there any questions?" he asked, looking from Henry to Janet and then to Sophia.

Sophia was the first to speak. "No, sir, not at this time. I'm a little overwhelmed, so I may have some later if you don't mind. I'm happy to sign my acceptance of the will now."

Janet could not restrain herself any longer. "This is absurd! I won't sign it," she yelled. "It's not fair! Edward's part should go to Henry, not Sophia, or get split between the two of us. She is no relation to Barbara at all, simply a trophy wife for Edward. She didn't leave me anything!"

Their solicitor looked shocked at her outburst, then said, "Maybe we should step outside and discuss this."

"No!" she stated again. "I don't need to step outside. I won't sign it!"

She was so loud and aggressive that the assembled group looked embarrassed.

Henry interceded. "Shut up, Janet. You're not even being asked to sign, and I will execute the damn document now." He was fuming with rage but did not want to give Sophia any excuse to take more control than she had just been given. Janet glared at her husband but stopped speaking.

Once the document was signed, Sir Joshua said quietly, "The boxes you see lined up on each side of the room are an accurate inventory of all the properties. Every piece has been cataloged and appraised by Sotheby's. Sophia, you will find an additional inventory for your personal properties at your new home.

"I have put together sets for both of you. The originals will remain here at our office, in case there are any missing pages," Sir Joshua concluded.

As Sophia was putting on her suit jacket, she casually asked Sir Joshua, "When can we gain access to Number Eleven?"

Hearing her question, Henry bellowed across the room, "You don't need that, Sophia. I am certain the lawyers will take care of everything." Then to no one in particular, he added, "See? She is overwhelmed already. Unfit for the task."

With a look of total disdain Sophia responded, "I cannot do the job I've been tasked with if I don't go to the property."

"What if you steal something?" he said, so crudely that all present, including some individuals still in the gallery, were taken aback.

Then Sir Joshua interceded. "Henry, Sophia is correct. She can't do her job without access. It will be an even longer process if you do not honor your recent signature and start jousting and contesting. If you wish to go with Sophia, then by all means, you have the right to see the building."

Sophia went around the table to thank Sir Joshua. She was slightly surprised when he took her arm and ushered her into his private office just off the conference room. "As a trustee," he said, seeing Henry start toward them.

At Sir Joshua's rebuff, Henry turned and stomped away to find his attorney.

In his large mahogany-paneled office filled with art and photos of himself with his famous clients, Sir Joshua paused, looking at Sophia's attractive features slightly shadowed with worry, and then began speaking. "This is not an ordinary trusteeship, Sophia. From today forward, you control 60 percent of a multimillion-dollar corporation. The details of your personal estate balance will be found in Kensington. This is not ordinary power. In fact, it is immense power, especially in the hands of one young woman. Don't ever forget that. Believe me, Henry will never let you forget your duty.

"My advice is to take it slow and start with Number Eleven. Your instincts to start the viewing today are sound. I urge you not to be hurried by others. From the basement to the attic, that building, including the retainers who serve it, holds generations of information and wealth historically and monetarily, some of which is not written in the pages of this will. Most importantly, from now on, I firmly counsel you to choose your friends and confidants very wisely."

Sophia was slightly confused at Sir Joshua's characterization of the will. She thought she had just inherited 66 percent of the estate and still had no idea of its value. Not wanting to seem ignorant, she decided not to question his statement about "60 percent of a multimillion-dollar corporation."

Instead, Sophia said simply to Sir Joshua, "Thank you for that advice, sir. It is a perspective I shall endeavor to keep in the forefront of my mind. And thank you for your faith in me as the sole trustee—I will not disappoint either you or Barbara's trust in me."

"Oh, Sophia, while I believe you can handle the job better than anyone, I advocated very strongly that we share the job equally, but Barbara was insistent that it be you and you alone. I think from what I have seen so far, you will be perfect. However, whenever you need guidance, I will be available. I am looking forward to working with you."

Chapter 6

Number Eleven Grosvenor Square

Sophia, Henry, and Janet, along with their attorneys, walked out of the lawyer's office to a sunny London afternoon. The sky was a pale blue with white wisps of clouds. The city's noise was a cloak that covered everyone's different moods.

Sophia hailed a taxi and, nodding toward Henry, said, "Shall we take one cab?" It was more of a rhetorical question. Their legal teams had followed their clients outside and were also waiting for cabs, but it was rush hour.

"No, we'll take two," said Henry gruffly. "This is a total waste of time."

By now Sophia was becoming angry at Henry's attitude. As the first cab arrived, and she started to get into it, her lawyer David, who had heard the exchange, jumped into her taxi. "You don't mind if I join you, do you? The other lawyers are also joining us. I overheard them," he said with a lopsided grin.

"Mind? Of course not. I need you there."

"You know, Sophia," he said gently as the cab moved away from the curve, "they are clearly going to try to eat you alive."

"I know, David, but don't worry," she said with a twinkle in her eyes. "They will find I'm tricky to chew. You'll see."

Sophia saw Henry get into the next cab, pushing his wife in front of him. "God, he is so mean to her that I almost feel sorry for her," she said, nodding toward Janet.

As Sophia stepped out of the car at Number Eleven Grosvenor Square, her hair blew in the breeze. Pushing it out of her face, she got her first honest glimpse of the property, and a look of astonishment spread across her face.

"My God," she breathed, "this is, er, was Barbara's home?" Before her was a stunning massive neoclassical mansion, built in the late 1700s and situated on an entire city block. The imposing brick building was four stories tall with twelve-over-twelve windows framed by three-story pediments. "How big is this building?" she asked no one in particular. There were no words as they walked up the steep stairs to the building that initially had been built during the reign of King George V. Sophia simply stared at it as would a child, in total awe.

A tall gray-haired liveried footman Sophia recognized as one of the men from the gallery met them at the entrance. "Welcome," he said. "May I take your coat and bag?"

"Yes, thank you," she stumbled, still at a loss for words. Remembering her manners, she extended her hand, saying, "I'm Sophia Lawrence, and you are?"

"Frazer," he replied in a slight Scottish brogue. "Again, welcome."

David was smiling.

"I take it you knew?" she whispered to him as Henry came up behind them.

He nodded in the affirmative before turning his head to hide a chuckle.

"May I take your coat and bag?" the footman asked Janet.

"No," she snapped, glaring down her nose at the footman's outstretched hand, as if inspecting it for dirt.

The massive stark-white entry hall occupied almost a quarter of the building's length. Its white marble floors gleamed, and in front of them was a massive dual arched staircase swathed in a red carpet. In between the two arched stairs was a massive round table with an equally large bouquet of fresh flowers. Above the table was a two-story-high Gainsborough painting. To the right of one staircase were several marble obelisks displaying artifacts contained in glass cloches. To the left of the other staircase was a full suit of medieval knight's armor.

The footman began to give them a tour that felt more like a history lesson, though Janet kept interrupting the poor man. Walking through the house, as stunning as it was, Sophia understood why Barbara had not wanted to live here. She saw extraordinarily little of her late mother-in-law on display. Instead, the whole place felt like a memorial to the Duke of Devon, her father.

Like Sophia, Janet was in shock. Unlike Sophia, who stayed quietly in awe, Janet was driven to talk constantly. She prattled about absolutely nothing. "Why didn't we know about this, Henry?" and "You must have known," then "What are we going to do with it?" and "Oh my, is that a Renoir? That cannot be the painting Sophia got. It's not fair."

"Shut up, Janet!" Henry finally barked. And she did, if only for a time. "What's that worth?" was her most common question. The footman, trying to be noncommittal, said as little as possible about values. Even before the group left the entry hall, Henry and Janet were snarling at each other and everyone else.

Remaining quiet as they made their way from room to room, Sophia looked at the mansion with an eye to the details of the furnishings. Deep-blue Aubusson carpets covered expansive marble floors, and antique furniture filled the rooms. The walls were laden with art; every flat surface had been filled.

The footman explained that the duke had collected many of the artifacts during his time in India and the Middle East, while the older artifacts had been collected by the previous duke and duchess during their time spent in both Egypt and Persia.

Henry was out of patience before they reached the second floor. He thundered, "Janet, we should all leave now. There is nothing more to do tonight, and I have an important dinner meeting to attend, which will sort all of this out quickly."

Sophia couldn't contain her laughter. "Henry, you go off to your *impotent* dinner," she said, deliberately mispronouncing the word. "I will still tour the house before I go back to my hotel. As for sorting it out quickly"—she turned her head to one side—"I believe that the instructions for how this was to be sorted were read to us today. The only thing I can assure you is that nothing will be sorted out over dinner tonight."

Then she noticed Janet putting a silver cup with Henry's initials into her purse.

"One thing, though, before you two run away," said Sophia. "How are we going to decide which personal mementos each of us wants? The will says we each pick a piece, so how do we determine who goes first?"

"You can go first," said Janet quickly, clearly unsure whether Sophia had seen her put the cup in her purse.

"Fine," said Sophia, pausing for effect. "Do you want to consider that piece of silver in your purse your first choice?"

All chatter in the room ceased, as everyone, especially the attorneys, stared at Janet. She wailed to no one in particular, "What do you mean?"

As calmly as possible, Sophia walked to Janet's oversized Louis Vuitton bag and pulled out a small silver loving cup. "I suggest that we put the silver cup back and tackle who gets what tomorrow," she said. Then, looking over her glasses with a stern, schoolmarm look, she added, "Henry, would you, Janet, and your lawyer meet me here tomorrow at 9:00 a.m. so we can decide on a methodology and begin the division of jewelry and mementos? I am happy to let Janet have a day looking around before she starts … goes first."

Embarrassed, Henry said sarcastically, "That's kind of you, Sophia. We will see you tomorrow." Turning their backs to her, they left the building.

David and Sophia continued to tour the house. Finally, Sophia asked, "How long do you think it will take me to sell and then empty this entire"—she paused, not knowing what to call this place, though for a moment she thought "mausoleum"—"building?"

"I don't know," he said. "It's pretty dammed big, even by English standards."

40

She wondered aloud, "Do I need a new appraisal of the value of everything in here? Or can I use the existing ones?"

David frowned. "I would have said use the old ones, but given what I have seen of Henry, you may need to update the valuation of the art, and that will not be quick or inexpensive."

As they arrived downstairs, Frazer announced that tea was being served in the library. The library was a small, intimate room covered in deep-red wallpaper. A large Georgian desk took up one side of the room and was flanked by two comfortable chairs. On the other side of the room, in front of the fireplace, were another two chairs with a table set for tea in between. An exquisite pair of seascapes, the Turners Sophia had just inherited, hung over the white and gray marble fireplace.

As the footman ushered them into the room, Sophia turned to David, saying, "I have several questions for you. First, does the estate pay for things we need to sort out the division of property, like storage, appraisals, brokerage fees?"

"Yes," said David, "anything you need within reason."

Sophia smiled. "The first thing I would like to do is hire a stenographer and videographer to record what we say and do when we're in this house. After that stunt of Janet's, you never know what can happen."

David laughed. "You're right there. I can arrange that for you. Sir Joshua has several on his staff."

"Second," she said, "do you have any contacts at Sotheby's? I suspect that most antiques and paintings will be best disposed of via auction."

"Got you covered. My friend Serina Winston, Sir Joshua's daughter, is the VP in charge of auctions as well as a specialist in both Impressionist and old masters' paintings. She can also steer you to potential buyers who prefer private sales."

"Third is a little more complex," she said. "How long is probate in the UK? What are the estate tax laws?"

David laughed. "That's what Sir Joshua and I are here for, Sophia. The short answer is that probate can take anywhere from three to twelve months from when you apply. The taxes are 40 percent of the value and must be paid in full before probate ends. There will be other tax considerations for the rest of the properties, which Barbara's accountancy firm will take care of."

Sophia felt relieved. Changing the subject, she said, "We don't own the land here, right? Am I correct that the Duke of Westminster owns it? I'd love to meet his agents and find out about the land lease."

David said quietly, "I can set that meeting up if you like. Let me make a couple of phone calls. Are you still at the Connaught?"

"I was going to move into the flat in Kensington. Now I think it will be better to wait until probate has started. When I booked my hotel, it was with the idea that the Connaught would be away from the fray." She smiled as she said it. "I clearly didn't have any idea where the fray would be."

"So you picked the cheap hotel on the outskirts of town?" he laughed. Just then his phone rang, and he stepped away to answer it privately. He returned with a big grin on his face. "You're on. We have a meeting for drinks tonight at your hotel with Uncle Gerald. It's your lucky day—he is in town."

She smiled and said, "I assume your uncle Gerald's surname is Grosvenor, and he's my new landlord."

Chapter 7

Meeting Westminster

*S*ophia walked into the iconic Coburg Bar at the Connaught wearing a stunning green silk dress and beige court heels. The emerald green showed off her fair coloring and reddish-blond hair, which she had brushed and slightly curled to make it look a little less windblown. David looked impressed as he and the older gentleman next to him stood to greet her.

"Sophia, please meet my uncle Gerald, the Sixth Duke of Westminster."

"A pleasure, Your Grace," Sophia murmured with a slight curtsy.

The older man took her hands and pressed kisses on each cheek. "Please, call me Gerald." He was a good-looking older man, slightly portly with dark hair flecked with a few strands of gray.

She relaxed and smiled. Both men ordered drinks while Sophia ordered wine. They were sitting at a table in the public lounge and not the private room Gerald had requested. The waiter had apologized, saying it had already been reserved by another party.

Looking at Sophia with captivating blue eyes, the duke teased, "I hear you're now my tenant. Great to have you."

Laughing nervously, she replied, "I may be more of a custodian for hopefully a brief period. I became aware of my partial ownership only today." Searching for something to say, she continued, "Can you shed some light on Barbara Devon's father and why she still owns the place?"

"Oh, I can," said Gerald, "but that is a long story that would take an entire evening. Are you free?" He looked first at David and then at Sophia.

"Yes," she said, "I am." *In more ways than one,* she thought, shooting a glance at his nephew.

"Devon was a character who served his country with distinction. He reveled in exploring foreign lands, looking for the next big business deal…"

Before the duke could finish, Henry and Janet stormed into the lounge with their bedraggled lawyer in tow. Henry was now wearing a navy-blue suit, and Janet had on a slightly too short and too low-cut black beaded cocktail dress.

"Shit," said Sophia softly. "I'm sorry, sir. That's my new nemesis." She slightly nodded to Henry as he saw her.

The duke, God love him, said, "I will introduce myself, Sophia. Follow my lead."

As Henry came toward them, she smiled. "Imagine seeing you here. I thought you were staying at the Berkeley?"

"Well, yes," he said, looking a tad embarrassed.

The duke stood up and, extending his hand to Henry, said, "Nice to meet you. I'm David's uncle Jerry."

"Hello," said Henry distractedly as he turned his back on the older man.

The maître d' moved toward the table, saying to Henry, "I don't mean to hurry you, sir, but your private room is ready. Your guests will be arriving soon. They are always very prompt."

Janet stuck her nose up in the air and gave a haughty look to Sophia and Uncle Jerry as she turned to walk away.

Sophia was giggling at Henry's rude treatment of the duke when a tall Middle Eastern man walked through the entrance into the room. He was dressed in a dark navy suit, a white shirt, and a red striped tie. He had dark curly hair, slightly on the long side, and almost jet-black eyes, and his striking good looks took Sophia's breath away. He was the most handsome man Sophia had ever laid eyes on. Behind him were four men, all wearing traditional Arabian thobes covered with black vests.

"Aha," said Gerald. "The prince of thieves has arrived. And I believe he is headed to the private room with your in-laws, Sophia. It's getting a bit crowded in here, isn't it? Let's adjourn to my private suite for further discussion."

The maître d' moved forward, ushering the prince's party toward the private room, but not before the man locked eyes on Sophia. His gaze was mesmerizing. Sophia then realized she was staring, and as she looked away, she saw a hint of a smile cross his face.

Signaling the waiter to tell him they were leaving, Gerald whispered something to the concierge, who grinned and replied with military precision, "Yes, sir."

They rode up to the duke's penthouse in silence while Gerald and David exchanged conspiratorial glances. As soon as they walked in and the door closed, the duke ushered Sophia to an intimate dining table already set with starched white linen and fine china for three. After she was seated, Sophia's curiosity finally got the better of her. "OK, you two, who is the prince of thieves?"

"When David told me today that you had inherited Number Eleven, he mentioned that this would be a hard separation. So I did some in-house investigation. We keep track of parties who are seriously interested in our properties. Prince Abdullah has some interest in the property. As of today, that's little more than cocktail party gossip."

Sophia said tartly, "I only feel a little on the back foot here, but not completely. As David will attest, when I was told the building was on leased land, I assumed you were the landlord." She also thought, *Nice to have Uncle Jerry in your camp.* She also guessed that the choice of David as her lawyer had been set up by Sir Joshua.

"I confirmed with the maître d' that Henry is dining with the prince. They don't know that I already have an offer pending on the property from King Fayed of the UAE. He wants to house their new embassy on the site. It is a substantial offer that has several added benefits."

The conversation stopped as a uniformed waiter served them wine. When he had left the room, a by now very curious Sophia said, "And how much is the offer, may I ask?"

"The offer for the entire property is slightly over thirteen million pounds. The man Henry is dining with wants to offer around a third of that for just the center section. He does not know the entire property is preserved through the National Trust and cannot be sold in sections."

The duke looked at Sophia. "I realize that you knew nothing of this when the day dawned, but ... my bet is within days, Henry will come to you with a lowball offer for a quick sale. So how do you want to answer that?"

"Do you mean how will I answer Henry, or which offer will I accept?" she asked. "To Henry, I'm just going to say that as the executor of the estate, I will get back to him when I have all the facts. The deal to be done appears to be with the UAE, unless you have others interested."

As she sat sipping her wine, she turned and asked, "Do you have a right of first refusal in your leases?"

The duke smiled at her question. "I do, but I won't exercise it. I am happy to collect my land rent."

"And who," she asked again, "is the prince of thieves?"

"He is Abdullah bin Abbas of Arabia," said Gerald. "Even though he is only thirty-seven years old, he is heir to the throne. Ironically, he spends as much time in England and Scotland as in Arabia. As an undergraduate at Oxford, he read at the prestigious University College, graduating with top honors, in addition to graduating from Sandhurst and LSE.

"Technically, he is officially attached to the Arabian embassy as a special envoy. However, he is also a very shrewd businessman and ruthless at the bargaining table. He successfully runs his personal finances and those of his father through a company called Royal Holdings."

They continued chatting throughout the elegant dinner. As dessert was being served, the maître d' from the restaurant came into the suite to whisper something to the duke.

The duke smiled and turned to Sophia. "I hear that the prince did not even stay for dinner; he left directly after drinks. His man of business dined with your in-laws, Sophia."

"That seems a little strange. Guess that meeting didn't go according to plan," she said with a bemused look on her face.

At dinner's end, David walked her down to her suite, where she immediately fell into a deep sleep. She awoke at five the next morning, after eight glorious hours of rest. After the maid had served her breakfast, she sipped her coffee and looked out over the balcony to the park below, pondering yesterday's developments and wondering what today would bring.

Exactly three weeks had passed since Edward's death, and her entire world had turned upside down. It was almost incomprehensible. It wasn't that she didn't grieve for Edward or Barbara—she did. Yet in the six days since her landing in Ireland, there had been little time to think about her husband's death. While she was alone at night in her luxury room, feelings of guilt engulfed her. During the day, however, she was only focused on business—and now the prince.

Chapter 8

Number Eleven—July 1992

Sophia walked up the steep front stairs of Number Eleven to be greeted by the Frazer the footman. "The others are already here, ma'am," he said, nodding toward the drawing room.

After exchanging pleasantries with him, Sophia looked at Frazer carefully and asked, "Are we all in a good mood this morning?"

"I can't say they're particularly high, as it were, ma'am."

Squaring her shoulders, she went off to find Henry and Janet and their lawyers in the elegant pale blue drawing room. The room went silent as Sophia walked in.

"Sophia, how kind of you to join us on time," Henry said sarcastically.

She let the jab slide. "Sorry, I was busy attending to details. And speaking of details, before we get to work today, I think it is necessary to set some ground rules for how the division of the personal property will proceed."

"You don't have to worry about that," said Henry. "My legal team is starting the probate process today."

Sophia shook her head. "Henry, do you ever listen to anyone or even to yourself? It is neither your job nor your lawyer's. It's mine. How many times are we going to go over this? I have also hired a videographer and stenographer to document our conversations."

Henry had turned bright red at this little speech. "Sophia, you can't take the will that literally. It's not really your job. It simply determines how much you benefit from the results, and even that may be in question. The lawyers will do all the negotiations and organizing of the sales, especially when selling commercial real estate, which you know nothing about. As of last night, we have a buyer for this property, the art, and maybe some of the other buildings in the portfolio. We don't need photographers and videographers."

Sophia shook her head. "Henry, after yesterday"—she looked squarely at Janet —"I want everything we agreed upon to be documented immediately, hence the stenographer and videographer. After all, memories are often tricky, sometimes even flawed! And I seriously doubt that you sold anything at your drinks meeting last night."

A red-faced Henry was starting to respond when everyone heard Sir Joshua clear his throat. He had been standing in the doorway, watching Henry go after Sophia.

He said in a low voice, "Excuse me, Henry. The will is clear. The entire job is Sophia's to do as she sees fit within the confines of probate, trusts, and taxes."

"But she doesn't know anything about commercial real estate like this," snarled Henry. "She is just a dumb blonde."

"The will is clear, and Barbara freely gave her the authority by making her the sole trustee," said Sir Joshua. "If Sophia needs assistance, she can draw upon Barbara's innumerable resources."

Sophia took this as her cue to step in. "Thank you, and while we're all here, I do have a question. Where do the suits of armor and the archaeological objects fall? Are they personal property or joint property?"

Henry blurted out impatiently, "Oh, Sophia, you are so stupid. You can have all the crap you like."

She tried, unsuccessfully, to hide a smile, thinking that rocks from King Tut's tomb and medieval armor just might have some value. "So you agree that the armor and, as you call them, old rocks or, as I call them, archaeological artifacts are my personal property."

49

Sophia turned to see the stenographer sitting quietly in the corner, taking notes.

"Yes," snarled Henry. "But you need to get all that junk out of here soon, so this building can be sold."

"Henry, I seriously doubt the moving company will arrive anytime soon. I have made up a list of categories that I was not certain were personal or joint property."

"See, I told you she can't make a decision," Henry interrupted. "Just let the professionals get on with it. If you don't stop making things difficult, I'll cut you out entirely."

Sir Joshua moved forward. "Be careful, Henry. You can't do anything without proof, and if you think what I have seen so far is at all a problem for Sophia, think again."

Turning to her sister-in-law, Sophia said, "Janet, why don't we start dividing the jewelry and personal mementos stored in the safe?"

The footman, who was to become ever-present in Sophia's life, had organized all forty sets of jewelry on a black velvet cushion, filling the massive table with a dazzling if slightly overwhelming display. Diamonds combined with precious stones in every color of the rainbow were laid out to view. With all the jewelry on the table, it became clear just how extravagant these pieces were. No one except the royals wore jewels like this anymore.

The first set of jewelry was a series of rubies: tiara, necklaces, earrings, and bracelets. Wining, Janet said, "I want that."

Next was a full set of small marquis-cut emeralds and diamonds, and while Sophia loved emeralds, she knew she already had one set. "Oh," cried Janet "maybe I want that too."

Janet was like a child with a shiny new toy, exclaiming, "I want!" at the first one and then the next one and then the next one. At the end of the day, when Janet still had not decided on one set, Sophia said sarcastically, "Janet, you stay here, and I'm going to get some other work done." It took less than two hours for her to decide when there was no one around to complain to.

It was the beginning of the third week when Henry, who had not been around, arrived at Number Eleven, raced into the marble foyer, and demanded everyone stop what they were doing.

"Sophia," he bellowed, "why did you hire Sotheby's? You should have hired Christie's. I insist you do so immediately! I want Christie's to auction our portion!"

"It doesn't work that way, Henry."

It was an unusual interruption because for the past week, Henry had been conspicuously absent from Number Eleven. Janet, on the other hand, had remained present. Once they had finished the division of the jewelry, there had been nothing for Janet to do, yet still she would arrive around ten every morning, spend two hours moping about the building, and then leave around lunchtime to go shopping. Sophia and Henry were totally estranged, and while it bothered Sophia, there was far too much work to dwell on it.

As Uncle Jerry had predicted, it didn't take long for two offers to roll in on the property. A scant three weeks from the reading of the will, David faxed her a written offer from the prince of thieves.

He had placed some unusual demands on the offer. He wanted a five-year break in the ground lease from the Duke of Westminster. Astonishingly, the price also included the purchase of the art and furniture in the building in their entirety—all for the supposedly attractive price of eight million pounds. Sophia shook her head, muttering, "Henry, Henry, Henry."

She scribbled a note across the top of the fax—"No!"—and quickly sent it back to David.

Henry called five minutes later with the same news, threatening Sophia that the offer would expire if she didn't sign it immediately. "He is an important prince! Don't screw this up."

"Stop trying to pressure me. To begin with, the art will never be part of this sale. That is nonnegotiable, so you should tell the prince to take it off the table."

"I can't tell him anything, Sophia," Henry yelled. "I don't know him."

"Really," she deadpanned. "Who did you have drinks with at the Connaught?" Not waiting for him to answer, she continued.

"Second, the Italian embassy and the Duke of Westminster, our landlord, need to be signatories to this agreement."

Henry's voice got suddenly quiet, but Sophia could hear the rage simmering just below the surface. "I'm confident it will be fine, Sophia. That's not for you to worry about. Why won't you just let the lawyers deal with it?"

She laughed. "Clearly, your lawyers have the wrong information. My lawyer has the offer, and when he picks himself up off the floor from laughing, I'll call you and tell you what he says." This time she was the one who hung up.

About twenty minutes later, David called with the second offer. This one was from the UAE. They wanted the entire property to house their embassy.

Their terms were simple and straightforward. Their offer was twice the prince's offer, with a request for only a one-year ground rent holiday. Their cover letter stated that they understood the enormity of the moving job faced by the heirs of the Duke of Devon and could be flexible on a closing date. In addition, they had agreements pre-negotiated with the Italian embassy.

That night Sophia returned to her elegant pale-green suite intent on having a relaxing evening of bad TV and room service before calling it an early evening. However, a last-minute phone call from David inviting her out for a night on the town, complete with a little playful guilting about wasting a Friday night in London, changed her plans. Now she was heading out to meet him at the Ritz.

She had dressed carefully in a vintage pale blue sheath Dior dress that Barbara had given her years ago, but she had resisted the temptation to wear a piece of flashy jewelry. When she arrived at the Ritz and realized how many celebrities were dining there and that there were photographers outside, she was glad of that decision.

As Sophia looked around the magnificent art deco room with its stunning oriental carpet and matching red velvet chairs, she recognized that the diners were a who's who of English society and diplomats. Keeping her eyes on David, so as not to be caught staring at some starlet or lord, she said, "This is very heady company for a girl like me."

"I have a surprise for you," he said, pointing to the small blue box at her place setting.

Upon opening it, she found a key for her new home.

Seeing the smile on her face, he added, "And I have a second surprise for you. It turns out you qualify for the title that goes with the property in Scotland. You are now the Countess of Carrick."

Looking dumbfounded, she exclaimed, "I'm a countess? How did that happen?"

Before David could answer, the Italian ambassador spied them from across the room and, after receiving a nod of approval from David, approached the table. He introduced himself to Sophia.

He was a tall, swarthy man with dark straight hair and aviator glasses. He was, Sophia noted, quite good-looking. "I am delighted to meet my new landlady. I believe I have some of your art on loan. May I call and set up a time for you to come view more of your collection?"

"Why, yes, I would enjoy that." She smiled shyly at the man, again noting his beguiling Italian dark looks and aviator glasses. He seemed to be flirting with Sophia, and she wondered if he was subtly asking her out on a date. After a few more minutes of small talk, he left them to return to his table.

While Sophia and David were finishing dessert, there was a scuffle of photographers and flashing light bulbs outside—a press scrum, David called it. The source of the chaos became clear when the prince of thieves walked in, accompanied by a well-known movie star. Sophia watched him move across the room dressed in a black Italian suit and white shirt without a tie. *Good God*, she thought, *he doesn't walk—he prowls!* His date trailed behind him, posing for the paparazzi, seemingly oblivious to who her companion was.

The prince spied Sophia and David and gave them a brief nod. His eyes again locked on Sophia's, and he gave her a broad smile. As he walked past their table, she noticed his long black lashes and slightly arched aquiline nose. Before he and his entourage moved into the private dining room, she noticed again that his hair was slightly on the long side yet impeccably groomed.

The following day, in addition to the pictures of the prince and his date, the tabloids also ran a small but rather good photo of Sophia and David, with the caption "Duke of Westminster's Nephew Has a New Mystery Lady." They also ran a picture of Sophia and the Italian ambassador with the headline "New International Relationships."

Monday morning, Henry called, shouting from the moment she answered the phone. Once he had slowed down enough for Sophia to get a word in edgewise, she said, "Good morning, Henry! What seems to be the problem now?"

Ignoring her greeting entirely, he raged on. "You turned down the offer last Friday. That was a good deal for us. What game are you playing at, Sophia?" He was so angry he was sputtering. To make matters worse, Sophia laughed at him, which only fueled his anger.

"Henry, to quote a phrase you often use, shut up! As of Friday, I am in possession of a different offer with better terms—for more money. And by the way," Sophia said, raising her voice now too, "where in the hell do you get off trying to give away extraordinarily valuable art to your *prince of thieves*?"

She heard the phone click. Henry had hung up on her.

Within one month, Sophia was well on her way to organizing the estate. Henry and Janet had finally returned to the USA, but their lawyer was an ever-present watchdog wherever Sophia went. She sometimes wondered if she was being followed.

Chapter 9

A New Home in London

While waiting to pay her bill at the Connaught, Sophia was stunned to find a note from the Duke of Westminster waiving the charges. She made a mental note to immediately send a thank-you note to His Grace. Then, hailing a cab, she headed for Kensington.

When she arrived, she found that the flat was as stunning as she had remembered. The staff seemed to have been waiting for her arrival and greeted her warmly. Standing in the formal entryway, she instantly felt at home. Memories from previous visits almost overwhelmed her. Had her last visit really been only a year ago?

There was a blank space over the fireplace in the main salon that she assumed was where the Sisley from Grosvenor Square would hang. The two oils on the other side of the room were also Sisleys. They were in perfect harmony with the Georgian antiques, the Savonnerie rug, and the rare Rose Medallion china in the Chippendale cabinet.

Brightly patterned yellow chintz fabric covered the two large sofas in the center of the room, which faced each other across a mahogany butler's tray table. The antique porcelain lamps were shaded in cream silk. Everywhere, there was the gleam of silver and crystal. Fresh flowers placed in bowls had opened up, and the air was fragrant with their pungent scents.

The staff of three at the flat consisted of Max, the footman and butler; Mrs. Kelly, the elderly cook; and Mrs. O'Brian, the housekeeper. They were long-term employees who had spent decades doting on Barbara and who knew Sophia from her frequent visits. It seemed they had missed this aspect of their lives and were excited to take Sophia on a house tour the minute she arrived.

Walking around the home, she realized that it could take her years to go through the contents of this house alone. Even though it felt comfortable, like home, she still felt disconnected from reality. When she had dreamed of a new life, it had always entailed doing fun activities—sailing, parties, things of that nature. So far this new life was singularly focused on the endless details of settling the estate.

The house was sprawled out across two lots on the tiny oval street. The entrance was a two-story space with a large circular staircase leading up to the second floor. On one side of the entry was the formal living room, and on the other was the formal dining area. In the back of the formal dining area sat a lovely sitting room facing the gardens, which was used as an informal place to take meals.

Upstairs was a mirror layout, with an extensive library on one side and the master suite, including a spa tub and steam shower, on the other. The area behind the center hallway was a small sitting room accessed from the library and the bedroom, with a mini coffee bar set up for wine and drinks.

The walls in the library, which Sophia had visited on many occasions, were painted a soft shade of green that somehow highlighted the exceptional tiger maple woodwork in the room. At the center of the room was a sizable French oak desk with curved legs from the Louis XIII period. All around the desk, and taking up a majority of the room, were a series of massive floor-to-ceiling bookcases topped with a carved pediment. Below the bookshelves were cupboards with doors trimmed in the same dental moldings as the pediments.

The opposite wall held a massive fireplace flanked by two additional cases. Above the fireplace hung Sir Joshua Reynolds's portrait of the second Duchess of Devon and her children. It was such a realistic painting that the whites in the dresses seemed to shimmer, as if they were natural satin. Sophia wondered what relationship this painting had to her. It seemed that all the people who had suddenly become a part of her life were in some way or another interrelated.

The street side of the library had tall, mullioned windows overlooking the street, while the garden side had French doors that led out onto a balcony that ran the entire length of the house, overlooking the garden.

The master suite was a pale creamy yellow, with a French-style carved marble mantel. Two chairs with a table in between provided seating. The bed was king-size, with what Sophia thought were new, immaculate white Frette linens. She looked at the stunning Wellington campaign chests lining the opposite walls and the elegant Chippendale side tables used as nightstands. The drawers were empty, and peeking behind the picture over the mantel, she saw one of the two safes that she knew existed in the house.

She walked back toward the dressing area and realized that Barbara's clothing still hung there. The housekeeper had just entered the room and was quick to explain that the staff hadn't known what to do with the fabulous designer dresses.

"We did clear out her privates," the housekeeper said, pointing to the chest. "We ... we," she said, shuddering, "didn't have much instruction, except for the one time Mrs. Lawrence stopped by."

Sophia stopped in her tracks. "And when was that?" she asked as calmly as she could.

"It was the day before she left, I think. She told the cook she needed a few things, but the cook wouldn't let her in. They had a big row. I hope that was OK. She said she was coming back. Max said the house was all yours, and we should take care of it as Sir Joshua had instructed us."

"Thank you," Sophia said. "I'm sorry I didn't come sooner." Sheepishly, she added, "I just didn't want to upset the apple cart. Not to worry, everything will be fine now."

"I apologize, and stop me if this is inconsiderate. We were all sort of wondering what you'd like to be called ... on account of ... well ... your husband and all?"

Without thinking on it, Sophia said, "I supposed I'd just expected you to call me Sophia."

If Mrs. O'Brian was slightly surprised by the casual nature of this, she showed no signs of it save for a slight twitch at the corners of her mouth before she nodded.

Just then the elderly cook walked in. "I've been looking for you two. I have tea, sandwiches, and scones downstairs. And clotted cream, Miss ... um ..." The elderly Mrs. Kelly trailed off.

"Sophia," the housekeeper prompted.

"Works for me," Sophia said, shrugging. If calling her "Miss" made them more comfortable, she'd just have to roll with it. "I'll be right down, you two, and please join me in the small dining area," she concluded. "I want to take a quick look at these dresses if you don't mind."

"Oh, ma'am, we have a listing of them that Miss Barbara left. There are all sorts of lists and letters in the desk in the library."

Searching through the top drawer, Sophia found the original list of clothing in Barbara's beautiful penmanship and took it down to tea. There were hundreds of outfits, many of them from couture houses such as Dior and Chanel and even a few from the highly collectible House of Worth.

What in heaven's name was she going to do with all of this clothing? she thought. It was too valuable to give away. While she and Barbara were the same size, she could not envision a time when she would wear a fraction of these dresses, no matter how storied they were.

Turning back to Mrs. Kelly, she said, "I guess there will be a lot of work sorting out just the clothing, and I am certain there are even more outfits at Number Eleven and the cottage in Scotland. When I go north, would you be able to join me there? Do you know anything about the house in Scotland?"

"Well, we know a little, ma'am. We're all from Scotland. In fact, we've all got houses in the village."

"You do? That's great! I'm so excited to have your help!" Sophia realized, partially from the surprise on both of their faces and partially from the warm feeling in her stomach, that this was the first time in a long time she had felt her customary enthusiasm.

After tea Sophia was looking out over the garden surrounded by ancient boxwood trees that blocked out all of the neighbors. Behind the garden was a car house with a bright red Mini Cooper.

The garage was accessed through a long, brick, covered patio area with arches facing the garden. It provided a covered walkway in any weather. Closer to the house, there was an open patio with retractable awnings. The second floor had a stunning deck with a canopy.

"Do we have a gardener?" Sophia asked Mrs. O'Brian.

"Max, the footman, doubles as the gardener. He loves it."

Sophia next toured the third floor and the attic. The third floor had three guest rooms with en suite bathrooms. She had stayed in one of these rooms often and was pleased to see that all the guest rooms were in immaculate shape.

"To celebrate tonight, may I ask all of you, as a favor to me, to have dinner in the small dining area? Consider it a family-style supper. I want to get to know you all better."

"Dinner?" Max queried, looking dubious.

Sophia pouted. "Come on, guys. We're going to have to be a little less formal around here, especially when I'm the only one here."

Dinner in the little sunroom turned out to be fun for everyone. After a few moments of awkwardness, everyone was thrilled to sit and tell little stories about Barbara, as well as a few about Edward in his younger years. Amazingly, they left out any mention of Henry. It was as if the staff understood some of the pain that Sophia was contending with.

As dinner finished, Mrs. Kelly finally asked the question that everyone had been thinking about. "Ah, miss, if you don't mind my asking, are you going to keep this house or sell it?"

She smiled. "I am going to keep it. I still have a lot of moving parts to figure out, but I love London, so yes, my plan is to keep it. I don't yet know if I will live here full-time, but I will be here a good part of the year."

Truth be told, she had not thought about this until Mrs. Kelly asked the question.

After dinner, Sophia retired upstairs with a glass of wine. It was a warm summer's night, and she sat on the elegant deck overlooking the garden as the events of the last few weeks ran through her mind. Seeing Henry daily had reminded her of the worst of her husband. Yet tonight she was relaxed and feeling more confident than she had felt since her arrival.

Chapter 10

The Bombing

*T*he next evening, Sophia sat down at the elegant partner's desk in her new library. The desk was an ornate French style and was polished to perfection. She ran her fingers across the top, once again taking in all the decor in the room. Opening the top drawer, she found the first letter from Barbara.

Dear Sophia,

I realize that if you are reading this, your life is in somewhat of a turmoil. Please don't despair. As you now know, I left you the major portion of my estate. I also realize that the marital relationship between you and my stepson Edward can best be described as broken.

This is the first of several letters that may help you understand how your vast inheritance came to pass. My father and my grandfather were both unique men, but my mother and grandmother, the duchesses, were always the power in the family. I was born the third child, the first and only girl, at the beginning of the Great War. It was a frightful war, and the scars left on the men who were lucky, or sometimes unlucky, enough to return home became the pain of our generation.

During the war, my grandfather sat in the House of Lords, later serving in the diplomatic corps in various positions. My father was in the army. With manpower in short supply, it was mostly left to the women to run the nation's business, especially hospitals, as well as provide food and comfort to the wounded. I was raised to always serve my country.

My grandmother was a lady-in-waiting to Queen Victoria. For her services to her queen, she was gifted the Queen's Diamonds, which you will find in the safe. Neither duchess was exceptionally faithful to her duke; then again, neither were their dukes faithful to them. As was the custom of the time, they did their duty and were the ultimate in discretion. Other liaisons ultimately resulted in some of the properties that you will now control.

After my grandmother died, my father took a diplomatic posting to India. Despite their differences, my mother, my father, and I moved to an outpost in the Punjab.

While history will not show the myriad things my mother did in her time in India, it was not all balls with the raja. She worked for the people of India, often traveling and putting herself in danger.

While her paramours were not glamorous, she did have quite a few, and one was the source of the Raj Emeralds. My father never seemed to mind her partners. He was more of a man's man and spent endless time with his regiment and fellow officers. When not with his men, he was amassing a significant collection of artifacts and antiquities, which are all stored in the attic at Number Eleven.

By the time the Germans began their second march through Europe, I was educated and well traveled and thought I was the future of the nation. I had graduated from Cambridge, having studied English as well as European and Persian history. This made me a likely candidate for a job at MI5.

I met many young men at the canteens and soirees I attended during the war. I had one grand passion and three—yes, Sophia, three—lovers in my life. My first love was Zalove, the young son of a Yugoslavian count. Our passion was not extraordinary, but I was young and reckless. In fact, we continually disagreed about everything, especially the war. We separated after a year, when our affair became a society scandal.

My grand passion came in the late 1950s. For four glorious years, I lived a perfect existence. It was the only time I knew great love, the feeling of being one with another human being. He was the man who gifted me the King's Rubies.

And then in 1961, in a heartbeat, it was gone. My past caught up with me when Zalove was uncovered and charged with espionage and treason. He was convicted and hanged, but the damage had been done.

Given my war work, it was assumed that I had been the leak. I was tried without any real evidence other than our illicit affair. I still believe that it was no one's business but our own, yet I was sentenced to a two-year jail term. I am certain that Churchill somehow intervened on my behalf to shorten the sentence, even though he was out of power.

When I was released from prison, I married David Lawrence and rarely looked back. While my mother never believed my innocence, my father always did and never cast me out.

This house is my home. I give it to you and only you, Sophia, with my fondest wish that you will make it your home. I know you and Edward do not always see eye to eye. I am hopeful that at some point in the future, you can be here to heal and move forward toward your destiny.

All my love,
Barbara

How strange, thought Sophia as she replaced the letter. She never saw the tiny button on the side of the drawer. Having read the letter, she opened the safe with the combination that Sir Joshua had provided her. Inside were boxes of jewelry, first the Raj Emeralds, then the stunning Victoria Diamonds, and finally, the most beautiful of them all, the King's Rubies, surrounded by hundreds of diamonds. As she gazed at the stones, she wondered about the stories Barbara had not mentioned in her letter. All three were stunning, but the King's Rubies were the most beautiful and totally impractical jewelry she had ever laid eyes on. Placing them back in the safe, she went to sleep dreaming of diamonds.

Early the next morning, in the wee hours before dawn, she was awakened when her house was rocked by an explosion that shattered the glass of her living room window. Sophia at first was so shocked that she was frozen with fear. Then the wail of sirens pushed her in to action. Jumping out of bed, she saw the burning car directly between her home and the house next door.

Dressed only in white linen pajamas, she managed to don a sailing jacket and slip on loafers. Grabbing her purse, she left the house with the staff. They hurried across the road to the crescent's flower garden.

The scene on the street was chaos. The car was burning, and the sounds of the arriving police and emergency medical vehicles pierced the air. To her surprise, Sophia saw the handsome prince, along with six or seven other men, exit the next-door building's side door farthest away from the car. He stopped at the sidewalk to look around and saw Sophia sitting on the bench in the garden.

She watched him wave away all but one of his guards. Soon the tall, handsome prince dressed in jeans was walking toward her, saying, "We meet again."

Her reddish-blond hair was rumpled, as if she had just gotten out of bed. His first thought was *I would love to see her in bed.* She looked adorable and very sexy. Her glasses had fallen down her nose, and she looked up and over them, not saying anything.

Uncertain of how to start the conversation and knowing full well that what he was going to say was not true, he said it anyway. "I believe we met over dinner at the Connaught with your husband."

Finally, after a few seconds, she said, "You must be mistaken. I am Sophia Lawrence. I did see you not too long ago at the Connaught and the Ritz; however, I can assure you that we have never had dinner together."

"You are correct," he said. "Nice to meet you, Sophia."

As he gazed down at her, he decided she was a perfect china doll—fair, creamy skin, deep-blue eyes, and pert nose. But her gaze, riveted on the burning car, held a hint of steel.

Realizing Sophia did not want to chat, the prince sat down next to her on the bench. One of his guards stood directly behind him. Most of the others stood a discreet distance back, surrounding the prince and Sophia in a semicircle. Yet another guard was talking to the police. Seeing the prince's men essentially surrounding Sophia, the four members of her household joined them, pushing their way in to stand behind their employer. She was surprised and said hello when Frazer and the rest of the household staff from Number Eleven arrived a scant fifteen minutes from the time the bomb went off and joined the team now surrounding Abdullah and Sophia at a discreet distance.

Finally, the prince said, "It appears we are next-door neighbors. We should be cleared to return to our homes shortly." Seeing her still studying the car, he asked, "What are you thinking, Sophia?"

"I am wondering why someone left a car bomb here—and who? Aren't you?" she asked, glancing up at him.

"I am," he said quietly, just as a Rover with diplomatic plates drove up to the crescent. Seeing the car, he waved the occupants away.

"I take it they wanted you to join them in the car," she giggled. "They want to take their pampered prince away?"

"I just said no," he replied, "and I'm a prince but hardly pampered." As he spoke, he gestured no again with his hand.

She giggled in response and said, "I hope this isn't a usual occurrence."

His hand slightly brushed her arm when he said, "Which do you mean, Sophia—a bombing or sitting in the park with me at midnight?"

His comment made her giggle again, this time nervously, and she turned to look up at him with a slightly arched eyebrow. The sight of his dark eyes and wide smile looking down at her took her breath away and for a moment rendered her speechless. Then he turned and said something in Arabic to his guard.

"Do you mind if my guards do a quick search of your garden to make certain it is secure?" he asked. "I will have them board up your window also. It will be replaced in the morning."

Sophia looked at him, thinking, *He is my neighbor?* Then finally, she said with a smile, "No, I don't mind. In fact, thank you. I appreciate that."

Fortunately, no one had been injured in the blast. The device had been detonated remotely, and the streets had been empty at the time of the explosion. By now the fire was subsiding, and the bomb squad had ascertained that no more cars would explode. The guards returned and announced that both houses and the homes on either side of theirs were clear.

The prince walked Sophia to her door, where he gave her a small bow and said, "It is safe now, Sophia. Pleased to meet you, even if under trying circumstances."

Just then, a reporter raced up to her and pushed his microphone in her face, saying, "Madam, this must be terrifying."

Sophia looked at him as if to say, *You're an idiot.*

The prince took the opportunity to move away into the darkness. Still, he heard her answer.

"Well, I imagine that the Blitz would have been more terrifying. Don't you think?"

He laughed out loud at her comment as he watched Sophia turn on her heels and stomp into her home.

Sophia invited her household to join her in the solarium, asking Mrs. O'Brian if it would be possible to provide everyone with a spot of tea.

She could hear the four women gossiping about the prince and his entourage from the kitchen. The phrase "good-looking" and a vivid description of the way he had looked at Sophia filtered out across the now early-morning air. Outside, her male staff was interested only in why a bomb had been left in front of her house if it had been intended for the prince.

Upon returning to his house, the prince immediately asked his head of security to please find out all he could on Ms. Sophia Lawrence. And how was she related to that Rochester doctor he'd had dinner with a while ago? He was still uncertain as to the reason his purchase offer on Number Eleven had been refused. He had heard rumors that the UAE had been the successful bidder, yet he had not discovered the terms of the deal.

The offer he had presented had been the one the doctor, who'd claimed to be the estate's sole trustee, had requested. The prince did not really need the property, and he had agreed to split the art collection for a generous kickback to the doctor, not really knowing what the art was. The art description had been so significant that he had assumed, given the price the doctor was asking, that most of the art was simply well-done reproductions.

The next day, his head of security arrived with the answer to his questions. "Your Grace," he started, "your neighbor is the sole trustee for Number Eleven and the Castle Carrick, your neighbor in Scotland. She is Dr. Lawrence's former sister-in-law. Her husband died recently, so she is the heir to two-thirds of the estate. Furthermore, I have it on good authority that the UAE has a contract. It turns out the art may be worth more than the building."

Abdullah shook his head, asking, "And why did we not know this sooner? That was an apparent failure on the part of your so-called intelligence. You say my neighbor is the sole trustee for the Devon estate?"

"Yes, sir, the one you met last night."

"Then I guess we should make it a point to get to know our neighbors. Would you not agree? From now on, I want to know her every movement."

The next day, his men watched Sophia's house, and when she went out for her daily walk, the prince decided to stroll around the crescent, starting in the opposite direction. So it happened that they ran into each other again.

She was dressed for exercise, in a black jogging suit and white trainers. Strands of hair had pulled loose from her ponytail and were windblown around her face. He saw bright blue eyes, almost navy, looking out of oversized glasses.

"Ah, Sophia, I see we meet again," he exclaimed.

Smiling, she slightly wondered at seeing him again. "Yes, Your Highness, but this is much nicer than during a bombing. Thank you again for your help last night. I have heard that the bomb was meant as a warning to you. I hope they do not confuse our homes. They do look rather similar." Without pausing for a breath, she continued. "Or maybe your security could be stepped up to take better care of our tranquil neighborhood."

Slightly chagrined, the prince nodded. "We are looking into it. And yes, we are adding more security that covers the entire crescent." Smoothly, he continued, "The good news is that it will be safe to walk around at any time of the day or night."

Smiling shyly, as she felt he was teasing or flirting with her, she shook her head, saying, "Safe from whom?"

They had completed the loop and were back at her front door by now. He left her to continue to his house, saying, "Hopefully, we will walk again, Sophia."

Chapter 11

Stolen Goods

*S*ophia spent the weekend after the bombing riding in the country at the Duke of Westminster's estate in Gloucestershire. It was a wonderful break from the long hours of work she had been putting in, made all the more enjoyable by meeting Duchess Caroline, the duke's petite blonde wife. Still, Monday morning she woke up thinking about what needed to be done to auction off furniture and decided to call her contact, Serina Winston, at Sotheby's.

"Hi!" she said as her friend came on the line. "I have a quick question. Is there any chance you could send me a furniture guru for a few days to tell me what we might have at Governor Square? Originally, I thought that I would use some of the furniture in the Kensington flat. Now that I'm here, I see that I don't need any more furniture in this house."

"As a matter of fact, I was just thinking about you. We are hosting an exclusive preview tomorrow night for our sale this weekend," Serina said. "The who's who of furniture buyers and dealers will be here, and I can take you around, provide introductions, and show you what is selling and what's not. That may be more important."

Sophia asked, "What time and which showroom?"

"It starts at five, but most don't arrive until six or so, and it usually goes until eight. We can grab a bite to eat afterward if you like. Oh, I almost forgot—we do have two new items from Scotland. You might be interested in them."

Sophia's internal antenna went straight up. "Really, what are they?"

"Two massive Jacobean hall tables. Strangely, one of them has 'Carrick' carved into the wood underneath. Isn't that near where your castle is?"

"Yes," Sophia said. "In fact, for now Carrick is my castle. How did you get these?"

"They are owned by a foreign consignee. He has something to do with a prince. We just put them on consignment. They were delivered last week. Why do you ask?"

Sophia sighed. "If you could, fax me a photo. I think I better stop by and look at them this morning if you don't mind."

Some sixth sense told both women that something might be wrong. Serina said, "I'll clear my calendar. See you at eleven. Does that work for you?"

"That would be great," Sophia said and rang off.

She went upstairs and found the box labeled "Carrick furniture." Just then her fax beeped, and it was a photo from Sotheby's. She pulled out the inventory book, opened the first page, and saw the tables. The tables in the faxed photo were precisely like the ones in the entry hall of Carrick Castle. She shook her head and called David.

"Hi," she said without preamble. "I have a problem. Any chance you can stop by my house this morning?"

Her second call was to the head of her Scottish security team. After she quickly briefed him on the situation, she requested that he go into the entry hall and take a photo with a date on it and fax it to her immediately. "Also, can you overnight me the entry hall security footage from when you started? Better yet, can you call me back and talk me through the footage on the phone?"

A fuzzy photo of a large entry hall with two gilt mirrors but no tables arrived within a minute. Her security team viewed the footage with her on the phone before sending it off. She began with the security system's start date, and as she had suspected, there already had been no entry hall tables then. In the photo, the walls also were very discolored, as if art had been hanging above them.

"Can you get a photo of the dusty areas and fax it to me? I know it won't be great, but it will have to do. And then can you courier the tape and photos to me please?"

Shit, she thought, *this situation is going to be awful.* The minute the word "prince" had been mentioned, she had known this was somehow related to Henry's failed bid for Grosvenor Square.

David arrived, and she asked him to join her in the plush formal library upstairs. "We have had a theft in Scotland! Oh, do you want some coffee or tea? Sorry, I forget my manners."

Knowing that the security Sophia had put in place was very thorough, he frowned.

Seeing his furrowed brow, she said, "Remember, it took me two weeks to add that security. I think this happened the first week, when Henry was not at Number Eleven." She printed out the pictures and put them in order on the massive desk for David to see.

"This is not a simple theft," David said. "Not only were they taken from you, but now they are auctioning them. If Sotheby's sold them by mistake, then they would have an awful time with the press for accepting stolen goods."

Sophia shook her head. "And then Henry could say that it was my fault, which would be breaking the will, right?"

"He could try, but as of now, we don't have any proof it was Henry."

Running her hand through her reddish-blond curls, Sophia continued, "Assuming it is him, then what do we do? I'm not trying to cheat them out of their fair share. He can't seem to keep himself from doing the wrong thing."

David looked at Sophia's worried face through his aviator glasses, then said, "Relax, Sophia, it will all work out in the end. I suggest you go look at the furniture at Sotheby's. I'm confident you have enough information to persuade them to hold off auctioning these late additions until their provenance is settled. After all, the last thing they want is a PR mess or, worse, to lose all your upcoming business."

Thanking him, she smiled and said, "I'm off to Sotheby's. I'll call to brief you on my meeting."

As she walked up to the door of Sotheby's, a footman liveried in green and gold immediately opened it. "Welcome, Ms. Lawrence," he said. "Ms. Winston is waiting for you in the collection room. Right this way."

Serina Winston, a tall, willowy brunette who was slightly younger than Sophia, got up from her elegant French writing desk as Sophia was shown into her office. Over the last few weeks, the women had started to develop a friendship. "I'm so sorry to drag you out on this rainy morning, but …" Serina's voice trailed off as she led Sophia into the room next to her office.

One look, and Sophia knew they were her tables. "I have no idea how this happened," she said to Serina. "Here are my photographs." She took the pictures and faxes out of her large Louis Vuitton purse. "The first set, Sotheby's took years ago; the second one was taken when I hired the security firm; and the last photograph is from this morning. Since then, my security firm has scoured the grounds and rooms, and these two tables are not on the estate."

Serina sighed, bending down to show her the carving "Carrick" under one of the tables.

"So what do we do now?" Sophia asked.

Serina's shoulders slumped. "I'm not certain I know yet. The head of security is waiting in our conference room along with our senior VP." As they entered the conference room filled with Georgian antiques and artifacts, everyone stood up for Sophia while a young lady offered her coffee or tea.

Once everyone was seated, Sophia decided to start the conversation. "As you may know, I believe that I am the rightful owner of the two Jacobean tables you recently took on consignment. My initial proof is here," she said, handing the photos to the very austere-looking gray-headed man who was the head of security. "However," she said, pausing and looking at the VP, "it is not my intention to make a scene about this, so I am eager to hear your thoughts on what we should we do."

The VP, a young sandy-blond man with gray eyes, answered quickly. "The first thing we are going to do is pull the two pieces from this weekend's auction. We have not quite figured out what to say to either the consignee or, if asked, the press."

"I may be able to help you with this problem. What do you think the consignee would say if you told him you have not confirmed the provenance and need more time? I am certain he can't provide you that information. And who, by the way, is the actual consignee?"

The VP sighed heavily, shaking his head. "I am really not at liberty to say."

Sophia had been anticipating this. Looking at him over her glasses, she said, "Then we have two choices: either you can leak me the name, so I can have my security firm quietly investigate, or sadly, I will have to report the property stolen." Tilting her head sideways, she continued, "Scotland Yard, lawyers, the press, tabloids." She stopped talking to let the words sink in before continuing.

"I know that Prince Abdullah wanted to purchase Number Eleven," she said. They all knew what she was referring to. "If"— again, she let the word hang—"I can find out who provided entry to the thief, then I am confident my attorney David Grosvenor and his uncle, the Duke of Westminster, can help me come to a resolution that will avoid any bad PR. In fact, we may just be able to avoid any press at all."

Serina hid a smile.

"So," the VP said, clearing his throat, "I am hearing you say that you simply want us to pull them from this auction and wait, as well as quietly drop the consignee's name?"

"Yes. And in exchange, I will not report them stolen, for now. I will also need your assurance that in the future, you will be more careful with items from both Number Eleven and Carrick if they come to you from any source other than myself."

They all agreed. Sophia left the auction house with the consignee's name: Prince Abdullah. She decided that time was of the essence in finding out what was really going on up north. It was time to visit Carrick Castle.

Chapter 12

First Time to Scotland

On the flight to Edinburgh, Sophia studied the portion of Barbara's will pertaining to Carrick Castle.

Carrick Castle is a beautiful place that holds many cherished memories from my early childhood. It is an old castle and a manor house surrounded by substantial land. It harkens back to medieval times. So it is also something of a dinosaur. However, it is more than a historic if somewhat run-down building. It is, in fact, a small township in Perthshire. Therefore, my primary concern is to ensure that the village remains intact and economically viable. First, each inhabitant of the village shall have the right to purchase their home at a quarter of the fair market value or to continue to rent for the rest of their lifetime. Income from these rents shall be put in a trust fund managed by a duly elected town council. Sophia as trustee will be the nominal head of the trust for two years or until it can run as an independent township. The trust is funded with two million pounds to endow the roads and infrastructure of the village.

While the castle and the manor house were joint property, the dower house, or the cottage, as it was referred to, was in Sophia's name. Sophia had called her security team with her arrival information, and upon landing in Edinburgh, she drove directly to the castle. Carrick was an almost three-hour drive north of the capital, and the beautiful Scottish countryside was in full bloom, with delightful lavender flowers and surprisingly clear blue skies.

The road toward the castle went up a slight hill, at the top of which was a gated entrance, which was open. She stopped at the entrance and stared in awe. Two turrets, one intact, one half-demolished, loomed above, jutting into the sky like daggers.

As she drove down the long entrance, the castle and surrounding land began to unfold before her. It was a remote Gothic building perched on a hill above a loch in Perthshire—five thousand lush acres. Off to the south were an additional five thousand acres on which sat the manor house. To the right of the castle were five thousand acres of lush farmland. Toward the left of the entrance was another road with a small sign saying "Carrick Manor." The top of the manor house could just be seen in the distance.

The castle itself initially had been a Stewart stronghold in the Highlands, before being abandoned in the 1600s. Later, it had been partially restored when the manor house was built to be a true Edwardian gentlemen's estate.

The farmers and workers from the estate were now residents in the remote village of Carrick. Filled with well-kept thatched cottages, the village was a magical space. The moment Sophia set eyes on this place, she knew she didn't really want to sell any of it.

By the time she arrived, it was noon. After meeting the security team and the three members of the household staff, she took a quick tour of the castle itself. Half the building was standing as a monument to time. The other half was in ruins, with large tape barriers announcing danger. The staff showed her the significant rooms of the castle. The grand entry was a massive hall with a vaulted Gothic ceiling. This was where the tables had been. This hall led into three other great rooms. The only rooms with any light streaming into them were the two front great rooms, having been modified, if somewhat poorly, to have large multipaned windows.

Sophia chose the brightest of these as a place to sit and discuss the theft with her security team. After a lengthy discussion, they agreed to review all the tapes the next day. So Sophia decided to carry on to the manor house.

She was standing on the keep steps, getting ready to leave, when she spied a broken and battered black Rolls Royce speeding down the long driveway. The noise from its exhaust would have let anyone nearby know it was coming long before the wreck was in sight.

The driver who climbed out was a short, pudgy man with balding gray and red hair and a pockmarked, reddish face. Her security guard said with a great deal of disdain in his soft Scottish lilt, "I see the Earl of Morven has arrived—to meet you, I assume."

Sophia stood still, slightly taken aback as the little man came bounding up the steps.

"Sophia Lawrence, I presume," he said without preamble. "I am the Earl of Morven, your neighbor to the north—better than that shady Arab prince Abdullah you've got to the south."

Sophia bristled at the use of the word "shady," even though she was shocked to learn they were neighbors here as well. It was all she could do to keep her features composed.

She took an instant dislike to this man. Still, trying not to forget her manners, she answered somewhat offhandedly, "Nice to meet you, Your Grace. I would love to stay and chat. However, I am on a schedule and must be at my next appointment."

The earl was possibly the ugliest man she had ever laid eyes on. His eyes were puffy, his face pockmarked. His dress was disheveled, and he had the all-too-familiar air of bullish drunkenness. He stumbled forward to shake her hand, and there it was: his breath was heavy with stale booze. Inexplicably, he tried to kiss her lips!

She turned quickly to avoid him. Again, she said in a very perfunctory way, "Lovely to meet you. I really must be going. Maybe we can have tea the next time I am in country." *Not likely*, she thought, but it was a reasonable effort at manners.

He looked askance, then realized he had been dismissed said, "Yes, that would be jolly." Turning around, he returned to his car and raced off back down the drive, almost hitting a couple of trees on the way out.

She muttered, "We don't need to spend time with him."

Upon hearing her words, the security guard added in his strong Scottish brogue, "He's a bad one at that."

With nothing more to do about the tables until the next morning, Sophia asked if there was someone who could give her a tour of the village and the other buildings on the property.

Her next stop was the manor house. It was everything she had imagined it would be from the pictures. The long and leafy tree–lined avenue culminated in a large forecourt area. Built in 1771, the house was a significant three-story, three-sectioned structure with twelve-pane sash windows across the two lower stories and a pediment subtly projecting from the central section. The center section opened to a spectacular entrance hall with hardwood parquet flooring and a massive stone fireplace with a molded surround. It was everything she'd imagined save for one oddity: there was no art in the entry hall.

The housekeeper met her at the door, saying that she would love to show her the house and that Lamote, the de facto head of the village, would be joining them shortly. The rooms to the right consisted of a formal living room in front and a proper library on the back. These were wrapped by an impressive grand ballroom with a stunning view of the loch.

The sweeping staircase ascended from the hall to the second floor, which held a giant master suite to the right and four smaller suites on the left. The center room over the kitchen was an additional sun-filled library that Sophia instantly fell in love with. The back of the house had a lovely Palladian-style patio with a ceiling that kept the worst gales from bashing against the house in winter.

About a mile from the main house, situated down path through a field of wildflowers, sat a white stucco four-bedroom cottage. Originally the dower house, the cottage was situated on a prominent knoll near the loch, and looking up a larger hill, she had a dramatic view of the large towers of the prince of thieves' property.

Sophia stared at Abdullah's massive Georgian mansion, wondering at the strange circumstance that made him a neighbor both here and in London. Lost deep in thought, she was pulled out of her reverie when a strapping young man with shaggy brown hair roughly her own age approached her.

"Welcome to Carrick. I'm Lamote. Would you like to see the village?"

"I would love to," she replied. "This place is so magical. I wish I had come here sooner."

Lamote escorted her to a slightly aging Range Rover to drive her down the hill to the village.

Carrick Village was a little village set on the edge of the loch. Neat, tidy homes with thatched roofs lined the one main street. The street had lamps at each house and was a tar-sealed road. At the end of the street was a cobblestone square with a small church, a school, a fire station, and a local mercantile. Lamote parked in the square and invited her to walk down to the loch and a small beach where the villagers had gathered to meet her.

She was charmed at the openness and warmth of the fifty or so people there, including the volunteer fire chief and the local pastor. They told her how happy they were to meet her, and she chatted with each of them.

After tea and smoked salmon sandwiches at the beach, seeing that Sophia looked tired, Lamote drove her back to the manor house. That evening, she sat sipping a glass of wine while reading the Scottish tabloids full of the latest gossip all about the Earl of Morven.

The next morning, she spent several hours reviewing the tapes and finding nothing to prove or disprove the theft. She finally asked a security guard, "Do we have a game camera on the property, the ones used to spot deer movements?"

"Why, yes, we do, ma'am, I had not thought to look at them. I will bring them in now."

At this point, the elderly cook walked in, saying, "Excuse me, ma'am. I couldn't help but overhear. If we knew exactly what you were looking for, we might better help."

"Well, you might be just the person to ask," she said. "I am wondering who was on the property before the security team arrived. Was there anyone you didn't know?"

"Yes, ma'am," she said. "The first visit was from Henry, your brother-in-law, and a foreign man—an Arab, I think. He was dressed in those robes, white they were. Oh, and the earl was here with him also. But … not at the same time as Mr. Lawrence. They were here for a couple of hours. Then a few weeks later, my daughter who works at the manor house saw him—the Arab, I mean—with a loading van. They drove right down this driveway, turned around, and went to the back buildings, the ones behind the manor house."

"When was that?" Sophia asked.

"Well," said the housekeeper, looking up to the ceiling for a moment, "it was right after Mr. Henry was here with the Arab man."

Now they were getting somewhere. "Let's see that footage," said Sophia.

They found the footage she was hoping for from the first week. First, a white van traveled down the drive. The driver was clearly Middle Eastern given his dress, but Sophia did not recognize him. Then the garden footage clearly showed the two Jacobean tables being moved into the van. The second participant in this theft was an unexpected face: it was the Earl of Morven.

"Well," she said to the security guard as they reviewed the tapes again, "we need both photos and copies of this tape. Then we need to secure both tapes in the safe."

"Yes, ma'am," he said. "You do understand," he stuttered, "that these are before our time. I have never seen the Arabian man, but of course, I have seen the earl."

Sophia gave him a warm smile. "I understand."

As her security man gazed out the window toward the drive, he spied a familiar car arriving. "And I think, ma'am, the earl has come to collect his tea."

The Earl of Morven stumbled into the front hall of the castle, clearly still drunk from his previous night's binge.

"And to what do I owe this dubious honor?" Sophia asked sarcastically, not getting up to greet him.

"Why, I am here for my tea, Sophia, and I have a business proposition for you."

"Oh? Do you now?" Looking at her security guard, she asked, "Would it be too much of an imposition to ask for a spot of late-morning tea? No scones, thank you, just a tea service."

"Yes, ma'am," he said. He left the door ajar as he exited the room.

"Well, Your Grace, what is your business proposition?" she asked, thinking it would be best to get this over with quickly.

He lurched slightly toward her and said, "You know, Sophia, since we are neighbors, I thought maybe we should become more friendly." Leering, he went on. "You might even become a countess."

She burst out laughing. In hindsight she would realize this probably had been a mistake, but she couldn't help herself. The inquiry was so outlandish and sudden, and the thought so preposterous, that she had no other response.

Trying to gather her wits, she said, "You do realize that in Scotland, I am already a countess? Surely, there's no need to be a countess squared." She was still laughing and missed his dangerous scowl. "Besides," she managed between her laughs, "I believe you're already married. Am I mistaken?"

Then lurching toward her, close enough that she could again smell his putrid breath, he said, "Our lands would be bigger than that dirty towelhead in a dress to the south. We could crush him with our acreage."

How dare you use that kind of language? she thought, but she somehow managed to hold her tongue, though the emotions were etched clearly across her face. Changing the subject, she said, "I read your story in all the gossip sheets last night. Marriage? You must be joking. I have no interest in marriage. So your business plan is officially, and *forever*, off the table."

"Sophia, you would be my countess!" he slurred indignantly.

"More like the Countess of Chaos," she snapped back. By now, Sophia was furious and wanted him off her property immediately.

Without the faculties or the sobriety to conjure a response, he lurched toward her drunkenly again and seized the front of her blouse. The sudden motion set him off balance, and he stumbled backward, ripping the blouse as he fell and collapsing into a befuddled heap on the floor about the time her security guard came running in.

"You're out of here, you blighter!" the guard said and physically pushed him out the door.

By now, the earl was running, stumbling for his car, and as it raced down the drive, other security men followed him to make certain he had left the property.

The housekeeper arrived with tea, and the footman brought Sophia her overnight bag so she could change her shirt.

"Can we *please* try to keep today's unpleasant events between us?" she asked. "The last thing I need is gossip."

They answered, "Yes, ma'am," in unison.

It was only after tea, when Sophia was wandering around the entry hall, that she noticed the large areas outlined with faded paint indicating where art once had hung. Not wanting to miss her plane, she thanked the staff and left for Edinburgh. While driving she pondered all she knew, especially about Abdullah.

Section 2

Chapter 13

Getting to Know Him

On her first night home from Scotland, Sophia slept fitfully. Around five in the morning, she awoke to the sound of loud voices speaking in Arabic outside. Looking out of her window, a move she would later regret, thinking there might have been another bomb, she saw the princes' men towing a car away from between the two homes. All of a sudden, she had a vision of another bomb detonating.

The next morning, a large "no parking" sign had been placed in front of the house. *Odd*, she thought as she dressed and went to get a cup of coffee.

The prince was waiting for her as she left her house for her morning walk. Soon their walks would become a daily ritual. He was a ravishingly handsome man—tall, with dark curly hair on the slightly shaggy side and dark piercing eyes—and very witty. He always wore Western dress jeans and a button-down shirt. Atypically, for a Middle Eastern man, he always was clean-shaven or was at least within a few days of a shave. Their conversations were interesting, engaging even, but always superficial—often about London, his other homes in the UK, or his horses.

Soon they were chatting away like old friends. On the third walk, Sophia asked him about his country. "Your Grace," she started, "or should I call you Your Highness? I know you're from Arabia. Could you tell me more about your country—its history, geography, and religion? I find I'm woefully uneducated about your kingdom."

"Please, when it is just the two of us, call me Abdullah. The history of my country is longer than a trip around this crescent, so I suggest we expand our walks over to the Serpentine and back."

Smiling impishly, she said, "The Serpentine it is. I enjoy running there."

"You do know, Sophia, that this is a first for me. In our country we never would be allowed to go walking or running in public with a woman. You can feel safe—my security guards have now taken up running." He gave her a wide smile, and they started to run.

Despite being a little wary of the prince, she enjoyed her morning exercise. His ever-present bodyguards, always behind them, served as a safety mechanism, and he never made a pass at her. Her one question, of course, was not covered in one morning's walk. These walks soon turned into an hour every morning and included running parts of the lovely paths through Kensington Gardens and around the palace itself.

Sophia realized she needed to act on the tables still sitting at Sotheby's, yet for some reason, maybe fear, she did not broach the subject with the prince. She was hoping, probably against hope, that he did not know about them—that somehow, it was all a misunderstanding. Yet realistically, she understood that Henry was involved and that eventually the information must be discussed with all the parties.

One morning as they were finishing their walk, on a whim she invited him in for coffee. He looked slightly torn for a moment before shaking his head. He didn't look her in the eyes when he did it. After another moment he spoke.

"I'm afraid I cannot come to your home, but you are more than welcome to accompany me to mine."

"What, you're afraid I'll poison you?" The second it came out of her mouth, she regretted the remark. Her hands flew to her mouth.

The scowl of anger that briefly flitted across his face was almost instantly replaced by laughter, mostly at her embarrassment. However, he knew Sophia's words held a hint of truth, so throwing caution to the wind, he said, "Fine, Sophia, coffee in your garden it is."

On the walk through Sophia's home to her garden, Abdullah spied and stopped to look at the Sisley, a stunning oil painting of Lady's Cove in Wales, now hanging in the sun-drenched yellow living room. "How did you acquire the Sisley I saw in your drawing room? I thought that all the art from Number Eleven was going up for auction."

Sophia was surprised that he had mentioned Number Eleven. She smiled as she said tartly, "Not all the art. Several pieces were given to me. The Sisley is one of them."

Her cook served coffee on the patio in the ivy-covered garden, eyeing the prince slightly askance, especially since Sophia had graciously motioned two of the security men through the house, offering them coffee as well.

Finally, he asked, "And the pair of Turners from Scotland are among them as well?" he asked, his face slightly furrowed with a frown.

"Yes," she replied. "How did you know that? They were never part of the sale of the property. The art was never included. And from the minute we knew about the collection, those five were always mine. And for that matter, how did you know about Scotland?"

"Sophia, you know that you are my neighbor in Scotland to the north, right?"

She regarded him distrustfully. What was his angle here? It was a little odd that they had never talked about her inheritance or Number Eleven since the night of the bombing. Sophia decided it best to take the proverbial bull by the horns and come out with it. "Why did you include the art in your offer anyway? To the best of my knowledge, you didn't tour the house."

He smiled. "You're right—I did not. I looked at the inventory I was presented and said yes. The artists were all well known to me. And I saw you the night I was at the Connaught, correct? You were with Westminster, I believe? Did you know I was only at the meeting for drinks? I left before dinner."

He spoke smoothly and confidently, and now he was eyeing Sophia with a sort of hungry curiosity. She was a lovely lady, fun, composed, and an excellent walking companion.

"Yes," she said, "I was there and did know." She suddenly giggled.

"What's so funny, Sophia?"

Without thinking, she said, "And he called you..." Then she stopped talking.

"He called me what, Sophia?"

She had been about to say "the prince of thieves" and knew that would be an insult. So she extemporized and said, "Oh, he just said you were a tough negotiator. That's all."

"And what's funny about that? Do you think it was inaccurate?" His dark eyes, the ones that always seemed to look through her, narrowed as he spoke.

"Oh, Your Highness, I am so sorry. Just forget I laughed. Nervous laughter, that's all."

"I make you nervous?" he said, placing the flat of his hand across his broad chest. "Why is that, Sophia?"

She blushed and stammered, "No, er, yes. Again, I'm sorry, Your Highness."

He put his hands up to shush her and allowed a white-toothed smile to spread across his face. "My name is Abdullah. Please start again."

She bit her lower lip and looked him straight in the eye. "Oh, Abdullah, I am so sorry. What I was going to say was ..." She was staring him straight in the eye, and he could see she might actually cry. "The prince of thieves," she finally blurted, followed by another rush of words, mostly "I am so sorry."

He burst out laughing, which provided Sophia with some relief. "Sophia, do not worry. I've been called far worse. Coming from Westminster, that is almost a compliment. Leave it to the English aristocracy to make literary allusions with their racism."

Sophia shook her head and changed the subject. "Are you off to the country this weekend?" They had spoken before of his country estate in Gloucestershire, which he maintained for his two daughters and wife.

"I am. I enjoy riding on my property. It and my property in Scotland are places where I can be alone, without guards, places where I can contemplate. Do you have any interest in horses, Sophia?"

She laughed. "Not really. I did ride a little as a child, and I even went riding a few weeks ago with the Westminsters, but my sport is sailing. In fact, I will be in Palma racing this week."

Sensing she was changing the subject, he added, "You should come to the country one weekend and meet my family. I think you would like to get to know my wife. You could ride and see my collection of horses. We have a magnificent string of Irish racehorses."

"That would be wonderful," she responded, feeling confident that the proffered invitation would never really arrive. "I'm excited about taking the entire week off. We are sailing for the season championships. Everyone I know will be there."

"Will you be safe traveling alone, Sophia?" he asked. While he had never shared the thought with Sophia, he had suspicions about whom the car bomb had been intended for.

"I'll be fine," she said. "I leave tomorrow morning. I'll be back in a week. The flight is Heathrow to Palma, nonstop."

"What do you do on the boat?" he asked, his eyebrows pushed together in a worried look. "How big is it?"

"I navigate, and it is forty feet." Sensing some fear in his voice, she added, "Don't worry, I'll be fine."

Upon returning home, Abdullah called his security team and dispatched one of his English men to Palma to shadow Sophia. "Just make certain she is safe" were his instructions. For the entire week she was gone, he called the man every day and asked for updates.

Sophia's week went by quickly. On the flight back, all she could think about was how fun it had been to see her friends, sail, and on the last night, party and dance until 3:00 a.m. Doug, her financial advisor from New York and owner of the boat, had grilled her on her time in London. While he knew about Sophia's inheritance, he also had read about Henry and Janet on Page Six and was a little worried about Sophia.

It was only later that week that Abdullah finally had the chance to ask the security guard about Sophia's trip to Palma.

"Did she have a love interest?" he asked.

"No, sir. However, she has many friends. She is a great sailor. They won the event and did not even have to sail the last day, so Sophia sailed with Juan. She drove for him and won that race also. At the awards party she and her teammates and Juan and his crew danced up a storm until 3:00 a.m. The—"

Just then, Abdullah's phone rang, and he excused the security guard to take the call. That meant he missed what would have been the last sentence of the verbal report: "The king of Spain adores her."

Chapter 14

Meeting Princess Rima— September 1992

Sophia had been back in London for a week when the invite to dinner from Their Royal Highnesses Abdullah and Rima arrived from a uniformed courier.

Sitting in her study, with the golden afternoon light setting the room ablaze, Sophia flipped the invitation over and over in her hands. Sophia had unfinished business with the prince. After looking over the tapes again, all she really knew was that a foreign man had helped move the tables and art—and that Sotheby's had said they were on consignment for Abdullah.

Her dilemma came from the realization that she actually liked him and that she really did want to go to dinner. And could she be blamed? He was witty and intelligent and treated her not only like a lady, but also like a person and an equal, despite their obvious differences in standing. Maybe she thought getting to know his wife would provide her with an insight into how to get around the problem of the tables without causing bad feelings with their Royal Highnesses.

She walked next door at promptly seven thirty and was ushered into the foyer by a footman uniformed in black with a gold waistcoat.

Princess Rima bint Abbas was a petite raven-haired woman with the most vivid green eyes Sophia had ever seen. She walked into the foyer from a sitting room and greeted Sophia warmly in a soft French accent.

Extending her hand, she said, "I am Rima. Welcome to our home. Please join me for an aperitif. I am afraid that Abdullah will not be joining us this evening. He was called away unexpectedly on business. You do not mind, do you?" She asked the question in a shy, almost demure tone of voice.

"Of course, I don't," Sophia said without hesitation. "It was meeting you that I was most looking forward to this evening."

Rima relaxed and ushered her into a small sitting room apart from the main salon. It was filled with art and furnished with ottomans, silk pillows, and small, low sofas, all sitting atop elegant Persian rugs. The tables along the walls were stunning French antiques, mostly demilune style with elegant bronze rococo embellishments. "This is my room," said Rima. "It reminds me of home."

Slightly at a loss for what to say, Sophia asked, "Are you originally from Arabia also? His Highness has been educating me about your home, giving me a history lesson during our morning walks."

"No, I was originally born in Syria," she replied. "But Abdullah and I were engaged at my birth and married when I was very young. Arabia is now my home."

Then Rima put Sophia immediately at ease by saying, "Please call him Abdullah in private. And yes, he enjoys your morning walks. He always arrives home with a spring in his step. I hope you enjoy his nonstop history lesson as much as he enjoys giving it. His walks give me a peaceful time in the morning to work without Abdullah looking over my shoulder, asking endless questions."

"What is your work?" Sophia asked, hoping she was not prying.

"I own a boutique hotel chain." Then laughing, she said, "It is Carrick Inc., named after the village where I hear we also have neighboring homes."

Sophia nodded. "Yes, an unusual coincidence."

Without commenting on the irony of their being neighbors in two countries, Rima continued. "We have several luxury hotels in France, England, Scotland, and India. It keeps me busy and happy."

Then changing the subject, she asked, "How do you find life in London? Is it different from the States?"

"I love London," Sophia said before stopping to search for words. For some reason, she trusted this woman, and she continued. "It seems liberating to start a new life."

"How so?" asked Rima.

"Last June, before I arrived in London, I had just spent fifteen days sailing across the Atlantic in a small boat, wondering what to do with my life and my miserable marriage, only to arrive in Ireland to find that my husband, whom I was planning on divorcing, and my mother-in-law had both died. I knew my marriage was over even before I left for Ireland, but I still felt guilty. Then I simply became sad and slightly terrified. Now I am learning to live with what I call my unplanned reinvention." Then Sophia asked, "How do you find life in England?"

Before Rima could answer, they were interrupted by a slew of uniformed servants carrying trays of delicious-smelling food into the formal dining room. The employees set the service up as a buffet and bowed before exiting the room.

The simple buffet turned into an elegant five-course meal that lasted for several hours, each course served with a different fabulous French wine. The women carried on with small talk, discussing the latest sale at Harrods and the art collection on display in the room, nothing too personal. By the end of the meal, both women had consumed a sufficient quantity of wine to diminish any inhibitions they might have had, and Sophia's curiosity got the better of her.

"I'm sorry to be so personal," she said, "but I thought alcohol was forbidden in your culture. Our consumption of wine tonight would indicate otherwise."

Just then a footman announced that the cheese course was served in the sitting room. The women adjourned to the lovely, cozy space where cheese had been set out with a bottle of Chateau Yquem. Rima smiled and nodded to the servers as they left, before turning back to Sophia. Her smile was gone and had been replaced by a pensive expression.

"You asked earlier how I find life in England and about the serving of alcohol at this meal. Sometimes I feel like I am living in two worlds, the West and the East. Since I was a young girl, I have been living this way and have grown used to it.

"I love England and my work because it takes me away from Arabia. I fear my husband may have glossed over some of the more problematic issues in our society during your daily walks."

Sophia asked, "Why do you wish to be away from your home?"—without really thinking that this might be too personal a question.

Looking down, deep in thought, Rima answered, "I want to share my story with you, Sophia. Because I believe you are worthy."

Worthy. It was a strange word to use, yet Sophia felt somehow honored by its mystery and grandeur.

"Abdullah and I were engaged to be married when he was seven and I was a newborn. It was our fathers' attempt to end the multigenerational feud between our families. Their plan worked, for a time.

"After my father's death, my brother, as the eldest male, became the leader of our family. He had always been ambitious, fatally so at times, and so too at this time, for it was his dream to rule the kingdom.

"That was not what had been carefully arranged in our marriage contract. It had always been agreed that Abdullah would eventually become crown prince and run the country when the time came. I had been taught from an early age that it was his destiny. In fact, it was *our* destiny.

"When I turned twelve, my brother and his uncle decided that the only way to break the long-standing marriage contract was to make certain I was no longer an eligible bride. He assumed—and in most cases, it would have been true—that if I disgraced our house, then the marriage would be called off. So he arranged for his men to rape me."

Sophia looked at her with horror written across her face. Rima appeared to not notice and continued.

"And after they were done, he did so himself. When I screamed, they gagged me. I almost suffocated. I will not bore or embarrass you with any more excruciating details, but Abdullah was told by one of my servants.

"He found me in the desert. After the rape, I had been mutilated." She paused. "I was almost dead. All I remember is pain and blood. He took me back to his family palace. The king, his father, was incensed.

"Abdullah was only eighteen years old, but he stood his ground, saying our marriage was his destiny, and insisted we marry immediately. The next day, we were married, and I was shown to the nation on the palace's balcony. While still angry at my family, the king never took his anger out on me. Abdullah took me to an exclusive private hospital in Switzerland.

"I was lost, scared, and married. Abdullah was at Oxford at the time, and every weekend except for the few during which he traveled to home, he would come to Switzerland. The hospital healed me physically as best they could, after which Abdullah enrolled me in an equally private Swiss school. He had his sisters and cousins enroll in the same school, so I would have friends. We were all allowed to learn about things that no one in our country is ever taught. And over those six years, Abdullah and I became fast friends. His kindness helped me heal emotionally. At first, I did not understand why I needed a school or a special hospital, but as I became older, it became abundantly clear how much damage had been done to me internally.

"Finally, I was as healthy as I would ever be and was very well educated both in Arabian culture and in that of the West. I spoke multiple languages, understood customs and history, and excelled in business. Despite all of these successes, I was still very frightened and lonely.

"On my eighteenth birthday, Abdullah and I traveled back to our country for what he said was my homecoming, to show the country what a perfect princess I had become."

Throughout this story Sophia had been looking at Rima. *How in dear God*, she thought, *can she sit here and explain this so calmly?*

Rima poured them both the last of the Yquem and continued. "I never saw my brother again. I was told he had been lost in a fierce sandstorm and died in the great desert of Arabia. I'm sure you understand what that means. And frankly, I did not care. I still don't.

"Abdullah finished his master's work at Oxford, and I enrolled in the Sorbonne. On our holidays we would travel the world—India, Paris, Rome, Hong Kong, the United States. And it was all platonic. We would forget we were married and think of each other as brother and sister. And we became the best of friends. Then he would mention destiny, and I would remember—destiny, a big and heavy word. However, traveling with Abdullah served one excellent purpose: it improved my health and my confidence.

"Over the years Abdullah and I have learned to cope with our private issues, with how badly broken I still am. He has been continually supportive of my business activities and allows me as much time away from Arabia as possible.

"That is a long, painful way to answer the question of why I love living in England."

As Rima had told her story, Sophia had sat quietly, intently listening to her words. "I am exceptionally touched that you chose to share your story with me, Your Highness. Yet I am equally if not more touched by your strength in the face of all adversity."

"What a generous and kind response, Sophia. Thank you."

When the evening ended, both women felt they had become fast friends. In the end, as Rima said goodbye, she placed a kiss on each of Sophia's cheeks and then said softly, "Never be afraid of your destiny, or of Abdullah. He is part of your journey. Allah will approve and, if necessary, forgive."

Upon returning home, Sophia walked into her study and sat down on the sofa, contemplating what she had learned about Rima's childhood. From everything she knew, she realized that Rima's problems had not ended with her hospitalization. They must continue with her every day. And Sophia realized they must have affected Abdullah greatly also.

Chapter 15

Life in London—October 1992

*T*he clock was ticking. Sophia had less than three months before the UAE wanted to take possession. Given the enormity of this task, she decided to defer another trip to Scotland. Then she remembered the art on loan to the Italian embassy. Not knowing their plans, she called the embassy and asked to speak to the ambassador. He took her call immediately.

As she stumbled over her question, he put her at ease by saying, "I assume you are calling about the art we have on loan."

"Yes," she said, "I am. I wish I weren't, but ..."

He said, "They are not in the buildings at Number Eleven. Sophia, please come to my residence, and I will show you what pieces are yours. I will hate to lose them as I adore all of them. Are you free for dinner?"

Her time in London was certainly taking on a life of its own—first Uncle Jerry, then the Ritz, her neighbor Prince Abdullah, racing in Spain, shooting parties, and now dinner with the Italian ambassador. She went to her computer to learn more about Antonio Scala.

His driver picked her up promptly at 7:30 p.m. Dressed in a white silk sheath dress and matching coat, she wore a stunning sapphire necklace and earrings. By eight, she was drinking prosecco in the formal drawing room at his residence. He was as delightful as she had remembered, one of the most charming men she had ever met. He had straight dark-brown hair and wore aviator glasses, and her research had shown that he was the same age as Sophia and single.

"You look stunning this evening, Sophia," he had said as he greeted her.

His kisses slipped a little from the normal to the more sensual. Sophia smiled warmly at the man, trying to gauge his mood.

He walked her through a tour of the residence, showing her the seven pieces that were on loan. They were all stunning oils by grade A artists, including a Turner and a unique Sargent. He told her why he especially loved the Venetian paintings since they all included his home, a palace in San Marco Venice. The Sardinian one also included his castle on the island.

Antonio mentioned over dinner that he would like to purchase all of the paintings and was willing to pay a fair market price. She told him she would have to think about her answer and changed the subject to his home in Italy.

"I would love to have you visit my homes in Italy, Sophia. We could always go to Venice for a long weekend."

While this sounded fun, Sophia surmised that he wanted her to be more than just a house guest. She demurred, saying, "I would love to, but for now, I need to focus on my work."

The dinner passed quickly with a lively conversation. After dinner, Sophia and Antonio sat in the drawing room, sipping on port. He was seated close to her on the love seat, facing the Canaletto.

"I love this one the most," he said. "It is a scene from my home in Venice. The people seem so in love and full of pleasure. It would be my pleasure to show you my home, Sophia. Will you please come away with me for a long weekend? I can show you this in real life."

The painting was erotic, and there was no mistaking the invitation this time. Again, she demurred. "I'm so sorry, Antonio. The sheer volume of work and other things I have to get done just keep me in London right now."

"Oh, Sophia, my pet," he said as he leaned over. He kissed her, and Sophia was so starved for affection that she began to kiss him back. Then his hand slid up under her dress, groping. This pulled her back to reality, and she squirmed, trying to get away.

"No, Antonio. No, I can't do this."

By now she was pinned on the sofa. She started to push him off, but he held her down, saying, "Shush, Sophia, this will be good."

"No," she repeated. "I really mean no." This time she pushed him away. As his hand slid out from under her dress, he ripped the hem. The sound of the silk tearing served to jar them both back to reality.

Sophia stood up, a little wobbly. "I need to leave now," she said as calmly as possible. Her hair was a mess, her dress was torn, and she was exceedingly uncomfortable.

"I'm sorry, Sophia. I didn't mean … But really, we're both adults. We could make good music. You're beautiful and soon to be rich—a winning combination."

The look of pure rage on her face brought him up short. "Besides," he added, "there is the deal to consider. Don't you think?"

Sophia pulled her cell phone out of her bag to call a cab.

"My driver can take you home, Sophia," he said quietly, realizing he had gone too far.

"No, thank you!" She turned on her heels and left.

"Sophia, you have not answered my question!"

As she walked out the door, she called back, "And I have no intention of ever doing so."

On the ride home, as she calmed down, she decided he would not do anything about the sale because it would not be in his best interest.

Early the following day, she penned a polite note to Antonio, thanking him for a lovely dinner and requesting that the art be returned as soon as possible. She wrote in parting, "I am happy to arrange for Sotheby's to package up the pictures at your earliest convenience."

She was just finishing writing up a report to Henry, even though such reports seemed to create more chaos and animosity than anything else, when her email beeped: "You've got mail." It was Henry.

> *Sophia,*

> *I insist that you begin releasing the funds in the bank to us immediately to get us through this troubling time. We are building a new house on the lake, and need the cash immediately. My wiring instructions are below.*

She sighed. How like him to demand something impossible.

It took her three days and several rounds with Henry and then her attorneys before this most recent debate was settled. The entire process unnerved Sophia. Why, she wondered, was Henry so combative and mean?

Just when she thought she had it settled, he started again. Henry called her yelling at the top of his lungs. "I want to separate out the art and the properties like you and Janet did with the jewelry, half to us and half to you."

"Henry, I see your math skills are off today. Let's start by working on your division. The split is two-thirds to me and one-third to you. Are you contesting that fact?"

There was silence on the other end of the line.

"Sorry, Henry, the answer is no. And as trustee I have the right and the responsibility to say that. And I will add some of the furniture from my estate into the auction, maybe even some Jacobean tables and furniture from Scotland."

Even though he was taken aback at her comment about furniture from Scotland, he replied, "If you do that, you little bitch, I'll see you in court."

Later that day, she received a call from Sir Joshua, telling her they had quashed the latest attempt from Henry's attorneys.

Chapter 16

Walking with the Prince

Walking with Abdullah had become a daily occurrence. The few times he had been out of town, he had mentioned his travel plans in advance and even specifically told her when he would be back. He had even taken to walking to her door and waiting patiently for her when she was late, with seldom a complaint.

It was a brisk fall day, and the leaves on the trees in Hyde Park were a striking orange and gold color. Sophia and Abdullah were taking their usual early-morning jog around Hyde Park. He had been in Arabia for the past week.

"You seem troubled, Sophia. Is it something I might be able to help with? Even by just listening?"

"I am," she sighed. "My outlaws have become so combative, and it takes so long to get anything done. Henry and I are constantly fighting. We end up bickering about every painting. Yesterday, it was the Renoir versus the Monet. It's just absurd."

She looked up at him and smiled. "I'm sorry. That sounds so silly when you deal with important problems all the time. Tell me more about your trip. I'm sure it was far more interesting than my problems with Henry."

He then proudly told her all about the economic reforms he wished to implement in his country. He explained, "While today we supply 28 percent of the world's oil, I do not believe we can always count on that income for my country. I am working hard on new developments so that in the future we will not just depend on the pumping of oil, but also will profit from its movement."

On their next morning walk, another glorious fall day, Abdullah wanted to discuss Islam. Often the change in subject matter from one day to the next made Sophia's head spin. After a few usual pleasantries—"lovely day" and "how are you?" type chatter—he said, "I was thinking about my religion this morning at prayer. Do you know much about Islam as a religion, Sophia?"

She looked up at him, making a funny face. "I am afraid I must plead woeful ignorance, Abdullah. But I have a feeling you will now educate me."

"If you like," he said. "I'm a Sunni Muslim, but we are not backward. Nor are we a violent religion. I believe it is a sacred duty to correctly interpret all religions and their wisdom for the modern world."

"That is a noble ambition, but how do you achieve that in the real world?" she asked.

"I also believe that the Quran's promotion of peace and respect is to be strictly obeyed, and that means that all religious beliefs should be tolerated.

"One way to achieve change in the real world is to have meaningful dialogue and discussion about Islam and other religions worldwide. The violent actions of an extreme minority have obscured the dignity and peaceful teachings of my faith. Given my position and privilege in life, it is my responsibility to have these global discussions."

She stopped walking and turned to face him. "That is such a great global goal, not just for your religion but for all religions. But given that so much of religion is local, how will you attempt to achieve this? And how will you get the more radical factions"—she held up her hands to forestall any comment—"to agree within your or any other religion, let alone across ecumenical lines?"

"That is a very good question, Sophia, one that I study and ponder often. Now let's go back to running, shall we?"

As they began running again, she thought of and asked another question. "This may be naive, but you speak of peace, yet didn't your country just finish a war with Iraq, with the United States' backing?"

"That was a very defensive posture for us. Iraq was the aggressor. We are very much engaged with your US military to develop strategic protection from our enemies in the region. And oh, my dear, we have many."

They had been running at a slow pace while deeply engaged in this conversation. Sophia had been listening intently, and when they arrived at the crosswalk at Queen's Gate leaving the park, she instinctively looked left, not right. Not seeing any traffic coming from her left, she started to cross the street. Abdullah saw the speeding cab approaching from their right and grabbed her, yanking her back up onto the curb.

As he pulled her to safety, she stumbled, falling toward him. To keep her from falling, he instinctively wrapped his arms around her, holding her close as he whispered in her ear, "Are you hurt, Sophia?"

It was the first time he had ever touched her. Maybe it was from fear, but Sophia felt shock waves run through her body. Slightly out of breath, she leaned closer into him and his arms. Then she blushed and tried to say some form of thank-you, but she couldn't quite find her tongue.

Feeling the warmth of her body in his arms. Abdullah slowly set her to rights and away from his now excited body, saying, "It's fine, Sophia." Then slowly, he added, "I hope I can always be around to help you."

The incident was soon pushed into the back of her mind.

A few days later, they were walking toward Kensington Palace and the park when she showed him a few photos of the artifacts that had been found at Number Eleven and asked him what he thought. He was fascinated and added a great deal of information on what they were and how they fit into the history of the Middle East.

"I would purchase those from you if you want, Sophia," he said quietly.

She laughed. "Why, thank you. I will keep that offer in mind, but I had a different idea."

"And that idea is?" he asked.

"I was thinking about donating them to a museum so I could acquire a tax deduction."

By now they had entered the park and were heading toward Rotten Row. "I will ponder your hardship, Sophia," he said teasingly. Changing the subject, he asked casually, "How was your big date with the Italian ambassador last week?"

Sophia glanced at him askance. "Not great," she said, also casually, she hoped. "He thinks a great deal of himself and really just wanted a discount deal on the art." She turned away from him so he would not see her face.

Abdullah knew immediately that she was lying. He put his hand on her cheek and turned her face toward him, which again sent shock waves through her body. Quietly, he said, "Sophia, tell me what happened."

She looked at him carefully, gazing into his eyes. She began haltingly at first. "I don't understand how you always know … sometimes I feel like you're having me followed. Dinner was lovely. My art is stunning—another Turner, a Canaletto, two Adams, and—"

He cut her off. "I was not looking for a description of your very prestigious and ever-expanding art collection, Sophia. And yes, I know you came home in a cab and ran up your steps like a frightened camel. You left here in a chauffeur-driven car. So what happened?"

He had been honest with her, so it was her turn to be honest with him. "After dinner, he made a pass at me. And I said no. He became furious and tried to be forceful. By the time he finally got the point that no was no, the hem of my dress was ripped, and I had a bloody lip. Then to make matters worse, he threatened me with queering the deal on the building. So I called a cab and came home."

The look on Abdullah's face was white-hot anger. She could see it in his eyes and then heard it in his voice. "I will—"

She put up her hand and shook her head no before he could finish the thought. "Please don't do anything on my behalf. I appreciate your concern, but I don't think he would really do anything rash.

The art is on loan, documented, and insured. He has already signed the deal. Just let him calm down without a fuss, and all will be well."

"Sophia, please promise me you will tell me if this happens again. And"—he held his hands in the air for silence—"I will happily match any terms if there is any problem with Number Eleven. Your deal will close, but consider me your backup. I am only interested in your safety."

"Thank you, Abdullah," she said quietly. "I appreciate your support." Then she giggled. "A frightened camel?" Sophia blushed and then added, "And it's not the first time I have received an offbeat offer. One guy asked me out to the Ritz for dinner but told me he could not pay because his father hadn't given him his monthly allowance."

Abdullah tried to hide the grin but was unsuccessful. "And what did you say, Sophia?"

Giggling again, she answered, "I told him my dad didn't give me an allowance, so we would have to scrap any dinner or date plans."

Laughing out loud, Abdullah said, "Now let's run this section, please." And they set off jogging across the park.

As they walked home from the park through the tree-lined streets, he said, "Enough about me and my country. What about you before you came to London?"

"I was raised in California. My father was a sea captain. He taught at a maritime college. That's why I enjoy sailing so much."

"What kind of ships, Sophia?"

"Big container ships mostly. Some of my friends ran tankers. I even learned about cargo handling and ships' stability when I was a child. I used to grade my father's papers. Thinking back, his students must have been appalled. I was only fourteen."

Abdullah laughed. "So you come by your sailing from your father."

"Yes," she said with a wistful look. "He taught me how to sail. He even built our family sailboat in our backyard."

"Why?" he asked.

She frowned slightly and then said honestly, "Abdullah, I grew up normal, not a princess. It was the only way we could afford it."

He had to think about that for a minute. "But now you live in London."

"I know, but this is all so new for me. When I arrived in London, I had no idea about Number Eleven, my house, or the art."

"Where did you go to school to learn?" he asked. "You are"—he paused, searching for the right words—"well educated."

She answered, "I went to Harvard and did graduate work at William and Mary in Virginia. I studied geology and geophysics and did my master's in oceanography and marine engineering. For my first job out of college, I worked for the Army Corps of Engineers, building harbors.

"My father was in the navy, so I was raised all over the world. It left me with a different perspective. Then when I was in high school, he went to work as a civilian, ironically carrying ammunition to Vietnam. At the end of the war, he came home with a Cambodian general whom he'd saved from persecution by smuggling him into the US. He lived with us for several months. The discussions at our dinner table informed my current beliefs—like your sentiment of Islam accepting all beliefs. I wish it could be true for all. But enough about me. Where did you go to school?"

"Oxford, LSE, and Sandhurst. Pretty typical for my family," he replied. By now they had arrived back at Sophia's door, so Abdullah asked, "Are you going to Number Eleven today?"

"I am, continuing my art education. I'll be an expert before I'm done," she quipped.

"Can I give you a ride to work? I have a meeting in the city. What time do you wish to go in, Sophia?"

Looking at her watch, she said, "About an hour—does that fit your schedule?"

"Perfectly. I'll pick you up then."

When they later arrived at Number Eleven, Sophia turned to Abdullah. "Would you like a tour of this mausoleum?"

"I'd love one," he replied.

After a three-hour tour, she said, "So what do you think?"

He smiled a goofy grin and said, "I wish I had met you first. I would have offered more."

Laughing, she replied, "Sorry, that ship has sailed, my friend."

Two days later, she read in the *Daily Mail* that the Italian ambassador was being recalled to Rome and posted to a new billet. She knew how that had occurred and thought, *Oh my, anywhere might as well be Siberia for him.* She also had a quirk of apprehension at the vast power and reach of her prince, as she was beginning to think of him.

Abdullah had gone back to Arabia for two weeks. When he returned, he immediately sent Sophia a note saying he was back and asking if she was free to walk the next morning.

The next morning, Sophia was up and dressed early. By the time their appointed meeting arrived, she had been pacing her sitting room, glancing out the window in anticipation. When she saw him walking toward her house, she literally bounded down the stairs.

"How was your trip?" she asked.

"I went home to celebrate the Prophet's birthday," he replied. "It is a special time that I use to study the Quran."

Knowing that this would lead him into an interesting lecture, she replied, "Really! Tell me more. What did you learn?"

"I was studying what the Prophet says about marriage," he replied. "You know, Sophia, that the Quran holds that men and women have equal moral agency, and they both receive equal rewards in Paradise. Muhammad married many wives, maybe nine or ten, depending on the differing accounts. Rima was chosen to be my bride at her birth. You know her story from age six. I have kept this story a secret from the world. Only I and now you know our full story. But all marriages in our country, especially in the upper echelon, have some political aspect to strengthen our tribes. This again was to be my destiny. Someday I will be king, and life will be different. But for now, we enjoy our walks, Sophia. They bring me great joy and tranquility."

"Yes," she answered slowly, uncertain of what this conversation meant to her, if anything. Finally, almost at a loss for words, she said, "But fortunately for you, Rima is strong and loves you dearly."

Abdullah turned away, but not before she saw the look of despair etched in his face.

That night was Sophia's cook Mrs. Kelly's night off. Coming home around five, Sophia did not feel like making herself dinner, so she quickly changed and walked out of her home toward a nice little Indian restaurant three blocks from her house.

As she was walking into the very plain restaurant, she noticed a man who looked like one of Abdullah's guards sit down on a bench across the street. She wondered, not for the first time, if he was having her followed.

Perhaps five minutes passed before Abdullah and Rima strode into the tiny restaurant. *Well, I guess that answers that question,* she thought. *But why?* she wondered.

Sitting down at her table without any preamble, Abdullah said in a gruff voice, "Why are you here alone, Sophia?"

Rima followed on with a more polite question. "Is the food good? I love Indian food."

Sophia's mouth opened slightly as she looked over her glasses at Abdullah. Then she smiled and shook her head. "Because I am hungry, and it is Mrs. Kelly's night off!" Looking toward Rima, she answered, "Yes, the food is great. Would you two care to join me?" As an afterthought, she impishly turned to Abdullah and said, "I got my allowance today, so it's my treat."

Rima had heard the story, and they both laughed.

"Wait one second," Sophia said as she left the table to find the owner.

When she came back, they were moved into the back room with beads hung as privacy curtains. "I know this is not quite as ornate as our homes, but I thought it would be more comfortable if we were tucked away in here," she said.

After dinner that evening, as they were walking back to their respective homes, surrounded by bodyguards, Rima said, "Sophia, how often does Mrs. Kelly have the night off?"

"Once a week," said Sophia. "She goes to visit her grandchildren. Why do you ask?"

"Every Thursday?" questioned Rima.

"Yes, as a matter of fact."

"From now on, every Thursday you must come to our house. I will even order Indian from that lovely restaurant." With a twinkle in her eye, she added, "And when Abdullah is not here, you should join me for a private shopping trip at Harrods. The food halls and the restaurants have delicious food."

Chapter 17

The Westminsters' Dinner Dance

*I*t was early November, and Sophia was attending a dinner dance at Grosvenor House, the London home of the Duke and Duchess of Westminster. She arrived at her appointed time in a chauffeur-driven Bentley. Sophia was slightly apprehensive about attending this function alone, but Sir Joshua had assured her it would be easy. She was quickly ushered down a long red carpet by a uniformed footman to the entrance, where she was announced to the assembled guests and greeted warmly by the Duke and Duchess of Westminster.

After her formal introduction to the duchess, she gazed out over the crowd at the who's who of the British aristocracy. Looking for someone she knew in the crush, she spotted Barbara's attorney, Sir Joshua Reynolds, coming toward her.

"Sophia," he said, "you look lovely, my dear. Join me for a walk around so I can introduce you to some of my friends."

Sophia had dressed carefully in an antique Indian gown that she had redesigned and recut to look more modern. It was a beautiful shade of turquoise blue, with blue-green bugle beads across the bodice. The sleeves came down to a large cuff with a tight pearl-beaded wrist. The bodice was cut like that of a belly dancer costume but was also wrapped around the back, so no skin showed. She had accessorized with a pair of sapphire-and-diamond earrings and necklace.

The soiree was held in the Westminsters' elegant pale blue and gold-embellished ballroom. Ablaze with massive crystal chandlers, the room was sparkling. The walls of the stunning room dating from the Georgian period were covered in massive gold-leaf rococo embellishments.

As the evening progressed, she began feeling more comfortable than when she had entered. She had just finished dancing with the duke, and they were walking off the floor toward his wife the duchess, when she looked up and saw a familiar ruddy, bloated face.

Sophia muttered quietly, "Shit. Why is he here?"

"Who?" said the duke.

"My neighbor from Scotland," she whispered to Grosvenor.

"Stiff upper lip, my dear. Take my arm," the duke said as he walked up to the earl. "I would like to introduce you to Lady Sophia Lawrence, the Countess of Carrick," he said to Morven.

"We've met," he said, slurring his words. "She's my bitchy neighbor as opposed to the dirty Arab neighbor."

The earl shot a glance at his wife, who shot a glance at the security detail. They immediately removed the very drunken earl to an anteroom to try to sober him up.

As Sophia and the duke moved forward, she commented, "I hate it when anyone make comments like that."

"There, there, Sophia. We all know you're not a bitch."

She turned and looked at the duke with wide eyes. "I mean the comments about Abdullah. Just because he is a foreigner is no reason to make slurs like 'dirty Arab.' It's just not right."

"You are very correct, Sophia, but there are many prejudices that run deep in this country. Whereas in your country that small but vocal group has tended to focus on people of color, ours tends to focus on other ethnic minorities."

Sophia replied, "But the more affluent society does not seem to shun Middle Eastern individuals. Look at the owner of Harrods, King Hussain of Jordan, and even King Fisal or Abdullah."

"Sometimes yes, sometimes no. I like the prince of thieves, despite my very private nickname for him. But others are jealous of his wealth." Then looking carefully at Sophia, he continued, "Since when do you—?" Before he could finish the thought, he spied Abdullah and Rima being escorted toward the stairs that led to the ballroom. "And speaking of which, he has just arrived."

Sophia smiled as Rima and Abdullah were formally announced and entered the room, moving down a flight of stairs toward their hostess, the duchess.

With a wave and a polite nod, and with Sophia on his arm, the duke started making his way across the dance floor and through the mass of partygoers, toward his newly arrived guests. Sophia took this opportunity to excuse herself and head in the opposite direction to find a powder room.

As Abdullah and Rima were announced, the prince spied Sophia. Bending down, he whispered to Rima, "I see Sophia is here."

She smiled while looking at Sophia, saying, "Patience, my prince. Oh my, she looks stunning in that dress."

"Yes, she does," Abdullah whispered hurriedly before he greeted his host and hostess.

As Sophia turned to walk across the room, Abdullah's gaze was utterly unguarded. He might as well have been alone in the room. For one moment the truth of his unadulterated love was written across his face.

The duke, possibly understanding the gaze, hastened to his side to interrupt his thought.

"Welcome, Your Highness," he said urgently, watching Sophia disappear around a corner toward the restroom, a look of concern leaving his face as Abdullah finally met his gaze.

Sophia had made a hasty retreat to compose herself. She was convinced her heart had skipped a beat at the sight of Abdullah in a formal tuxedo. *My God, he is handsome,* she thought. However, she got lost finding the powder room and stumbled upon a small book-filled wood-paneled library. Still wanting to take a second to compose herself and hoping Westminster had not noticed her reaction, she stepped inside.

Then she heard a voice. "So you've decided to take me up on my proposal after all," he slurred. The earl stumbled toward her forcefully, grabbing her arm. She tried to pull away from him, but his grip tightened. Now he was blocking the door.

"Stop it, Your Grace," she said. "Let me pass."

"I'm going to have you," he said, "right here and now."

As Morven lurched toward her again, the door was opened by two security men. Saying something unintelligible to the guards, he inexplicably lurched for her again and was immediately picked up by the scruff of his neck by a tall guard wearing the prince's royal emblem. Sophia recognized the guard from her walks and mouthed the words "thank you."

By this point Westminster had entered the room, exclaiming, "Are you all right, Sophia? Did he hurt you?"

"No harm done," she said shakily. "I am fine."

Behind Westminster she could see Duchess Caroline, Rima, and a very angry Abdullah. Rima was holding his hands to keep him from dashing into the room and talking to him in Arabic in a highly animated voice.

"Honest, I am fine. Morven is mad I won't accept his proposal." As she said this, she kept glancing over Westminster's shoulder toward Rima and Abdullah.

Duchess Caroline, seeing this, said, "Come now, Sophia. I have an introduction to make. Sophia, Countess of Carrick, I would like you to meet Prince Abdullah bin Abbas of Arabia and his wife Princess Rima bint Abbas."

Sophia automatically dropped into a small curtsy to the royals. "It is a pleasure to meet you both, Your Highnesses." Her eyes were twinkling as she spoke.

Westminster walked up behind Sophia and whispered in her ear, "I think anyone and everyone in the room by now knows you have met Their Highnesses."

Giving a sheepish look to the duke, she said, "I have, but your duchess wanted to give me a formal introduction, and I saw no reason not to oblige her. And how did you know that?"

"You have tenderly called him Abdullah all night long, my friend," he whispered into her ear, laughing. He did not mention that he had seen the look on Abdullah's face when he saw Sophia.

Abdullah chimed in, saying, "And I too appreciate the duchess's introduction, as I did not know my neighbor was the Countess of Carrick."

Later that evening, she was chatting with Rima and Abdullah when a waltz started. "Come, Sophia," he said. "I wish to do something else I can never do in my own country."

She eyed him with curiosity. "What is that, Your Highness?"

"Dance with you publicly." And with that he put her arm over his and escorted her onto the dance floor.

She felt like she was floating on air. Nearing the dance floor, she took a deep breath as he took her into his arms, and they started to waltz. He was an excellent dancer, and his steps to the waltz were flawless.

Swirling around the floor, she almost felt dizzy but matched his lead step for step. As the dance progressed, his right hand moved a little lower than necessary down her back. Yet she started to relax. He also held her closer than polite protocol usually dictated. To Sophia it was intoxicating.

At first her eyes were focused straight ahead at the lapel of his tux. As she relaxed, she looked up into his face. Seeing his wide smile, she responded with one of her own and then said, "Is there anything you don't do well?"

He smiled down at her, thinking about her question and wanting to kiss the top of her pert nose. Instead he replied, "Not in public." Then he added with a clearly flirtatious glint in his eyes, "And there are many things I do in private where my skills are far better than my dancing ability."

She smiled even as she arched her eyebrows, as if questioning or maybe daring him.

As they finished the dance, he said, "Don't tease me, Sophia. I might embarrass us both right here in Westminster ballroom."

She blushed a noticeably deep shade of red as Abdullah ushered her off the dance floor, his arm still around her.

While they had been dancing, Rima, the Westminsters, and Sir Joshua had been watching them from the edge of the dance floor. Rima smiled and said to the duchess, "They make a lovely couple."

The duchess was gobsmacked at the comment and looked over at Rima with arched, questioning eyebrows, while Sir Joshua said to no one in particular, "Yes, they do!"

Smiling like a Cheshire cat, the duke interjected, saying, "I suggest we go meet them before they embarrass themselves."

The next Sunday, there was a pheasant shoot at the Westminsters' to which Rima and Abdullah were also invited. The stands for the participants were set up in a semicircle away from the copse of trees from which the birds would be driven. Each participant had a loader to keep reloading their shotguns if necessary. Sophia was the only woman shooting. After Sophia drew stand number two, the prince, breaking protocol, immediately asked his host if he could take stand number three. The duke agreed with a nod, placing Abdullah in stand number three next to Sophia. Then Abdullah added, "I wish to be able to back up Sophia, in case she misses one."

The duke walked away, saying, "I doubt that will be necessary, Your Highness."

Sophia just shook her head and scowled at both men.

The first flock of pheasants flew straight down Sophia's lane. She used five guns and shot every bird with one shot, ten birds in all. Westminster was laughing out loud when the show was over.

"No more in my lane," she said breezily. Then, turning to Abdullah, she said, just loud enough for Westminster to hear, "May I back you up, Your Highness?"

The entire field could hear Abdullah's laughter.

The duke looked over at Sophia and Abdullah. *My goodness,* he thought, *he is so smitten with her, and she with him. I wonder where this will lead.* Then shaking his head, he began to worry about Sophia.

Chapter 18

Drama in the Highlands

Over the years at Eleven Grosvenor Square, there had been fewer and fewer staff. The current team of four consisted of a butler, an elderly housekeeper/cook, and two footmen who also worked as handymen. Sophia had, despite Henry's protests, decided to keep this team in place until after the sale. Yet she worried about what would happen to them after.

Sophia was having tea in the library of Number Eleven, sitting in a lovely French chair, when the footman Frazer entered the room with a serious look on his face and asked if he could have a word.

"Of course, Frazer," she replied. "You look worried. Is there something wrong?"

Slowly, he began to speak in his strong Scottish brogue, low and quiet. "Ma'am, until this week, we had all planned to move home after this house sold. We just lived here to take care of the house for Miss Barbara. We were planning to purchase our own homes, just like the will said we could, and then we received this notice." He handed her a piece of paper.

She looked outside at the gray rainy day. Then with a sense of dread, she opened the letter to read it.

> *Due to the unfortunate death of Lady Barbara Devon Lawrence, over the next few months, the*

Castle Carrick, the Carrick manor house, and the properties in the village are to be sold on behalf of the Lawrence family. While not yet certain of the time frame, we felt it was prudent to inform every tenant that their leases will not be renewed and that they should immediately begin to look for both housing and employment elsewhere.

The signature on the letter belonged to the Earl of Morven.

Sophia sat in the library, her tea forgotten, shaking her head in dismay. As she had been reading, the elderly cook had joined Frazer, and when she looked up at the two elderly employees, they both had the saddest eyes she had ever seen.

Finally, the footman spoke. "We just didn't think you could or would do this to us, madam. We were all in the gallery during the reading of the will and thought we heard you would be in charge. Some of us discussed going to Sir Joshua, but we decided to see if you could explain this to us. We've heard it's your friend the prince who is buying the property for Morven."

For a minute Sophia was speechless. She shook her head, and her voice cracked when she said, "I have no idea what this is really about. I can assure you all that it is not true, and you will be able to move back to Carrick and purchase your homes. This is not what Barbara wanted, and I have done nothing to even attempt to sell either the castle or the manor house. Please bear with me. I will go to Scotland tonight and sort out how this notice even came to exist."

As Sophia rode home, she closed her eyes and placed her hands on her head, willing herself to think clearly. All she really wanted to do was sit by herself and cry. Arriving home, she realized that the staff at the flat would have received the same damn letter.

Max, the butler, met her at the door, saying, "We know you're upset, Miss Sophia. Frazer called us from Number Eleven. Mrs. Kelly is fixing you a spot of tea."

"Thank you," she said. "If you don't mind, I'll be down shortly. I just need to compose myself." She headed to her study upstairs.

When she entered her study, the chesterfield sofa called her to sit down and try to relax and think rationally. Tears welled up in her eyes, and trying to keep from crying, she laid her head down on a pillow. She knew that the earl was involved, and maybe even Abdullah somehow was too.

Looking back, she realized that despite all the time she had spent with Abdullah, they had never discussed the Jacobean tables still sitting at Sotheby's. She smiled, thinking about the delightful evenings and walks they had shared over the last few months, but she also wondered if she hadn't swept the issue under the rug. *Why did I ignore the tables for so long?*

Mrs. Kelly found her half an hour later, still lying on the sofa, tear stains on her cheeks. "I've brought you some tea, miss," she said. "Don't fret. We all know you're going to solve the problems—it just takes time."

Sipping her tea with a faraway look in her eyes, she thought of taking the train to Scotland that night. But before that, if possible, she needed to have a chat with the prince.

Deciding to take a chance that he was home, she washed her face and slowly headed next door.

Standing in Abdullah's entryway, she looked at all the fine antiques and artifacts on display. The label for one of the artifacts said it was from Mesopotamia. *With all these trappings of wealth and power*, she thought, *why two tables?* She was nervously biting her fingernail, trying to decide how to start the conversation, when he entered.

As Abdullah entered the foyer, a smile spread across his face. "This is a lovely surprise, Sophia. How can I help you?"

When she turned to face him, and he saw her puffy eyes and angry stance, his smile vanished and was replaced by a frown.

"What is wrong?" he asked softly.

"I have two massive problems, and I don't know if you are part of the problem or part of the solution. If you have the time, I would like to outline the facts and find out what you honestly know."

He looked at her expectantly as he said, "Go ahead, Sophia."

She started speaking in as calm a voice as she could muster. "Let's start with the Jacobean tables sitting at Sotheby's with your name attached as the consignee. How did you come by them, and do you know they are mine?"

He looked at her and slowly said, "I will tell you whom I bought them from, and by now, I do know that they are part of your estate. I bought them from your brother-in-law as well as a few pieces of art."

"Art?" Sophia repeated, raising her voice. "What art did you buy?" This day had started out badly enough, but now he had also bought art?

"Before I made the offer on Number Eleven, Henry claimed the Scottish property was his. As you know, he is the eye surgeon to my father as well as many other royals in the Middle East, so my family had no reason to distrust him. I have a bill of sale if you would like to see it." His eyes were narrowed in anger, his voice low but calm, as he continued. "Yet by now I do distrust him. I am sorry I did not speak to you about this sooner, for fear of upsetting you. You have had so much to deal with."

Crossing her arms across her chest, her voice dripping with sarcasm, she said, "You didn't think owning property that is partially mine would upset me, did you? In case you're wondering, it upset me a great deal and still does. But you said you had a bill of sale. Do you happen to know where that bill of sale is, and would you care to share it with me?"

"One second," he said. He walked out of the room, pressed a button on an intercom, and angrily shouted into it in Arabic. Turning back to her, he said, "The bill of sale will be here shortly. Can I offer you an iced tea?" He ushered her into the living room and poured her a glass of tea.

Seemingly at a loss for words, Abdullah handed her the glass, saying, "I realize 'I'm sorry' seems very shallow right now. But if it makes you feel better, I was working on a plan to return the tables and the art to you. We can call it a misunderstanding. Ironically, it was. But you said you had two problems."

Again raising her voice, she said, "You have not answered my question yet! What art did you purchase?" She stared at him and then, trying to calm down, took a sip of tea.

Abdullah looked at her, realizing she honestly didn't know. "*The Officer of the Regiment* by Gainsborough and the Cullens One and Two by Turner," he said quietly. "They will be returned to your home today. They are at my estate in Scotland."

She was shocked and had to work to keep herself from screaming at the top of her lungs. Taking a deep breath, she said, "They are not even part of the estate. They are mine. Henry stole those paintings."

Abdullah ran his hands through his hair. He too was now shocked, and his face was turning red, but composing himself, he managed to say calmly, "I am so sorry, Sophia. I had no idea. I honestly believed him."

Just then, Abdullah's man of business, a short stocky man with menacing black eyes, walked into the room with the bill of sale. Sophia looked up as he handed the paper to Abdullah, and all of the color drained from her face. Her hand started to tremble, and the teacup slipped from her fingers.

It shattered on the floor, spilling onto the elegant white carpet. Almost immediately, a group of servants raced to clean up the glass. Abdullah snatched the paper out of the man's hands and ushered Sophia into the hallway.

"Sophia, what is wrong? You look like you have seen a ghost! Please tell me."

She willed her hands to stop shaking as she took the bill of sale. It was signed by Henry Lawrence of behalf of the Devon Lawrence estate as a trustee.

Looking at her now clearly frightened face, Abdullah realized something else was very wrong. Uncertain of what it could be, but seeing her fear, he put his hand on her back. "Sophia," he said calmly, "it has stopped raining. Let's go for a walk around our little circle so you can tell me your problems. I want to help you as much as I can. Honestly, I had no idea it was your art."

As they slowly walked around the crescent, she finally managed to speak. "I realize you can give me back the tables and the art, but ..." There were tears in her eyes, still unshed but shimmering.

Abdullah did not know what to say. He put his arm around her to console her and then finally spoke. "I beg you to forgive me, Sophia. Honestly, I had no idea it was your art. It will be returned immediately."

Shaking her head, she turned her face toward him. The tears continued pooling in her eyes as she started to speak. "The first time I went to Scotland, we found a videotape. It shows your man of business loading the tables for transport with the Earl of Morven." Speaking at a rapid-fire pace, she continued, "I tried to keep it out of the press that the tables were at Sotheby's, but today I received this letter." She handed a crumpled page to him to read.

As he read the letter, the look of pure rage on his face served only to increase her fear. Seeing this, he softened his features, but underneath his calm facade was pure rage. "Why is the earl involved in this?" he asked.

"Because he will stop at almost nothing to try and harm me. He's broke and wanted me to marry him, to combine forces, as he said, against you. But you saw him at the Westminsters'. He kept repeating he wanted to marry me and make a big estate. He did not like my answer, and like the first time I met him, it got a little rough."

Abdullah gently took her arm and turned her toward him. "How rough?"

Sophia blushed, and a tear finally dropped down her cheek. "He tried to force himself on me."

To hide his anger from her, he pulled her into his arms and held her. "Sophia, as you must know, I have had a couple of paramours, but I do not believe in forcing myself on a woman. I find it abhorrent in any form, and I am angry that he tried."

After a long silence in which she tried to compose herself, she said, "This is one part of the problem that is not laid at your feet, Abdullah, except to let you be informed."

The prince looked over her shoulder at the garden in the little crescent and appeared to be thinking. Finally, with a twinkle in his eye, he said, "I think I may have a way of dealing with the earl. Could you please leave that to me? Consider it a form of apology for any problems I have inadvertently caused."

"But none of that solves the issue of the letter. Morven has told people in the village that you are paying him to buy the land."

His voice was gruff when he said, "I can assure you, Sophia, that I am not trying or even thinking about purchasing your property in Scotland." They were on their fourth lap around the little loop by now. "It appears to me that your first matter of business is to assure the village that you are in charge and will not betray them. I think we need to go to Scotland immediately."

"I was planning on taking the overnight train."

"Why don't we fly up together? The plane is more comfortable than the train," he said with a smile.

"I was leaving tonight."

Looking up at the sky, he said, "When can you be ready? The sky is clearing, and I will have the plane set for one thirty this afternoon. Is that enough time? I inadvertently helped create this mess, so I will help you sort it out, Sophia. A simple plane ride is the least I can do."

As they completed the circle, he put his arm around her and turned her toward him. His chin was resting on her head as he again looked out across the gardens. The electric feeling was there, and he held her for a long time before he spoke again. "I have a couple of business calls to make, and then I will pick you up."

Then taking her face in both of his hands, he said softly, almost stammering, "I cannot express how ashamed I am. Since we met, I have always wanted to help you, not hurt you. And I have never wanted to see the fear I saw in your face today. You are a lovely lady. And while I have often dreamed of making love to you, you are safe with me."

His touch, his hand on her face, had completely unraveled her. She looked up into his face in amazement. "I believe it is prudent for me to pass on your offer," she said. Then she heard herself say to him, "Amazingly, Abdullah, I do feel safe with you."

As he turned to walk next door, he called back, "But if you ever want to make my dreams come true, I would finally be a happy man."

Still shaking her head, she walked inside.

The prince was fuming when he walked into his house. After he had calmed himself, his first call was to the Duke of Westminster. He did not waste any words when he got Gerald Grosvenor on the phone.

"Your Grace, I know we did not get off on the right footing after the offer on Number Eleven, but we have a mutual friend, Ms. Sophia, who needs our help. Please hear me out."

His phone call with the duke took ten minutes. His second call was to his Swiss banker. That call was a series of orders barked out in anger, and his banker assured him the job would be done within the day.

The third call was to his government's head of secret service. After another string of barked orders, he went upstairs to gather a few things for his upcoming trip to Scotland.

He and Sophia arrived at Stansted Airport and boarded a Learjet for Scotland. Abdullah took the pilot's seat and motioned for Sophia to join him in the copilot's chair.

"You fly?" she asked.

"Yes," he said. "I was trained at Sandhurst, and I'm licensed for every plane I own. For now, Sophia, leave your troubles behind." As they banked out to the north, Abdullah dipped one wing and then the other. "It's a habit of mine. I wave at the tower or others when I can. It's a type of signature."

It was a glorious flight over the Lake District, including a low-altitude diversion to see the Duke of Devonshire's storied estate, Chatsworth. Then they headed west over the outer islands of the Hebrides, circling the Cullen Mountains on the Isle of Skye, where the Turner landscapes had been painted. From the Isle of Skye, they flew low over Loch Ness, from the bottom to the top, before turning back to the northwest toward the Highlands.

As they approached Abdullah's private landing strip, it was almost sunset. The sky had turned a vivid purple, making the russet red of the moors stand out against the pine trees.

Seeing the vivid colors, Sophia gasped in delight. "It is so beautiful up here."

For the entire trip, Abdullah had kept up a stream of chatter about the country they were flying over. Finally, he asked, "Sophia, how will you get to the village?"

"I have a car in Scotland," she said. "I can drive from the manor to the village."

"You do know that in my country women are not allowed to drive," he replied. "I would appreciate it if you took a driver with you. Take one of my cars, or one of your security men."

"But we're not in your country. And I can drive. Besides, your cars all have diplomatic plates. You don't think the village would know whose car it is?" she asked in a teasing manner. "And why are you worried about my safety?"

"It is in my nature to worry, Sophia," he responded tersely.

As they landed, the prince said, "I will be here if you need any help, but I would think your visit to the village should be without me." Thinking about their last conversation, he then led her to a car and showed her to the driver's seat before getting in on the passenger side. By now he was laughing. "You can drive yourself home, Sophia. And I will then bring my car back from your house."

For the first time that day, she actually giggled. "Do you ever take anything seriously?"

"I do," he said. "I just try not to show it to the world. Just a few select special people." And then he winked at her.

As they arrived at the manor house, she turned to him and laid her hand on his, saying, "Thank you, Abdullah, and please say hello to Rima for me. I hope we can visit each other while I am here."

She entered the manor house, where the housekeeper was waiting. The reception she received was polite but frosty. "You've had a phone call from Mr. Henry," the cook said. "He requested that you call him back."

Sighing, Sophia went into the study and closed the door to make the call. There were no polite hellos before Henry started yelling.

"The earl is going to buy the whole damn thing, Sophia!"

"And what was he planning on buying it with?" she yelled. "You do understand he has no money, right? He's broke!"

"Sophia, the earl has means. He told me so. He says the Arab will pay."

Sophia laughed out loud. "You mean the same one to whom you sold the tables and the art you stole from me?"

She waited for his reply, but he had hung up.

Sitting in the dimly lit study, she considered the call. She wondered why Henry thought Abdullah would buy the property. In the back of her mind, she wondered if she was the one being duped. Something Sir Joshua had said popped into her mind: *Be careful whom you trust, Sophia.*

She finally called her attorney David to update him on the day's events. As she finished her story, he asked, "Can you really trust your prince, Sophia?"

Uncertain why she was so confident, she said emphatically, "Yes, David, I can!"

After a strained dinner alone, she went to bed. She pondered the events of the day, and her last thought before drifting into a restless sleep was *Why does Abdullah think he has to keep me safe?*

Chapter 19

A Visit to the Village

The following morning, Sophia was driven to the village of Carrick by her security officer. As she had done on her first visit, she admired the quaint main street, with its row of thatched homes with colorful doorways, that led to the neat cobblestone town square. The flowers were gone, replaced by fall harvest decorations.

She had called Lamote, the de facto head of the village, and left him a message, but he had not returned her call.

Sophia instructed her driver to stay in the car when she exited in front of the local school. She was greeted by a teacher and a group of young children on the playground.

Sophia introduced herself. "I'm Sophia Lawrence, the trustee for Barbara Lawrence's estate. Is Lamote around?"

Immediately, the children began yelling, and then one young boy threw a stick at her. A moment later, a rotten egg hit her in the head and dripped down her face. Finally, two rocks hit her in the eye. Although the rocks stung, she motioned her driver to stay in the car.

The teacher tried to gain control of the children, ordering them inside. Once the children were inside, the young teacher said, "I am so sorry. Are you all right?" But then she turned and said, "You're Sophia Lawrence?"

"Yes," she replied, "and I am trying to find Lamote to discuss a problem."

The teacher glared at her. "You're the one throwing us out of our homes."

Sophia heaved a sigh and shook her head. "No one will be thrown out of their homes. It is a large misunderstanding that I would like to correct. Again, do you know where I can find Lamote?"

The teacher frowned and looked confused. "But we had a letter from you and the Earl of Morven. He said that the village would be sold to that Arab."

Sophia looked at the teacher and said, "I have seen the letter, and yes, it says the trustee for the estate is selling the property, including the village, to the earl. However, as the trustee, I did not authorize that letter. It is simply not true. I understand why you all are upset, but I am trying to get to the bottom of this fiasco, if you could all bear with me."

Realizing there was now a trickle of blood on her cheek, she glared at the young lady and continued, "Of course, from what I have seen so far, you have nothing but heathens in your charge. After all, I am now the one with a black eye and rotten egg all over my face and hair."

The teacher managed to look chagrined.

"When I was here two months ago, I thought that Lamote was in charge of the village. That is why I am looking for him, to clear up this mess."

By now, the young lady was totally confused and embarrassed. "Yes, I can show you to his house."

After a brief walk through the village, they arrived at a tidy little white stucco cottage with bright red window frames. All the way, Sophia could see curtains being pulled aside and felt the eyes inside following her every movement.

When Lamote answered the door, his pale blue eyes were guarded. His dark, untrimmed brown hair was longer than on her last visit, and he had grown a beard, which made him look as wild as the moors that surrounded the village.

"What da ye want?" he snarled.

"I am here to clear up this mistake," said Sophia.

"A mistake, ye call it?" he snapped at her. Finally noticing her disheveled appearance and the egg yolk in her hair, he asked, "Did someone throw something at you?"

"Yes, eggs, rocks, and sticks, but it's OK—no lasting harm done. More importantly, yesterday I was told about a letter you received. I am here to tell you it is not true and to try and clear up the obvious hard feelings."

"Well," he said in a thick Gaelic brogue, "how come is that ye wha sent it dinnae ken whit it says?"

Sophia was having trouble understanding the man and was so exasperated that she could have screamed. Mustering some reserve of calm, she finally said, "Given what I have seen, I cannot see how you think I sent it. It was signed by the Earl of Morven. As you know, I'm the sole executor of Barbara's estate. You know that selling the whole village and kicking everyone out is not what she wanted."

"I was at the reading of the will," he said, "and I heard what she wanted, but she is dead, and you are just doing what you want without her around. We have proof that the letter is real and that Mr. Henry agreed to sell to Morven."

He walked over to a small antique desk, pulled out a large envelope, and handed it to Sophia. It was from Rochester, Minnesota, and addressed to the "Mayor of the Village." The cover letter inside was printed on stationery from the Rochester office of Henry's law firm. Enclosed was a signed sales agreement between the trust and the earl for the entire contents of the castle, manor house, and village.

Sophia shook her head. "When did you receive this letter?"

Thoughtfully, the man answered, "About a week ago."

Sophia felt overwhelmed. All she wanted to do was sit down and maybe finally just have a good cry. "Can you tell me who else we need to talk to in the village? The whole issue of what the will stipulates is a long story, and I would rather not repeat it twenty times and have anything become a rumor." With a wry smile, she added, "I think you have enough of those already."

Then a thought struck her. "Didn't anyone else from the manor house or the castle attend the reading of the will? They would have known this was not true."

"Well, there is the pastor of the church, the head of the store, and the fire department."

"Can you call them to join us? And may I use your washroom to try and remove the rotten egg?" She was shown a washroom but could only manage to get the egg off her face. The dried egg was stuck to her hair, so she pulled it back into a ponytail, to deal with later.

All this while, she was thinking about the letter and wondering what Henry and the earl were up to. Why would Henry pick on the village? she wondered. She returned to the living room just as another man arrived, followed by the priest. She stepped out to her car, which also had been hit by rotten eggs, to grab her briefcase and tell her security man she was OK.

When everyone had arrived, Sophia began. "Gentlemen, there has been a terrible misunderstanding. I know you received a letter from a solicitor and the Earl of Morven purporting to control Barbara Lawrence's estate. However, that letter is incorrect and does not follow Barbara's last wishes at all."

One of the men started to speak, and Sophia held up her hand. "Let me finish, please."

Taking the page she had copied from Barbara's will, she read it aloud to them. They all wore a perplexed look.

"As you can see, and as I believe several of you heard at the reading of the will, it was always Barbara's intention to take care of the village. As the executor of this estate, it is my job to make certain this document is followed.

"Of course, it would be helpful if you gentlemen and the village would help me with a plan. And if we could stop the rotten egg and rock throwing, that also would be appreciated."

The portly priest laughed at this remark. Seeing the bruises forming on Sophia's face and eye, several of the men said there would be hell to pay at home that night for their children's part in the rock throwing. Then they all started talking at once, but Sophia did not interrupt. She just wanted to listen.

"But I thought that foreign guy wi' th' earl said the earl was going to buy it?" said the chief of the fire department.

Sophia sat up straighter, trying to understand their words.

"That is what he said," chimed in the shopkeeper. "And he said Mr. Henry was in charge 'cause of Mr. Edward's death."

"Gentlemen," Sophia interrupted quietly, "whom are you talking about?"

The room went still, and then the fire chief cleared his throat. "Well, ma'am, right after Ms. Barbara passed, a foreign gentleman came here with Mr. Henry, looking at the castle and the manor house.

"Mr. Henry had official-looking papers saying he was the executor, just like you do. And after he finished touring the castle, they had a big truck come up here and take away some art and furniture from the castle and the manor house. The same foreign man was with the Earl of Morven. Then this week we got this letter."

Sophia turned to the fire chief. "What exactly did the papers look like?"

"It was exactly like yours, ma'am, except it said Mr. Henry and his agent were in charge."

"You mean it looked like a will?"

"Yes, ma'am," said the priest.

While the others were talking, Lamote had gone into another room. When he returned, he set a pile of papers in front of Sophia. It was a nearly exact copy of the will, but without any mention of Sophia anywhere, just Henry and Edward. The instructions for the disposition of the village also had been removed. They had even copied the seal.

She looked at Lamote. "Is this your only copy? I would like a copy of it, please."

The men looked at her as if she were a two-headed beast.

Finally losing the last of her patience, she said, "Let's put a stop to this now. Which one of you gentlemen would like to call Sir

Joshua Reynolds in London and ask him who the estate's executor is? And while you're at it, ask him if the village is being sold."

"I will," said Lamote. "I do have a feeling I should have done so before."

Sophia shook her head. "But what does the earl have to do with this? Does anyone want to hazard a guess or tell me something about him I don't already know?"

"He's a right rotter," said the fire chief. "They say he killed his first wife."

Everyone in the group, even the priest, nodded.

In complete exasperation, she said, "If he is so bad, why did you believe him?"

"Well," said the priest, "he is an earl, and these were his ancestral lands long ago. He claims he has no money, but by divorcing his second wife, he will have money, and he wants his lands back."

"Wait!" She raised her voice, her tone incredulous. "And based on this, you believed him?" Her impatience was showing, but it did not hurt her cause at all.

She continued, "I was here two months ago—met most of you." By now she was on fire and lecturing the assembled group. "Lamote, we have exchanged several faxes. I have helped repair the infrastructure in the village. Then last week, you … you …" She was about to say "idiots" but stopped herself. "Last week you get this letter and believe it. Lamote, why didn't you tell me about the other will? And where in God's name did you think the earl could get the money to purchase the castle and the lands?" Her hands were on her hips, and she was glaring at the group over her glasses, waiting for an answer.

The police chief said, "My son, who will be getting the hiding of his life, helped them move. He says the Arab told the earl he could get the money from his boss."

"Which Arab?" she said, pushing harder than she'd expected.

"The short, fat one he was with. He's the sheik, right?"

Sophia shook her head. "Thank you, gentlemen. I have the information I need. I will be working on solving the problem, but now I am going home to finish cleaning up." She pointed again to the dried egg yolk in her hair.

After a moment, she added, "I believe you all should know that the man with the earl was not the sheik. He was simply an employee. And I have no intention of selling anything to the Earl of Morven, ever!"

With that she spun on her heels and walked out the door.

Chapter 20

Show Down with a Prince

*A*rriving home, she spied a horse and rider cresting the ridge to the south. The white of the massive animal stood out against the red of the moors. The animal was galloping like the devil was at his heels.

Ah, my friendly prince, she thought. *I have a beef to hash out with you.*

As Abdullah pulled up on his horse, he could see Sophia standing with her arms crossed, glaring at him. He understood her obvious anger.

While Sophia had been at the village, Abdullah had spent his day looking for answers as to how he had been duped into purchasing stolen goods. What he'd found was a folder outlining the full extent of the perfidy his man of business had gone to with Henry Lawrence.

"He's gone, Sophia. You never need to worry about him again. You will never see him again."

A chill went down her spine, and she shouted, "Goddamn it, Abdullah! I wanted to believe you. And then I find out—"

"Yes, I know, Sophia," he said, dismounting his horse. His hair was windblown, and his magnificent white horse was sweating. "Sophia, I have found a copy of the correct will that was given to my man of business by Henry, along with blank stationery with his legal team's address. At the time, Henry told everyone—even the king via fax—that he was in charge, and because he was a trusted man, they believed him."

"Henry told your father?" Incredulity was audible in her voice.

"Independent of the king or myself, it was my man of business and Henry who forged the document that they have in the village. My man not only stole the tables and art but also agreed that I would purchase the property in the earl's name.

"I only learned of this today. As I said, you never need to worry about him again. He is on his way home to my country and will be dealt with there."

Her blood ran cold as she just stared at Abdullah. She wanted to believe him, yet there were so many moving pieces. Then looking at his handsome face, she broke down and started to cry.

Through her tears she screamed, "Damn you! I believed you. I wanted to trust you. I even thought about what you said the other night. And now you want me to believe that you didn't know? I'm not stupid, Abdullah!"

He reached for her, but she pulled away. "Sophia, I'm sorry. I honestly didn't know the full extent of his dishonesty. When I learned about the earl—"

By now, Sophia was sobbing hysterically—gut-wrenching tears and sobs that had not been shed for six months.

He reached for her again. "Shush, I won't hurt you. Honest, I won't." His hands were softly rubbing her back. "We have become very close. I have fallen … It's OK, Sophia, you can cry."

The sobs came, one wave after another, crushing her body as she doubled over and started to fall to the ground. Abdullah caught her, dropped to his knees, and held her.

She kept saying, "I wanted to believe you, I wanted to trust you, I thought you were my friend."

When the sobbing subsided, Abdullah picked her up and carried her inside of the manor house. The housekeeper, who had been watching Sophia cry, led Abdullah to the study where a fire was roaring, and hot tea was ready to be served.

As he gently placed her on the sofa, he said, "It will be dark soon. I must be heading back. Would you do us the honor of joining Rima and me tonight for a casual dinner?"

Sophia nodded in the affirmative. "Yes, I would like that," she said, a tiny smile crossing her lips. "What time? I need to wash my hair."

It was then that he noticed just how disheveled she looked. On top of that, she had a bruise and dried blood on her cheek and near her eye. Dropping down to the floor on his knee, he whispered, "What happened?"

"I had a fight with a bunch of rocks and rotten eggs," she mumbled. "I'll tell you about it later."

The staff was noticeably friendlier. The village gossip had informed them that Sophia was trying to help, not hurt them. And there was something about the prince that they did not understand. Something seemed different.

The housekeeper poured her tea and kindly said, "I have a bath drawn when you are ready, miss. The entire village wishes to apologize for the eggs and rocks thrown at you today."

Taking her tea upstairs, she sank into the warm bath. She wondered if Abdullah really wanted to buy the property. But it made no sense. He could have made an offer for it through her. She had almost fallen asleep when she heard a clock chime and realized it was seven o'clock—time to get dressed. She chose a casual pair of silk slacks and a white silk shirt and added some simple gold jewelry. She pulled her hair back in a ponytail.

She entered Abdullah's vast Georgian pile on top of the hillside at slightly past eight. Turrets stood out on the back and front wings of the mansion, giving it a slightly forbidding look. The entire facade was white sandstone, with an imposing two-story round Palladian entrance. The entry foyer was small, but coming through into the main house revealed a grand staircase adorned with fabulous art. A pair of Caravaggios hung on either side of the staircase.

Upstairs, the house was split into two wings, east and west, one for guests and one for the family. On one side of the foyer was a stunning sitting room; on the other side was an equally stunning dining room.

"Welcome, Sophia." Rima's outstretched arms enveloped her in a warm hug. "I am so glad you're here."

Sophia found the hug very comforting after her trials of the day. "Sorry I am late," she murmured. "I had some egg on my face."

"Abdullah will be down shortly. I hear that you weren't the only one with egg on your face today—that even my husband metaphorically also had egg on his face. I am so sorry about the troubles you faced, especially my family's part. The bruises and cuts on your face look like they hurt. I will get you salve to ease the pain."

"Thank you. That would be nice. Right now, I feel like I am bruised all over."

"You know, Sophia, my husband is a just man, even though he is a force to be reckoned with when crossed."

"I've gathered that," said Sophia slowly. "I do believe he is just. Ironically, circumstances have put us slightly at odds on a couple of occasions. It has been hard not to cross him."

"I know," she said. "Abdullah does not blame you. You have become very dear to him. I hear he even made a pass at you."

Sophia was shocked at this disclosure. Smiling, she said, "Yes, but it was kinder than most I have received recently. I declined, just not with the violence that accompanied the other instances. But I'm certain he told you that also."

"He did. I am sorry about the earl." Rima smiled. "We have very different ways in our country, Sophia. If you change your mind, I can show you how to navigate our customs."

Sophia cocked her head to one side, a habit when she did not know what to say. "Thank you, Rima. I hope we can all just stay good friends and neighbors."

"I am certain no matter what you decide, that will always be true. Now, before we talk business, I must get you the salve. It has special oils that will stop the bruise from becoming too dark." Then changing the subject, she added, "As you may or may not know, I am a board member of the Scottish National Trust."

"I didn't know," Sophia said. "Interesting …"

As Rima left, Abdullah entered the room. "Ahh, Sophia, you look much better than this afternoon. Egg yolk in your hair does not become you. Please, never wear yellow. It's not your color."

She giggled impetuously.

"I heard my wife mentioning her connection to the Scottish National Trust. I must tell you both of an interesting conversation I had with the Duke of Westminster."

"Uncle Jerry!" Sophia said. "I am all ears to hear his advice."

"He will arrange to purchase the castle from you. This means that portion of the estate will become a trust property, and it will, in turn, provide you with a large tax deduction for the balance of your estate."

"Interesting. I would love to hear more," Sophia replied.

Rima returned with the salve and handed the jar to Abdullah. "This is for Sophia's bruise. But I … I don't want to hurt her. I will go check on our dinner."

"Oh, I can put it on," Sophia said quickly.

Abdullah had already opened the jar and was sitting in front of her. "This won't hurt, Sophia, I promise. Close your eyes and breathe in the scent."

Then he touched her cheek, the one that was not bruised. Electricity surged through her from his fingers. Yet he did not stop. Very gently, he massaged her bruised face with the cream. It smelled of sandalwood and something else, and under the gentle massaging, which expanded to her forehead, her other cheek, her entire face, and her neck, she finally started to relax. As he continued to massage her neck and face, he pulled her ponytail out to let her hair flow freely. "I like it down," he said.

Then he changed the subject. "Rima came up with the idea of expanding the use of the manor, making into a hotel. It could be managed under her existing hotel chain banner, with both of you as partners. I am hoping you will consider this idea."

When Rima returned, he finished Sophia's massage, got up, went to the bar, and poured three glasses of Pol Roger champagne. "This will help the bruising also," he joked. "A toast to a future grand hotel for my ladies!"

They bantered and exchanged ideas about turning the manor house into a hotel until late into the night. Rima's excitement was contagious. Finally, exhaustion overcame Sophia, and Abdullah drove her home.

The next morning, she met with her security team to explain who had stolen the art and the tables. She requested every second of footage with the Earl of Morven in it. After that meeting, she called her attorneys to tell them the story of the fake documents and the beginnings of her plan.

"This is serious," said David. "There are only a few people who have copies of the document. It will be easy to prove it's a fake, but who faked it?"

Sophia sighed. "I think someone who used to work for Abdullah and Henry. But I'm pretty sure he is no longer in the UK." She failed to add "and is most likely dead." "But …" She paused. "I don't think that man is important. We are working on a plan. I need to get the attorneys to a meeting here, all of them.

"Abdullah has already spoken to Uncle Jerry, so he can fill you in on the details of their part of the plan. The duke needs to be here also. When do you think we can meet? This meeting may be long, so everyone can stay at the manor house—well, everyone but Henry and his team."

"Sophia," David said, "are you really on a first-name basis with the prince?"

"Do you mean Abdullah, sometimes known as the prince of thieves?" She giggled. "Yes. He has become a close friend of mine. So when can we all meet?"

"Shouldn't be more than three or four days," said David. "I'll set it up. But what about the prince's part in this?"

"David, I have just told you it will be fine. Your uncle Jerry is helping with the plan. And please do nothing that will in any way bring on the press. All I need is to set up a meeting with Henry's legal team in Scotland at the castle in four days' time. I will see you then."

"I understand, Sophia, but please be careful."

Her next call was to Sir Joshua to explain in detail Henry's actions, as well as Abdullah's explanation that it was only his man of business who had played a part and that Abdullah had not been involved directly.

"You realize, Sophia," said Sir Joshua, "that Henry's actions mean the will is broken, and you will become the sole heir to the entire estate, both in Scotland and in London."

"I do," she replied.

He continued with measured words. "Can I also assume that given he had no direct knowledge of the theft or the forgery, you will not be trying to take any action against the prince?"

"You can," she slowly replied, wondering how he knew this.

"That is good, Sophia. I would hate to have the press get hold of this incident, for everyone's sake."

"I agree," she replied. "And this is where I have a question. Is it not in my purview, as the sole trustee, to decide not to kick Henry out completely? What if we have an iron-clad agreement from both Henry and his legal team? After all, they're both complicit."

She continued, "I have an idea that I can make work. Why don't you join me in Scotland on Friday? If after what you hear, you believe that Barbara would be upset, then you can always overrule me."

"I will be there, Sophia, as will young David. We will get the lawyers there, but what about Henry?"

"Just leave him to me," she said. As she got off the phone, she realized this showdown had been coming for a long time.

Soon after, Abdullah arrived at the manor unexpectedly. "I came by to see how you are feeling today," he said. "Did you get a good night's rest?"

"I did, but I got up early to work on a plan. Come in. Would you like to hear it?"

"I would enjoy that, Sophia. I am all ears," he said.

"You are not all ears—eyes and legs, maybe—but not ears."

"Are you flirting with me, Sophia?"

"No," she said, laughing.

They sat in Sophia's study, working on a plan for the properties, for over three hours. When they were finished, Sophia said, "This should work. However, if Henry fights me on this, there will be negative press.

"I would like to have you present at the meeting when I present my ultimatum. I think it may add more weight to the gravity of the situation, your being a prince and all. You'll be sitting right next to Westminster."

He laughed at her words—*a prince and all.* "Yes, Sophia, I am happy to attend. I have meetings today in London, but Rima would love to have you join her again tonight for a girls' dinner. And Sophia, if we must threaten the press or even have some, I will still back you."

"Tell Rima I will see her tonight. And ... Abdullah ... wait ... I want to say how much I appreciate your help and honesty. As you know, I heard this morning that the Scottish National Trust has a new benefactor to purchase and endow significant buildings." With a whisper, she concluded, "Thank you."

Chapter 21

Henry to Scotland

*I*t was blowing a full gale when Henry, Janet, and their entire legal team arrived at the castle.

Henry's brow furrowed as he noticed the two Jacobean tables on either side of the entry hall, with the two Turner seascapes hung over them. He understood immediately that trouble was brewing.

After the visitors had spent ten minutes waiting in the entry hall, the liveried footman Frazer, from Number Eleven, ushered Henry and his legal team into the sitting room. Sophia sat on the side of the table farthest from the door, flanked on either side by her lawyers, David and Sir Joshua. Slightly behind but next to Sophia sat two imposing oversized Jacobean chairs, behind which were the two massive Gainsborough paintings.

Sophia did not welcome Henry as the footman showed the group into the room. Her face was calm; for once, every thought was not written across her features. When everyone was seated, Sophia started to speak.

"Gentlemen, I assume by now you all realize that you have broken the terms of the last will and testament of Barbara Devon Lawrence."

At first, the room was quiet. Henry and his American attorneys paled slightly while the British legal contingent looked at her with a perplexed stare.

Janet broke the silence by yelling, "No, he hasn't! You're up to your old tricks again, Sophia."

Sophia just looked down her glasses with disdain at the woman.

Henry followed with his typical response. "Shut up, Janet." In a slightly calmer voice, Henry said, "Sophia, I have no idea what you are talking about."

Uncharitably for Sophia, she looked Henry straight in the eye and said, "Henry, shut up and listen very carefully, as I am not in the mood to repeat myself." Then, nodding to the footman, she said, "Can you escort the other gentlemen into the room please?"

Sir Joshua smiled, and Henry looked petrified when Prince Abdullah and the Duke of Westminster walked in, taking the two seats behind Sophia.

Janet mumbled, "It's all his fault."

A pause fell over the room. Sophia's jaw visibly tightened, and her eyes flashed dangerously as she looked at her former sister-in-law, appalled. Sophia was about to speak, to say something in defense of Abdullah, but a slight shake of his head made her bite her tongue.

With a new fury burning inside her, she turned to Henry. "I assume, based on your wife's ... insight ... that no introduction is necessary." Then with a flourish, she laid a tape recorder on the table and pushed the button to start recording.

"First, I wish to state for the record who is in attendance at this meeting. The Duke of Westminster and His Royal Highness Prince Abdullah bin Abbas of Arabia—"

Before she could finish, Henry yelled, "You can't use this recording, Sophia. It's illegal."

She shrugged. "Its existence is more important to me than its legality. And Henry, you may get away with yelling in your operating room, but you cannot yell here." Then she continued speaking to the group, her eyes never leaving Henry's. "Mr. Henry Lawrence having violated the terms of the last will and testament of Barbara Devon Lawrence"—she paused for effect—"it is my obligation as trustee to enact the clause that states, 'The party who by any means fails the intent of this document shall immediately forfeit their rights to receive any portion of the will.'"

Janet was in tears. "That means that all the proceeds from the jewelry will go to charity," she wailed.

"I'll contest!" shouted Henry.

"Contest what, Henry? That you stole my individual possessions? That you sold them and accepted the funds? Or are you going to contest your part in forging the will and distributing it to the village? Someone in this room had to provide a true copy of the will to be forged. Someone had to provide your attorneys' letterhead and envelopes."

She slowly placed copies of all the documents on the table. "Those actions constitute multiple crimes, here in the UK, in Arabia, and in the United States, whether or not your lawyers have aided and abetted you."

Henry looked toward Abdullah, who actually smirked at him.

Sophia continued, "I don't think there is a doubt in anyone's mind that your actions have broken the will. But far more than any economic loss you may incur from these actions ..." She paused and turned to look at Abdullah, who nodded. "If I were to go to Scotland Yard with this information, there would be other severe consequences. It could include loss of your medical license and jail time for you and Janet—not to mention the shame your children will face. Are you honestly going to risk everything?"

Henry now had a trickle of sweat running down his cheek.

Sophia continued relentlessly. "Here is how I intend to proceed. I will donate Castle Carrick to the Scottish National Trust. I will retain all the art from Scotland. The manor house, now under my sole ownership, will become a lifestyle hotel. This will ensure that many of the villagers are employed. Since I will be taking a loss on this property, I will deduct that amount from your proceeds of the sale of Number Eleven. I will also deduct the funds you received for the sale of the art to His Royal Highness from your share of Number Eleven."

Henry started to say something, but Sophia stopped him. "Henry, I am being very generous. The will states that you forfeit everything.

I have simply outlined your forfeiting the Scottish portion of the inheritance. You will still have your portion of the real estate trust. You can try to contest, but at that point, with the full blessing of everyone in this room"—she paused, turning around to look at the group of men around her, who nodded encouragingly—"I will call Scotland Yard. You see, I have enough evidence without the recording. I think your attorneys will advise you that I am being very generous with all of you. One final note. I will execute a full release for all parties, conditional upon two things. One, none of the parties can ever make any claim on me, my heirs, or the estate, and two, no one outside of this room may discuss this with anyone. If one word of today's meeting leaks to the press, you are agreeing by signing that the rest of the estate is immediately forfeited."

Sir Joshua was amazed. She was being very generous. Then looking around the room, he realized the nuanced but subtle hand of both Westminster and Abdullah.

"Maybe you would like some time to discuss these papers before you and your legal team sign." Looking toward Westminster, she said, "Gentlemen, I suggest we adjourn."

Prince Abdullah stood up and asked Sophia if he could speak. She nodded.

He looked at Henry with steely black eyes and a demonic grin. He rested his hand on Sophia's shoulder, then said, "I have given this a great deal of thought, and because several parties misled me, as a form of compensation to Sophia for her losses, I am taking the following actions. First, as you must have noticed, I have returned the art and tables to Sophia, and she will refund me on Henry's behalf for the payment I made."

Henry stuttered, "But … I borrowed against that money."

"Second," he said, ignoring Henry, "I will be donating additional art from my personal collection to the national museum in her name. Most importantly, I urge everyone in the room to consider the consequences of their actions. I sincerely hope no one thinks that Sophia was bluffing when she stated we could and would take this to a higher authority in several countries." He emphasized the word *we*. "And finally, I would also like to provide a meaningful cash donation to the village endowment. Does that meet your approval, Sophia?"

The duke and Sir Joshua exchanged conspiratorial glances.

Sophia's eyes were dancing as she said, "Yes, Your Highness. Shall we adjourn now and discuss the exact definition of the word 'meaningful'?"

The Duke of Westminster chuckled.

As Sophia's team left the room, they could hear Janet crying, but Henry's UK attorneys were doing all the talking.

"You will take this offer, Henry," they heard a lawyer say before the door was shut.

While Sophia had tea and juice drinks served on the enclosed back porch, she quietly said to Abdullah, "You don't have to donate to the village, you know."

"I know," he said with a twinkle in his eye, "but I have my eye on another property lease in Mayfair, and I am hoping to help my cause with Westminster."

Henry and Janet left that evening without ever saying another word to Sophia. Henry's UK lawyers merely handed her the signed papers. Before the attorneys left, the senior partner turned to Sophia and said, "Thank you. You do know we were not a party to this."

She nodded as she walked them to the door. Then Henry's attorney turned to Sophia again and said, "But there is one thing I am confused about. I thought the Earl of Morven was going to purchase the entire property. What happened to that deal?"

"I believe he lost his backing. I don't think he has a great deal of cash available to do a deal like this." The full truth, Sophia knew, was that the Scottish National Bank had foreclosed on Morven's estates, and the prince has purchased them from the bank.

Later that week, she flew back to London with Rima. Abdullah had gone to Arabia on business. On the way home Sophia explained that her visa was expiring, so she needed to return to the United States and intended to spend the holidays in Rhode Island. She had convinced herself that Christmas at home would be lovely. She would decorate her house, go to parties at her clubs, and entertain her friends.

Sadly, from the moment she set foot in her Newport home, she realized this would be a different holiday than she had envisioned. The lovely antique farmhouse seemed somehow unfinished. She was in no mood to decorate the tree. And there was something about her friends that was different. She could not quite put her finger on the change, but it was noticeable.

Every morning, she walked the beach in front of her home. But it did not, she realized, bring her the same comfort as running in Hyde Park with Abdullah did. As the days moved toward Christmas, it became more apparent to Sophia that Newport, maybe even the United States, was no longer her home. Almost daily, she received gift baskets from Rima and Abdullah filled with food, flowers, and jewelry. It was a strange yet wonderful combination. This led her to think about Abdullah almost endlessly. On the day after Christmas, she mentioned to Rima that she had received her resident visa and couldn't wait to get back to London.

"We have a lot of work to do in Scotland, chérie. I am excited to see your ideas and plans for Carrick. This year, we need to push very hard to open the new property for the summer season. I have an idea. I'll be in Paris for New Year's Eve with my sisters. The plane is in New York, so I can have it stop in Rhode Island to pick you up. That way, you will be in Scotland when I arrive at the end of the month."

Initially, Sophia hesitated. Yet she had already declined offers to New Year's Eve parties, since the holiday was her former wedding anniversary. The one thing she was certain of was that she did not want to attend the same old boring parties that had been the mainstay of her life with Edward for the last decade. She went for one final walk along the beach in front of her home with that in mind.

The winter waves crashed on the beach, and despite the blue sky above, the day was bitterly cold. As she slowly wandered back to her lovely antique farmhouse, she knew it was time to move on, time to continue the change that had started in England. Fundamentally, she was bored in Newport. At night alone, she ended up dreaming of Abdullah. *You should make a clean break*, she thought. The more she considered this idea, the happier she became.

With that in mind, she called Rima back, said she would love a ride on the plane, and thanked her for the offer.

Section 3

Chapter 22

A Date with Destiny

*P*acking for her move to England, Sophia included all the lovely gifts Rima and Abdullah had sent her while sensing her sadness over the holidays. The story behind the jewelry was touching. When Janet had put her jewelry up for auction at Christie's, they had advised her that vintage jewelry was trending in the markets and that it would bring an exorbitant price. Ironically, Sotheby's had advised Sophia precisely the opposite.

When the jewelry did not sell at Christie's, one anonymous buyer had been willing to purchase three of the sets after the sale. Rima paid roughly half the initial bid price.

Rima then had taken the jewelry to Tiffany's in New York and had them rework the pieces into stunning modern necklaces and earring sets. During the holidays, Sophia had received a collection of contemporary jewelry, sometimes from Abdullah, sometimes from Rima, sometimes from both. Each set had a nautical theme. There was a hammered gold lighthouse with diamonds for the lights, marquis-cut emeralds, and diamonds as pendants made to look like skylights on ancient ships. She had indulged in a private chuckle over receiving the jewelry back reinvented. Karma, she decided.

When the day of departure came, she had dressed carefully for her flight, as usual, wearing winter-white wide-legged wool pants and a matching sweater topped with a beige and white jacket from Chanel. She accessorized with beige court shoes and a matching Birkin. She also carried a large portfolio case, which matched her handbag and held her work on the hotel. Her jewelry consisted of a striking gold necklace and gold and emerald earrings, crafted to look like anchor chains.

The limousine drove to the end of the runway where the G3 was parked, ready for takeoff. Sophia had no idea the changes that were about to occur as she gracefully boarded the Gulfstream. If she had, she might have raced back to Newport to hide.

A uniformed flight attendant greeted her warmly and asked what her beverage preference would be once they were airborne. Captain Winston, the pilot, greeted her with a clipped Scottish accent. "Welcome aboard, ma'am. We look to have a good flight today. Time in the air will be about six or seven hours, depending upon tailwinds." The plane was stunning but not ornate, with white Italian leather and beige suede mixed with warm wood tables, similar to the Learjet in which Abdullah had flown her to Scotland.

Thanking them both as the door shut behind her, Sophia looked aft for a comfortable seat. Abdullah was standing in the back of the plane. He was dressed in a white linen shirt, open at the collar— almost entirely unbuttoned, in fact—and navy-blue slacks. Tall and as ruggedly handsome as ever, he had his hands set on his slim hips. He smiled and said quietly, "Welcome, *mon amour.* Are you ready to face your destiny?"

Sophia was only mildly surprised at his presence. There was that word again, *destiny.* It crossed her mind to run. Intuitively, she understood that he would have let her go. One small part of her brain said, *Leave now, Sophia.* Yet another said, *No … I don't want to. I should have expected this.* She remembered Rima's words—she had said that the plane would be returning from New York, and she would be in Paris. She had not said that the plane would be empty, simply that she would not be on board.

Finally, Sophia nodded and smiled shyly. "Yes, I am ready, Your Highness."

Slowly, they walked toward each other. He sat on a plush double-sized white suede sofa, motioning Sophia to sit next to him. When he buckled the seat belt around her waist, his hand lingered on her hip, a stunningly intimate move. The simple touch, just like the day in Kensington Gardens, sent a shock wave through her body.

His scent, a combination of ylang-ylang and sandalwood, calmed her nerves.

"Are you ready to make my dreams come true?" His voice sounded like a cat's purr—no, not a cat's, a lion's.

The double entendre was not lost on her. Looking directly into his lust-filled eyes, Sophia heard herself saying, "Yes, my prince, I am ready to fulfill your every dream."

Almost on cue, as he clicked her seat belt into place, the engines roared, and the plane began to taxi down the runway. His hand was splayed across her stomach, moving in a slow massage as a feeling of amazing sexuality rolled through her. As the jet continued its roll down the tarmac, he matter-of-factly said, "Then we begin."

The flight attendant came forward, and Abdullah said something to her in Arabic that Sophia did not understand. She nodded and moved away toward the crew quarters at the front of the plane.

"How were your holidays, Sophia?" he asked politely. "Plenty of parties with friends?"

She sighed. "No, not really. Most of my friends did not have much of consequence to say to me. It was like being in a different and slightly foreign world. Gossip about Newport, two small galas, a few quiet dinners with close friends. It seems that Henry and Janet have often been seen on Page Six. And so, by association, have I. My acquaintances were quick to tell me about it."

She then continued, "Fortunately for me, I did have one set of friends who were not in town but who somehow managed to provide the most extraordinary gifts—gorgeous flowers, food baskets, and some of the most magnificent jewelry I have ever owned. And as you know, I own a lot of jewelry." She touched his cheek as she quietly said, "Thank you."

"You're welcome. Purchasing Barbara's jewels and repurposing them was Rima's idea. I guided the designer to make them perfect for you. I thought they might be a more modern and wearable style. You look lovely today, *mon amour.*"

My love—it was a new term of endearment that was not lost on Sophia's dazed brain. "I did work quite a bit on the designs for the new hotel," she offered. "Rima has seen most of my ideas. Would you care to review some of them?"

"I would. Did you bring them with you?"

As she looked around for her portfolio, Abdullah stood up and took it out of the overhead bin where it had been stored. *He has the grace of a lion*, she thought. *And … he looks as if he is about to pounce.*

It was around noon on the Eastern Seaboard. With a seven-hour flight ahead, they would not land until early morning in Scotland.

After laying the portfolio on the table in front of them, he took her hand. "Sophia." The way he said her name sounded like a caress.

She froze, the portfolio forgotten. He turned her head with his hand, caressing her cheek. He spoke more slowly than was his custom, giving weight to his every word. "I will never hurt you, Sophia. That is not my way. I need you." He emphasized the word *need*. "Rima knows and understands. This was somewhat even her idea.

"But I want—no, I need—you to want me also. I will give you everything, protect you forever, and take us to our private destiny. For us to work, you must want me also."

There was an unspoken meaning in his words. Afraid to utter a sound that would break the spell, she leaned into him, her breasts pressing against his shirt, and began kissing him.

It was a timid kiss at first, but he took her mouth like a starved man. Her entire body was on fire as his hand slid over the outside of her sweater across her breasts.

"I take it that is a yes, Sophia," he murmured, pulling away from her kiss.

Speechless, she found that the only word she could utter came out as a low moan. "Please."

He held her close, his chin resting on the top of her head. "I am not a small man, Sophia, nor an easy one. But I will bring you great pleasure everywhere, take you to places you have never been, in ways you've never known. You must promise, even unfairly so, that you will be all mine and only mine from now on, forever!"

She heard his words clearly and understood their meaning. Without equivocation, she nodded her assent, saying softly, "I will make your dreams come true, forever!" She realized that she wanted this, regardless of the myriad unknown consequences.

Guiding her into the master cabin and shutting the door behind them, he said, "Sophia, I will undress you." It was a tone of voice she would learn to love—soft, simple words said as part question, part thoughtful request, and part command.

Raising her hands over her head, he removed the cashmere sweater and then slid the white slacks down over her hips. Kissing her naval while removing the slacks, he said, "No pantyhose, Sophia. That is good. Please never wear them."

As she stood in the cabin in only her bra and panties, her hair fell in reddish-golden curls around her shoulders. One nipple had escaped the white Italian lace bra, and he caressed it with a single finger while unbuckling his pants with his other hand.

Sophia leaned forward, burying her face in his chest, eyes closed. He cupped her face with one hand, and she smelled spices on his fingertips. She impulsively licked one of his fingers and pulled it into her mouth. She deeply inhaled the smell of his hands and chest, a powerful, soft, masculine scent.

"Open your eyes, Sophia. Feast your eyes as I do mine."

She looked at his face, a chiseled profile with luminous deep-set eyes. His normally clean-shaven chin had a slight five o'clock shadow. The few hairs on his chest were a curly black. He was completely naked. Her eyes followed his chest downward, taking in his well-muscled torso, his lean abs, and the cut of his V, down to the proof of his desire for her. At seeing him, she inhaled slightly.

"There may be pain, Sophia. Be it emotional, spiritual, or even physical, pain can serve as one of life's great teachers. It comes and goes. It is part of the cycle of passion, and only when you experience some pain can you fully feel gratification and satisfaction. My job, Sophia, is to make you feel so completely satisfied that no one else will ever do. My job, Sophia, is to teach you."

Standing naked in his cabin, forty thousand feet above the earth, she felt herself shattering into a thousand pieces. His words, his caresses, and his kisses had made her feel a sexual excitement and tension she had never felt before. She was instantly ready to accept all of him.

Then with the grace of a tiger, he lifted her up and slid her down over himself. She gasped at the feeling, but he held her still. Her arms went around his neck, and her legs wrapped around his back. Slowly, ever so slowly and deliberately, he pushed deep inside of her, pulled out, then drove again.

Sophia was on fire. She had no frame of reference, nothing with which to compare this passion, this feeling of being alive, the connection of the moment. All previous interactions could be described as only—well, there were no words.

They would not leave the cabin for the balance of the flight. Making love with Abdullah was a feeling of waves washing over her, breaking as they climaxed, and then reforming only to break over her again and again.

His stamina was prodigious. With his attention always focused on her needs, they made love for hours. His ability to vary the pace, first going slow and then building, then slowing again, led them both to stay in a state of heightened arousal. His erection never flagged as he took her to a climax time and again. He let her feel the explosion of what seemed to be every nerve in her body and then started again. He was in complete control of her every feeling and emotion.

He was correct—sometimes there was a small amount of pain, which immediately was replaced by a building sensation that she quickly learned would grow. Several times, Sophia felt herself climax so intensely that she was certain she had briefly blacked out. Sleep was not on the agenda.

He whispered in ear, "I did not mean to cause you any pain, Sophia. Are you satisfied?"

"The pain of accepting you, my prodigious prince, is always forgotten with the pleasure you provide."

He smiled at the alliteration and held her close until finally she dozed off in a deep, sexually infused sleep.

Abdullah watched her as they flew across the Atlantic. Her golden, almost red curls fell around her head. Watching her sleep, he realized he had never been this sated or emotionally content in his life. The feelings that welled up inside were so strong. *So this is what true love feels like,* he thought, laying his head next to hers to rest. Two hours out of Scotland, he awoke and slid into her, slowly bringing her again to a climax.

"We are almost home," he murmured, getting out of the king-size bed. "Time to get dressed."

She looked toward the bathroom, and he said, "Please, do not shower. I want you as you are when we get home. For now, you are me, and I am you."

Again, there was that tone, question, request, or command. Sophia did not dwell on this. Quite simply, she was so intoxicated with sexual desire that she didn't care what he asked—she would obey.

"When we get home, we will eventually perform a ritual washing after sexual activity. For the next three weeks, you will be spending every second of the day by my side, Sophia. I have dreamed of possessing you fully, and you must possess all of me. There will be nothing between us. We must consummate our union in every manner possible. This will heighten our experience and bring us closer together."

It was a calm command, not a request. This time there was no doubt. She nodded her head in agreement. Again, she did not care. Twin flames of fear and desire danced inside her, intertwining to the point where she could not tell them apart. She knew Rima would not be back in Scotland until the twenty-first. The thought of Rima made her sit up with a stricken look on her face. What had she done?

As if reading her thoughts, he comforted her. "Do not fret, *mon amour.* Rima knows what we have done here," he said, sweeping his arm across the bed. "She wanted this to happen. She dreams of us being passionate and fulfilled together both when she is with us and when she is not."

Not sure of precisely what the last part meant—*All three of us?* she thought—she looked quizzical.

Now dressed in jeans and a white collared shirt, he turned to leave the room. "You are fulfilled, are you not, Sophia?" This time it was a soft question.

"Yes, Your Highness," she said, lightly kissing his hand. "I am fulfilled in many ways."

"Join me when you are ready. Happy New Year, Sophia. It will be our first of many together. I think I will take a look at your portfolio now." He smiled down at her and left the cabin.

The cold cerulean-blue sky was cloudless as they disembarked from the plane. The crew bade the prince and Sophia a polite goodbye, the captain wondering about the lovely lady. Was she truly Abdullah's second wife?

The flight attendant confirmed that she had been asked to witness documentation to that effect. Then she added quietly, "They will not immediately make this public. I believe this is also an affair of the heart for him."

Thinking out loud, the captain said, "I hope this is a good thing, not trouble." He had been the prince's lead pilot for over ten years and knew of the growing political and social issues that the prince and Rima faced at home.

Chapter 23

Highlands Paradise— January 1, 1995

hey rode from the private airstrip to Abdullah's large Georgian mansion in peaceful silence. Abdullah was thinking about the last few months of his life and how he had dreamed of being with Sophia.

He knew Sophia was overwhelmed that Rima understood his wish to marry her. She would be in a state of shock when she learned how often and in what a straightforward manner Rima had not only encouraged him but even coached him: "Take her in my sunroom. Sophia will understand it comes with my approval."

As a son of Islam, he must now ascertain her understanding of her promise on the plane. He worried that the promise had been extracted without a complete understanding of what it entailed. In his mind, though she did not yet know this, Sophia was not a girlfriend or a mistress. She was his second wife.

"Woo her," Rima had said. "You want to anyway. Let her have a choice, and slowly as a part of our family, she will become quietly yet truthfully and then publicly your second wife."

His duty as a prince was clear. He must not fornicate with someone he was not married to, and that marriage must be public. "So," Rima had suggested, "you must marry Sophia. It will not be a hardship, Abdullah. You're already in love with her. We have a strong partnership, Abdullah. You have taken care of me, and we have grown together. But we never fell in love. Oh yes, I do love you, yet … I want you to have fulfillment—and in a manner that does not involve sneaking around behind everyone's back two or three times a year simply to prove your virility.

"You need a second wife—one who loves you, one who respects you for who you are as a person, not for a kingdom or title. Please do this for me."

Somewhere in the recesses of their minds, Abdullah and Rima knew that Sophia might not have a happy and fulfilling life in their Middle Eastern world. Yet Sophia was in many ways the perfect wife number two. She could even give him another child, a thought that excited him beyond belief.

For months Abdullah had carried on a debate with himself, analyzing the different cultural and social issues surrounding a potential marriage to Sophia. What would happen when he became crown prince and then king? Would Sophia be happy leaving most of her Western ways behind? And most importantly, would his people accept her? In the end, he knew first and foremost that his country was his final destiny.

Now he was filled with a feeling of peace and happiness that he had never known in his entire life.

As they entered his home, he drew Sophia to Rima's Persian sitting room. He gently pulled her down to a floor divan and began kissing her again. He felt an overwhelming urge to ask her again to marry him, to explain to her that now she was, in the eyes of God, married to him and only him. And he conceded that maybe, just maybe, he should use the word marriage.

Looking at her sitting on the sofa, he realized with a startling clarity that Rima had been right. He had fallen in love with Sophia. He slid his hand gently down her back. "Sophia," he murmured, "I have a secret to tell you, one I have never spoken to any other woman in my life."

She looked up at him, a shy smile on her face.

"Sophia …" He stumbled over the words. "I have been falling in love with you for months. I want you to be my wife." There, he had said it. The genie was out of the bottle and could never be replaced.

Then he was kissing her again, words forgotten. Gently, he pulled her down on the pile of soft, plush pillows, never breaking the kiss. The word "please" formed on his lips. He whispered the word as if it were a prayer, a word he was sure he had never used before in this situation. He felt slightly off-center, a very unusual feeling for him.

Sophia ran her hands through Abdullah's hair, as if feeling his thoughts, and gazed into his eyes. This only served to inflame them both. He wrapped his arms around her and held her close.

"I … I … I," she stuttered.

"Shush," he murmured. "Don't say a word, *mon amour.*"

Sophia's head was spinning with half-formed thoughts. His wife? Conflicting emotions were at war in her mind. Should she stop and be safe or continue and feel the full extent of the pleasure she knew was coming? Part of her screamed, *This will end in disaster!* At the same time, she felt enveloped in a strong feeling of peace. Maybe, just maybe, this was indeed a safe and right path.

Her sharp intake of breath when his hand touched the skin of her flat stomach made him break the kiss. Fear was etched on his face. What if she stopped and said no? Would he have the strength to do as she asked?

"Please," he said again, his voice as soft as the kiss and just as sensual. His hand slowly moved toward her breast. Her intake of breath was almost a sob. He gently rubbed her nipple. Her breath was ragged. While his thumb drew circles on her nipple, his other hand slid down her stomach and below her lacy panties, which were damp and smelled of their lovemaking on the plane. He pulled back, looking at her with a question in his eyes.

Again, he felt a powerful urge to hear her consent. He needed her more than anything. But in his very being, he needed to know that she wanted him—not for money or power but for himself. Had Sophia fully understood the importance of the word "forever" on the plane? Did she genuinely wish to be married to him and only him?

Sophia looked deep into his eyes, answering his question. With the slightest nod of her head, she moved again to kiss him.

He had never been this out of control with a woman before, and it frightened him. He could feel her spasms and kissed her to keep her from screaming his name. It came out as an exotic-sounding moan—"Dullah."

Later, he carried her upstairs to his room. He had done Rima's bidding. They had made love in her sacred room. Now he wanted Sophia in *his* bed, *his* room. The room was plush, a masculine space, the floors covered in multiple layers of burgundy silk Persian carpets. His bed was a custom king-size with a padded headboard. A crystal chandelier gave a soft glitter to the otherwise stark space. Filled with his smells, it was fit for a king. He laid her on the bed and resumed undressing her. Slowly removing her panties, he continued caressing her and kissing her everywhere.

It was amazing to Sophia. They had performed this ritual just a few minutes ago, yet it seemed brand-new and equally exciting. She moaned when his lips touched her nipples and his hand slid to her inner thigh. She wanted to touch him yet could only reach his chest. She toyed with his nipple, gasping as he raised her legs above his shoulders and again made love to her.

She felt ready to instantly explode. Rhythmically moving, she felt her pleasure grow again, this time more powerfully. Abdullah's thrusts took her over the edge, and he yelled out her name in pleasure as she tightened around him.

Holding her in his arms and coming slightly back to his senses, he realized how hard it would be, most likely impossible, to ever give this woman up.

"Sophia, we must talk. On the plane, you promised, even if unfairly, that you would be all mine and only mine from now on. The word was 'forever.' What does the word 'forever' mean to you?"

"Forever means always, never-ending," she said slowly.

"In my country it means marriage."

She raised her head to gaze into his eyes.

He continued speaking softly. "You know, Sophia, in my country it is customary to marry before consummating the act of marriage.

In fact, it is more than a tradition; it's almost law. It would bring great shame upon my entire family if they knew what we have done without being married."

Sophia's brow furrowed, and her lip turned down. "Marriage," she finally managed to say. "You already have a wife."

Abdullah pulled her close. "Yes, I am married to Rima. We were married in Arabia. In my country polygamy is not illegal. Even the Prophet had four, maybe more, wives. As long as we treat each wife equally, it is legal in the eyes of Allah.

"Rima and I were never married in Europe, so would you do me the honor of marrying me tomorrow? It would be a small civil ceremony here in Scotland with a justice of the peace." He pulled out a small box and opened it, presenting her with the largest emerald-cut diamond she had ever seen.

Sophia was in shock. Her stomach hurt, and her heart was pounding so wildly that she thought he must be feeling it.

"Rima has agreed to this," he said. "We have her full blessing."

Sophia closed her eyes, trying desperately to calm herself. Then she looked up at Abdullah's face etched in fear.

"I did promise," she said slowly, "though I did not truly understand all of the implications you just mentioned at that time."

He held his breath, waiting for her to repudiate him.

Sophia would never know where the following words came from—maybe somewhere deep in her soul—but she heard herself say, "I love you. I will gladly become your second wife."

The smile on his face lit up the room. "I promise you, Sophia, I will always keep you safe, take care of your every need. You will always feel pleasure with me, Sophia."

Then he slid himself into her. She was wet and ready for him, but true to his word, some pain still ran through her like a shock. Instead of pulling back, Sophia put her arms around him, pulling him in even further. This inflamed him even more, and then she felt the white-hot heat of pleasure begin.

Sophia had been falling in love with Abdullah for months. Now she understood that she would always love this man, no matter what the future held. It was as if a spell had been cast over them.

She realized again that there was a wonderful feeling of calm settling over her that she had never felt in her entire life. She still did not know what this promise truly entailed, but she reasoned it would not be a hardship because she was in love.

Later that evening, still in his palatial bedchamber, Abdullah thought Sophia was looking pensive. Bending over her and looking deep into her eyes, he said, "What is bothering you, *mon amour*?"

"I was wondering about my ... our promise."

He stiffened.

Sophia turned to look at him and saw shock on his face. "I have no intentions of breaking our vow. Rather, I'm wondering about the more mundane, modern bits of how to make this work on a day-to-day basis. What exactly does this mean to our daily life and the outside world?" Finally, she said, almost mumbling, "Please, Abdullah, can this be our secret, not shared with anyone?"

He looked down at her, smiling. "For a while, it can be a quiet truth, *mon amour*. Remember, Rima already knows, as I never keep secrets from her. I can promise you that I will never, ever keep secrets from you either and that I will always treat both of you equally—because I love you."

Abdullah continued, "Understand, my love, my new hope for our future, and do not fret. The words and the vows we share—I will honor them for you as well. I will love you forever." Then to lighten the mood, he said, "Do you remember the first time I touched you, Sophia?"

"Yes, when you saved me from being run over coming out of Queen's Gate. I think my heart skipped a beat."

"I think my heart must have stopped too," he said, pulling her closer, "because that was the only thing keeping me from trying to take you then and there."

Laughing, she said, "That would have been a scene—a total PR nightmare!"

He laughed. "When did you fall in love with me?"

"At first, I was attracted, walking around our tiny crescent. Maybe even before that—like the first time I laid eyes on you. I knew I had fallen in Scotland. I saw you riding across the moor, and as angry as I was, I wanted you. My anger stemmed from the fact that I thought you were my friend and had betrayed me. When you held me, I knew I was wrong, that your feelings had nothing to do with tables or art. They were just for me."

He looked down at her, smiling. "Yes, in Scotland. For much the same reason, that was also when I knew. Your exact words just hit me like lightning. No one has ever wanted me only for me."

The following morning, Abdullah was holding her close, looking at the small scar on her breast. "Did that hurt, Sophia?"

"Physically, not really, even though it took four surgeries to remove all of the cancer. The real pain was emotional. I had a tough time coping with the very public degradation my husband heaped on me." Then remembering that Arabian men often discarded their women for sickness and physical flaws, she said cautiously, "What do you think?"

"I think," he said, smiling down at her, "that I love you just the way you are." As if sensing her fear of something, he continued. "Sophia, remember, today is our civil marriage service. While I also want you to have a traditional ceremony in Arabia, I feel the need to have something more concrete now, and I think it would make you feel more at ease also."

Her impish grin returned. "Abdullah, have you arranged this already?"

He nodded yes.

"Oh my," she said as a smile lit up her entire face. "What shall I wear?"

They were married in Scotland by a justice of the peace, standing in the elegant dark green library at Abdullah's mansion. Despite the chill of the wind, it was a sunny winter day. Sophia wore a long white woolen kaftan embroidered in gold beads that she had found in the attic of the manor house. Abdullah's Scottish head pilot, Captain Winston, was the sole witness. Abdullah slipped a gold band on her finger that was engraved: "I love you forever. Dullah."

After the short ceremony he took her arm and guided her toward the sofa in front of the roaring fireplace. In addition to the roaring fire, candlelight flickered off the walls. Going down on his knees in front of her, he said, "Before our meal, I have written you a wedding poem, Sophia. May I recite it for you now?"

His gaze was so intense and so sincere that her eyes grew big and welled up with tears as he took her hands and began reciting.

"I have never known such joy as the passion that we share
I have never known such peace as sleeping in your arms
I have never known such comfort as your kisses in the dawn
I vow to love you forever
I vow to follow your love wherever it may take me
I love you, Sophia, with all my heart and soul."

She let the tears fall, and then, kissing him on his forehead, she repeated his words back to him.

His eyes were glistening when she finished. They sat just gazing at each other, amid the firelight dancing across the room, for a long time.

The first week flew by. They rode his horses and explored the valleys and lochs of the Highlands. Sophia had never actually seen the entire Carrick Estate from boundary to boundary. Abdullah wrapped her in furs when the snow came, and it was like riding in a cocoon. When the wild windswept highland gales arrived, they stayed cuddled in the warmth of the massive fireplace in the library.

He read her the Quran, with the verses and stories teaching her the ways of his world. He wrote her more love poems in Arabic. Gradually, she began learning how to speak and read the language. Through this, Sophia slowly developed a deeper understanding of his life. They spoke of political and social upheavals in his country and the broader region. He told her of his inner fears about his kingdom being overthrown by radicals.

One day Abdullah wanted to chat about the laws in Arabia. "We don't have freedom of speech, especially for women, even though we revere family. We have many arcane laws and punishments."

"I have read about some of these. They sound pretty oppressive to me. But when you make a decision to live in a country, you need to obey its laws," she replied thoughtfully. "Are you planning on trying to change them when you become king?"

He replied slowly, "Things are beginning to change. The largest impediment to change is the committee on virtue and vice. However, we must always work with all factions within our country to assure stability. Sometimes, simply to keep our reign stable and family secure, even I find it necessary to turn a blind eye."

As she learned about the complexities of life in Arabia, she began to appreciate more and more how Rima's devastating childhood had led to their current situation. *Abdullah and his two wives*, she thought, yet sometimes she wondered how this would work in more practical and social terms.

At the end of the second week, their passion had not abated. They were having lunch when he started chatting about his time in India. "During my gap year, I traveled to India to study literature. I was young enough that the only book I cared to study was the *Kama Sutra*. Did you know, Sophia, that female sexual satisfaction, including simultaneous orgasms, is not only encouraged but demanded by some religions?"

"For the last week, with your help, I seem to be discovering that for myself," she responded teasingly.

Later that afternoon, they were stepping into the rough-hewn cedar sauna when he gently pushed her toward the sauna jets. He was behind her, holding her breasts in his hands. She realized that she was reacting to the water jets, and then streams of pleasure began to wash over her.

She could feel his massive erection, and somehow, she knew this coupling would be different. They had read about this in the *Kama Sutra* at lunch. Very softly, he whispered in her ear, "May I please, Sophia? Will you fulfill this dream for me?" Then he added, "It is your call, my love. I do not wish to hurt you."

She nodded yes.

He was very gentle, slowly easing himself inside her. Anal sex was a new experience for him that excited him beyond belief. His movements were careful and gentle.

When Sophia did not join his movements, he feared that she was feeling some pain, which in fact she was. He slowed his movements down, and eventually, she began to return his thrusts.

They climaxed together as he gently squeezed her nipples, until a milky substance was dripping out of them. Feeling it, he turned her around and sucked both of her breasts. She climaxed again.

She was dazed as they finished. He pulled her gently into his arms, picked her up, and carried her to their bed. After drying her with a towel, he held her close, kissing her neck. Looking down at her lovely face, he said, "I love you, Sophia." Then he noticed a tear run down her cheek. "Did I hurt you?" he asked. "I did not intend anything other than pleasure, *mon amour.*"

She tried to talk as images from her childhood assailed her. "When ... wh ... wh ... tee ... co ..." She could not get any words out and finally stopped trying.

Abdullah had no idea what to do. It was clear she was upset, and he thought he understood why, but what to do now?

Sophia turned toward him, held him tightly, and finally cried herself to sleep in his arms. Awakening the next morning, still wrapped in his arms, she remembered the night before. Abdullah was already awake and watching her sleep with a look of confusion etched across his face. Her eyes were puffy from last night's tears, and he kissed them gently.

"I will never do that again, Sophia. In no way did I mean to hurt you. Do you want to talk about what upset you?"

She shook her head no and then leaned into him with a long, passionate kiss. Abdullah was confused and decided not to say any more at this time.

They had now been together for three weeks. Part of Sophia was still in a sexually infused coma, but she was fretting over what would happen next. She had often thought about how safe she felt here and was afraid that feeling of safety would end.

Abdullah was beginning to sense her moods. "Sophia, what are you troubled about?"

Pausing, she looked at him. "My future?"

Abdullah smiled. "Your future is safe with me, Sophia. You are my wife. You have your own money and lands. At some point we will move to Arabia, and you will meet my family and my country. For now I wish to give you this time to become accustomed to being my wife. We will travel back to our homes in London and to your new home in Gloucestershire. Does that help ease your fears?"

She replied in a squeak, "A little." However, there was no conviction behind her answer.

After thinking for a moment, he said, "Sophia, remember our previous conversation about being a wife? I pray we shall have a child. When we consummate our love with a child, you will raise him as a Muslim. You must convert to our faith immediately. And when your cycle comes—prayers to Allah that is never or only once or twice—then we will separate for that time. You may go to London, or I will travel home.

"I suggest that we—I mean you and Rima—begin work on the hotel at your manor house this week. That way, you can move into the west wing here, and we can be together without raising too many ugly rumors in the village. Everything else in our life will stay the same for now."

She nodded her head, uncertain yet not disliking the answer she had just received.

"Would you like to have my child, Sophia?" It was the gentle and kind Abdullah speaking.

"I have thought about it because it is obvious that I have not practiced any form of birth control. Yes, I would love to give you a child, a son. And yes, I will convert to your religion. From what you have taught me and what I have read, I do believe in the Prophet's words. Still, not knowing all of the implications that it would hold for the three of us plus your existing children, I am slightly afraid."

"When we need to, Sophia, we will cross that bridge together, hand in hand."

Once again, the tone of his words had soothed away her fears, and she was at peace.

On the evening of the twentieth, Sophia said to Abdullah, "My love, I know that Rima will be returning tomorrow."

They were sitting in the library reading, and without looking up, Abdullah responded in a desultory fashion, "She knows, Sophia."

"Yes, I am aware," she said with a smile, "and in truth, I am quite comfortable with that fact. Yet she may wish to speak with you, her husband, without my presence intruding. I think it is time I went back to my cottage. I am certain she and I will also speak. I'm not suggesting a secret, my love, just a modicum of privacy for all of us so as not to cause any embarrassment."

He nodded his agreement. "No secrets, Sophia!"

Chapter 24

Rima Returns to Scotland

Sophia drove herself in her dark blue Range Rover to her small four-bedroom thatched-roof cottage at dawn. As the water filled her large soaking tub, she sipped a cup of strong Arabian coffee and studied her language book. She was thinking, *Arabic will be a complicated language to learn.*

She heard the plane overhead, and looking outside, she saw the little Learjet winging its way toward the airstrip. Rima was back. She sighed. *Well,* she thought, *that was a lovely interlude, but honestly, how am I supposed to stay calm? She is both my friend and his wife—his other wife.*

Thanking the captain of the Lear, Rima walked toward her husband, who was waiting for her on the tarmac. A new aura enveloped him; he had a softer smile and a sense of peace she had never seen. Now she was certain that her assessment of Sophia had been correct.

"You look rested and rejuvenated, my husband. I see you have enjoyed your fortnight with, I assume, your second wife. Is my assumption correct?" She looked at him shyly with a smile.

"You are correct, and I can assure you there will *never* be a wife number three. Between the two of you, I could die today a spiritually and sexually sated man."

171

She gave him a beautiful smile that showed the sun's warmth, and he pulled her close in a tender embrace.

"No regrets, my wife?" he said over the top of her petite dark head.

"No, my prince, no regrets. There have been days in our life when I have yearned with jealousy and longing for what I cannot have. And at the same time, you and our family are always first in my mind. Then I hurt for what you have not had. If Sophia brings you that with the understanding of what is truth, then I pray thanks to God, we have found her, for in some ways, it is my salvation as well as yours."

And then she stopped. "Let us go to our Scottish hideaway, shall we? I want to hear everything." They rode in companionable silence toward the manor.

Rima went immediately to her sitting room. She could smell Sophia's Chanel perfume, and she smiled. She settled herself on a cushion, one that reeked of perfume. "Why is Sophia not here?" she asked. Her absence made Rima sad. She'd much rather have had them both here now—to see their eyes, hold their hands, and reassure them all was well and would continue to be so.

Abdullah thought, *She is a little wistful,* and he reminded himself not to boast; that would be hurtful. "She wanted to give us some time alone, to talk is what she said."

"I assume your sexual encounters were to your satisfaction?"

He smiled sheepishly, and then being totally honest, he said, "Extraordinarily so. Plentiful and satisfying in every way. I believe that Sophia called it 'prodigious.'"

"Children?" she asked.

"We used no contraception and certainly consummated our marriage enough times that it could be possible. We'll know soon, for this cycle will end within the week."

"Did you ask?" Rima asked with her eyebrow raised.

"Yes, my love. I did ask. But seriously, Rima, I may be in love, but I still can count weeks in a monthly cycle."

They both laughed.

I even started teaching her the Quran. She is an avid student and is now also ordered to perform daily yoga with you."

"So she really did agree to be your wife, knowing what it meant. Did you explain to her that we will be equals?"

"I was very clear and very concise. And she was equally so. She had some fears that you would be angry with her, but now I believe she is simply a little cautious about exactly how we will navigate a new situation for all. She has no interest in competing with you and is more concerned about your friendship than anything else. She is extraordinarily happy to become my wife. She did not equivocate at all. She wants to spend more time entirely understanding how she will fit in, but she clearly expects, and is looking forward to, being with us forever. She is eager to see you, but ... she said that given the circumstances, she wanted you to have the sanctity of our home to discuss this alone, to not be influenced by her presence."

Rima simply smiled.

"I have told her she can move into the west wing. Is that satisfactory to you?"

Rima looked at him and shook her head. "Why the west wing? Will she not live with us?"

"On this matter, I'll do whatever you want, my wife," he responded. "But it may initially make for less embarrassment on her part. And it gives her a place to live during her cycle."

Rima frowned. "No, she is your wife, your exclusive sexual partner, and our equal intellectual and spiritual partner in every way. I insist she must live with us. I have the room to your left, and she can have the room to your right. There is already a door between all three. Does that work for you?"

"Yes," he said, smiling. He knew where he would be sleeping from now on but kept quiet out of respect.

"You will sleep with her whenever you wish. I am genuinely grateful."

He knew she meant this. For their entire marriage, their love life had existed in the hands of a fertility doctor and in occasional oral intercourse initiated by Rima. Rima was so desperate to please him that despite the pain on her part, and hence the lack of excitement on his part, that this always entailed, he had, to use a Western phrase, faked it for her sake.

"She will be here for dinner," he said.

"Then we must celebrate your marriage."

At the cottage, Sophia was anxious. She had told Abdullah she would return for dinner but was now totally uncertain of where she was spending the night afterward. *This can't be,* she thought, and then she remembered Rima's words on the phone: *You are the beacon of joy I have been waiting for.*

Sophia, dressed in a long flannel shirt dress, arrived precisely at six and was greeted at the door by Rima, who was dressed in exactly the same dress. The two women laughed at the sight of each other.

"You're home," Rima said as she embraced Sophia in a warm hug.

At that moment, Sophia realized yes, she was at home.

"Come, we are celebrating!"

The petite lady ushered her into the cozy sitting room, brought her a glass of champagne, and took one herself. "Sit down, my friend. Now, you must tell me all. Is he a perfect sexual partner in every way? Is he not a perfect husband? I am going to adore having you as my equal."

Sophia almost spit out her champagne. Then she just burst out in a delightful peal of laughter. This openness and honesty were foreign to Sophia, and she was slowly beginning to comprehend that this was precisely as it seemed—open and honest, no hidden agenda.

"Yes," she finally stammered out.

"Did he cause you pain, Sophia?" It was an odd and even more intimate question.

Honesty, Sophia—the thought went off in her brain like a light bulb. "Yes," she said simply, "but always followed by pleasure. And …" She looked searchingly at Rima. This was a secret she had wanted to share with someone for many years.

Sensing something coming, Rima held her tongue.

"My deceased husband used to often cause me pain. He would force me to dress in black underclothing, sometimes lace, mostly leather. He would use painful clips on my nipples and other tools elsewhere. He would often spank me, and not just on my buttocks. The spanking would go on until I was red, sometimes with a small whip that could reach more delicate parts, and I would bleed. Then when I was frightened and dry, he would force himself on me. Because of this, I do understand pain, and Ab ... Ab ..." She could not get his name out without stuttering. Finally, she said, "Abdullah never gave me anything but pleasure."

"Oh, my dear," Rima said, moving to hold Sophia, who had by now started to cry. "I am so sorry."

More sobs engulfed Sophia as she continued. "Like you, I was raped as a child. Unlike you, I was not brutally damaged physically. But when I was twelve years old, I was an elite athlete. Every week my coach would rape me in the back of his car. Yet he never took my virginity. It was always painful. I was too scared to tell my parents, so they never knew."

More engulfing sobs overtook her as she cried in Rima's arms. "I have never told another soul because I blocked it out and did not remember until a recent night. I tried to tell Ab ... Ab ..." She stuttered again. "I tried to explain what I remembered, but I was totally incoherent. Then I was so afraid he would find me shameful, and the safety I felt would go away."

Abdullah was standing quietly in the doorway, listening to the rest of Sophia's story. He now felt great shame at how he had taken her in the sauna. Yes, it had been consensual, and she had felt pleasure, but in hindsight, it had been unnecessary of him, filling no purpose other than his own ego. He silently vowed to make it up to her.

Then, in a low growl, he said, "I will kill them."

Sophia looked up, recovering her wits. "Too late. They are both long gone." She knew with certainty he was not kidding.

"We have decided that you will not live in the west wing."

Sophia looked stricken.

"Instead," he went on, "Rima has made up the room on the left-hand side of mine. She is to my right. From now on, I will be sharing your bed there."

She blushed a deep red, and Rima laughed. The sound of her laughter made Sophia smile.

"What were you thinking just then?" Rima asked.

"Well, that I love your laughter. It is like the twinkling of a star coming to life. Your face lights up, and the sound is delightful."

"Why, thank you. That is a beautiful compliment."

"You're welcome, my friend."

"Would my wife please pour me a glass of champagne?" Abdullah interjected.

They both stood up at once, and again laughter filled the room.

"I see there may be some things I need to learn also," he said smoothly, moving toward the drinks table.

Dinner was filled with delightful conversation, some about art, some about the renovation, and Rima filled them in on gossip and news from home. Sophia realized that Rima was skillfully teaching her about the rest of their family as she did this. A prelude, she supposed.

After dinner, Abdullah excused himself, as did Rima, claiming jet lag. *From Paris?* thought Sophia. *Not likely.* But she had some reading she wanted to finish, and they all adjourned to their rooms.

Her room was more than spacious. French country antique furniture was covered in luxurious stark-white Egyptian linen, and silk and cashmere pillows and throws in pale champagne and white gave the room an ethereal glow. The closet contained some of her clothing, and the drawers had been filled with her Italian lace undergarments. A white lawn nightgown and robe were laid out on the bed.

She heard a shower running, and about half an hour later, Abdullah entered with a towel wrapped around his waist. He leaned over her shoulder, kissing her neck. "Good book," he said. She was reading the Quran.

"So I am told. All part of my next advanced degree," she quipped.

"How many of those do you have, Sophia?" he asked, pulling down her robe while still kissing the back of her neck.

"One baccalaureate, two master's, and part of a doctorate, all in science—geology, geophysics, marine engineering, and oceanography," she replied. "All of which completely failed to prepare me for what I am doing now."

He picked her up and laid her on the bed. "Sophia," he said haltingly. "I was saddened to hear about your past tonight. I didn't know, or I would not have, and I should not have. It was my ego. Please forgive me."

"I know that, Abdullah. There is no need for forgiveness. I love you."

He held her close. "One strong, enduring lesson I have learned from Rima is that the pain of your past can make you a stronger, better person. Neither Rima's rape and circumcision nor your rape was in any way your fault."

"I do understand that, as I said before—bad but distant memories."

He leaned down to kiss her, and conversation ended for now.

The next morning, she felt shy at breakfast but was soon put at ease by Rima's enthusiasm. Rima was wearing yoga clothing and an oversized sweatshirt and was full of plans for the day.

"First we will do an hour of yoga," she said. "Then I would like to tour the building today, top to bottom. And I wish to see the furniture. If any of it needs repair, and we are to be open in the spring, we should get started on that project. And we need to finalize our partnership paperwork. I have a draft, but you need to study it. You can send the papers to your lawyer if you like. But they were drawn up by Sir Joshua. We also need a strategy for including the village and local craftsmen and artisans in the process." She added quietly, "I'm afraid the village does not like Abdullah and me as much as they do you, Sophia."

"Well," Sophia said, knowing this was true, "we'll just have to win them over with our charm and exuberance."

Abdullah, who was watching this lively exchange, smiled. If anyone could stage and win a charm offensive, it was Sophia.

The week went by in a flurry of activity. After dawn prayers and yoga, Abdullah rode with the ladies every morning before they went off to the castle, the manor, or the village to work.

There was more than enough great antique furniture. Many pieces needed minor repairs, and only a few needed significant repairs or reworking to fit into their plan. "If we need more," said

Sophia brightly, "I have storage areas full of antiques in London. I also have an idea about who can help us with this work from the village. Let me make a quick phone call." She came back smiling. "Come with me, my friend," she said, and the two women jumped into her Rover.

Lamote had wanted to see Sophia again and had heard she was back. He had also heard she was now living with the prince and his wife. He thought this was odd, but the manor staff said that given the scope of the renovation, the manor was truthfully in no state to be lived in.

Sophia performed the necessary introductions. "You know my partner in this venture, Her Royal Highness Rima," she said. And then she launched, as only Sophia could, into what she needed. Finally, she asked Lamote, "Can you help? I would love it if the labor could come from the village."

"Sophia, from what I have heard, most of the labor is already coming from the village. And the people you have not hired are now working over at the Earl's old wreck." He looked at Rima. "I believe that is your husband's doing, correct?"

"Do we have full employment yet?" Sophia questioned.

"Close, but not yet. In answer to your question, I do have some older men who are qualified and, with my oversight, would do an excellent job."

"Great. Do you have time to view the furniture today? We have so many pieces that need to be finished by the late spring. I need to see if this job can even be accomplished in our time frame."

"Lead on," he said, grabbing his coat and car keys. He had wanted to see the renovation but had not wanted to pry. The village had given planning consent, and so far everyone was thrilled at the progress being made on the project.

Rima and Sophia were relaxed as they took Lamote through the rooms and showed him the renovation plans. By the time the tour was finished, Rima had enchanted him, a good first step in thawing the village's negative feelings.

Chapter 25

Acknowledgment of a Marriage—Spring 1993

*D*uring the spring of 1993, Sophia's life settled into a joyous pattern. For three weeks each month, she and Rima worked on the hotel in Scotland and with the village, whose residents were finally beginning to accept Rima. Both women helped the villagers start new businesses or expand existing ones. They took the time to work with each individual, to encourage them to grow outside the confines of Carrick.

Every month, when Sophia would start her menstrual cycle, she and Rima would travel London or visit some of Rima's other hotels in France and England.

In London they had opened an old forgotten door in the backyard long covered with ivy, so they could move freely between their two homes without going outside to the street.

Abdullah and Sophia continued to walk or run in Hyde Park. One morning, coming back from a run, he said, "Do you feel comfortable converting to Islam yet, Sophia?"

She thought about this a while and said, "Yes, but could you explain exactly what it entails?"

"It is an easy ceremony called a shahada. With Rima and myself as witnesses, you will declare your faith with conviction, repeating the words of the Prophet in front of an imam."

179

"That seems almost too easy," she quipped.

"We could all go to the Shah Jahan Mosque in Woking on Saturday if you wish." His voice was low, almost pleading.

Turning to him with a bounce in her step, she said, "That would be lovely."

That Saturday, on a sunny but cold day, Sophia dressed in a black pantsuit with a silk head covering borrowed from Rima, and they entered the oldest mosque in England. In front of the imam, Sophia repeated the words "Ashadu an la ilaha illa illa-ilah, wa ashadu anna muhammadan rasul ullah" in Arabic. This translated to "There is no God but God (there is none worthy of worship but Allah), and Muhammad is the messenger of Allah."

The next week, Abdullah had returned to Arabia for a week, and Sophia joined her friend Doug for a sailing regatta in Florida. At first Abdullah had been very uncertain that Doug could maintain Sophia's security. After a long and sometimes uncomfortable phone conversation with Doug, he had grudgingly agreed that if they chartered a powerboat to house the crew, and if Doug promised Sophia would wear a hat and sunglasses while sailing, it would be, in Abdullah's words, "safe enough."

When Sophia arrived in Miami on the G3, she was quickly whisked through customs and onto a smaller private plane for the short trip to Key West. Doug met her at the airport and said, "Sophia, I am thrilled to hear of your marriage! Now would you like to explain the rest of the story?"

Tilting her head to one side and fluttering her eyelashes, she said pertly, "I fell in love."

She was so comical, even Doug had to laugh. "Let's chat over dinner tonight," he said. So later that night, Sophia explained to Doug everything that had occurred in the last three months.

During this trip to Arabia, Abdullah had the time to contemplate the turn his life had taken through his marrying Sophia. Physically and intellectually, he adored spending time with Sophia. They often chatted about his investments in his private company Royal Holdings, and he found her insights into which stocks to pick useful. At her suggestion, he had invested in more technology stocks, which were doing very well. She was well educated in both business and, maybe more importantly, Western political intrigue.

He had heard rumors that the Devon Estates controlled vast portions of several multinational companies with which he was involved. Yet in the now three months they had been married, all he had ever heard about was art. While he enjoyed collecting art himself, he wondered if his information had been incorrect.

With Abdullah away, Sophia too had time to contemplate the turn her life had taken. She thought, *I guess that I have learned to love people as individuals, including myself, instead of judging them against a set of prescribed standards. And I certainly am a different person than I was a year ago.*

It was early April when Sophia arrived back in London, the day before Abdullah arrived from Arabia. Sophia and Rima were sitting in the comfortable Persian sitting area when he arrived. He immediately announced, "We are going to the Ritz tonight for dinner."

"Lovely," they said in unison.

Sophia followed on with "What will I wear?"

Abdullah, who was in great spirits because his meetings had gone so well and his work was unusually calm, said, "Jewelry, Sophia. We know you have jewelry."

She laughed. "I somehow don't think you want me dressed in only diamonds."

It was unusual for them to have this flirtatious play with Rima present, but she chimed in. "I will wear the rubies, and you the emeralds, Sophia, but what else?"

Laughing, he announced that dinner would be at seven thirty and then left the room.

After they stopped laughing, Sophia excused herself, muttering, "I really do need to figure out what to wear."

That night, instead of entering through the private entrance at the back of the Ritz, the three of them exited the limousine and walked in the front entrance, past the usual scrum of paparazzi. The flashbulbs were blinding as they were quickly whisked into the calm of the lobby and escorted toward the restaurant.

Upon entering the restaurant with its elegant pale-green Louis XVI surroundings, they noticed several diners who were acquaintances of either Abdullah's or Sophia's. The Duke of Westminster nodded toward the group, acknowledging their presence, and stood to greet them as they passed. Sophia responded to the older man's greeting with a warm hug.

Looking down at her left hand and seeing the newly acquired diamond and gold band, he whispered in her ear, "I see the rumors are true, Sophia."

Quietly, but in a voice loud enough for others to hear, she answered, "Yes, Your Grace. This time the rumors are true. Abdullah and I were married in Scotland in January. I am now Abdullah's wife."

The duke smiled and greeted the prince and Rima warmly. Still, he was not certain if he should say congratulations in front of Rima or not.

Once they were seated, they were offered the finest Pol Roger champagne to begin their meal, and when both Abdullah and Rima declined, Sophia also declined.

Abdullah said softly, "You may have a glass, Sophia."

Knowing that especially here, the walls had ears, she replied demurely, "No, thank you, Your Highness."

Chapter 26

Three Days of Mayhem

Sophia had one last task to complete before her estate could be finalized: the division of Barbara's property portfolio. Sitting at her elegant Empire desk on a blustery April day, she was attempting to divide the portfolio in an equitable manner.

Abdullah arrived home from work and bounded into Sophia's study with his normal exuberance. Wrapping his arms around her and then massaging her tight neck while running his other hand through her hair, he said, "And how was your day, my princess?"

Sophia leaned back, feeling his touch, and uttered some noise that sounded like a cross between a purr or a moan. Finally, she said, "I have finished my property division plan. Do you want to look at it?"

He had been itching to help Sophia with this portion of her estate. "Of course, I will help. I am here to be of service to my princess."

As she showed him the plan, Abdullah was thoughtful. "There are some very prestigious properties here," he said. "What if we take a tour to see them in person?"

"Great idea. I haven't seen them all yet either," she said. "Now about that service of a princess," she giggled.

A couple of days later, Sophia, Abdullah, Uncle Jerry, and Sir Joshua toured the properties together. The first thing Sir Joshua noticed was the diamond and gold band on Sophia's finger.

"Are the rumors true?" he asked, looking pointedly at Sophia's left hand and then to Abdullah. Uncle Jerry stood back, crossing his arms, to see how they would answer.

"They are," Sophia giggled as Abdullah put his arm protectively around her.

Smiling at the attorney, Abdullah said, "Yes, meet my wife, Princess Sophia bint Abbas.

"Congratulations!" the attorney said, beaming as he shook Abdullah's hand. Then he wrapped his arms around Sophia in a hug, whispering in her ear, "A brilliant match."

They soon came to one of the lots in central London with an Esso station on it.

"Ah," Sophia exclaimed, "one of the problem children."

"Why is that?" asked Abdullah.

"Well, Esso has notified us they will not renew their lease, and we are responsible for the cleanup—the very expensive cleanup."

"Oh, I am certain that can be overcome," said Uncle Jerry.

Abdullah nodded his agreement as both men smiled at each other, while Sir Joshua watched them with a look of glee.

"Really?" she said. "How?"

Uncle Jerry spoke first. "BP will lease the lot from you, Sophia."

Then Abdullah chimed in. "Or Aratex will lease it."

"How can you two know that?" she asked, perplexed.

"Well," said Jerry, chuckling, "I'm the chairman of the board of BP."

Abdullah was laughing.

She turned to her husband and looked at him askance.

"And I know the chairman of Aratex," he said.

"Hm," she said, attempting to frown, though a small smile still crossed her face. "OK, I guess that's one problem solved."

"But," said Abdullah, "Aratex wouldn't do it for Henry."

Westminster chimed in. "Neither will BP. Remember, Sophia, he is not your friend. He is your enemy."

184

After a good deal of debate, Henry eventually arrived in England to divide the property. They would use Sir Joshua as a proxy for Edward.

Henry stormed into the meeting, yelling, "You're trying to sell the property, Sophia. You've taken him to every property behind my back. See, she is not fit for a business meeting. I have been telling all of you this for months."

Sophia shook her head and remained silent.

Still, Henry continued. "You're trying, probably unsuccessfully since you screwed him out of the last deal, to sell the lot to that towelhead. Or is it you're just his whore?"

One of the junior attorneys from Latham said, "Hear, hear!" to Henry's comments.

Then the room went silent. Sophia's mouth was actually open, in shock not at what Henry had just said, but at the naked hatred and jealousy she saw in his eyes. *Abdullah is right*, she realized. *He is my enemy.*

Clearing his throat, Sir Joshua said, "Stop! I want everyone in this room to listen very well to my next statement. While I will not repeat myself, I am at this point more than happy to act on it."

"The lady you seem to think it is now fun to swear at and mock is Her Royal Highness, Princess Sophia bint Abbas. Her husband and her kingdom are important allies of both Britain and the USA. If anyone makes one more disparaging remark about Her Royal Highness during these negotiations, I will consider the will broken, and all properties will go to Sophia." Then turning to Sophia, he said gently, "You may continue, Your Highness."

Finally, the Watkins senior partner said, "Shall we begin?"

Methodically, they went through the list of properties, first Henry, then Sir Joshua, then Sophia. Henry's legal team had, in fact, reviewed the documents and were actively and even aggressively suggesting which properties he should choose, but he was insisting on doing it his way. Every time, he went for the high-rent property.

Henry's first and second choice was one of the petrol stations located in central London. He made the decision quickly and looked over at Sophia with a smug glare. *Good luck with that*, Sophia thought.

Mr. Watkins was surprised, as was Henry's other lawyer, who had advised him against it. He now reminded him, "You do realize that this lease will expire shortly, and we have been informed by the tenant they will not renew. It also has been declared a hazardous waste site. You and you alone will be responsible for any cleanup on the site after the tenant vacates."

"We'll see about that," snarled Henry. "It's the one I want."

At the end of the day, the division was completed, and it was left to the legal team to redraw the trust agreements. Henry said goodbye to his lawyers and left the room without a word to Sophia, Sir Joshua, or Watkins and Smith.

She was still seated with her lawyers when her phone rang. Henry was yelling about the petrol stations, saying he had changed his mind.

She replied very calmly, "I have had enough of your histrionics. I will separate the properties and send you my final decision. If you want to have one more meeting, we can reconvene tomorrow at 10:00 a.m."

"Fine!" he yelled. "Tomorrow you can buy my portion of the whole portfolio based on your damn evaluations. The fucking will does provide for that, and I want my cash now!"

The house was quiet when Sophia arrived home. She was sitting in her library, surrounded by piles of papers and files, staring at the fireplace with a vacant gaze, when Abdullah strode into the room.

Seeing her worried look, he put his arm around her shoulder, asking, "How did your meeting with Dr. Henry go?"

"Very, very, poorly. In the end, he just blew up, saying I should buy him out for one-third of the value of the trust."

"I thought you said you could not sell the properties for five years," Abdullah mused, "according to the will."

"We can't sell them. But I do have the right to buy them from Henry. In her infinite wisdom, Barbara gave me the right of first refusal on the properties."

"Are these the properties?" he said, pointing to a stack of disorganized papers on her desk. "May I look at them again? I do know something about property," he said with a devilish grin.

As she looked up at him, he gave her a quick kiss on the nose. Smiling, she said, "Of course, you can. As you know from your tour, there are some are great properties. Do you have any bright ideas for this conundrum, my prince?"

He looked at the map and smiled. "Why, Sophia, I can solve this one very easily."

"You can't buy them from me," she said with a sigh. She was learning very quickly that money was Abdullah's answer to every problem.

"Do you mind if I sit and review these again?"

She smiled. "I would love that, my prince. Would you like a cup of tea?"

They sat in the two plush chairs in her library in companionable silence, both reading documents for around thirty minutes, until Abdullah said, "Sophia, come here, please. These are the properties I find interesting." He held up three sheets of paper as he stood and moved to the sofa. "The rest are all excellent investments, but these three are special. Yet I do not see how two of them fit into the estate. The deeds are not to the Devon Real Estate Trust."

She left her desk and went over to the large chesterfield sofa and sat down next to him. "Which ones?"

"As you know, I like the dirty lots in London, but I want to know more about Nockatunga Holdings, the cattle and sheep station in Australia. What did you say earlier about Henry wanting you to buy his one-third out? Which ones of these did Henry pick?"

Sophia laughed and said, "In the end, none of those three. He said, 'Who wants some stupid cows and sheep in Australia?'"

Abdullah could not keep from laughing.

She continued, "And as for the purchase, he wants me to pay him one-third of the stated value in cash."

Becoming serious, Abdullah said gruffly, "How much?"

"But you can't buy them," she said, "and I don't have that kind of cash."

"Spare me the details of your poverty, Sophia. When is your next meeting?"

"Tomorrow. I have a meeting at nine with Sir Joshua and then at ten with Henry and his legal team." She shrugged her shoulders. "One last try."

"I suggest that you say yes to Henry's thoughtful offer, whatever it is."

Sophia opened her mouth to retort. But he took her arms and pulled her into a big hug, saying, "Shush, I will happily give or lend you the money. If you don't want to take my gift, then we can have a legal note, and if you are pushed on where you got the money, you can say that you borrowed it. When and if they ask from whom, tell them it is none of their damn business. I will arrange for a petrol company to take over the city leases. But you once said there was also a private stock portfolio?"

"Yes," she said. "Sir Joshua mentioned it to me privately at our first meeting. I have never found any indication of any stocks while going through all of these boxes." She threw her arms out to indicate the piles of boxes and papers that cluttered every surface of the library.

Abdullah missed her gesture as he was focused on one paper. "What do you know about Nockatunga Holdings?" he asked again.

"Well," she said, "it is a large sheep and cattle station in Australia. They also own property in Sydney and Melbourne. They are all rented. The station is also partially leased to Aratex. They don't, however, pay all that much rent. Oh, and Aratex leases the top half of the high-rise in Sydney for almost nothing also."

Sophia met with Sir Joshua at his office the following morning.

"Sophia, before our next meeting, have you looked at all of the documents and letters that Barbara left you? I don't mean the joint ones. I mean the private stocks and the letters she wrote. She insisted that you should know the whole story."

"I never found them," said Sophia in complete exasperation. "Where are they?"

"She told me they were in the top drawer in her desk."

"I only found one letter there," said Sophia.

"Have you heard of hidden compartments?" asked Sir Joshua. He smiled and continued, "We need to have our last short meeting with Henry now."

Her final meeting with Henry and his legal team was an unmitigated failure. He stomped in, and after calling her a slew of names—slut, whore, and an Arab's prostitute—he reiterated that he wanted a buyout and started to stomp out again.

Drawing from some secret reserve of calm she didn't know she possessed, Sophia said to Henry's lawyer, "The amount I'll pay will be on my initial property division. There is no other offer on the table. Your client has walked out of this meeting, thereby nullifying the will as well as the secondary conditions from the Scotland agreement. Please remember that your lawyers are also liable and signatories to that agreement. If Henry disagrees, then my husband and I are perfectly willing to reinvestigate the Scottish matter."

Turning to her lawyer David, she said, "This estate is now ready to be finalized."

Sophia was shaking her head as she walked up the steps to her house. All she could think was *I have stumbled down a rabbit hole into mayhem.* She was seething at the slurs directed first at Abdullah and now at herself.

Abdullah met her at the door with a smile and wrapped her in his big arms and kissed her. With his arm around her as they walked up the stairs to Sophia's study, he grinned, saying, "I have something exciting to show you! How did today go, my princess?"

Shaking her head sadly as they entered the library, she said, "I've had such a bad day that a drink may be in order."

Just then, Mrs. Kelly walked in, saying, "Tea, Your Highness? Oh, Ms. Sophia, you're home. Would you like tea also?"

Sophia accepted the offer from Mrs. Kelly, who left the room.

Then Sophia looked around. New tables had appeared in front of the windows of her study, her papers had been moved, and her desk had been rearranged. "Abdullah, what have you done to my study?"

"You didn't answer my question. How did your day go?" he said, ignoring her question.

She sat down on the big chesterfield and said, "Awful! I finally agreed to buy him out. I guess I will need that loan."

"*Jyid,*" he said with a broad grin. "Good in Arabic."

She had already been seething when she came in, but it was Abdullah's smile that pushed her over the edge. "How can you say 'good'?" She continued rapidly, without pause. "I'm trying to solve that last part of this fucking entanglement, and you say *jyid!*" She mimicked the word in Arabic.

"Ah, Sophia, I could hear you from next door. Is tea ready?" Rima entered the room as Mrs. Kelly was returning.

"Sanity," Sophia mumbled. "I've lost my sanity. And then Henry called me a slew of names, and at the end, he said I was your whore." Tears were beginning to form in the corners of her eyes. "So you see, my sanity is truly in question. I am sitting here in my library with my husband and my husband's wife. My former brother-in-law, who stole and lied to me, is calling me names. I have fallen down a fucking rabbit hole."

Just then a cell phone on the desk rang. Abdullah reached for it, but Sophia beat him to it. "That's mine," he barked.

As Sophia handed the phone to him, she saw that the caller was Sir Joshua.

"Yes, sir, she's home. A little rattled. But leave it with me. I think I have found the solution you may be looking for. One of us will call you back. But since Sophia is standing here glaring at me, I need to ring off."

There was a pause while he listened to Sir Joshua.

"Oh, but did I hear correctly what Henry called her? I'm sure you understand that I find that slur to my wife highly offensive and unacceptable. If you see or hear from Henry, tell him he is no longer the surgeon to our country, and the funding for his eye institute has just been revoked!" He then hung up on Sir Joshua.

Sophia's mouth was hanging open, and Rima was laughing, but Abdullah's eyes were flashing with white-hot anger.

Now with her tea in hand, Sophia wheeled on Abdullah. "What have you done to my library? Where are all my neat piles of paper?"

He said gently, "Calm down, Sophia. I have only rearranged them."

Sophia glanced over to see Mrs. Kelly and Rima looking at the two of them with what looked like smiles on their faces.

Before she could start again, he said, "I have simply rearranged the piles into first country and then property type.

"You have some hidden gems here," he continued, laughing. "And I have found the rest of the letters from Barbara."

"Where?"

"They were in the top drawer of your desk, Sophia."

"You went into my desk? My personal papers?" She was yelling now, and again Rima and Mrs. Kelly were standing in the corner, laughing.

"Yes, my princess, my wife," he said quietly.

"Don't 'princess' me. Those are my personal papers, and you said that—"

"Peace, Sophia. We all know you had a horrid day, but if you would please slow down and trust me—"

"No!" she yelled, and the tears started to fall.

By now, Rima was no longer laughing, and Mrs. Kelley was nervously eyeing the door.

Abdullah walked over and put his arm around Sophia while rubbing her back with his other hand. "Sophia, I did not read the papers on your desk. I suspected, with the help of your lawyer, Sir Joshua, that the desk had a hidden compartment."

Listening to Abdullah's calm voice as he massaged her neck, Sophia was slowly calming down.

"Look at me, Sophia," he said as he gently turned her so she was looking directly into his eyes. "I have not hurt you. I did not meddle, even though I understand you think I did. I did look at the rest of your properties, as you asked me to, and I found some hidden gems. More of them are not in the Devon Realty Trust. They are yours alone."

"How do you even know Sir Joshua?"

"He is also my personal lawyer," confessed Abdullah. He pulled her down onto the sofa, stroking her hair and holding her tight to his chest. "Let me tell you a story, Sophia. Once upon a time, there was a little girl in Arabia. She married a rich prince, and as part of her wedding present, he bought her a hotel in Agra, near the Taj Mahal. It had almost perfect views of the building. But there was a piece of land in between the two, and no one knew who owned it. It was in a blind trust. For years the prince and princess looked for the owner of the trust to no avail.

"Then one day the prince fell in love and married his true love. The princesses formed a hotel group, and all three were living happy and fulfilling lives. The prince loved Princess Sophia with his whole heart. This was not an arranged marriage in which they had developed an affection, but rather a case of two people who had fallen desperately and hopelessly in love.

"And one day, while helping the love of his life with a business project, he stumbled across a title to a blind trust that owned land and buildings in Agra. So you see, the princess owns the land that the other princess wants.

"When the prince found this out, he was very excited and called Princess Sophia to tell her, but she did not answer her phone. So he called his lawyer to tell him. And the lawyer said, 'Aha, Sophia has finally found the rest of the documents.' After a little conversation, he figured out that this land was not part of the joint estate, even though the papers were stuck in the joint ownership file.

"Next, instead of doing princely things like running a kingdom, the prince spent the entire day playing file clerk for the princess."

As Abdullah slowly massaged the back of her neck, Sophia had finally started to relax, and at that comment, she giggled.

"What he found was amazing!" Abdullah continued. "And I think from what our friend Sir Joshua says, the best part is in the letter on your desk—unread!"

"I told Henry I would buy him out. I wanted so badly to do this on my own without your help and your very thoughtful offer."

As she was speaking, he pulled her close, saying, "Shush. That is one of the many reasons I love you, Sophia. The money for the loan will be in your bank account tomorrow.

"Oh my God," she said, jumping up.

"Oh, So-phi-a," he sing-songed, "you just ran away from me."

She turned and pulled him up off the sofa as she kissed him. "Come, my love, please read it with me."

Abdullah was still holding her hand tightly, looking at her with a gleam in his eye.

"No," she said, reading the sexy glint in his eyes. "It will be hours before we read that letter if you start this now. Before you totally distract me, let us see what you found."

They sat side by side on the sofa, Abdullah's arm around her, as Sophia opened the letter.

Chapter 27

Aratex

Dear Sophia,

Every item tells a story. Every picture was someone's passion when they were painting it. Homes, buildings, pieces of land, and even stock certificates hold the stories of their owners' lives. Sometimes they are happy, sometimes sad, yet every story is unique.

The possessions I have left to you and you alone are my story. The joint properties are the stories of the old dukes and can be found in the attics of the houses. Everything that became an essential part of my story is found here at my home.

Without further ado, let me fill you in on a few details.

Nockatunga Holdings is a vast cattle and sheep station in Queensland, Australia. The Nockat family owned it for several generations. It is a wild and sometimes winsome place. I genuinely suggest you visit it as soon as possible, Sophia. Your interest in travel should be piqued by now and may set you on another journey.

Anyway, it is the story of how we acquired Nockatunga that is the most interesting. The Nockat boys were twins who left home to help the world during the Great War. Being Australian, they were sent to fight on the border of the Ottoman Empire at the battle of Gallipoli. We all know what a historic failure the battle was. It was surprising that my friend Winston ever made it back into office after that. Thank God he did. Still, there were families of the dead and wounded who never forgave him.

Fortunately, the Nockat boys managed to survive the battle with the help of their commanding officer, my father. It had been nip and tuck, they always said when telling the story. "There were Turks wielding swords, beheading all those in sight," they said. "The blood was running to the sea when Devon saw that a small pod of us were alive. He grabbed three men on horseback, commanding them to follow, and with two rifles each, they fought their way into our midst. Each rider took two men, and triple-mounted, the horses moved toward the evacuation line. Still, we all soldiered on. Our Australian division was the first to land on the peninsula in 1915 and the last to leave in 1916, and Devon was with us the entire time."

The Nockat brothers served my father for a year. He had saved their lives, and at some point they saved his. They showed their gratitude by gifting my father a vast tract of land in Queensland, Australia.

The Ottoman Empire was changing rapidly. My father considered both of the boys the sons he no longer had. After the war, they jointly opened trade with Turkey, Arabia, and eventually Egypt and England.

It was in 1921 that this story took another turn. When my parents traveled to Australia, they were keen to see the Nockatunga station. While there, something must have happened, because they departed Queensland early, never to return. I have always wondered whether, maybe surmised that, my mother fell in love with the eldest brother in the Nockat family, because upon his death in World War II, she, not my father, inherited another vast tract of land in Sydney and the rest of the station. That is why the deed to the station runs in two different documents.

Early in 1936, oil was discovered at Nockatunga. At the same time, my father put together a joint project with a young oilman from Texas and a Bedouin sheik. By combining all of their resources, they had enough money and rich oil land to form Aratex Oil.

For the decade-plus between 1940 and 1955, my father was rarely home. By now, his business ranged worldwide and covered a vast scope that included shipbuilding, shipping, oil, mining, coal, and a host of new technologies that were beginning, including airplanes and electronics. Aratex Oil and the land it owns are part of these legacy holdings. I inherited my 60 percent stake in what is now called Aratex Holdings from my father.

Through a blind trust, I also own 14 percent of Royal Holdings. I do not vote my shares; instead, my trustee Sir Joshua provides a proxy to the chairman of the board of each venture.

Sophia turned to look up at Abdullah. His lips were pursed together, his eyes questioning.

You may also be wondering about a series of leases in a company called Nortex that we hold from the Norwegian government. We were posted to the Norwegian embassy when I was a little girl. In World War II, I briefly worked with the Norwegians

*undercover for MI5, and the leases were a gift to me
from the new king of Norway for the risks I took to
protect his country.*

Sophia finished the letter and sat very still. She was remembering back to the first day, to the reading of the will. "You now control 60 percent of a multinational company," Sir Joshua had read aloud. She had thought he intended to say 66 percent, meaning the split of the Devon estate. But he had been referring to Aratex. *Be careful whom you trust.* The only thing she was certain of was that Sir Joshua knew far more than he had ever let on.

Attached with a paper clip were copies of the stock certificates for Aratex Corporation, of which Sophia was now a 60 percent owner, and a stock certificate for 14 percent of Royal Holdings— Abdullah's private company.

Abdullah also appeared stunned by the contents of the letter but was the first to finally speak. "Sophia, Sir Joshua Reynolds has been my British lawyer since I came to this country to study. He was at school with my father."

"I don't understand," she said slowly. "Does this mean I own 14 percent of your company? Is this *that* Royal Holdings? And I know nothing about Aratex other than it is a big, privately owned company." She stood up and started pacing the room.

Abdullah looked as though he wanted to howl in pain. How had this happened? he thought.

Finally, she stopped pacing. Sophia stood in front of Abdullah, her eyes blazing. "It's either fucking destiny, my prince, or you are Machiavelli. There are far too many coincidences here for me to believe they are all accidental. How would you like to divulge"—she pointed a finger at his chest—"the honest truth for once?"

"Sophia, which coincidence are you referring to? Of course, I knew that Sir Joshua was the trustee for Aratex and Royal Holdings. Sophia, he never divulged who his client was. What he did do was put me in touch many years ago with an eye doctor named Henry Lawrence, long before you and I met. No one knew about this except Sir Joshua.

"Coincidences, some. But what are you suggesting about Machiavelli? Are you saying I used you?" He stood up, came close, and held her arms. She could feel his heart beating with anger.

Sophia continued, "You claim it is an accident that you are my neighbor. Really. You are sleeping with me—married me! There are far too many coincidences."

"First, Sophia," he said, raising his voice slightly, "I was given Number Five/Six by my father. Again, Sir Joshua did the transaction. Nonetheless, I am certain that my father knew the Duke of Devon. My father was the Bedouin who was the third partner in Aratex, and I am the other 40 percent owner!"

Sophia was shocked and about to speak when he continued.

"But please, Sophia, do not deny me! Make no mistake. I fell in love with you, walking around this little crescent. And ever since New Year's Eve, all I have done is fall more in love with you. Please, Sophia, believe me."

She looked into his eyes. Anger, rage, love, and fear—every emotion a man could feel showed on his chiseled features. The electricity in his touch made her forget everything else she had intended to say.

"Oh, Abdullah," she said as she began to sob against his chest. "I have no intention of ever denying you anything. I am just so confused." The rest of what she might have said was lost in a kiss.

He picked her up and carried her into their bedroom. Eventually, she cried herself to sleep in his arms.

In the wee hours of the morning, when Sophia awoke, Abdullah was sound asleep next to her, his arm still wrapped around her in a protective embrace. As she gazed at his handsome, chiseled profile, she was overwhelmed with a gnawing uncertainty. Had he known before? How could he have not known? What did owning Aratex really mean? Sir Joshua's words kept running around her head; he had said something about her inheriting "immense power" for someone so young. Use it wisely, be careful, he had said. The overriding question in her mind as the sun rose was had she been careful enough?

By five, sleep still eluded her, so she quietly rose and went into the breakfast room to reread the letter. Then she began reading the Aratex annual reports. She started with the reports from the 1950s, when Barbara had inherited the property, and finished the last one from 1992 around nine. She was fascinated. The company was far more diverse than she had thought. Its largest division was oil production, shipping—both tankers and containers—and port facilities. Aratex controlled much of the world's oil reserves. Over the years the corporation had branched into technology. The division called Aratech owned satellite, electronics, aerospace, and chip manufacturing entities. One separate division was a defense weapons-manufacturing facility in the USA, while still another division, Arapharma, ran advanced medical and pharmaceutical laboratories, as well as a private hospital in Switzerland.

Her mind was swirling with questions. She was staring out at the garden, biting her lower lip while deep in thought, when Abdullah walked into the breakfast room.

"You look troubled, Princess," he said, lightly kissing her on the head.

She had a rueful smile on her face when she said, "I have been up all morning thinking, worrying, reading about Aratex."

"Oh, my love, no need for you to fret," he said.

Inside, Sophia thought, *Now there is a problem in the making,* but she continued speaking. "I feel I have a responsibility to learn and understand more about Aratex. Monday morning I am going to set up a meeting with Sir Joshua."

Abdullah was taken aback by this new turn of events. He had been single-handedly running Aratex with Sir Joshua's blessing for close to a decade. Not once had the wily solicitor let on that Abdullah's unknown partner was his neighbor, or especially his new wife. And again he wondered about the car bomb. Finally, his thoughts turned to Sophia. What did she know about running a company this large and complex? Nothing!

Instead of voicing these concerns to Sophia, he said calmly, "What will you be meeting with Sir Joshua about?"

"I need a will. What happens if something happens to me? Now it's not just cash and buildings; it's a major stake in a massive worldwide company."

Abdullah was about to say, *Well, I am your husband*, but then realized that that might be the issue. Leaning over to take Sophia's hand, he said, "Anything you wish is fine with me, even though I would be interested in knowing what you are thinking."

She sighed. "For now all I want to do is learn. I would like to see the buildings, the offices, even some of the port facilities. Clearly, you have been running the company for some time, and that will not change. Will you teach me more than just what can be found in an annual report?"

Then she just looked at him. Shaking her head, she said quietly, "Abdullah, you honestly didn't know? How could that be, really?"

So, he thought, *the problem is now on the table.* "Sophia, what are you asking?"

"Did you marry me for Aratex?" And then the tears started to fall.

He stood up and went to her, bending down so he could look into her eyes. Wrapping his arms around her and kissing her forehead, he said, "I guessed at your being involved in Aratex about forty-eight hours ago. Remember when I said I had found deeds to a couple of buildings that were not in trust?"

"Yes," she said, nodding.

"One of those is the Aratex building. I have an office there. So I started to have my suspicions. To answer your question, my beautiful wife whom I love with all my heart, I did not marry you for Aratex. I married you for love."

Trying to break the tension between them, he joked, "Now let's get the next camel out on the table. Whom, other than me, do you want to leave your 60 percent share of Aratex to in case of your demise?"

She shook her head and, with tears streaming down her cheeks, said, "I don't honestly know." Then she added in almost a whisper, "Abdullah, was the bomb meant for me? Who was responsible?"

Still holding her close, he said, "I honestly don't know, Sophia. At first I thought it was Henry. But it now appears that the bomb was not intended to kill; it was most likely a warning of some sort. Since then, I have stepped up security and made every effort to protect you, even before you became my wife."

Sophia held on to him tightly as she continued in a frightened voice. "Because if it was meant for me, they most likely knew about Aratex before I did, and how would they know that? It had to be leak from somewhere, and if so, where?"

"I suggest that your first idea was a good one. Meet with Sir Joshua and see what his thoughts are. The entire idea of a will is a good one. Don't be surprised when I meet with Sir Joshua to update mine as well."

Sensing that this conversation was over for now, Sophia changed the subject. "Did I read that we are building a new tanker, *Trader II*? And that we own the *Trader*? I knew the first *Trader*; a friend of mine was the captain."

When Sophia had seen the photo in the annual report, she had been astounded. She remembered her close friend going by her on the tug at her father's funeral and the radio saying, "This is the *Trader*, outbound for Dubai."

However, Abdullah was not listening. Rather, he was thinking about what Sophia would do with her 60 percent.

Chapter 28

Sophia's Will

*T*he next day was a gray, rainy Monday, and Sophia awoke early. Her mood matched the weather, and realizing that Abdullah again was in a deep sleep, she crept out of bed and went to her study. She quietly locked the door and sat down to read again the letters from Barbara. No matter how she looked at it, Abdullah must have known something. Had she really been that blind?

She had so many questions and realized that maybe Sir Joshua, if he was honest, could give her the answers. As soon as it was remotely civilized to do so, she called his private home line. He answered on the first ring, almost as if he had been waiting for her call.

Without a preamble or even a polite hello, she said, "I would like to have a meeting this morning. Do you have time?"

"I am pretty well scheduled, but I can make fifteen minutes for you at nine. I judge that this is about the balance of your inheritance?" he replied.

"Yes, it is. I will see you at nine with questions."

At 8:45 a.m., she walked into the austere offices of Winston and Reynolds. Sir Joshua was waiting for her and quickly escorted her into his mahogany-paneled private office, where he offered her a seat across from his desk.

She waited for him to be seated at his large partners desk, and then, her voice filled with sarcasm, she said, "I take it our early start means we have thirty minutes now, Sir Joshua. As you might have gathered, I have many questions.

"First and maybe foremost, did Abdullah know of my share of Aratex before yesterday?"

Sir Joshua looked at her carefully, and she held his gaze. "I do not think so," he answered.

"Did his father?"

"Again, I do not know for certain. However, he may have suspected."

"Was the bomb intended for me?"

"Yes, we believe it was a warning, and that is why I say I am not certain of the answer to the other two questions."

She stood up and paced the room as she spoke. "You mean to tell me that both you and Abdullah knew the bomb might have been intended for me, and neither of you happened to mention it?" By the end of the sentence, her voice was raised.

Turning to face him and placing her hands on his desk, she snarled, "I am your client. Don't you think you had a responsibility to tell me? Why didn't you push me to find the papers before this week?" She was seething with anger. "You certainly knew of their existence and the relationship."

"Well, that's a complex question. First, I did not know of your marriage to Abdullah until recently. And I do sanction it with all of its possible pitfalls. As a lawyer it is my job to keep the counsel of my clients to myself. It is the essence of what we do. So while I knew of the extent of the holdings and the other partners, it was not within my power to tell you sooner.

"As for not pointing you toward the letters earlier, there has been so much turmoil with Henry that I felt it was best to let the natural course of events progress, hoping that you could finalize the estate with him first. Last week, when you agreed to purchase the last parts from Henry, I decided that for both sets of my, you and Abdullah and my friend the king, it was time for the Aratex secret to be found. I knew the letters were in a drawer, and I told you about them. How was I to know that your husband would find them first?"

"Was my marriage to Abdullah part of the natural course of events, or did you arrange that too?"

"Sophia, that is not fair. I had no idea you and Abdullah even knew each other, let alone were married in Scotland."

"That's not true. You knew that I was Abdullah's next-door neighbor. For Christ's sake, you stood next to the Westminsters and watched us dance at their party last fall. At a minimum, you clearly knew that he and I were acquainted."

"Well, that again is not fair, Sophia. Just because you had a dance—"

"Oh, spare me," she interjected, her temper taking over. "How many other women did he dance with that night? Or ever in public? Even I knew it was a statement. I just didn't know what it meant!"

"I hardly call the Westminsters' home public, but I do see your point. I promise you, I honestly did not think of it."

Sophia rolled her eyes in disbelief and began pacing the room again. "Let's go back to the bombing, shall we? What do you know, and am I safe in my current situation?"

"What I know with any certainty is this. The bomb was not the IRA. It was not intended to kill, given its location and the time and method of explosion. It was not connected to any official Arabian royal protection—and yes, that was looked into by the UK authorities at my instigation."

"Why, pray tell, would you have looked into this?" she snarled at him.

Actually raising his voice, Sir Joshua said, "Sophia, I knew you had inherited Aratex. And I knew what it meant. You do realize what you actually control, don't you? Of course, I would look into it!"

"What do you mean by that, what I control?" she said scornfully.

Finally, in complete exasperation, he slammed his fist on his desk and yelled at her. "Sophia, with your husband's share, you control almost 40 percent of the world's oil reserves."

At this outburst she stood very still, staring at him with a shocked expression on her face. Unusually for Sophia, words eluded her, so when she said nothing, the lawyer continued.

"I do believe you are safe and that Abdullah has every intention of keeping you safe."

"That is all well and good, but how do I know I can trust you?" she asked quietly.

"Fair question, Sophia. The best answer I can give you is that Barbara trusted me, and she left the estate to you and you alone. I assume she would have wanted you to trust me."

Sophia did not think this was a great answer; still, it might be the only one she could believe for now. Changing the subject, she said, "I need a will."

"That is a good idea," he replied. "Who will be the beneficiary?" he asked, almost too calmly.

"For now the sole beneficiary will be Abdullah, or if he is deceased, his heirs in equal proportion, regardless of gender. If I should die before the age of fifty from anything, including natural causes, then the shares of Aratex shall be in a trust, with my financial advisor Douglas, my attorney David Grosvenor, David's uncle the Duke of Westminster, and yourself as equal trustees for a period of fifteen years.

"I do not know yet if I will tell Abdullah about my decision. If I do, there will be a mutual disclosure about both of our wills, with you as a witness. I will demand to see Abdullah's will and agree to him reading mine. As of now, I do not know if Abdullah is going to include me in his private estate if he dies. I do know he is planning on discussing this with you soon."

Just then the phone rang, and Sir Joshua answered it.

"Yes, Your Highness, she is here. We are discussing the final portion of her estate. She is safe, Your Highness. Yes, I will remind her." As he hung up, he said, "I am certain you know who that was. He is on his way here to take you to Aratex headquarters here in London.

"Let me assure you, he was concerned only for your safety, not knowing where you were. Ironically, I realize now that you may be

205

safer with Abdullah than with anyone else. You do see that, don't you, Sophia? There are very few individuals who have the capability to provide for your safety the way he does."

"I would have thought, given my inheritance, that I could hire an entire army to protect myself!"

Sir Joshua was still exasperated when he said, "Sophia, you could hire security. What you cannot hire is the intelligence of an entire country and its allies to protect you. For you, owning Aratex will curtail many of your freedoms—not just being an Arabian princess, but being Mrs. Aratex! I will have your papers ready for you to sign tomorrow. Do you have any other questions?"

As she sat back down across from Sir Joshua, she finally smiled and said, "Yes, one. Is the pilot Captain Winston related to your law firm?"

"Yes, he is my nephew. My sister was married to Lawrence Winston, the other partner in the law firm."

"So my security is not just in Abdullah's hands; it's in yours as well?"

"Yes, Sophia, that is true. And as I said, you are as safe as we can make you." Sir Joshua paused before continuing. "One more thing," he said kindly, coming around to her seat and putting a hand on her shoulder. "Give your husband a chance. Let him show you the balance of your inheritance. After all, he has single-handedly grown it to what it is today. He has—to the exclusion of attention to friends, family, and until you, even love—worked tirelessly to make this company what it is today. As his wife, can you please try to be proud of him?"

Sophia nodded silently.

Abdullah met her at the entry of the building, a pained look on his face. As they walked to the waiting car, Abdullah turned to her, saying, "I was worried about your safety." His eyes were so forlorn as he continued. "I was actually afraid you had left me." Then he added, "I would like to take you on a tour of your new company and buildings, *mon amour.*"

Once they were both seated in the car, she took his hands in hers and kissed them. With an almost impish grin, she looked into his face still filled with fear. "Dullah, would you please show me our new company and buildings, the one you as the chairman of the board run for our family?"

Slowly, his taut features relaxed, and he smiled, realizing that for now the storm had passed.

They drove into the lower level of the building through a gated and guarded entrance. "Only my car has passage through this entrance," he said. "I will have your car put on the list."

Abdullah then whisked her away in a guarded private elevator to the top floor of the building, saying, "I have a surprise for you. There are two offices on this floor. I think this one should be yours, Sophia."

Shyly, she looked into a large, spacious office furnished with modern furniture. It looked as if it was just waiting for a person. She did realize that this would make a far better office for the real estate and other business deals than her study at home. The furniture looked new.

"This is a lovely space," she said, coming to stand next to him and looking out the windows at the stunning view of London. Turning to Abdullah, she said, "Tell me again, you really did not know I was Aratex before we married?"

He continued without answering her question. "Your buildings stretch four city blocks in either direction, and these top floors can be accessed only by the helipad or the garage we parked in."

"Our buildings," she corrected him. "But you didn't answer my question."

He turned toward her and, taking her arms, looked her squarely in the eyes. "No, Sophia, I did not know. I did suspect there might be some relationship after I looked into the bombing. But I had no way of knowing. And Sir Joshua did not tell me.

"Now, let me show you the conference room. It is where we will have our board meetings. And the first one will be next month."

As they walked down an open staircase, she saw that the conference room was an equally stunning space, with views out over the city and a giant Danish modern table and chairs. A sideboard filled the entire back wall. Ironically, there was only one flag in the room, an Arabian one. *Might need to change that*, she thought, but for now she kept quiet.

"What is below us?" she asked.

"Aratex takes up the top twelve floors of the building. There are three empty floors below us and then the executive offices of Aratex."

"Why are there three empty floors?" she asked.

"I have no idea. That's the way it's always been. Now here is my office," he said, showing her into a smart, elegant space, again with modern office furniture. The only difference between hers and his was the myriad framed photos of her and Abdullah sitting in the massive bookcase behind his desk.

"When did you take these?" she said, looking at photos of them running in Hyde Park and in Scotland, even one of them dancing at the Westminsters'.

He blushed. "I had my guards take them. They make me happy." He was thinking of telling her the truth—that he used to come here and dream about her. A sixth sense said that might not be quite the right thing to say and could be misconstrued.

Over the next month, Sophia and Abdullah spent most of their days at Aratex. The first day, she set up a computer, moved and organized her real estate paperwork, and met their executive secretary. He made it a point to introduce her to every one of the department heads, but only as his wife. Abdullah was busy collecting and reading reports from the department heads for the board meeting.

He would first read the report and write comments in the margins. Then he would give the report to Sophia to read. One day she spent the entire day reading the shipping and port facilities report. In the afternoon she bounded into Abdullah's office, saying, "I have a heap of questions. Do you have the time to chat?"

They sat comfortably in the two chairs in front of his desk while she riddled him with questions. "How many of our tankers have or will have double bottoms? Do we own or lease the land in our port facilities? What is our plan for OPA 90, the new oil spill regulation in the US?"

"Why are you asking these questions?" he queried. "How do you know about oil spill and shipping regulations?"

"I told you my father was a sea captain, and my first job out of college was at the US Army Corps of Engineers, building harbors," she tartly replied.

From this day forward, at first tentatively, they began working together as a team. She would ask questions, and when Abdullah did not know the answers, he would ask the appropriate division head. In the process he came to learn more about Sophia's knowledge, especially of the shipping industry and port facilities.

They were having lunch in the Aratex boardroom when Abdullah brought up the subject of Sophia's security. "I have been thinking about your security, Sophia," he announced as the waiters left the room, having delivered their lunch.

"Why now?" she quipped. "We're sitting in Fortress Aratex!" This was her private nickname for the building.

Deliberately keeping his voice calm and low, he said, "Because our security uncovered another potential threat this morning."

Sophia took in a breath and set her hand on her chin, looking straight at Abdullah. She could feel her heartbeat quickening, but she worked to equal his calm demeanor. "Tell me more details please," she said quietly.

"They found another car with a bomb attached in the same place as the last one, about an hour ago."

"How do they know it was meant for me?" she asked.

"They don't," he replied. "But it was clearly near the room where we sleep," he said candidly.

Sophia had not moved one inch during this conversation, but she now stood up and began pacing the conference room. Finally, she asked, "And what are we going to do to enhance"—she turned around and looked at Abdullah—"our security?"

"We are, of course, investigating," he said. He stood up and walked over to join her at the window. They looked out to the city as he put his arm around her. "My bankers are now negotiating the purchase of the rest of the properties on our street so there will be no cars allowed to park, and it will become gated. However, I am worried about your safety when you travel."

"You mean when I ask to go sailing again, don't you?" she said, turning toward him.

He shook his head with a rueful look on his face. "Yes, I do mean sailing."

"Hit me with it," she said, fearing that this was the end to the sailing adventures that she had loved for decades.

His answer surprised her. "While I would like you to limit your sailing, Sophia, and only sail with Douglas, Captain Winston has drawn up a sailing protection plan. We will enact it whenever you join Doug. I have also instructed our bankers to purchase a large power yacht, and it will serve as your accommodations when you do a regatta. Doug and your crew will be able to join you. You will also have on-the-water security during events. Are you OK with that, Sophia?"

She wrapped her arm around his waist and leaned into him. "Yes, I'm OK with it. I do wonder why every solution is to buy something—more houses, big yachts, whatever. But I'm OK."

"Aren't you concerned about your safety, Sophia?" he asked, now kissing the top of her head.

"No, not really, Dullah," she said, using her new private name for him. "Ever since my little chat a couple of weeks ago with Sir Joshua, I realize that you've been keeping me secure since even before we married. I can't even walk to Harrods without an entourage. I guess I have become rather fatalistic about it. As long as you do everything you can to keep me safe, I can't spend my every waking hour worrying. So I don't."

With that she leaned up and kissed him and thanked him for the yacht. She was going to ask what kind, but the kiss was more important right now.

The next day, she arrived at Aratex without Abdullah, who had gone to a meeting at the embassy. On her desk was a framed photo and large portfolio of pictures of a fifty-two-meter navy-blue Feadship with a simple note: "I love you. Dullah."

She sat at her desk for a long time, thinking about how lucky she was, before calling her friend Douglas to have a nice long chat.

Two weeks later, the first Aratex board meeting was an eye-opener for Sophia. Sir Joshua attended as well. Each department head individually provided their quarterly briefing, after which Abdullah asked questions, before asking Sophia and Sir Joshua if they had any questions of their own. For the first few briefings, for Aratech and the pharma company, Sophia had no questions. But when they came to the briefings on Aratex Shipping and Aratex Oil, she did have a few.

It crossed her mind to hold her questions, but the dismissive tone of these two department heads rankled her. Finally, she asked the head of Aratex Shipping how the company was responding to OPA 90, the landmark oil-spill legislation passed after the Exxon Valdez accident.

His response was clipped. "We have complied with the intent of the law in every port and on every ship. As you may not know, that law applies only to the United States. Most of our shipping is international."

Deciding that this was not the time to engage in debate, she stayed quiet the rest of the meeting. However, in her mind she began formulating a plan for some new business.

Section 4

Chapter 29

Arabia

*A*lmost a year after Edward's death, Sophia, dressed in a white dress and navy jacket, walked out of the Old Bailey to a blindingly blue English sky. The relief she felt showed on her relaxed features and in her demeanor. While not friendly, Henry had at least shaken her hand as they said goodbye. The press took Henry and Janet's photos as Sophia discreetly slid into her limousine.

Let them brag, she thought. *Now I can get on with my new life with Abdullah.*

On her ride home, two of the pillars of the Quran kept running through her head: almsgiving, or giving back, and taxation of 20 percent annually. She had vowed that morning at her dawn prayers never to forget their importance.

"Rima, Dullah, I'm free. It's finished!" She danced into her home to find them waiting for her in the sitting room. "And guess what?" she said gleefully. "I have a present for you, my Rima. We have a new property in the Cotswolds for Carrick and a piece of land in Agra, India."

Both Abdullah and Rima understood how desperate Sophia was to be equal in her business ventures with Rima. What they both saw as she entered the house was her joy at focusing on sharing as opposed to the pain and anger of fighting with Henry.

"Well, my dears," said Abdullah, "it seems we must celebrate. I suggest Pol Roger here before dinner at the Connaught. I have taken the liberty of inviting a few friends."

"Let me guess—the Grosvenors and Sir Joshua?" Sophia said impishly.

Two weeks later, it was a typical gray London day. The windows were flecked with the first drops of rain. Rima and Sophia were sitting at the breakfast table, which was adorned in a thick white tablecloth and set with fine china. The banquet behind the table was sagging under the weight of the breakfast spread, including bowls of cut fruit, a chafing dish of scrambled eggs topped with fresh herbs, and another chafing dish full of Abdullah's favorite savory lamb sausages.

Strong Arabian coffee in hand, Sophia and Rima were happily planning a day of shopping when Abdullah stormed into the breakfast room. His robe was open, and he was clad in nothing save a pair of well-fitting boxers, his hair still a mess from the night before and his eyes filled with white-hot anger.

He threw a copy of the *Financial Times* onto the table and growled, "The nerve of these British journalists is astounding."

The headline read, "British American heiress sells her soul to an Arab prince."

Sophia gasped in dismay. "Oh my God!"

She heard the rattle of china behind her as Mrs. O'Brian, their housekeeper, entered the room with another tray of breakfast delicacies, kippered herring and tomatoes. Turning toward the woman, Sophia saw her mouth agape, a look of shock on her face, and her hands shaking as she stared at the almost naked Abdullah.

Rima turned to follow Sophia's gaze and saw the same expression on Mrs. O'Brian's face. The two women burst out in gales of laughter.

Fortunately for poor Mrs. O'Brian, the now red-faced and embarrassed Abdullah moved quickly and grabbed the tray before it smashed to the ground. Pulling his robe around himself, a chagrined prince then left to get dressed. He could hear Rima and Sophia laughing as they went to find Mrs. O'Brian and explain.

When Abdullah returned downstairs, he had managed to find the humor in the scene and was also resigned to the press. He said quietly, "Sophia, it is time that we move to Arabia and formally make you a princess."

Turning to Rima, he said, "Could you please go to Paris with Sophia and purchase an Arabian wardrobe? The plane will be waiting for you at the airport. I will call home and start planning the celebration."

Then turning again to Sophia, he continued, "On the plane please make a list of guests you wish to invite, especially the male guests who will bear witness with my father. I suggest Westminster and Sir Joshua and your friend Douglas, the man who handles your finances in the USA. Is he the man you wish to have hold your dower? Go get ready now, and we will discuss this again tonight."

Sophia thought about this briefly before answering. "Yes, I should make Doug and Sir Joshua trustees for all of my accounts."

"That, my princess, is a very good idea. Will you call Sir Joshua, or shall I?"

"I can do it, thank you. But what dower?"

Abdullah smiled. "In Arabia, husbands give dower money to their bride's family. In your case it will be held by your financial advisor."

As the chauffeured Range Rover drove them to the private terminal at Stansted Airport, Sophia asked, "Could you explain to me the sudden urgency here? I just don't understand."

"I think Abdullah is worried that the king as well as other people in the kingdom might have seen the *Financial Times* and wants to forestall any issues with the religious authorities before we arrive." Changing the subject, Rima said, "Now I will make a list for what we shall serve for your wedding party."

Throughout the short plane ride, the women discussed in detail preparations for feeding everyone. Rima finished the food list and handed it to Sophia.

As she read the list, Sophia realized there would be enough food to feed a small army. There were over forty different elegant appetizers, including Norwegian salmon, Russian caviar, and

Danish cheeses. The main menu to be served featured steak and lamb, including a traditional lamb kabsa, and a variety of vegetable dishes. Sophia grimaced when she saw camel on the menu. Rima had listed an array of drinks, including alcohol-free bubbly, lassi, and fruit juice, and had noted that somewhere, there would be hidden champagne. Dessert would consist of countless types of pastries and a traditional wedding cake.

"Wait, I don't get this mention of champagne," Sophia exclaimed. "They do not allow alcohol in Arabia. Isn't this flouting the rules because of royal status?"

"Yes," Rima replied. "But it happens all the time in many ways, with far worse than champagne."

Upon landing at a private airfield outside the city of Paris, they were whisked away in a limousine to a private atelier on the Rue de Faubourg, right next to the main Chanel boutique. The sign on the door was in Arabic. This was, Rima told her, the chosen boutique for Arabian royals to purchase their dreaded veils.

For hours the two women tried on one black robe after another. Some were made from heavy woven cloth, and others were made from the finest thin chiffon. Some had gold embroidery; others, light silver and gray patterns woven into silk cloth. A few, the ones Sophia liked the best, were a dark navy blue.

Rima showed Sophia how to don the garment gracefully by throwing it over her shoulders and, maybe equally important, how to take it off quickly.

"I can get used to this," Sophia said. "Do I have a scarf to go with the abaya?"

"Yes, there will be a scarf, but next we need to fit your veil."

A hairstylist was brought in to show Sophia how to put her hair up so her reddish-blond locks would not sneak out of the scarf. There were essentially three weights of cloth for the veil: heavy, medium, and light. All of them covered Sophia's eyes except for small slits.

Trying to walk toward Rima in a medium-weight fabric veil, Sophia tripped over the abaya. She exclaimed, "How the hell do you walk anywhere in this contraption? I can't see where I'm going."

Next she tried the heavyweight veil and actually fell to the floor, landing hard on her hands before flopping over and sitting up.

Rima laughed, saying, "You'll get used to it."

By now Sophia was frustrated and muttered, "I should make Abdullah buy me a damn seeing-eye dog to go with this outfit." She tore off the veil, destroying her new hairstyle.

Rima, sensing that Sophia was getting angry and trying to calm her down, said, "You only have to wear it outside the palace. Once we are inside with women, we take it off."

But as Sophia picked herself up off the floor, she was still irritated and not yet ready to let the veil conversation go. "Tell me why I am wearing this. I just don't get it."

Rima paused, a thoughtful look on her face, and finally said, "The way we dress in public for those other than our families is part tradition and part religion. From a religious viewpoint, there are several passages in the Quran urging women to cover their bodies from the neck to the wrist and foot, or in some places, only the veiling of their hair is encouraged, as well as loose garments covering the whole body to ensure purity.

"Yet with the expanded powers of the committee for vice and virtue came the strong requirement"—she held her hands up and made quotation marks—"that you must fully veil in front of any man who is not your husband, brother, father, or sometimes close cousin.

"Traditionally, however, long robes and coverings served as protection for skin and clothing from the sun and harsh sand."

Sophia was still grumpy and sarcastically said, "I failed the purity test before I became part of this family. And I could easily cover myself from head to toe in black without this." She flailed the garment around her for effect.

Feeling very uncomfortable and desperate to change the conversation, Rima asked, "Now should we go next door and see what they have there for wedding dresses?"

"I think I have had enough shopping for one day. Let's go to the Ritz for tea before we fly home," Sophia suggested.

The two women walked and window-shopped the short distance around the corner to the Ritz Hotel, located on the elegant Place Vendôme. The doorman greeted them as old friends and ushered them into an exclusive private dining space in front of the fireplace in the Salon Proust, away from prying eyes. The plush chairs and warm wood ambiance served to calm Sophia, and the women chatted amiably, sipping tea and eating cucumber sandwiches, until the piles of packages arrived, all the contents now tailored to fit Sophia. As soon as the last package arrived, their Egyptian driver whisked them back to the airport for the short flight home to London.

On the plane, Sophia compiled a list of around twenty of her closest friends. She was thinking about having her sailing friend Juan Carlos stand up for her instead of Sir Joshua.

When Sophia and Rima arrived home, Abdullah met them at the front door and immediately requested that Sophia join him in his formal study. Abdullah's study was painted dark gray, which added to its somber tone. As they entered the room, Abdullah looked pensive.

He drew her next to him on a black velvet sofa and took both her hands. He had an unsettling look on his face. "Sophia, we need to talk about Arabia. I have tried to tell you about our country, but I may not have portrayed parts of my country to you accurately."

"How do you mean?" she asked.

"Sophia," Abdullah said, "I want to make certain you understand exactly what this move to Arabia will mean for your lifestyle.

"We will be married again in a traditional Arabian wedding ceremony twelve days after arriving. Once we have been formally married, with only my father, an imam, and the men who handle your dower in attendance, I will host a grand party for you. There actually will be two parties, one for the women and one for the men. About a month later, we will go on our first extended tour.

"When we get to Arabia, your life will be different," he said slowly. "You must always wear your abaya and your veil in public, and you can never—and I do mean never—let a man other than me, the men of our family, and the servants see your face. I know this will seem foreign to you, but that is the law in my country."

She nodded her head as he continued.

"Ever since the war, my country has been trying to modernize without becoming Westernized. We have made many changes, especially in educating middle-class women. Many of them are not wearing a full veil, but rather simply wearing headscarves and abayas.

"However, as royals, we must be seen to be following the rules of the committee on virtue and vice. And as the future king, I am held to a higher standard than most.

"While in our private villa, in the areas for women, you can take off your veil, but in those areas that are coed, you must be careful. This is because we never know who may be visiting—there may be a special guest who is a non-family member or a businessman."

With a hint of exasperation in her voice, she said, "I tripped and fell when I was trying on my new wardrobe today. How can I be expected to see through the veil, even to go from room to room?"

"Our private villa is quite large. Most of the time, you will see only me, my father, and a couple of very close aunts and cousins and will not be required to veil. The rest of your days, when I am at work, you will spend alone, with Rima, or in the company of female family members. I do understand how strange this must seem, but it is our law."

"Is it true," she asked, "that when I go shopping, I need to take a driver and a guard?"

"Most of the time when you go shopping, Rima will accompany you. Your driver is a nice Egyptian man who has been with our family for decades. He is also one of your protection officers."

For this entire conversation Sophia had looked at Abdullah carefully. Sensing his worry, she gripped his hand tightly and said, "I understand. I have read about this, and I'll comply with our country's laws."

Abdullah sighed. "Sadly, even among women you may not voice your opinion on our laws and customs or on our political policies. You may feel like a golden prisoner, Sophia. For that I am sorry. But we will have time together every morning, and I will have most lunches at the palace with you and, of course, dinner and every night." The happy glint had returned to his eyes. "We'll also travel a great deal, to places where the rules are less strict."

She leaned into him. "Abdullah, I agreed to be your wife. This is merely part of what I agreed to."

He put his arm around her, saying, "Thank you, *mon amour*. I cannot tell you how happy you make me. After our wedding parties, we will take our honeymoon. But the first few weeks will be the time for you to work with the royal court, to learn the ways of Arabia. Rima will be a great help to you in learning the ways of the court.

"I know you and Rima would wish for change in Arabia. I would also, but please, Sophia, for both your safety and mine, obey these rules."

Sophia thought this sounded ominous but kept silent.

"Now for more pleasant subjects. I have hired the *Vogue* photographer Mario Testino to take our wedding photos. He is free to shoot any photographs he wants, but we will release only the appropriate ones, those without your face showing. The rest will be our private treasures.

"Oh, one more thing—you may work on our private business and charity work in the palace, but there will be no work outside of the palace. In Arabia I am your guardian on all things, and you must obey me. You will not have any funds separate from mine in Arabia."

Looking into his eyes with distress written across her face, she said, "I understand your words, Abdullah, but I am slightly confused. How can a country with this much wealth be this backward, especially when it comes to women?"

His dark eyes appeared to be searching her soul when he said, "Sophia, I love you so much and want you and our family to be happy with our future. Learning the ways and traditions of a new culture will not always be easy. After you get to know some of my cousins, we will have private dinners with a few select and trusted relatives. And when we have children, I pray your days will be so full, and you will be so fulfilled raising our son, that you will not fret about these things."

Caressing his cheek, she responded, "I love you with all my heart, Abdullah. I will work to strike a balance. And I too long to give you a son."

"Do you have any other questions?" he asked gently.

"No," she replied. "I'm certain it will all work out."

As she sat curled up next to him, his hands massaging her arms, she consoled herself with the thought *I love, and I am loved. Whatever the future holds, he loves me, and my future is with him forever, with all the possible consequences.*

She had read much about the customs of Arabian society yet had believed that much of it must be slightly apocryphal. Sophia would soon come to understand that this was the truth in Arabia.

After a light dinner, where Rima made them all laugh, recounting the story of Sophia wanting a seeing-eye dog, they all retired early. Sensing some tension from the day's events, Abdullah held Sophia in his arms, softly whispering Arabic love poems to her as she fell asleep. Sophia slept restfully, dreaming of having a son with Abdullah.

The next morning, the houses were in a frenzy, readying the family for the move. Sophia had always thought that the movements back and forth would be easy, yet the next day she had a visit from their head pilot, Captain Winston. Standing in the sunroom, he looked a little sheepish as he said in a slight Scottish brogue, "I need your passport for the upcoming trip."

"Of course," said Sophia, "let me go get it. Which one do you want?"

"You have more than one?"

"Yes, I have one American, one English, and one recently issued from Arabia."

As he followed her up the staircase to her relaxing wood-paneled library, the pilot looked deep in thought. "Princess Sophia, I hope I am not speaking out of turn. I believe you should use the Arabian one. I want to make sure you understand. This passport will not be returned to you. It will be kept locked away."

She frowned slightly, and he continued.

"So if you can, I suggest you quietly keep your other ones safe, even leave one here. And as a precaution, would you please put these extra signed letters of passage with your spare passport?"

Sophia took a little while to process and then said, "Captain, thank you. I will keep this conversation private, and I will leave my UK passport here at my home. While I believe all will be well, I appreciate both your concern and your constructive insight."

Two days later, the king's plane arrived to take them to Arabia. Wearing a black silk pantsuit with simple gold jewelry, Sophia boarded the plane as instructed, walking behind Abdullah and with Rima following her.

She was visibly shocked by her first glimpse of the plane's interior. Red, green, and gold brocade covered the walls. The first seat was a solid gold throne. Then she heard Abdullah say, "Father, I did not expect you."

"I know, son. I wanted to meet my new princess," he replied as a uniformed flight attendant ushered Sophia past the gold throne and into the main cabin.

Abdullah provided the introduction, and Sophia gave a very English curtsy, saying, "I am honored, Your Highness."

The king was a tall, slightly portly man with a full beard and mustache who looked to be around seventy years old. He was dressed traditionally in a white thobe covered with a long black and gold vest, or *bisht*, and a white headscarf, or *ghutra*, secured by a black *igal*. In the same calm, deep voice as his son, he said, "Please, Sophia, sit here next to me so we may chat."

Wide-eyed and glancing at Abdullah, who took the seat on the other side of the king, she sat where she was told.

Looking at Sophia, the king said, "I want to acquaint you with our closest relatives to help you understand our family system in the kingdom."

"I would love that information, Your Highness," Sophia said.

"I come from a small family by Arabian standards. Originally, I was one of five children, but my two brothers are deceased. Now it is just myself and two sisters. They are as different as night and day. Maya is my progressive sister, who spends at least half the year at her villa in France or traveling. Aria, my conservative and less progressive sister, rarely leaves her palace, even to join me next door in mine.

"Maya has six children, three boys and three girls. They were all educated overseas. In fact, Maya's eldest boy was in school at Oxford and London with Abdullah, Prince Kalide. I think you may have met him."

"Yes, I have," said Sophia, "but I did not actually know how he fit into the family."

The king continued, "Aria, my conservative sister, has three children, one boy and two girls. Her son Ramani is the head of the royal court. He is a little stuffy. I must tell you, he is very skeptical that my son married a foreigner. So my recommendation is for you to be very careful in what you say and do in front of Ramani. I would avoid any discussions of a personal nature, about business, or about your past."

Sophia was uncertain of how to respond to this. She decided to simply make a benign comment. "Yes, sir, I will remember and heed your advice."

As the plane crossed over the Mediterranean, Abdullah said quietly to Sophia, "Please join me in my stateroom. We need to change before disembarking."

Excusing herself, Sophia followed Abdullah to the aft of the plane.

Unlike the rest of the plane, his cabin was similar to the one on the G3, with plush white Italian suede covering the chairs and the walls. Finely woven Egyptian linen covered the bed. Once they were inside the cabin, he turned to her with a twinkle in his eye. "This is where it began, Sophia," he said. Quickly, he removed his clothing and then slowly began to undress her.

She said with some trepidation, "But your father?"

Abdullah laughed as he teased her nipples with his tongue, his fingers running up inside her with little flicker movements so intense that she could feel herself starting to tremble. Almost with one arm, he picked her up and laid her down on the king-size bed, finally saying, "He is a king, Sophia, not a saint."

She giggled at his remark, but she was still tense. He sensed this and slowly massaged her neck until she started to relax. As soon as he began to kiss her, Sophia was lost in his power. He felt her start to tremble and slid inside of her as she came.

"I need more of you, Sophia," he whispered. "Hold me inside of you, tighter." He felt her tighten around him and pushed deeper inside her.

She gasped out loud as he came inside of her. "Take me, Dullah."

Holding her to his chest, he murmured in her ear, "That was a quickie, Sophia. We will have to practice more later tonight. But now we must get ready for our arrival."

As Abdullah stood from the bed, he said, "I have something special for you, Sophia." Going to the closet, he unveiled a stunning gold and black abaya. It was really two layers, a very thin black layer over a medium layer of solid gold. The set included a gold- and jewel-trimmed veil and headscarf.

Sophia looked at him with a horrified expression. "It is stunning, Abdullah, but is this your idea of not making a statement?"

"No," he said sheepishly. "It is my father's idea. He has decided he wants to make a statement—that we are already lawfully wed, that we are not fornicating."

"Fornicating?" She arched an eyebrow.

"Our doing so before marriage would bring great shame to my family. So my father has arranged for a few of the trusted press and a receiving line of princes and princesses, all relatives, to meet us at the airport."

Sophia quickly showered and began to dress. Looking at Abdullah as he donned a freshly pressed white thobe and a long black vest with gold trim, she said, "What should I wear under this?"

With a sexy glint in his eyes, he smiled. "I am tempted to say nothing." Then pulling out a gold silk pantsuit, he said, "This will be a perfect outfit for when we reach the palace and you take that wretched garment off!"

"Whatever you say, *mon amour.*"

Minutes later, when she walked down the aisle of the plane, the king said, "Sophia, you look perfect."

"Are you both certain we want to make this big of a statement?" she asked.

"Yes!" the king exclaimed.

It was a bright, sunny day, with a light warm breeze blowing, as Sophia started down the steep steps from the plane. The glare hurt her eyes even with the veil, but she could make out a few cameras set up on the tarmac. With their backs to the press was a line of about ten women in black abayas and veils and thirty men in white thobes. But she barely noticed them because she was petrified she would trip and fall down the stairs leading from the plane. Somehow—she later would decide God had been watching out for her—she did not. Once on flat ground, she paused and peeked out from her veil. She realized there were many other people, almost all men in white thobes, behind the chain-link fence. She straightened her shoulders and, after a deep breath, walked the red carpet that had been rolled out for their arrival, alongside Abdullah and behind the king.

The king stopped at the podium that had been placed in front of the photographers. His speech was short and clear. "Please, my people, welcome home my son and his new wife." He motioned for Sophia and Abdullah to step forward. "From this day forward and forever, she is to be known as Princess Sophia bint Abbas al Arabia."

With that short speech, the press was ushered away by the security guards.

Their arrival at the airport was celebrated by forty of the immediate royal family with what could best be described as polite skepticism. But then Sophia wondered how she could actually know, since she could see only the faces of the men, who all wore an expression of curiosity. And of course, they could not see her expression either. Rima performed the introductions, and the women, all princesses, were polite, shaking her hand and saying welcome. The men, all princes, simply nodded after they embraced Abdullah, often bumping noses with him. Their names were a blur to Sophia.

The next day, the state press called her the golden princess. It was a nickname that would be with her for the rest of her life.

Chapter 30

Abdullah's Home

*A*bdullah was elated to be home in Arabia with Sophia. Upon returning home, the king had gone directly to his offices. Abdullah, Sophia, and Rima rode from the airport to the palace in a chauffeur-driven Bentley through the worst traffic jam Sophia had ever seen. Finally, the Bentley turned onto a lush tree-lined street, and they were driven through a heavy wrought iron gate amid thirty-foot-high stucco walls to an equally lush cobblestone courtyard. Here they were, in the desert, and it looked like a tropical paradise.

As soon as they were inside the villa, Rima, with a flair only she knew how to accomplish, removed her abaya. Sophia's attempt at imitating her friend actually sent Abdullah and Rima into gales of laughter. As she finally managed to disrobe and dropped the garment in a puddle at her feet, she regained her sense of humor and laughed with them. "I'll have to work on that," she muttered.

Without her veil, Sophia finally took a moment to look at her surroundings. The massive entry hall had twenty-foot-high ceilings, and its walls were covered in off-white and gold silk cloth. Gold-leaf neoclassical embellishments adorned the ceiling in a pattern reminiscent of Buckingham Palace. Priceless Impressionist art, including one of Monet's *Water Lilies*, hung on the wall. She gasped, recognizing some of the art from Number Eleven that she had sold at Sotheby's. Tables displayed equally ornate and priceless vases filled with fresh flowers and artifacts.

Rima rang a bell to order refreshments, and a uniformed servant arrived in what seemed like seconds.

"While we are waiting for refreshments, would you like to begin a tour of your new villa?" Rima asked Sophia with an almost impish grin. Then she giggled, adding, "Abdullah has been working on this project for months. It will be your private quarters with him."

Abdullah announced he had to go to his office and would be back for dinner.

Sophia and Abdullah's palace was magnificent for anyone who liked gold and white. As someone used to the staid world of antiques and British elegance, Sophia was not certain if she loved it or hated it.

Their private quarters were so large that at first Sophia was certain she would get lost finding her way around. It was a miniature city, with a theater, beauty salon, spa, indoor pool, and lush gardens. *All this for two people*, she thought. She would later find out this was a good thing, because she would rarely leave the palace grounds.

Next door, connected by a garden outside and a shared ballroom inside, and equally over-the-top was Rima's palace. Rima had added a few changes, but it was also white and gold, with a massive amount of marble and all the same amenities.

After the tour of Rima's palace, the two women were relaxing in the garden, and all Sophia could think of to say was "We really needed two hair salons."

Rima laughed. "It's a status thing," she said. "We have to have equally grand living spaces so Abdullah can prove to his family that he is treating us as equals."

Abdullah arrived home from his office late to find Sophia sound asleep in her new double-sized king bed. He paused at the door, just looking at her peaceful face, and wondered if he should waken her. As he slipped into bed, she stirred, and he could not resist the impulse to awaken her with kisses. He whispered, "It's time to make a baby, Sophia."

As she started to return his kisses, she could smell mouthwash and a hint of scotch on his breath. He pushed inside of her almost too forcefully, but she immediately tightened around him. He could feel her holding him and becoming wet. They made love until the dawn was peeking into the room through the partially opened curtains.

She was again sleeping soundly when he showered and left to join his father for morning prayers at the mosque next door. They walked down the tree-lined street in companionable silence, a ritual they had shared since Abdullah was a little boy. Abdullah had not yet had the opportunity to speak privately with his father. After walking back from the mosque, Abdullah and his father had strong Arabian coffee together on the men's porch overlooking the king's lush tropical garden.

"Sophia is a delight," his father said. "And she clearly loves you dearly. But what will she do when she is here?"

"She has expressed an interest in charity work, Your Highness— specifically, children's education and health care."

"That is good," said the king. "And what will you give her father for her dower? You must make certain she is cared for in every eventuality."

"Sadly, Sophia's father is deceased." Then Abdullah chuckled. "Sophia is a very well-heeled woman, Father. She has more than ample means to maintain any lifestyle she chooses."

"Will you give her jewelry?" he asked.

"Doubtful," said Abdullah. "I have already given her many jewels over the last few months. And she inherited so many that she cannot keep track of them without lists, lists, and more lists. The same is true for property and stocks. I have decided to gift her the one thing Sophia does not have in her name."

"What is that?"

"A charitable foundation, fully funded. As we speak, it is being formed, and it will be fully endowed with substantial cash and income-producing assets. It is to be called the Princess Sophia Trust."

"But Abdullah, if anything happens and you divorce, how will she pay bills from a charity?"

"First, I have no intention of ever divorcing Sophia. Equally, I have no intention of divorcing Rima. Both women know and agree to these facts. They are actually best of friends. As I said, she is in her own right already set for life. Her inheritance from Barbara Devon Lawrence is very substantial. Did you know she owns 60 percent of a little company called Aratex and 14 percent of our Royal Holdings?"

The king looked at his son and quickly looked away. He was gazing at a rock pool with a painfully sad look on his face. "Will she convert?" the king asked quietly.

"She already has, my father. She and Rima are presently at prayers as we speak. We witnessed her shahada at the mosque in England."

"But does she truly follow our ways? Does she honestly believe?"

"Yes, for the most part, she follows our ways. She is learning Arabic, studies the Quran endlessly, and prays at least three times a day. And if for some reason she must miss a prayer, I have seen her slowly turn toward the east, if only to briefly stop and contemplate. She has this interesting ability to be in a crowd and at the same time far away.

"As for believing, she does believe in the truths of Mohammad. Of course, she will be shocked, as we are, by the more radical of our clerics. I am hoping to keep some of their worst offenses from her. She has been ordered to never let loose her opinion in public or even among the family. Yet one of her most endearing traits is her complete lack of bigotry and prejudice. She will not tolerate one unkind word regarding any ethnic group. This could pose a problem in large family gatherings. I will also say that Sophia is a perpetual motion machine."

"What about children?" the king asked.

Abdullah chuckled. "Father, as I said, Sophia is a perpetual motion machine. I can assure you, I try to wear her out every night, working to make a baby. This has the added advantage of keeping her asleep past dawn. But to answer your question seriously, we are both working studiously on that." But he had a slightly haunted look in his eyes as he continued. "So far she has not become pregnant."

"And what of Rima? Will she adjust to this change?"

"Father," he said quietly, "Rima actually endorsed these actions. I have and will always treat my wives equally, and I adore my two daughters. While I am sad at not having a son yet, as I said, Sophia and I are working on this."

"So you sleep only with Sophia?"

"Yes, Father, I sleep only with Sophia. It would actually amaze you to know how few women I have actually known in my forty-one years. And I actually go to sleep with my wife. I find her presence soothes my mind."

Again, the king pressed, "What about Rima?"

"We all dine together every morning and evening. Sophia spends much of her day with Rima. I walk with Rima most days, and we talk and often spend hours alone peacefully. Truthfully, Father, I am more comfortable with Rima now than ever. We even share more tenderness."

"I am not convinced, my son," the king said, "but I will leave this in your capable hands to manage."

Sophia had been in residence for only a week when the king sent a handwritten note requesting a private meeting. She donned her abaya, and a gold-and-green-uniformed servant escorted her to the king's courtyard. While she was waiting for his arrival, another attendant poured coffee. The courtyard was a vast, lush space filled with tropical plants and moss, interspersed with waterfalls that fell into deep rock pools. There were tropical birds chattering away in large cages. Sophia did not need to close her eyes to believe she was in the Amazon.

When the king entered, she greeted him formally, saying, "Good afternoon, Your Highness."

"Good afternoon, my lovely princess daughter-in-law. Thank you for joining me. Please, there is no need to be so formal when we are alone. Please call me Father."

Sophia was delighted at his response and smiled shyly. "Thank you, Father." Changing the subject, she said, "What a stunning garden!"

He proceeded to show her all of the finer points of the garden and then asked her if she would like one exactly like it.

Without thinking, she said, "Of course! It is a work of art."

And then the king changed the subject. "How did you meet my son, Sophia?"

Her eyes twinkled. "Well, I saw him twice before we met. The first time was at the Connaught bar. I was with the Duke of Westminster and his nephew, who is part of my legal team."

"Why were you there with your lawyers?" he asked.

"Oh, it was after the reading of the will. I had just finished learning that I was the major stakeholder in the Devon estate, through my late husband, and all that entailed. Then I saw him again at the Ritz."

Sophia rambled on for several minutes, explaining how she had met Abdullah. Most of her monologue came out as a run-on sentence, and the king sat quietly listening to her.

"I see," said the king thoughtfully but with a smile on his face. "It was destiny! But one more thing—how did you come to be the primary heir to the Devon estate?"

"My former husband was Barbara Devon Lawrence's stepson. I had sailed across the Atlantic only to find out they both had died when I was sailing."

"An amazing story, Sophia. As I said, it was destiny. I must go now. We will chat again soon."

The next day, Sophia was shocked to see construction workers tearing up her garden to remake it into a rain forest. When she queried Abdullah about it, he said, "My father insisted I build one for you."

Her comment in response both surprised and pleased him. "Please promise me that from now on you will ask me first. I truly do not need one more thing!"

Chapter 31

The Wedding

The week before the wedding, Abdullah announced he was going to the desert with his male cousins to receive petitions from the Bedouins. "It is a custom," he explained to Sophia. She was slightly amazed when she saw fifty or so assembled men getting into a caravan of cars and trucks.

Later that afternoon, when Rima walked into her study, Sophia asked, "What do they actually do in the desert?"

Rima sighed. "They fly falcons, ride camels, drink, talk, and converse with the Bedouins. Sometime a serving girl even comes back pregnant." She finished with a grimace.

Sophia looked horrified.

"Never from Abdullah," Rima quickly added. "And then the poor child is banished." Changing the subject, she said, "The royal court is in full flight, planning your celebration, *ma chérie*."

Not wanting to hear any more about the desert, Sophia quipped, "Better them than me. Have they decided yet what I should wear?" Sophia was completely out of sorts over her wedding dress, and she continued, "I have had problems convincing the stylist what colors I look good in. I want dusty rose pink, and they want pale baby pink or some white-and-gold creation that looks so heavy it may crush me."

"How did you resolve this impasse?" Rima asked.

"I sent for the dress I wish to be married in from England. It is one of Barbara's. The one I want to be married in is a dusky pink with more than ample gold trim, and it will look great with the ruby necklace—I am hoping to wear the ruby necklace that I inherited from Barbara. Do you think Abdullah will mind that it's not new? And what will you be wearing to my big event?"

"I … I will not be attending," she answered quietly.

"And may I ask why not? Don't you want to attend?"

"Oh, I do want to attend, but the royal court has decreed."

"The court decreed? I thought only the king could do that," Sophia said, scowling.

"I do not believe he has been or should be consulted," Rima answered. "The court does not want me to attend. Remember, some in this court do not like me. They believe that Abdullah never should have married me. Remember, that is why I spend so much time out of the country, *ma chérie*."

"But I need you here! Besides, you will be the only other woman who knows the Duchess of Westminster." She stopped talking and looked carefully at her friend. "Rima, you are not getting divorced from Abdullah, are you?"

"The court would like that," she replied, "but I have not agreed."

"Did Abdullah ask you for a divorce?"

"No, he has not. But … he has been busy."

"I've noticed that, and I understand it. But correct me if I'm wrong. If he does not want a divorce, and you do not, why would you?"

"Oh, *ma chérie*, I am sorry to burden you with my problems. When will that gorgeous dress arrive?"

"I believe it is arriving tomorrow," Sophia said, but she was worried for her friend and her friendship.

Later that week, when Abdullah came home from the desert, she decided to ask him about the matter. "My prince," she said, curling up next to him, "I have a protocol question that only you can answer. I am asking not to bother you with silly things but rather to ensure I do not do anything accidentally to upset the court."

He tousled her hair. "Oh, Sophia, I have spent my entire life upsetting the court. What is *mon amour*'s quandary?" he said, kissing her neck.

Taking a deep breath, she said, "Should Rima not be at our marriage party?"

Going still, he asked quietly, "Why do you ask?"

"Because when I asked her what she was going to wear, she mentioned she was not attending. She said that the court did not want her to attend."

"I will quietly look into this, Sophia. Let me handle this. You do want Rima there, don't you?"

"Of course, I do. And she wants to come. But she also ..." She trailed off without finishing the sentence.

"Finish, please, *mon amour*."

"She said the court wants you to divorce her."

"Not to worry, Sophia. I am not divorcing Rima, just as I will never divorce you. But Sophia, until you learn who your allies are, it is right to come to me with—what did you call it, a silly thing?" Changing the subject, he asked, "Now, what else did you do this week?"

"My dress and jewelry arrived. So we can get married now. I am hoping to wear the rubies from Barbara. Is that OK with you?"

Abdullah smiled. "Anything you want, Sophia."

The actual marriage occurred late afternoon on the day before the wedding party at the king's palace. Fully veiled, Sophia sat in one room with Rima. The men, the king, Abdullah, her friend Douglas Winthrop, the Duke of Westminster, and Sir Joshua met in another.

The imam from the local mosque officiated the ceremony. First, he witnessed the signing of the wedding contracts and the exchange of dower from Abdullah to Douglas. Then he went back and forth between the rooms, reciting a prayer from the Quran and giving a short speech on the importance of marriage.

Later that evening, in a break from tradition, Abdullah hosted a small, intimate dinner with himself, Sophia, Douglas, Sir Joshua, the duke and duchess, the king, and Rima in attendance. The dinner was served at the king's palace in a special tent in the tropical garden. Hundreds of small tea lights gave the tent an ethereal glow. Rose petals were strewn across the white linen—covered tables, which were set with gold china and gold eating utensils.

After dinner, Abdullah presented Sophia with her other dower. She opened the box, thinking, *I just don't need anything.* Inside the box was an envelope with gold lettering: "The Princess Sophia Royal Foundation for Charitable Giving." She opened it to see a card with the foundation logo, a handwritten note from Abdullah, and a substantial one-page balance sheet.

Her eyes welled up with tears. "Thank you, my prince," she said, her words coming out in a whisper. "It is the most thoughtful gift you could have given me."

"You may share, Sophia," he said.

She immediately turned to the king, handing him the note.

The king and Rima read it together. The king said, "I am proud of you, my son," as he handed the note to the duke and duchess and Douglas. Rima's smile showed the room her thoughts.

Duchess Caroline said, "Oh, Sophia, you will be a busy lady."

The duke commented, "Congratulations, Sophia. Now the real work begins."

"You are right on that count, Your Grace," she replied.

The five-course dinner, including fine French wine, was filled with laughter. At one point, Westminster said, "You know, Sophia, we might have made a mistake, not selling Number Eleven to Abdullah."

The king chimed in, "I second that. Can you undo that sale?"

"Noooo," Sophia said quickly. "That would mean I would have to deal with Henry."

The day of her wedding celebration dawned. It was a cloudless, blindingly sunny morning. Not a breath of air swirl around the gardens as Sophia said her morning prayers. As soon as Abdullah had left for breakfast, saying, "I will see you tonight, my princess," Rima bustled into her suite.

"It's your special day," she said gaily. "The staff has all assembled to prepare you for your wedding."

"Prepare?" she said quizzically, her glasses dropping down so she was looking over her nose. "It's only nine in the morning. Isn't it a little early?"

"No, *ma chérie*, the hair colorists and professional body-polishing specialists are all here to prep and bathe you. Then we will lunch and nap before hair and makeup. We will start with a bath to remove all your body hair. It is tradition. Then we will do lashes and eyebrows, followed by a long massage."

Soon Sophia found herself lying on a massage table as women spread a sweet-smelling honey goop all over every part of her body. Then without warning, they started with cloths that stuck to the goop, sort of like a Western waxing. Their first removal was her public hair.

She howled in pain, and Rima came rushing in. "What is wrong, Sophia?" she exclaimed.

"It hurts!" she ground out through clenched teeth. "Tell me again what tradition this is." But as she was talking, the body polishers continued working and removed the rest of the hair from her private parts.

With a small army of women working on the polishing project, it was quickly completed. Sophia finally managed to growl to Rima, "Why didn't your damn husband tell me about this tradition in our walks around Hyde Park?"

Rima simply burst into laughter, and at the sound of Rima laughing, Sophia joined in. The pain of the polish was soon forgotten with a two-hour massage that put Sophia to sleep. Then for two hours her hair was penned to become a very pretty shade of reddish-blond and brown. Her eyebrows were dyed to match her hair, and soon it was time for lunch. Around 7:00 p.m., after another long nap, Rima awakened Sophia to begin the process of dressing and donning her heavy ruby necklace.

Around eight in the evening, Sophia watched from upstairs as a long line of limousines dropped off 1,500 female relatives and wives of close business associates of the groom. An army of uniformed guards kept the guests from moving into the residence. They were led into the king's ballroom, which led out through open doors to the garden. The day before the event, a private plane full of thousands of pink and peach roses had arrived, and they filled the entire villa and the tent.

At ten in the evening, drums and singers announced the arrival of Sophia dressed in Barbara's dusty-rose lace dress, with a matching veil rimmed in gold and studded with tiny diamonds. The effect was a shimmering halo over Sophia's head.

The crowd of women gasped and cheered. The wedding was a typical Arabian event. The largest garden at the palace had been covered over in tents. Inside the tent was an atmosphere unlike anything Sophia had ever seen. It was hung with white silk brocade embroidered with gold. The wedding party was seated at a long table in the front of the room, before a large dance floor surrounded by other tables. Place settings were white china and crystal with gold utensils.

As she walked down a gold carpet like she was a model, she was greeted by loud shrieks and applause. A troop of female dancers arrived to entertain the ladies, followed by a break for eating from the scrumptious buffet, which held enough food for an army. After this, around 11:00 p.m., a lovely female singer arrived to entertain.

At the court's insistence, Abdullah's two aunts, Maya and Aria, were seated at the table with Sophia, Rima, and Duchess Caroline. Sophia had requested that she sit between Rima and Duchess Caroline. However, when she arrived at ten, the two aunts were seated next to Sophia's spot, with Rima and the duchess on the ends.

The one major glitch in the evening was Sophia's jewelry. At first all the women fawned over the "gorgeous rubies" with comments like "Where did you buy them?" and remarks about how lucky she was that Abdullah had gifted them to her and so on. The only person who failed to make any comment was Aria, the king's conservative sister, who looked at her and turned away to chat with another cousin.

"She doesn't like me!" Sophia whispered to Rima.

"No, she does not, but then again, she does not like me either," Rima replied.

The king arrived with Abdullah around one in the morning. Coming up to Sophia, the king said, "You look stunning, my ..." He stopped midsentence.

Sophia could see he was overcome by something and quickly said, "Thank you, Your Highness." But his look was so haunted that she asked, "Have I displeased you?"

"No, not at all, Sophia. Your necklace is ... stunning. I was dazzled by it."

Then Abdullah, dressed in a thobe and a black and gold coat, walked toward her and gently removed her long diamond-studded veil. A smile shone on his face as he whispered, "You are simply the most beautiful woman I have ever met."

With that he whisked her onto the dance floor for a waltz, to the clapping and chanting of the assembled women. He finished the dance by dipping Sophia back over his arm. As the dance ended, he walked her toward the wedding cake, a multitiered confection with vanilla frosting and decorated with edible gold leaf.

"Are you going to feed me?" he said.

"Yes," she said, her eyes twinkling. "But not so you wear it."

They turned their backs to the crowd and fed each other a piece of cake, licking each other's fingers and smiling and giggling like children.

Afterward, he kissed her gently on the nose. "I will see you in our bed at dawn," he said, before leaving to continue celebrating with his male guests.

The photos from Mario would later prove stunning. The official wedding photograph would show the back of Sophia's head as Abdullah wrapped her in his black and gold *bisht* in a light protective hug. The look on Abdullah's face showed all the warmth and love that could ever be captured in a photograph, despite the fact that Sophia's face could not be seen.

The private photo, however, did both subjects justice. For the rest of her life, Sophia would wonder every time she saw the photo how he had captured that one brilliant moment in time. At the end of the one waltz she and Abdullah had shared in front of all of the women, he had swung her around and bent her backward over his arm. She by now had such trust in Abdullah and his ability to hold her that she was completely relaxed. As she looked up at him, all she could see was the smile of love on his face. She was so totally relaxed, and the looks on both their faces showed not simply love and affection but also great, deep, abiding trust and respect.

By the time the wedding party was over at four in the morning, everyone was exhausted. Abdullah arrived back at the palace at six in the morning, drunk. Sophia thought the entire ceremony had been very odd.

Chapter 32

Artifacts on Tour

A few mornings later, Sophia had finished her prayers and was dressing for breakfast. Abdullah returned from his prayers and said, "I am working on our upcoming state visits today. Sophia, would you please join me after breakfast for a planning meeting?"

"Yes," she said breezily. "Will a member of the royal court be in attendance at this meeting?"

"Not for breakfast. That is just you and Rima and myself. The court will join us later. I wish you to meet my cousin Ramani again." Abdullah continued, "Each visit to our neighboring countries in the Middle East will be a state visit to introduce you to the other royal families." Then almost as an afterthought, he said, "Rima will not be joining us on state visits."

She sat on the bed wide-eyed and bit her lower lip.

"I sense you have a comment, Sophia?"

Slightly gulping, she smiled. "I think I need my own protocol officer. And is there a historian who can brief me? Why won't Rima be joining us? And what the hell am I going to wear?"

He burst out laughing. "I will organize your staff, Sophia. As for Rima, she despises state visits, and in some countries two wives are frowned on. It will be better for diplomacy if I arrive with only one."

She looked up at him, smiling, and said, "I am amazed, a little scared, and so excited that you would honor me this way. Yes, I am happy—deliriously so—but I need to make certain I do you and your father proud. Abdullah, do you remember the thousands of artifacts I found in the Devons' attic at Number Eleven?"

"Vaguely, Sophia. I can honestly say that I do not remember all the artifacts. It would be like trying to keep track of your jewelry."

"Stop teasing me," she said with a smile. She was now standing in their bedroom, wearing only her lace underwear. "I have far too many things in storage. So rather than sell them off for more"—she threw her hand in the air—"what if I took a few of the significant artifacts, and we donated them to the national museum in each country we go to for a state visit? You know, in Egypt we can gift King Tut artifacts, in Jordan ones from Petra. They don't—well, they shouldn't—belong to me or England."

Abdullah looked at her. "Oh, Sophia, that is a brilliant idea. Do we have a list of what you have in storage? Let's get Rima to help review it with us."

"Oh shit, she will be waiting for us. We're late!"

"Sophia, slow down. It is OK. Rima knows where I sleep at night. Remember, we are married."

"I know, but … I just never want to hurt her feelings."

"The fact, Sophia, that you even think about it means you will not, because you care." By now, he was dressed in his usual immaculate white thobe and striding out the door. "See you soon, *mon amour.*"

Sophia quickly dressed in a bright red, gold-embroidered kaftan and sandals before racing into her study to find three big binders filled with typed lists and photos. Grabbing all three, she hurried off to breakfast.

She was in such a hurry that running around a corner, she ran right smack into the king, dropping the binders in the process. "Oh, Your Highness, I am so sorry!"

Hearing her voice, Abdullah and Rima stood up and looked out into the hallway.

The old king was full of smiles. "Ah, Sophia, we meet again. But what are these?"

She stuttered, "Notebooks with lists and photos of artifacts I inherited from my mother-in-law, Barbara Lawrence. Some are very interesting, so I wanted to pick a few as gifts for our upcoming trips."

There was a sadness etched on the king's face that she did not notice. "Why, Sophia, I would love to help you with this project," he said as he escorted her into the breakfast room. "You don't mind if I join you, do you?" he asked Rima and Abdullah as he sat down in a vacant chair.

Abdullah almost spit out his food. This would be the first time he had ever had breakfast with his father—and, he was pretty confident, the first time the king had taken breakfast with a woman, let alone two of them. As Sophia was always inclined to do, she had somehow made his father feel relaxed and chatty. *Yes, chatty,* he thought. Stranger things might have happened, but not recently.

As servants rushed to provide the king a place setting, asking what he would like to be served, Sophia set the books on the banquet behind the dining table. Then the king stood up, saying, "You don't mind if I take a look at these now, do you, Sophia?"

"Not at all! I just need to figure out if there are items that will be good enough to give away as gifts. I think there are, but …"

The king had opened the book to a random page and stopped. "Oh, Sophia, I do not think you have to fret about that. This one is perfect for Egypt. I do not understand why you want to give these away."

"Your Highness, I cannot possibly display them all. They were kept in museum-quality storage for decades. Should they not return to their original, or might I say rightful, owners for all to admire and learn from their history? Or at least live somewhere in my home here on display?"

"That is very generous, Sophia, and I applaud this action. Once I have studied these books, we shall chat again. I will help you!" Sitting down, he ate his breakfast and then excused himself with a faraway look in his eye.

How very odd, Abdullah mused.

In the end, the king chose all of the gifts. Sophia was happy to have his input, and he seemed delighted to have her companionship. In addition, they made a plan for the rest of the artifacts. Within six months, the Princess Sophia wing would open in the national museum.

Chapter 33

The Desert

*I*t was the summer of 1993, a week after their wedding, when Abdullah announced, "Sophia, I would like to take you to the desert for our honeymoon."

The desert! Sophia had dreamed of visiting the desert since she met Abdullah. What would it be like to smell the air, live in a tent, and ride horses at breakneck speed without a care in the world? She thought it must be like the ocean without the water.

"That," said Sophia, "would be wonderful! Can we ride? I actually long for open freedom."

"I don't think you will find the freedom you long for, my pet, but I do think you will enjoy the vacation. I have invited my auntie Maya and her son Prince Kalide and his wife Noora to join us. Unfortunately, Rima has declined to attend, instead choosing to go to Europe. Even decades on, her memories of her childhood assault in the desert are too painful for her." At this, Abdullah sadly glanced away, as if in shame.

"I understand," she said, standing up to give Abdullah a hug. Then looking up at him with an impish grin, she added, "I imagine the desert is a different kind of freedom."

His smile slowly returned as he held her in a gentle embrace.

For the next few days, she watched in amazement as the court made plans for their trip. Special trucks were loaded with everything imaginable. Black goatskin tents would replace palaces, and everything else was packed and moved to a magnificent encampment near a wadi. Camels and horses were both transported.

She invited Maya and Noora to afternoon tea, so they could tell her what to expect. Both women were also in a state of high excitement. Over tea they chatted about the details of the upcoming trip.

Maya, with her long brown hair and chocolate-brown velvet eyes, was stunningly beautiful even at the age of fifty-five. She had grown up in a province near the desert and explained many of the customs to Sophia. Princess Noora, the tall black-haired beauty married to Prince Kalide, was around Sophia's age. She had been raised in the city and had gone away only infrequently, mostly to other capitals in the Middle East and Europe.

Maya's excitement was contagious. "We are all bringing our favorite horses, and we will also ride camels," she said. "It is so much fun. We will have hours to walk and ride without another person in sight. I love these trips where we can breathe fresh air without our veils."

"What should I pack to wear?" Sophia asked. She had learned that even if it was just for other women, Arabian women always dressed well.

At Noora's suggestion, all three women went to Sophia's closet to help her pack. They chose an array of colorful sundresses and light shawls as well as riding gear. Shoes were flat sandals and riding boots.

From the minute they left the next day, Sophia loved almost everything about the outing. They arrived in a convoy of cars, and immediately, all three women took off their robes and veils, almost in unison. They laughed when they realized all three of them had worn almost the same dress, just in different colors. As they waited for the servants to set up the tents and prepare dinner, they went for a walk in the dunes.

It was around sunset when Abdullah and Prince Kalide went out to find the ladies. Not far from the camp, the princes spotted them walking back across a golden expanse of setting sun and sand, arm in arm and laughing like young children.

"I'm so happy to see my wife enjoying the company of your wife and mother," Abdullah said.

"I am also," replied Kalide. "As you know, my mother spends a great deal of time in France, and Noora is often lonely. But now that I think about it, my mother has spent more time in the kingdom since Sophia arrived. This is a good thing."

That night, the five cousins enjoyed a light supper in their communal dining tent. Afterward, Abdullah escorted Sophia to their sleeping quarters with a familiar gleam in his eyes.

She was not surprised that Abdullah's tent was different from all the rest. Befitting a prince, he had special skylights made out of clear glass. During the day, they had shades to keep out the sun, but at night he opened them. "I like to see the stars," he said. "Are you ready to make love in the desert, my princess?"

"I told you it would be like sailing … the stars," she replied breezily.

"You can bathe first," he said, "while I make the tent cozy. Then I'll shower."

Her maid had drawn her a bath, and she sank into the hot scented water, relaxing and dreaming about the lovely day they had shared.

He walked into the bathroom naked and fully aroused. As he prepared to join her in the tub, she giggled, "Is this tub big enough for this act?"

Water splashed over the edge when he got in. "We will find out soon, *mon amour*," he said as he slid into tub and into her.

He massaged her breast lovingly, and she moved as he pulled her on top of him, fully entering her. He was so slow and deliberate that she was burning with desire. Every nerve in her body was on fire. "Please," she murmured in his ear.

"No, my love, too soon. I will wait until bed." He stood up, pulling her with him, and carried her to the king-size bed. As he dried her off with a towel, she inhaled the smell of ylang-ylang incense and noticed the small candles casting a romantic glow around the room. He finally threw back the covers and rolled into the bed, pulling her with him.

Sliding into her again, he said, "Sophia, you feel so good." He started slowly at first and then quickened the pace. Her legs were over his shoulders, her hands gripping his forearms, as she felt herself go over the edge. He kissed her to cover her cry of passion and came into her, throbbing, as he collapsed on top of her.

He held her close and then wrapped them both in a light sheet, holding her and kissing her neck until both their heart rates slowed down. Together they were watching Orion the mighty, Al Jabbar, rise in the east when Abdullah quietly said, "I love you, Sophia. More than life itself."

"I love you more," she said.

He held her close, whispering a love poem until she fell asleep.

The sun sets in the west for my love
The moon rises in the east for my love
Shooting stars race across the night sky for my love
I will follow the sun, moon, and stars around the world for my love.

The next morning, the small group set off for a ride across the sand dunes, with Sophia on her new horse and Abdullah on a large black stallion named Devil. Sophia was exhilarated to be unfettered by the dreaded abaya and veil. Their security guards formed a perimeter around them, so they had both privacy and protection. They ate a light picnic lunch near an old wadi, under the shade of a group of old acacia trees.

On their way back to camp, they were approached by a group of Bedouins, whom their security quickly sent away. Abdullah shouted at the women to stay where they were and reminded Sophia to put on her veil. The nearest rider delivered the hated black garments, and the women complied quickly. Then Abdullah and Kalide rode after the Bedouins. When Abdullah returned, he said that he and Kalide would be joining the Bedouin men in their tent tonight.

Turning to Sophia, he continued, "You do understand they are also my countrymen, and I must, if possible, interact with them and hear their petitions. Tonight will not be much fun for you and the other women. You and my cousins will be delivered to the Bedouin women's tent for food and entertainment. All three of you are ordered to wear your abaya and veil since we have no idea if anyone else will arrive. Your security guards will take care of you."

Even though this sounded odd, she answered, "It is fine, Abdullah. I am certain we can make do."

Maya leaned over to her with a twinkle in her velvet-brown eyes, saying, "That's an interesting way to say yes—*we can make do.*"

The air had a chill to it when the ladies dismounted their camels to join ten other women for dinner. The meal, consisting of roast camel and tabbouleh, was served in a tent that had been hastily cleaned. The guards were uncertain that the three princesses should even enter the tent, but Sophia insisted. She sat cross-legged on an offered seat of pillows and rugs, and after a few moments of uncomfortable silence, one of the Bedouin women asked very shyly, "Are you the golden princess?"

Sophia was at a loss for words, so Maya answered for her. "Yes, she is Abdullah's bride."

Immediately, excited loud chatter in a dialect that Sophia did not really understand ensued, and finally, Maya calmed them down enough so Sophia could ask a question. In Arabic, since she knew the language now, she said, "Tell me about your life in the desert." And then she added for some unknown reason, "How can we help you?"

Sophia had learned quickly that in Arabia people rarely spoke directly to answer questions. Several hours of comical conversation, with Maya helping with translation, provided a lovely evening. Finally, toward the end of the meal, the chief Bedouin's wife said to Sophia shyly, "I don't know if I am allowed to ask, but our village needs medical supplies. I am afraid my husband might forget to mention it to yours."

Over strong coffee and baklava, the women at first shyly and then in a great rush told Sophia about the medical needs for their children and themselves. Sophia had to remind herself to keep a straight face and not become visibly upset. This tribe had nothing, not even Band-Aids. When Sophia asked to see their first aid kit, she was told they did not have one. Carefully, Sophia had Maya explain to the women that she would begin working to help them through her foundation.

Beginning the day they returned from the desert, Sophia worked endlessly on what would become known as the Bedouin Hospital Project. Every morning, she would be up, showered, and dressed, poring over papers in her study, when Abdullah came back from his morning prayers. It was only two days after their return, when Abdullah found her in her study and came in to greet her with a soft kiss, that she said with an exuberant giggle, "Are you ready to hear my idea?"

A week after their arrival back, Sophia received an invite to a private tea with Princess Maya.

They met in Maya's sitting room, a bright, sunny room off her very English flower garden, filled with lovely French Empire antiques. It was a cloudless, hot Arabian day, without a breath of air.

After Maya greeted Sophia warmly, both women sat on a low divan in the elegant room while the servants poured tea and served small date cookies. Once the servants had left, the older woman said, "I have been thinking about our conversations with the women in the desert." Almost shyly, she added, "If you are going to provide some medical aid to these women, I would enjoy helping you with the project—if you would let me."

For the last week or so, Sophia had done nothing but think about and research ideas on how to provide assistance that would have the largest long-term impact, so she was thrilled with Maya's offer and immediately responded, "I would love to have your help, and I am anxious to hear your thoughts on what their needs are."

"I too have thought about this endlessly since our return," Maya said, sipping her tea. "These people need hospitals. Not big ones, but small local facilities with trained nurses, medicine, and first aid available. They often need midwives for childbirth. The problem is that they do not stay in any one place, instead living in tent encampments that move three and four times a year."

Sophia smiled. "I have thought of that. My idea would be to build and outfit a movable container that would hold the supplies and equipment. The actual facility could be in a separate tent, sort of like an army field hospital. It would move when they move or be located in a central place close enough to serve multiple tribes. I have asked Abdullah about this, and he believes it can be done."

"When will you start work on this?" Maya asked.

"I already have. I've asked Abdullah to help me with the specialized containers. He knows the director of a private hospital in Switzerland that will outfit them and ship them here. Do you think we should start with one or three? It might take a month or so to arrange the containers and ship them here. And I have no idea how to work with the women or the tribe to see if this fits their needs."

"I believe I can help with that," said an excited Maya. "Can you get Abdullah to join my family for dinner so we can discuss more details?"

Two days later, at a lively dinner at Maya's, the six cousins batted around many ideas. Kalide agreed to help liaise with the Bedouins, and Noora, Maya, Sophia, and Rima each took on different facets of the project. The creative use of Aratex containers eventually would become one of Sophia's lifelong charitable centerpieces.

Chapter 34

The Royal Court

*A*nother month went by, and with only two weeks left before their scheduled departure for their first trip, Sophia took steps to begin what Abdullah called a charm offensive on the royal court.

The first planning meeting with the royal court and Abdullah had gone rather poorly in Sophia's opinion. In fact, she had sat and listened for two hours, and neither her role nor her duties had ever been mentioned. Now, two weeks before they were to leave, she knew nothing about the schedule and had no idea what to pack or whom she would meet. She had complied with every request from the court for her wedding. But she was not about to go on her first state visit without being fully prepared.

Abdullah asked her why she had been so compliant before, and her answer surprised him. "Abdullah, you do realize that our wedding was not for me. It was for your family, your country, your court. Therefore, I agreed with everything!

"Now I need to get to know your cousin Prince Ramani, the head of the court. While I have met him, I am not certain we got off on the right foot. I was thinking I would ask him for a meeting to discuss the upcoming trip."

Abdullah ruffled her hair, saying, "Meet away, my princess. Just send him a polite note. I am certain it will be fine." In reality he was not at all certain; nevertheless, he decided to run with her idea. He knew the court was not particularly helpful to Sophia, as did his father. Still, at his insistence they had both taken a wait-and-see attitude.

That morning after prayers, he mentioned this upcoming meeting to his father.

"Son," he said sternly, "what is Sophia up to?"

"I believe it is called a charm offensive, Your Highness."

"I don't want her to get into any trouble. She is trying very hard and, even I can see, not always succeeding. Prince Ramani is not a big fan of hers. I don't want him starting trouble. When and where is this meeting?"

"I believe the main living room, today after the noon prayers. Now, my father, I must go off to work. And you?"

As Abdullah left the room, he heard the king muttering. "Yes, I have something very important to do today—save my daughter-in-law from my court."

The response to Sophia's meeting request was swift and courteous, maybe too courteous. Yes, Prince Ramani would be available and would rejoice in meeting Princess Sophia in the family living room this afternoon at one thirty.

Sophia, who was always punctual, arrived five minutes early with a notebook and pen. In very Arabian tradition, Prince Ramani was thirty minutes late. The tall but still slightly pudgy Ramani was accompanied by three princes and a princess, all relatives and all part of the royal household.

Ah, she thought, *multiple people to win over.* "Thank you all for coming," she said in English. "I was wondering if you could provide me more details regarding our upcoming trip. I wish to make certain that I do everything according to protocol. A detailed schedule would be most helpful."

Prince Ramani turned to his staff and said in Arabic, "Do we have a schedule for the princess?"

One of the princes answered, "No, sir, I thought she would just go to the evening functions. I don't think she should meet too many people. Do you?"

Ramani shrugged. "Not really. However, we run the risk of angering the king and Prince Abdullah with that strategy. You do know they actually sleep together."

One man responded, "Yes, real punta," and other two men laughed.

The princess managed to say, "I think in Jordan the queen is expecting to meet the princess. She wants to take her to Petra and other historical sites."

Then another prince interjected, "At least the queen can speak English to her, and she won't appear as a dumb mute. We also have invitations to several functions from Egypt and the UAE. It does seem that everyone wants to meet her, except she is just not worthy."

The third cousin then said, "Maybe she will swallow a fly and die."

Unknown to all in the room, the king was standing behind a closed curtain, listening. He was steaming with anger but held back, waiting to see what Sophia would do next.

Sophia was equally angry but waited until the conversation had a natural lull and then asked Prince Ramani in English, "Can I please have you translate what was said?"

"They said that in Jordan you will meet the queen, and the same may hold true for the First Lady of Egypt. It is unclear about the UAE."

Still smiling, she said in English, "Prince Ramani, could I have a private word with you please?"

He looked surprised, but still he said yes and motioned for his team to leave the room.

Sophia was remembering what the king had said about progressives versus conservatives at court. As the door closed, Sophia stood up, looked at Ramani, and smiled. In her most light and conversational tone, she said in English, "That went very poorly."

He started to speak, and she stopped him. "I hope we can try to keep the first part of this meeting secret. However, we have a large problem, and I will need your help to solve it." Then she said, "Why is it you and the court hate me? I have followed every rule given to me for months. The only thing I asked was to invite twenty of my close friends to the wedding. Instead, I was allowed to invite six. Why was that? Are my friends not good enough for this kingdom?"

Prince Ramani was speechless—she was speaking in fluent Arabic.

Now pacing around the room, Sophia continued. "I am highly educated and extremely intelligent, and I speak fluent Arabic, French, English, and Spanish. Why do you and much of your family hate me?"

Ramani looked down his beak-like nose at her closely. The sparkles in her eyes were not tears; instead they held a glint of fury. "You understood everything, Your Highness?"

She nodded slightly, shaking her head. "You mean that I am a dumb mute punta who should die swallowing a fly? I translate that into you all hate me!"

"I am so sorry, Your Highness," he said. "I have brought great shame on my mother and my uncle and cousin. Please forgive me."

"Ramani," she said, exasperated. "Your staff has even brought shame upon your camel, but that's not important. Right now we have a problem that you and I alone have to solve."

He watched her carefully, thinking she was correct. The shame and fear he felt were obvious on his face. So Sophia just waited.

She heard a small noise near the curtain and guessed it was the king. Ramani heard it also and looked in that direction. Sophia shook her head, her eyes pleading with him not to go over there. She was certain that could only end in disaster.

Finally, he said to her, "I think that we are all afraid and jealous of you. We have heard you are well educated. Yet you rarely speak. We are afraid that you will try to change our country, that when you travel, you will speak of the less impressive parts of our country. In the last months you have not made one statement about our country other than to say how nice the hospital is, or how lovely the desert is, or how pretty the palace is. Do you think you let us know you had a brain in that pretty little head?" As he said the last line, he prayed that the slight joke was taken as such.

Again in Arabic, Sophia said slowly, "What you say is true. However, I did not wish, as they say in my country, to rock the boat. I also am not fully briefed on all the issues of your country." Her mind was in turmoil. She could not get these words wrong now. Taking another deep breath, she said, "Rather than risk saying something out of turn, I deliberately say nothing.

"Of course, I would enjoy seeing women treated better. I hate my abaya, and the veil is torture. Nonetheless, this is your country. What right do I have to say you must change your culture a few months after moving here? I am the woman who married into this country, not the other way around. It is actually my responsibility as Abdullah's wife to do everything in my power to uphold the laws of this country."

Ramani was looking at her in a new light. "What things would you like to do, Princess Sophia?" he said quietly.

"I will need your help. First, when we travel abroad, I would like to work to show my new country Arabia to the West in the best possible light."

"But those will be the things that His Highness speaks about with the leaders of the country."

"Yes, they will be. And I will be lunching with the ladies. Now what do you think the countries' first ladies are going to ask me about? Do you think they all talk about couture gowns? And after our lunch what do you think they discuss with their husbands at night? It would appear to me that having us both singing the same tune would be good for diplomacy."

Continuing on with an impish grin, she said, "I know I don't have a brain in my pretty little head, so maybe if you would brief me on what Abdullah will be saying, I could avoid any mistakes."

Seeing the look on his face, Sophia giggled and said, "Now I am slightly teasing you, Ramani."

He sighed, saying, "I had not thought of that at all."

"Next there are the issues that we might as a country want assistance in, such as medical training for doctors and improvements to our ports."

Again Ramani said, "But those are the things—"

"Ramani, what do you know of me?" she said.

Then almost as if a light bulb had turned on, she remembered the king's words on the plane: *My recommendation is for you to be very careful in what you say and do in front of Ramani. I would avoid any discussions of a personal nature, about business, or about your past.*

"I know you are married to Abdullah, have a house next door to him in London, and had six people from your side at your wedding: the Westminsters, your friend Douglas, Sir Joshua, and Mr. Annan."

"Maybe we should start with my wedding guests," said Sophia. "Let us start with why I had only six guests—because your planner said those were the only people I could invite. I had an invite list of twenty people who wanted to come. You should ask your planner what he said to me when I handed him my list."

"Why don't you tell me, Princess?"

"Well, in summary, he said in Arabic that I was a gold digger who just wanted to meet people. In the end he said I could invite the six who came."

Continuing on, she said, "The reason was that your planner did not know those six people. He did know who the rest of the proposed guests were. He assumed I wanted to invite them so I could meet them. Unbeknownst to all of you, I knew everyone on that list, well enough to have their private phone numbers. I don't have to call the staff to get a phone call through. I just dial the number.

"Even so, do you know who those people I was allowed to invite are? No one ever asked me. You tell me not to be involved, yet I am involved in substantial issues of poverty, education, and the environment. I am now on three of Mr. Annan's committees."

Ramani frowned. "I do not know this Mr. Annan. I did not speak to him at your wedding. He was, according to my cousin Kalide, very nice and interesting."

"Prince Ramani," Sophia said quietly, "Mr. Annan is the head of the United Nations. My friend Douglas runs the largest charitable foundation in the world as well as a fund larger than your Royal Holdings, and the Westminsters are the duke and duchess of."

The shock on Ramani's face was evidence of the total breach of protocol that had occurred.

"What is wrong now, Ramani?" said Sophia, seeing his shocked expression.

"I am worried about the consequences of the protocol blunder my team and I committed."

"Ah, Prince Ramani," she said softly, "you have no need to worry about your—what did you call it? Protocol blunder? Because your dumb, mute, stupid princess made certain no one knew.

"Now I suggest we start over. I would like to have my meetings with the other first ladies include a combination of learning about their country's history and discussions about important social issues faced by everyone in the region, including health care and education for both the poor and refugees.

"What is important to me is the work of the Princess Sophia Foundation. You know that everything I have is run by Abdullah and the king. Yes, I am on committees, and yes, I recommend, but that is it. I want to represent Arabia in a strong and positive way without being in the limelight."

"Princess, while we are clearing the air, why did you wear a gold abaya when you arrived in Arabia?"

For the first time in this meeting, Sophia laughed. "Not guilty! I was given the abaya by the king and Abdullah to wear. All I did was their bidding. My guess, and it is only a guess, is that the king wanted to make a statement to protect me from gossip. Please notice, I have not worn it since."

Ramani nodded. "My mother was very angry about that outfit."

Sophia looked at Ramani, knowing how conservative his mother was. "Ramani, is there something I can do that would defuse your mother's anger? I am happy to enact any ideas you may have."

"Maybe. Could I persuade you and Abdullah to dine with his auntie?" he said with a smile.

"I am certain Abdullah will be fine with that. I think we should adjourn for the day, so you can try to calm your staff. Can we reschedule for tomorrow?"

With a nod, Ramani left the room. Sophia waited for the king to move the curtain and stroll into the room.

He sat, and Sophia waited for him to speak. Finally, he said, "I am angry at my court, Sophia, not at you."

She sighed. "Yes, Your Highness. But please, I do not think punishment will help my situation. And I hope I did not say too much. I tried to just stick with the foundation, not anything else."

He nodded slowly. "You are correct—punishment may not help. And yes, your answers were for the most part charming. What I am very interested in is who else was on your wedding list."

She grimaced. "Personal friends of mine. Two European princes and princesses, a king and queen, two CEOs of major banks and shipping companies. Several of them are sailing friends. None of them are individuals whom I met through Abdullah. I knew them all before I even moved to England."

"I assume I know many of these individuals, including the king and queen?" he said in a slightly raised voice.

"Oh, it is fine. They are not upset and see no slight from you."

"I must speak with Ramani," the king said in a thunderous voice.

Sophia covered her face with her hands. "I am hoping that this can be what Abdullah and I call a quiet truth. Yes, you know what went on in this room today. However, as of right now, no one is embarrassed or publicly shamed. If you speak to Ramani, it will start a snowball that will grow as it rolls downhill. They will all think I told you.

"If we keep this a secret, then Ramani can try to get the team to do the right thing without any hard feelings. They can think it is their idea. It will remove their fear."

"I will consider your words, Sophia, but now I'm off to work."

Later that afternoon, Sophia and Abdullah were invited to Ramani's mother's home to dine.

"I don't want to do this," Abdullah said harshly to Sophia.

She sighed and hugged him. "Remember the charm offensive? This is part of it. Just be kind for a few hours, and all will be well."

Sophia and Abdullah were ushered into Aria's villa by a footman uniformed in gold. They were just inside the door when the king arrived.

"Brother, I did not know you were coming," said a startled Aria. Her son Ramani looked slightly afraid.

"I know, my dear sister, but I was feeling left out, so I decided to join you. You don't have a problem with that, do you?"

"No, not at all. I was intending to start with drinks for the men in the garden and juice for the women in the salon."

The king replied smoothly, "Why don't we all sit in the garden? It is lovely this time of the evening."

The women sat in a group together. Ramani's wife, trying to break the ice, said, "Your wedding was lovely, Sophia, especially your ruby necklace."

"Yes," said Aria, "the necklace was truly impressive. Where did you get it?"

Before Sophia could answer, the king said, "I gave the King's Rubies to Abdullah to give to Sophia."

Abdullah chimed in, saying, "Yes, I was proud that you gifted them to me, Father, so I could gift them to Sophia."

Sophia knew the king and his son had just lied, but she managed to keep her mouth shut. But why? she wondered. What purpose did this lie serve?

But Aria was not ready to let the conversation about the rubies die.

Finally, the king cut her off, saying, "Enough jewelry chatter. I think every princess in this kingdom has enough to go around."

The rest of the dinner passed in what could only be described as awkward silence. The king and Ramani tried to fill in the gaps with discussions of the desert and Bedouin history. Sophia and Ramani's wife had a lovely chat about Parisian fashions. Only when Ramani's wife waxed enthusiastically about how she had hired the caterer that Sophia used at her wedding, Bijou II, for several parties and how wonderful they were, was Sophia mute.

In the end Ramani's tour became a victory for Sophia. While Abdullah was in his meetings, each first lady wanted to show her their country.

Egypt's first lady, Suzanne Mubarak, took her down the Nile on a trip through the pyramids. As the women chatted about the history and discovery of the ancient sites, Sophia inquired about Mrs. Mubarak's social concerns for her country. Upon hearing that children's health and education were at the top of Mrs. Mubarak's mind, Sophia shared her idea about portable hospitals. Within an afternoon of floating down the Nile, both women were excited to tell their husbands of a new partnership idea. Sophia's portable hospitals could be staffed by young Egyptian physicians.

In Jordan her reception was much the same. Queen Noor drove her to the archaeological sites in Petra, where they met the scientist working to preserve the site. The drive in the queen's Jeep, just the two of them, provided both women the time to engage in private conversation.

Finally, the queen quietly asked, "How are you finding life in Arabia?"

Sophia paused with her hands in front of her face, as if in prayer, before answering. "It is certainly different from what I am used to, but I am working to overlook the things I cannot change and focus instead on those things I can through my charity work."

"I can certainly understand that!" the queen responded. "And what are you focusing your charity work on?"

For the rest of the ride, the women discussed their different charities and goals for their positions in both of their newfound homes.

That night, over dinner by the sea in Acaba with Abdullah and the king of Jordan, they all discussed Sophia's idea of portable hospitals to service the ever-growing refugee problem.

Her days spent with the other first ladies proved to be interesting from both a cultural and a philanthropic perspective. From the first day, Abdullah would always mention that his wife was in charge of his family's philanthropic efforts, which afforded Sophia the opportunity to forge stronger bonds with each of the nations through the Princess Sophia Foundation.

Upon their return home, the king made it a point to say how pleased he was at the reception she had received. He noted that from what he had been told, her future philanthropy would be a major diplomatic coup, helping to cement sometimes-fraught relationships.

For the rest of the year, Sophia worked tirelessly with the king, his sister Maya, and sometimes Abdullah to develop her idea for rural health care. Soon requests for such facilities in other countries were flowing into the trust, many of which were funded.

Slowly through the year, by focusing on her charity work, Sophia developed a famous and mostly great relationship with the royal court. This and her generosity took her far in the kingdom, just not far enough.

Chapter 35

The Arabian Season

W̶hat Sophia called her "Arabian season" was filled with a unique combination of work and exercise. It was a strange custom that women did not exercise except for when they were young children, and they never learned sport. The royal family often took trips outside of the kingdom, where their female children were allowed to swim and play organized games, but in the country this was allowed only for men. It took almost a year for Sophia to find ways to exercise that did not break some custom.

Sailing was out because it was a coed sport. She tried single-handing a small boat once at their summer palace but could not see. Sailing in an abaya and veil just did not work. Swimming was allowed once she had Abdullah install a private female-only pool for her. But that took over a year to accomplish. When it was finished, it was more of an artificial lagoon surrounded by lush plants. Still, she and Rima enjoyed the solitude and could often be found there. Every attention to detail assured her complete privacy.

Work also had its challenges. She read as much as she could find on the issues she was interested in. But she was expressly forbidden to have any input on or fund any issues having to do with women's rights or with the laws of Arabia. This was stifling to Sophia. Abdullah had every Arabic newspaper delivered to his study every day. Often, she would sit and read what was happening in the country. Sometimes an article would appear about a man having his hand chopped off publicly for a small crime, often theft of food. Less frequent were accounts of men raping their female children and receiving only a mild three-month jail term.

It was only through her work with the hospitals that she really learned of the atrocities perpetrated against women. When she finally broke down and asked Abdullah privately about these atrocities, his initial response was anger. Then eventually, if she pressed carefully, his response would turn to a combination of pain and shame.

It usually ended with the same explanation: "I was educated in the West, Sophia. I understand the problems. But there is nothing I can do to change this now. Maybe when I am king, change will come, but not today!" And that response always signified that the discussion was at an end.

Her response was typical Sophia. She would throw herself into working on Carrick with Rima or push herself to find projects for her foundation that focused on less controversial but still important subjects.

By 1994, Sophia had grown into her roles as Abdullah's wife, the head of her foundation, and most importantly, Abdullah's private partner in Aratex. Individuals often divide the year into four seasons. For Sophia there were three: the English season, time spent in London and other foreign residences; the Arabian season, time spent in one of three palaces in the kingdom and the state; and the Aratex season, time spent on business travel around the world.

It was spring 1994 when Abdullah said, "Sophia, Ramani would like to meet with you to discuss our next trip. I have told him it is part state and part business. Remember, he thinks Aratex is solely mine. In addition, he will be joining us on this trip."

Prince Ramani joined her in the mixed garden of her villa. After some small talk, they got down to business.

Ramani started the conversation by saying, "You are aware of the Aratex meetings in Norway that the prince will attend alone."

While Sophia privately bristled at this comment, she kept silent.

"In addition the king would like to have you and His Highness to dinner with his son and daughter-in-law. I believe they sail?"

"Yes, they do. I am friends with the crown prince and his wife. Ironically, I do not know if they know that their Sophia Lawrence from competitive sailing has become Princess Sophia, or if they know about my association with Aratex."

Ramani laughed. "Your association with Aratex?"

Sophia glared at him over her glasses. "I am married to the chairman of the board."

Changing the subject, Ramani asked, "To avoid any embarrassment when you meet the prince, are you close enough friends to tell him, behind the diplomatic scenes, of your change in status?"

"Great question, well phrased. And yes, I am. I will send him a fax."

Abdullah and a small entourage flew to Norway from England. He piloted the plane with Sophia in the copilot seat. Over the North Sea he asked for permission to detour so Sophia could view their oil fields and lease. As they came down to a lower altitude, Sophia said, "Look at that gloss on the water! Is that oil?"

"Yes," he said. "Do you have your camera, Sophia? The big one? Please take photos."

Sophia clicked away as the oil just kept on coming. It became apparent that they were flying over a major spill. Fortunately, this area was not where their rigs were currently drilling. "I think this area has old BP wells that are supposedly capped," she said. "My map says it is not our lease and that only one section has been drilled. This could still be an ecological disaster affecting the entire region. The PR will be awful."

Sophia left the copilot seat and went aft to confer with the team. Without preamble she began, "We are going to face a slight PR issue when we arrive. There is a major oil spill that could cause a major ecological disaster. While they are not our rigs or our leased land, there will still be press inquiries."

Then, in a move unusual for Sophia, she barked an order. "Ramani, as soon as we land, I would like you to liaison with Aratex PR both in Norway and in London. For now I want no comment from the palace on the prince's private business. Please let Aratex PR take the lead."

Ramani was slightly taken aback at Sophia's authoritative tone. He also noticed that Abdullah was conversing with her as if she were his equal. Something told him to not challenge her and remain quiet.

"And please," she said, staring hard at Ramani as she finished, "leave my name out."

"Oh no, look, Your Highness!" Ramani exclaimed. They looked out the window to see the rig below them on fire.

As everyone started speaking, Sophia moved forward to retrieve her rig and lease maps. Abdullah, who had relinquished the flight controls to the other pilot on board, handed her the books.

"Who owns that rig?" she asked nervously.

"We do!" said Abdullah.

"Is that the royal we or a specific we, and if so, which we?"

"It is one of ours, the royal Aratex we. You can take a deep breath, Sophia. It is not leaking oil, just burning off gases. Our Norwegian escort is coming alongside us now." They looked out at the fighter jets that had come to escort them into Norwegian air space. "We're landing at the military base, not the commercial airport, in ten minutes. Buckle up, everyone."

The rest of the trip was fun yet thankfully uneventful. Sophia and the Norwegian prince sailed a charity regatta, which Sophia won. She teamed up with the Norwegian Center for Ocean Science as her charity.

When they arrived back in England two days later, Sophia was pensive. She finally said, "Abdullah, I have two thoughts from our trip to Norway and specifically the oil spills. If you remember, on the flight I sat there trying to help you when we found the spills and the flames out on our rigs. Yet absurdly, at the same time, I had to pretend I was a dumb blond and did not know anything about Aratex."

"I don't think you succeeded at that," said Abdullah. "You left Ramani with more questions than answers."

She smiled at his response. "Well, I am afraid that could become a problem and am wondering what to do about it."

"I will smooth it over for you, Sophia," he said gently. "What is your second thought?"

"This is a bit more long-term," she started. "Abdullah, you once told me you want to be more progressive. Given our responsibility to the oil industry and our responsibility for clean water, I was wondering, don't we need to invest in oil spill prevention and in training for oil spill cleanup? I have an idea for how Aratex Shipping and Aratex Oil could be front-runners. In the US they have passed the bill OPA 90—the Oil Pollution Act."

"I know what it is," said Abdullah. "Right now we are busy refitting our tanker fleet with double bottoms—at great expense, I might add. And we, unlike Exxon, have never had an oil spill!"

Ignoring his comment, Sophia went on to explain her idea for developing and installing a world-class oil spill cleanup and protection facility. "We could do it on one of those empty floors at the Aratex building," she said.

"That, my princess, is a great idea. Why don't we go over to the Aratex building? I think you have an office there and might need to use it more when we are in England."

For the next week they worked together at Aratex. They sketched out ideas, batting around what-if scenarios all day long, then running them buy them by members of their staff. Abdullah enjoyed every second of it. It was, he conceded, a bold and brave initiative.

Eventually, Abdullah asked, "But who will use it other than Aratex?"

"I am certain we could sell these services, even pre-sell them, to other oil companies. Arco, Chevron, and Exxon come to mind." She grinned. "They are the most affected by the new legislation now, but the future is coming soon!"

He adored working with Sophia, and in London they were more relaxed. He respected her ideas, and she adored his insights. He made love to her every night with a new poem. When her cycle was late, she rejoiced. But fearfully, she almost took to her bed.

For the next week, he held her gently, praying and hoping that she was pregnant. When it turned out she was just late, she cried for almost an entire day. Despite his sorrow, he comforted her instead of leaving, holding her close and caring for her every need.

It was only in England that she was free to work on her ideas for the company and slowly, with his support, bring them to fruition. The first oil spill protection simulator was completed in early 1995. It occupied an entire floor of the Aratex building and was connected directly to many of the ports via an experimental satellite conference system that Aratech had developed.

The opening of the simulator was attended by around one hundred individuals in the maritime industry from around the world. Sophia and Abdullah performed the ribbon cutting together, and it came as a surprise to Abdullah when Sophia began to introduce him to some of the attendees.

Chapter 36

Two Years On

*I*t was the spring of 1995. Sophia had now been married to Abdullah for two years.

Amazingly, the sexual passion between them had never waned. They had taken to cherishing their private time in the mornings and late evenings. To ensure their privacy, Sophia had reorganized their private living spaces at the palace, turning Abdullah's bedroom into a sitting room for Rima, Sophia, and Abdullah. No one else was allowed to use the space, except when the king would come to chat with Sophia.

It was during one of those afternoon visits from the king that he said to Sophia, "I hear you made a comment to Ramani about women's rights?"

Sophia paused at this statement, looking carefully at the king's expression. "You are right, Your Highness," she said slowly. "I said that I do not agree with how women are treated here. I should not have said that to Prince Ramani."

"Sophia," he said. "I feel you have more to say."

She frowned, pursing her lips and thinking. "Yes, Your Highness. I have never until today made any statement like that. I did follow it up by saying that I am fully behind the laws of this country and would never say anything like that publicly. However, I apologize for saying it to Ramani. It will not happen again."

"But?" the king said.

Her eyebrows lifted. "You must know that your laws regarding women and children are simply"—she hesitated—"draconian. Especially children. They can be raped and buried alive by family members without any retribution. I have never voiced these opinions because I am here to be Abdullah's wife. I would never willingly hurt him or you. And that is why I have focused on education and health care with my foundation. Again, I apologize. I should not have said anything to Ramani."

"Sophia, I know you are correct in your statements. If it were easy or even an option available to me, I would change this, as would Abdullah. For now, it is not. Please, my lovely daughter, be careful. I need you by Abdullah's side. You are good for him as a man." As the king walked away, he called back in a loud voice, "And I need a grandson!"

In the end this conversation served to make Sophia realize one change that had occurred over the years: they had spent less and less time trying to make a child.

That night, as they were getting ready for bed, Abdullah asked, "What did you do today, my princess?"

She thought, *I made a great faux pas with your court*, but aloud she said, "I studied the countries we are visiting for our next state visit, and I read your Aratex report. I am worried about the ports. From what I see, they need upgrading. I have a big idea for expanding our ports. Can you set aside some time to discuss it with me soon?"

"Define 'big,' Sophia."

"Restructuring every port we own to double our unloading and offloading capacity. About a billion. Any interest?" She was now leaning across his chest.

"Yes, I can give you an uninterrupted two hours tomorrow, Sophia. It will be my pleasure. I am interested to hear your wild ideas." He was smiling down at her with that about-to-pounce look she knew and loved. "But I am now tired. My brain is tired, Sophia."

Smiling, she rolled over, turning her back to him.

"Sophia," he said, "I said my brain, not my body, is tired."

"Yes, my prince, I heard you," she said as she rolled back over and kissed him. "I'm sorry you are too ti—" She did not get to finish the sentence as he pulled her on top of him. As he started to kiss her, she said, "Dullah, let's work a little harder at making a baby, please."

They did not sleep until sunrise.

The next day, she was thrilled when Abdullah called her, asking, "Sophia, when do you wish to meet and discuss your big ideas?"

He had decided it was essential to humor her on all things Aratex. He did not believe for one minute that there was a "big idea" that could even remotely cost a billion dollars. However, he thought it better to humor her than anger her and cause problems that could be avoided.

"I would like to meet you two days from now. May we use your conference room?" After they set a time, she hurriedly rang off.

Two days later, Abdullah was slightly stunned when he walked into the conference room to see it professionally set up with maps and enlarged photos of several Aratex ports.

Taking his place in the offered seat across the table from Sophia, he said with as much seriousness as he could muster, "So what is your idea, Sophia?" Out of the corner of his eye, behind Sophia, he saw a curtain move and knew his father was also in the room, listening.

"As you know," she said, "we—meaning Aratex—have several piers in the port of Rotterdam. As you wrote in your report, operations are slow and cumbersome for our ships, with no capacity to grow either in amount of cargo moved or in size of ships."

He was watching her formal slideshow, whose contents he realized were also included in a bound book in front of him. Looking around the room, he also noticed several blown-up photos of the major Aratex ports: Oslo, Amsterdam, and Oakland, California. Maybe it was his father's presence or the tone of Sophia's voice, but finally, Abdullah started to pay attention, to really listen.

Sophia saw the change in his body language and immediately understood that she finally had his full intellectual attention.

"Did you know that there is a way to halve our offloading and loading time for containers that would increase our shipping capacity by 75 percent per port?"

Fantasy, thought Abdullah, but he was listening.

"It turns out that we own a vast tract of waterfront land in Amsterdam, undeveloped. It also turns out that the controlling water depth in the harbor in Amsterdam is nine feet deeper than Rotterdam."

They both heard a shuffle, and then very quietly, Sophia said, "Your Highness, it would possibly be more comfortable if you would join us at the table. I am certain your son will not mind."

She knew all along, thought Abdullah as the king walked out rather sheepishly. Sophia made a place for him to sit and gave him a glass of water, a notebook, and a copy of the presentation.

"Now let me continue." The following slide was a drawing of a standard ship unloading containers. "Today in Rotterdam, we unload each box on one side of the ship, and when finished, we reload on the same side.

"It turns out that if we could offload both sides of the ship simultaneously, we would save 50 percent in time. While we cannot redo the port of Rotterdam, if we built a new terminal on our existing land in Amsterdam, we could do this." The next slide showed detailed drawings of ships offloading from both sides and the map of their land in Amsterdam, with an engineering sketch showing a new port development.

"It would be expensive, but with this being a port development, I am certain there are some government funds available somewhere. What do you think?"

Neither man knew what to say. Finally, the king had a question. "Where else do they do this, Sophia?"

"Nowhere, to my knowledge," she said. "Certainly not where Aratex ships dock."

Abdullah interjected rather gruffly, "How did you come up with this idea, Sophia? Who mentioned it to you?"

"No one. I dreamed it up myself—many years ago, actually."

In the back of his mind, he remembered discussions with Sophia about her college degrees and past work experience. What had her degrees been in? Oceanography and marine engineering? "Sophia, is this from your college days?"

She smiled. "Close. Actually, my first job."

"Which was?"

"I worked for a large American engineering firm specializing in building harbors and dams."

"Which one?" he growled.

Finally, laughing out loud, she said, "Abdullah, I have told you this. I worked for the US Army Corps of Engineers. I used to build harbors for them."

After looking at his son's face and at Sophia, the king burst out laughing. "You can count on my vote, Sophia. This is brilliant!"

Lightly, she asked, "Any thoughts, Abdullah?"

"Yes," he said, putting on a stern business face. "First, how many other ports can we revise? Second, how much per port? And finally, do you think there is any room for improvement?"

She smiled, saying, "About half, about three hundred million per port, and yes, there could be more efficient loading equipment and trailer management in the ports."

Abdullah looked at her, slightly dumbfounded, as his father said, "You asked, Abdullah. She answered." The king was laughing again.

Then changing the subject, Sophia said, "Before I go to my next meeting, have you looked at the two other reports I gave you a couple of days ago? They were the annual reports for Carrick Inc. and Bijou II."

Abdullah was ashamed to admit that he had not only not looked at them but had even thrown them out.

"In case you have misplaced them, I have included copies for your review in your package today."

"Sophia," he growled, "I don't even know what Bijou II is!"

"I know, but you have been busy doing princely things like running a kingdom, while I have been reorganizing my piles of papers, playing file clerk."

Her repetition of the words he had used in their one big fight over Sophia's property made him smile. "Ah, yes, about that loan, Sophia."

It was again her turn to laugh. "I paid it back in two months, Abdullah. Do you not look at your bank accounts?"

The king stood up. "I think it is time for me to leave. What is it you said, Sophia? I must do kingly things like running my kingdom."

They could hear him chuckling as he walked down the hall.

"OK, Sophia, your point is made. Please brief me on Carrick and Bijou II."

"Carrick is a castle," she said cheekily.

"Sophia," he growled.

"Carrick owns the real estate and runs the hotels. It now has ten hotels that Rima and I own together."

"Ten? I see it has grown in the last two years."

Smiling, she continued, "Now about Bijou II. One day in Paris, we decided that for doing big parties it would be more efficient to have all the bits needed—tents, china, coffee pots, et cetera—in one place and ship them to the event. So we went shopping. Then we rented some warehouse space from my trust, bought some sexy white containers from Aratex, and set them up as movable parties. We rent them out along with our planning services for weddings and things like that. They even catered our wedding and your auntie's party last year."

"Cute idea, Sophia, but how much money can that bring in?" he asked with some scorn in his voice, even though he actually felt foolish and was now becoming angry at himself.

She could feel his irritation. "Well, Abdullah, if you would read the reports, you would see that between the two, they are very profitable small companies."

Standing up, he walked over to her and in a low voice whispered in her ear. "Why did you keep this a secret from me, Sophia? And why did you embarrass me in front of my father?"

"I did not hide this from you. I have sent you every quarterly report. I sent you the plan, and I sent you a detailed memo on funding it. You did not comment, so I assumed you were honestly busy. As for embarrassing you, it was not intentional.

"You do not take my business ideas seriously when we are in bed. So … I asked for this meeting to make you see how serious I am. The fact that your father was here was an accident."

"Sophia, come to me," he growled.

"Please don't be upset with me," she whispered, almost afraid as she leaned into his chest.

Relaxing when he saw the fear in her face, he said, "I am not angry at you. I am angry at myself." He looked down at her and gave her a soft kiss. "May we have an early dinner tonight, Sophia? I want a date with my wife, and then I think I want to go to bed early."

Giggling, she kissed him back and said, "I don't want to be late for my meeting with Rima. Then we are off with Princess Aria to meet the Minister of Health's wife and tour the hospitals in the city." She added, "Prince Ramani set this up and is coming with us."

Abdullah looked at her carefully. "Could you do me a favor, Sophia? I would appreciate it if you would send me your daily schedule so I have some idea of what you are doing."

"My pleasure, Your Highness," she said breezily.

An hour later, Rima and Sophia were in deep discussion when the king arrived, requesting to speak with them.

"I am interested in your business ventures, ladies. First, Sophia, about Aratex—I have a few questions about how to accomplish this in ports other than Amsterdam."

"Well, Oakland may be the next logical port. Aratex is already there, relatively underdeveloped. We most likely could receive some tax breaks, maybe even financial support."

"Why not San Francisco?" he asked.

"San Francisco is a great city, but sadly, there is not enough land, and the access to the port is very hard, not a major freeway. In fact, it ends with a section hanging out over the bay. If Oakland does not work out, there is a great sugar pier further up the bay that could be an alternative."

"And how do you know of this place, this sugar pier?"

She laughed. "That is a long story. I used to drive a tug back and forth from there."

"I will wait to hear that story, Sophia. Are you and Abdullah free for dinner?"

Her eyes got big. "Not really, Your Highness. I have a date to rebuild a bridge with your son."

He laughed. "I thought that might happen. What about tomorrow night? What is the rest of your schedule for today?"

"After this meeting, Rima and I are off to meet your sister Aria and the wife of the Minister of Health to tour the hospital. I believe Aria wants me to put in a good word with you for a grant from the Lawrence Foundation."

"I cannot wait to hear how that goes." Then turning to Rima, he said, "I am proud of what you have achieved with Carrick, Rima. You do my son proud. Please join us tomorrow for dinner."

Rima looked shocked. Once the two women were alone, she said, "He has never given me a compliment or asked me to dine with him. Will miracles never cease?"

Chapter 37

Date Night

Sophia and Abdullah's date was to take place in the ballroom in the king's palace. Abdullah had sent her a note with the time and place. She raced to her closet and faced the standard dilemma over what to wear, finally deciding on a mid-length champagne-colored silk dress. She added heels and large diamond earrings from Abdullah.

Because the outfit was sleeveless, she wore her abaya and a head covering to walk to the ballroom. When she arrived, a buffet dinner was displayed on a side table under warming drawers. The table was set for two with candles, fine linen, and elegant crystal. Soft music played in the background. As Sophia entered, she removed her abaya and fluffed her hair with her fingers.

"Sophia," he said softly as he entered wearing a tuxedo. "Let me do that while we dance." They had danced only rarely before, and he was as accomplished a dancer as the best in the world.

He twirled her around the ballroom first in a waltz, and then the music progressed to a tango. "How do you know these steps, Sophia?"

She smiled. "I was a dancer when I was young."

"I was thinking that we could dance between dinner courses tonight."

Leaning back to look at his handsome face, she smiled. "Anything you want, *mon amour.*" Kissing him on the cheek, she whispered in a throaty voice, "Anything!"

During the first course, he regaled her with a story of searching through his papers to find the Carrick and Bijou notes. "Sophia, I am astounded the two of you have made this a real business. Tell me again how this happened."

"Well, you knew we were partners in Carrick Manor. Originally, I provided the property, and Rima the working capital. It soon became apparent that our tastes in restoration would require something more than nightly hotel rooms to make it profitable. We completely overspent the budget.

"Then one day we had a call from a gentleman in India whose daughter wanted to spend her honeymoon, with all her guests, at a private lodge in Scotland. We thought we had won the lottery.

"We brought some of the staff from Rima's French hotel up to work the event, and it was a raging success. And we charged the client extra for everything. Then when the estate settled, rather than Rima or you buying the land in Jaipur, we combined that land with the hotels.

"On our first trip to Paris, we decided to form Bijou II. We are, after all, two princesses with jewelry, hence the name Jewelry 2. That is when we decided to give you the shares as a gift for all of your help.

"I see. Now, Sophia, it is time to dance."

They worked their way through course after course, chatting and dancing. They waltzed and tangoed their way through dinner.

Before dessert, Abdullah said, "Now, my lovely, a little rock and roll. I am going to sing you a song." His choice was "Don't You Forget about Me," from *The Breakfast Club* movie. He had a mic ready and sang the entire song to her while they danced. They danced the song three times, making up dance moves to the words. In the end, exhausted, Abdullah suggested they adjourn for the evening.

"It would be my pleasure," she said, and arm in arm, they went back to their villa.

"We should practice that dance more. Let's all go to the palace on the seashore this weekend, Sophia. We'll relax, and maybe, if you are relaxed enough, we could make a child."

"Oh, Abdullah, I would love to have your children. But what if I can't? What if it never happens?" She had gone very pale at this thought.

He smiled at her. "We can figure that out, Sophia. I know of a very discreet clinic in Switzerland. I will arrange a visit." He leaned over her. All thoughts of conversation ended until he said one last thing. "Sophia, what am I to do about your punishment for embarrassing me in front of my father?"

Her eyes twinkled up at him. "Anything you wish, my prince. Maybe you could make love to me all night long until I am sleep-deprived."

He had a familiar glint in his eye when he said, "My pleasure and yours, my love."

She nodded yes, and he gently turned her over and slid inside of her.

As she went to sleep in his arms, as the sun rose, she heard him say, "We will make a baby, Sophia, I promise."

Chapter 38

State Visits, 1996 and 1997

*T*he largest disappointment in 1996 and 1997 would be that Sophia did not become pregnant. As promised she and Abdullah paid a visit to the Aratex hospital and clinic in Geneva. They were given an elegant private suite at the top of the building overlooking the lake. They tested her endlessly, harvested her eggs, and gave her dietary instructions—no alcohol, healthy food, and less starch—which she followed to the letter. The first month, Sophia was nervous, as was Abdullah. But the test showed nothing wrong with either of them. Month after month, they visited the clinic. She worried endlessly about the issues surrounding surrogacy, as it was forbidden by their religion. Yet still her eggs were safely frozen and stored in a vault in Switzerland to which only Sophia had the code.

One day in early 1996, Abdullah announced, "We're off to Washington, DC, next week, Sophia. Are you ready to enter into conversations with our port people in the US? We'll also go to New Jersey and make a quick trip to California."

"Really?" she said. "You liked my idea that much?"

"Yes, I did," he said, getting up from where he had been sitting to move closer to her. "After I got over my wounded ego because it wasn't my idea, I realized just how great it could be. When I thought about it, I realized just how much I respect the work you are doing for our little company." He gave her a grin. "So I've decided that part of our visits will include meeting the upper management at Aratex. There will come a day when they all will know your name, my love, and I think that maybe breaking them in slowly is the best idea."

To say Sophia was thrilled was an understatement.

Washington was so much fun. Sophia was fizzing like a little kid. They met with both the Clintons and the Gores. Sophia and Al Gore were both avid conservationists and had several lively discussions. Hillary was interested in how Sophia navigated Arabia as a blond American. And almost predictably, Bill tried to make a pass at Sophia, which she sidestepped with grace and, more importantly, without Abdullah knowing. At the state dinner Sophia became reacquainted with a friend from her Corps of Engineer days, Bill Cohen, who was now the secretary of defense.

From Washington, they went to New York. While Abdullah held meetings with the Arabian delegation, Sophia, who had been invited by Al Gore to join the UN committee on the environment as a member at large, went to a large environmental symposium.

The next day, they flew to San Francisco. It was a sparkling California day, and the hills around the bay were a golden brown under a blue sky when the limousine drove Sophia across the Bay Bridge to the Port of Oakland. Abdullah had arranged that she and the head of Aratex Shipping would attend the meeting without him, saying, "I have to meet with the Arabian consulate this morning."

As the car entered the port facility, she thought it looked both the same and different. She had been here many times before with her father, decades ago. Then she thought, *It's not different; you're different.* Their meeting was scheduled for 11:00 a.m. with several port and city officials, including the current mayor and former governor of the state, Jerry Brown.

Her team set up the conference room, and after coffee and small talk, she started the official meeting. The head of Aratex Shipping had been slightly dubious that Sophia should be doing the presentation, but when the mayor gave Sophia a kiss on the cheek, saying, "It's been a long time," he realized that maybe Abdullah had been correct. He had said, "This is Sophia's show. Let her run with it."

At the end of Sophia's presentation, Jerry Brown turned to her and said thoughtfully, "So am I correct that what you want from the city of Oakland is to purchase two tracts of land and receive a three-year tax break on all of your property while you work on the facilities?"

She nodded, finally saying, "Yes, that's all we want."

He smiled, looked around the room at the nodding heads, and said, "I think you have a deal, Sophia."

That afternoon, as she waltzed into their hotel suite, she was jubilant. "Abdullah, Abdullah, we just bought Oakland. We did it!"

He was so proud of her that he picked her up and swung her around the room, dancing. "Now, my lovely," Abdullah said when he was finished waltzing her around the room, "Rima and I have a surprise for you."

"You do? What, pray tell, are you two plotting?"

"We leave for the airport now. Your bags are packed, and you have clothing on the plane. Follow me!" he said, dancing out the door of their suite.

They boarded the 737, and Abdullah said, "After dinner, we will have a nice nap." He was almost giggling like a child. "We have to stop once to refuel, then one more nap, and then your surprise."

"Tell me now," she giggled. "The suspense is killing me." In response he tickled her, making her giggle even more.

They ate dinner quickly, Sophia commenting, with a toss of her head toward the stateroom, that she wanted her first nap. He proceeded to torture Sophia for hours with his fingers, until finally she was begging him to come inside of her, which he gladly obliged. Seventeen hours later, Abdullah woke Sophia from her sex-infused coma, saying, "Time to get dressed. We have a quick state visit, only one daytime reception, and then we're on to our final destination."

"State visit?" she mumbled. "I don't have anything to wear!"

He burst out laughing. "Look in your closet, Sophia. Rima has taken care of everything."

Still naked, she opened the closet. It was full of magnificent Indian-style saris and scarves, each labeled, with shoes and jewelry set in cloth bags.

She wheeled around and, with a squeal and a smile that felt like sunshine to Abdullah, said, "We're going to India?"

"Yes, *mon amour,* we are meeting Rima at your hotel in Agra. We both wanted you to see the Taj Mahal."

As they landed and pulled up to the jetway, Sophia spied Abdullah's G3 parked next to them. "You brought two planes here?" she asked. "That's over the top even for you," she said, giggling.

"I did!" He shrugged and gave a wide, white-toothed smile. "You'll see." He then began to regale her with stories of what he had learned studying the *Kama Sutra.*

"Stop!" she finally exclaimed. "If you keep talking about the *Kama Sutra,* I'll just want to go back to bed, not meet a prime minister."

He laughed so hard that the flight attendant came to ask him if he needed anything.

For the state visit she wore an elegant Indian-inspired peplum top and red skirt printed with a traditional Indian kalka pattern. As promised, the visit was short and sweet.

Within four hours they were boarding the G3 and heading for Agra to meet Rima. It was sunset when they landed. Abdullah had arranged for a low-pass flyby to see the Taj from the air. Sophia gasped at her first view of the massive Islamic mausoleum constructed of ivory-white marble.

Rima met them as they walked off the plane, holding hands. Sophia fell into Rima's arms.

"I've missed you, *ma chérie!*" both women exclaimed.

They walked together to the waiting limousine. Abdullah had one arm around each of them and was smiling like a Cheshire cat.

Sophia loved the hotel. Their private suite was a stunning replica of a Raj's royal palace in Jaipur. In their private dining room, waiters served them a multicourse Indian meal with wines for Germany. It was the most relaxed meal they had all shared in months. They finished the evening in the sitting room, sipping port while watching the moon rise over the Taj. Rima and Sophia were sitting on the plush sofa while Abdullah sat in a chair next to them.

The large moon capped the white marble dome that surrounded the tomb, the mausoleum for the woman it had been built to celebrate. Fingers of moonlight seemed to dance around the four freestanding minarets, making them seem as if they were dancers in the starry sky.

"They say," Abdullah noted, getting up from his chair, "that he built it for his favorite wife." Smiling at them as he sat down between them, he said, "I could try to build something as beautiful for my favorite and only wives."

He put his glass down and then wrapped his arms, one each, around the two women. Sophia thought this was a beautiful act of intimacy. Abdullah continued, "I have written a poem for the two most important people in my life:

> *I greet you every day with my heart in my hand,*
> *always ready to gift it to both of you.*
> *I kiss you both goodnight with my heart full*
> *because you have both led me to believe in love.*
> *Every night in my prayers my heart tells me to*
> *follow you,*
> *because together your love has led me to the most*
> *wonderful place,*
> *our life together.*
> *I know I will love you both forever, my wives,*
> *because you lead me with your strength."*

Both women had tears in their eyes when he finished.

Sometime later, Abdullah walked Rima to her room while Sophia quietly went to hers and Abdullah's. None of them wanted to break the spell of Dullah's poem.

When he returned to their room, Sophia quietly asked, "Is she all right?"

He smiled his broad smile, saying, "She is happier than I have seen her in months."

The next morning before dawn, Dullah awakened Sophia with soft kisses. "Time to get dressed, Princess. We have another surprise for you—the Taj Mahal at sunrise."

Sophia bounded out of bed and raced to the closet and was not even surprised to see all the outfits from the plane hanging there, ready to be worn.

"Oh, what to wear?" she giggled, just as Abdullah left the room and Rima entered.

Rima was wearing a stunning black silk dress with just the perfect amount of gold trim. "I am hoping, *chérie*, that you will wear the white version of my dress," she said almost shyly. "Abdullah has hired a photographer and wants photos from today."

"Then that, my Rima, is what I shall wear!" she announced with a smile. She quickly did her hair and makeup and donned the outfit.

As the trio walked across the park that Sophia had gifted to their hotel chain, she saw Mario Testino setting up for the photos. No one else was around except their guards, who stood a good distance back. They sat on the same cement bench as Princess Diana had three years ago. First, all three sat for the photo, then Rima and Sophia each had individual photos, and then at Abdullah's insistence, there was a photo of Abdullah and Rima and another one of Abdullah and Sophia. Finally, at Sophia's insistence, there was one photo of Rima and Sophia. It would always amaze Sophia how Mario had somehow captured the memory of the night before in the photo of the three of them, or maybe they themselves had exuded it.

They spent the rest of their Indian vacation traveling to different tourist sights in the region. And when it was time to go home, they all agreed it had been the most relaxed vacation any of them had ever had. But sadly, especially for Abdullah, work called. He told them on the last night that when he got home, he would become the prime minister of Arabia, the second-most important position in the kingdom.

From the day they arrived back, he began working like a man possessed, spending both days and long nights with his male staff. He tried, not always successfully, to spend time in the mornings and evenings with Sophia and Rima.

In Arabia Sophia's days were full, if highly programmed. After morning prayers and daily yoga, Sophia studied and worked on Aratex, educating herself on the various issues the company faced. By noon she often had a list of questions for Abdullah when he returned from a long day's work.

She always ate lunch with Rima. Sometimes Rima would organize a small group of other female relatives. These lunches rarely strayed from the topics of home decor, art, jewelry, fashion, or other possessions. Sophia described them to Abdullah as "boring but good for family PR." She quipped, "At least I know something about those subjects."

Other afternoons, she and Rima—and Maya when she was in the country—would meet in their private garden to discuss business or charity work, piloting how best to help others. To their amazement, the king would often join them, adding his recommendations. More and more, the king asked both Sophia and Rima's advice on which grants his own foundation should approve.

Around three, after afternoon prayer, Sophia would retire to her suite and often nap or read and bathe to be ready for her ever-energetic prince to return from work. He always wanted to share stories about his job and even many of his troubles within the kingdom. He was beginning to fear that the radicals were plotting to overthrow the monarchy, as they had done in Iran. She was an interested and compassionate listener.

After dinner they would adjourn, and business chat would end.

Nowadays, Abdullah rarely slept and often got up in the middle of the night, leaving her in a sex-filled, dreamy sleep, to read and work in their private study. Sophia always awoke to his pre-dawn kisses before he left for morning prayers with his father.

After her morning bath and prayers, Sophia would start the day again, always similar to the previous day but never boring.

Chapter 39

And Then They Called Her a Whore

*I*t was fall 1997. Abdullah was physically exhausted from work and travel. Coming home very late one night, he stood in their suite and said, "Sophia, I would like to go to the desert for a vacation. I believe the endless sea of sweeping sand will comfort me, make me remember why I love my country and my heritage. I know we spoke of going to London. Do you mind changing that plan?"

Looking at his haggard face, she replied, "If it is what you wish, then let us go to the desert."

After five years, Sophia had come to love the desert. Over the years they had explored every inch of the country, from the mountains to the sea. Sophia often thought she was living a dream from a different century. When she was home with Abdullah, they roamed the desert as they had the moors of Scotland. The difference was that tents replaced mansions, and deep-blue underground grottos replaced hot tubs. The roughness of the rock, silk on a sand surface, wild nonstop rides by moonlight in the desert: when they were together alone in the desert, it was as if he had designed their adventures around constant sexual stimulation.

What kept her firmly grounded in reality was the growing fear of Islamic uprising.

They were riding out together. She was seated in front of him on his massive black stallion Devil. Her mare followed along behind.

He pulled the horse to a stop, saying, "Turn around, please, Sophia." There was a devilish glint in his eyes.

She tilted her head, and he said, "No, face me with your pleasure." Turning her body around, he pulled her close, lifting her skirt. Almost immediately, he slid himself inside of her, and she gasped with pleasure. He whispered, "Hold on, my love."

As the horse galloped onward, she felt the rhythm of the horse through him inside of her. Her scarf was blown back, her hair free in the wild ride across the sand.

It was more than she could stand. She climaxed, expecting him to join her in their pleasure, and was surprised when with a superhuman effort, he held back and kept on riding hard. She came again, and again he held back. This pattern continued until Sophia wept with excitement. She was drenched in sweat and limp in his arms.

They stopped and climbed off the horse, and he bathed her now sore and bruised body in an oasis. "Did I hurt you?"

"No. However, you might have finally worn me out."

The sky was turning an inky black, and one by one the stars came out. He and Sophia headed back to the encampment under a skinny moon. They spent the night peacefully wrapped in each other's arms in their plush tent. They both awoke at dawn and spent a dreamy morning in bed. After bathing, they enjoyed a lazy brunch and spent most of the day reading poems to each other. On the third day of their vacation, it was too hot to ride until late in the afternoon. Sophia mounted her mare, and Abdullah mounted Devil. Four outriders left before them, and four followed behind them and quickly moved out to give the couple privacy.

By the time they started back toward camp, it was a sparkling moon-filled night. Her now blond hair was shining as bright as any beacon in the night when four men on horseback beset them. Thinking the men were Bedouins, Abdullah whispered, "Your veil, Sophia."

Somehow she managed to pull the black veil over her head. Abdullah quickened their pace to a gallop, and then Sophia's horse stumbled. He managed to lift her off her mount in one motion, seating her in front of himself. As he lifted her off the mare, she had grabbed the pistol that always sat loaded in her saddle.

Abdullah was worried and muttered, "Where are my fucking guards?" as the group of four men surrounded them. They were dressed all in black and wore face coverings—they were clearly not Bedouins. They were speaking in a dialect that Sophia could not completely understand, but from the moment she heard her name mentioned, it became clear that their intent was to harm her.

Finally, Abdullah pulled out his sword to fend them off. Sophia saw the glint of one of their knives and kicked it away as one man attempted to stab at her. The knife fell, stabbing the man's horse and making it rear. With all the commotion, Abdullah also was stabbed, and having failed at swordsmanship, he pulled a long pistol and commenced shooting with deadly accuracy.

A second man came lunging at Sophia. She shot him once. Another moved forward, stabbing her arm. In the commotion, as she shot at him, she missed, only killing his horse.

Abdullah and Sophia raced off across the desert, the stallion carrying them as if it were a rocket. They did not stop for what seemed like hours. The horse was drenched in sweat, yet sensing fear, Devil was reluctant too slow even for his master.

When they reached the encampment, Abdullah barked orders at his men but then collapsed as he dismounted his horse. Servants carried Abdullah into the tent, and Sophia immediately began to render first aid to Abdullah's wounds. Replacement guards moved both on horseback and in cars to find both the outriders and the attackers.

Gently, Sophia began to cut off Abdullah's pants to bandage his leg.

As she leaned over him, Abdullah quietly said, "Close your eyes, Sophia. I will kiss you. I have failed you today. I am so ashamed. I know that is not a strong enough word. Remember always, Sophia, that I will be true to you. And I will always have your safety first and foremost in my mind. I have committed an inhuman sin today. I did not keep you safe."

She started to speak, but his kiss stopped her words.

Finally, she broke the kiss, saying, "Please, my prince, may I tend to your wound?"

He complied and let her continue. The blood had stopped flowing, but still the gash was very deep. The sword had entered the top of his inner thigh. Sophia made a bandage out of linen and bound the wound using a cotton shirt.

When his guards returned, they came directly to him, ignoring the fact that Sophia was unveiled in the tent. After an animated discussion, they left, and Abdullah turned to Sophia. He said quietly, "Our guards were found slaughtered, but only three of the four attackers were found dead. They were from a radical religious group."

Abdullah put one hand on Sophia's cheek, and she put her hand on his. They sat gazing into each other's eyes filled with dismay and pain. Sadly, they both knew that this was only the beginning.

His men entered and then left to return quickly with a lifter. "No," he ordered, standing up. "I will ride! And Princess Sophia will ride with me!"

The tensions in the Middle East had been boiling over for years, since the Gulf War. Abdullah and Sophia both knew it was only a matter of time before the radicals would try again.

As they cantered back toward the city, another group of men, this time in jeeps and carrying automatic weapons, came rapidly toward them. Almost simultaneously, Abdullah's new, fully armed outriders surrounded the couple.

He held her tightly with his left arm while gripping the horse's reins in his right hand. "Put your scarf over your head, Sophia, to hide your hair. Keep your eyes and face down, and do not speak!" he said.

She complied instantly. In the next second, shots were fired into the air. She had a hard time not looking. The jeep's occupants were arguing for passage in Arabic.

"Let them pass," Abdullah said, and despite the anger from his guards, they were allowed to pass, to continue on their journey.

As the armed men drove away, Sophia heard the group yelling, "Abdullah's whore!" The words made her slump into him.

"I'm sorry, Sophia," he said in that low, calm voice she loved so much. "They may be my people, but unfortunately, I cannot always control them."

With a striking sense of clarity, she knew that her time with Abdullah and Rima was moving toward a conclusion.

They all had tried to delude themselves that Sophia would fit into their world. As they hurried home, watching the aurora borealis brighten the desert sky, she thought about her unwavering love for Abdullah. With all her heart she wanted to stay and be his forever wife. Yet she understood she would never realistically be safe here. It was, she knew, a matter of life and death for both of them.

The two-hour trip back to the city was slow, and she knew Abdullah was in agony. He rode into the palace upright, with pain etched across his face. As Sophia jumped down, Rima appeared.

"Quick," Sophia barked, "he needs a doctor."

The doctor was waiting behind Rima, and as Abdullah finally succumbed to his pain, his guards carried him into his chambers.

Sophia sat with Rima outside the door, fear etched on both of their faces. Finally, Rima turned to Sophia and noticed the bloodstain on Sophia's shirt for the first time. "Oh no! Sophia, you were injured also!" She quickly barked out an order in Arabic, and servants ran into the halls.

"No, I'm fine. It is just a scratch. Maybe I should go clean up."

Her maid led her away to her room, where a doctor soon appeared. Twenty stitches later, Sophia's arm and chest were wrapped in bandages. The knife had sliced her upper arm and right breast. She refused any pain medication.

Sophia must have lain down, for she awoke from a deep sleep to Rima shaking her shoulders. "Come quickly, Sophia. He is awake and will be fine. But he has lost a lot of blood. After you see him, the king commands that you come to his chamber."

No, she thought, *not yet.* Following Rima, she went into Abdullah's chamber. He was awake and sitting up in bed.

"My love," he said, with seemingly no thought to Rima standing on the other side of the room. "Again, what I said in the desert. I have failed you. My father wishes to see you. Please, Sophia, close your eyes, and I'll kiss you." The kiss was slow and tender. "Remember, I will always be true. Now the king commands, and even I cannot overrule him."

"I will always love you, my prince. Allah will forgive."

As Sophia held back tears, Rima led her to the king's chambers, saying, "You must be strong, Sophia, both calm and respectful."

"Thank you," she whispered as she was ushered in to see the visibly frail and aging king.

"Ah … Princess Sophia." The king stood up and hugged her. Looking at her mournful face, he said, "I hear you have had a bad day."

An understatement, she thought, keeping silent.

The king continued, "My son and I have both failed to protect you today. I ask your forgiveness. I love you, Sophia. You are almost everything a king could want in a daughter-in-law. The worst of my sins is that I have been untruthful with you. I love you like a daughter because once upon a time, I too loved an English woman."

Suddenly, lines from one of Barbara's letters came back to her: *The great love of my life was lost to me the day I was arrested. Yet he has stayed faithful, true, and in love with me to this day—always caring and always protecting from afar.* Still, she remained silent.

"I can see by your expression that you know of whom I will now speak."

Sophia nodded, wondering why she had not figured this out sooner. Abdullah's words in her study came back to her: he had told her that the Bedouin who had helped form Aratex was his father.

"You may have guessed, her name was Barbara. We met in London, and soon after, she traveled here. We were married in secret. Your palace was her palace for three years. It was simply the happiest time of my life. She returned to London for what was supposed to be a short stay.

"You know the official story of her giving photos to the KGB. And because she would not divulge anything, she went to jail.

"The long-hidden truth, Sophia, is that she did not give photos to a KGB agent. They were secret photos of our oil refinery defenses, and she gave them to me. The only way she could clear herself was by telling the court about us, and I had asked her to keep us secret. Rather than betray me, she went to jail.

"When she was released from jail, I took care of her by protecting Aratex. As you know, we jointly—but she mostly—owned Aratex.

"I wanted to care for her because I loved her. And she loved me. Sadly, our worlds were too far apart. I gifted her the Lawrence Foundation. Before she died, she gifted it back to me.

"When I learned of you and Abdullah, I was worried. Then I learned you were Barbara's heir. To me, it was fate that had brought you together, and I had hope and joy.

"You have brought more to our land than you might believe. And you and Abdullah will always be tied through Aratex.

"I think, Sophia, that you know what I must now do. Please remember, it is because I love you and fear for your safety, the safety of my son, and my kingdom. Regrettably, all the men who attacked you were not killed tonight, and as I understand it, you shot and killed one of the men. While you are in the country, even I as the king cannot protect you from the consequences of that action. Maybe in time, but certainly not tonight."

She nodded, trying to blink away the tears.

"For now, and hopefully not forever, I must ask that you leave the country. Men on both sides of a conflict you have nothing to do with have died today. I believe too much in peace to start a war, even for my favorite princess."

She nodded her head in agreement as she looked around the room, one she had been in many times before. Its ornate green and gold wall coverings and plush Persian rugs seemed somehow more garish to her than before. Yet she knew she would miss the king. He had always been kind, patiently teaching her a great deal about his country, the region, and the religion.

"The plane will be waiting at the airport. You may take anything you want. Items you leave here will still be your belongings. In time I hope you can return. You are, simply put, still a princess and a wife. And even if in the future you are not a wife, you will always be a princess. For now, maybe we should hold this as what you once termed a quiet truth."

"Your Highness," she said in a whisper, "I accept this fate. Please understand that while you may have my forgiveness, as I have forgiven Abdullah, I must share some of the blame. I do not owe you forgiveness. What I owe you and will abide by, no matter where or what, is ..." The tear finally fell. "You have my loyalty forever."

With that, the king stood up and hugged Sophia. And then, over the top of her head, he said, "Go with God, Sophia. I will always hold your heart and your loyalty near to mine, my princess."

She walked away with tears streaming down her face. Back in her room, she was surprised to find her maid packing for her.

"I requested it," said Rima. "I've included a few of the more personal photographs and small art pieces that I know were gifts. The plane will fly you to Scotland, and the car will be waiting when you arrive. Abdullah has been informed. I will see you again soon, Sophia. Please do not fret, *ma chérie*."

Sophia turned to Rima. "I understand. Please tell Abdullah I ..." She stopped, looking at the other woman.

"I will tell him you love him, Sophia. I have known that for a while now. And I assure you, he knows it also."

They walked arm in arm down the long hall to the rear driveway, where Sophia stepped into the Rover for her ride to the airport. Rima stood under the porte cochere, tears streaming down her lovely face.

The back window on the car was open, and as the Rover pulled away, she looked up toward Abdullah's room. He was standing at the window, and she heard his animal-like howl of pain across the courtyard. She was grateful when the driver rolled up the blackened windows.

She flew across the Mediterranean in a daze. Her thoughts were a jumble, yet surprisingly, she was not crying. She was almost oblivious when the crew told her that they needed to refuel and that there would be a short delay in Paris.

What had the king said? That this must be a quiet truth?

Finally, she gave up on thinking. It hurt too much. She pulled a romance novel out of her briefcase. It was the latest novel by Katherine Grey. That night in Kinsale seemed so long ago, indeed in a place far away. She smiled. *I was right. My life is better than all her books combined.* The book lay unread.

They had been on the ground for over two hours and still had not refueled when she heard the stairs rolling into place. She knew she had to disembark for them to refuel.

As the door opened, she heard the flight attendant say in a shocked voice, "Welcome, Your Highness."

Abdullah stepped onto the plane. He walked toward Sophia with a limp and a smile. He explained, "After some arm twisting, it was decided that I should recover from my injuries in Scotland."

Her smile lit up her face. "I take it we have enough fuel to continue." Sophia took his hand and led him back to their cabin. "You need your rest, my prince," she said softly.

"No, I need you, Sophia."

"Lie down, *mon amour.* I don't want you injured any more than you are. Does your father know?"

Abdullah smiled. "Yes, Sophia, he knows. The plane that brought me here is his. I think he understood when he, like half the kingdom, heard my howls of pain. And he truly loves you, Sophia. To him, you are still a princess, and with all his heart, he wants you to return someday."

"I heard your howls too," she said. "I almost died in the car."

"So my father ordered it. Rima took me to the car and sent her love."

Sophia shook her head in wonder. "She, my prince, is the saint in this trio."

He nodded in agreement. Drawing her close, he whispered, "You are the angel."

She smiled. "Are you in much pain?"

The twinkle in his eye returned. "Not the kind you think, my princess. The kind only you can cure. But tonight … I might need your help."

She smiled as an idea came to her. "I will endeavor to ease all of our pains." She moved her head down his stomach, knowing exactly what to do.

Chapter 40

Separation

*I*t was late November 1997. Sophia and Abdullah had been in Scotland a month when Rima arrived unannounced. "Abdullah, I come bearing life-changing news. I am so very sorry."

When Rima had finished telling him the news of his father's stroke in a matter-of-fact manner, she said, "Tell me, Abdullah, do you wish to hold Sophia to her promise? Will she be happy living in the East or, heaven forbid, living here without you? It might have worked if we had more time, but sadly, Allah has taken our time away."

He knew Rima was right. "No," he said in a whisper, "I will release her from her marriage vows." As he strode from the room, a tall, proud, yet heartbroken man, Rima realized that this was the first time she had ever seen him cry. And for the first time, she was uncertain if she had helped or hurt her husband.

Sophia heard the car drive up to the front entrance of the cottage. It was Abdullah. As he got out of the car, barking orders to his driver, he was in a hurry yet looked shattered. Sophia immediately knew that something was terribly wrong.

He walked in the front door, slammed it shut, and took her into his arms. "Sophia, Rima arrived with the news that my father has had a stroke. My time as a free man, a free prince, is over ..."

"You are now a king?" she asked.

"Not yet. A crown prince in waiting."

"You are leaving now?" It was not a question, more of a confirmation.

Again, he nodded.

Then picking her up in his arms, he carried her upstairs. The second he passed through the doorway, he set her down and began ripping off his clothing like a man possessed. Naked and fully aroused, he turned to her, raised her skirt, and pulled off both the skirt and her underpants while simultaneously pushing her back down on the large bed. As he entered her, he gasped, "Sophia, please understand, I must."

This time their lovemaking was filled with an all-consuming urgency. Sweat poured down his chest and back as he rode her harder than he had ever done before. His hands groped, pulling and pushing into every part of her body.

It was, again, that strange combination of both pain and pleasure. It was as if this was more than a sexual encounter—some sort of a ritual dance. She responded in kind to him, somehow understanding that this was what he needed. It was more than desire. Her breasts were throbbing with an intense combination of pain from his rough handling of her nipples and a desperate need when his hand moved to pinch her genitalia.

She felt she was in another universe, maybe heaven, maybe hell. Again, she blacked out when they jointly climaxed in each other's arms. She would have bruises on her body, and that deep, exotic feeling of need she had felt for him would last for hours.

He looked down at her, seeing a black bruise starting to rise on her arm. "I am sorry, Sophia. I never meant to hurt you." He screamed out, "Argh! I love you!" In a lower voice, he said, "But we both know ..." The words were left unspoken.

Sophia ran her fingers through his hair and said, "Goodbye, my king, *mon amour roi*," intuitively understanding that this goodbye was not only to him as a husband but also to the passion they had shared.

"Sophia, I will always love you, and if you ever need my help, you can call. I will be back and forth, but of course, it will be different. And here"—he put his hand on his heart—"I will always be your *mon amour roi*, and you my *mon amour reine*."

As he turned to leave, he said, "Rima sent her love and wanted you to know that she too will miss you. You know, Sophia, you may be the only true friend either of us has. And all of our business partnerships will remain the same. So I will see you again. It will just be different."

She took his hand. She wanted one last time to look at her prince, to see his dark, sultry features, to indelibly etch them in her mind forever. She realized he was about to become the king of Arabia, a man with millions of people in his sole care—a startling responsibility, even if it was one he had trained for all his life.

He looked at her with a hooded gaze, waiting for her to speak. Her face said she had something to say and was looking for the right words.

"I love you, Abdullah, and understand. I hope you know, you will always have my discretion, loyalty, and fealty, my liege. Go with Allah. It is your destiny."

He pulled her into his arms for one last embrace. Holding her gently, he felt her sag into his arms. He again had tears on his cheeks but managed to speak in his usual low, calm voice. "I am sure you know that I will not hold you to our marriage vows, Sophia. You are too young and have too much life ahead of you. You have too much to give to the world. It would, in the end, cripple you, and I could not bear to see that happen. Not all my people have been educated at Oxford and the Sorbonne. And unfortunately, we know now there are many people who would like to see us both dead.

"It is my sincere wish that you can recover in time and find your destiny. I hope you can find it in your heart to forgive me for the hurt I have caused yet still believe in the good we have shared. Please, if only for the memory of what we have shared, I pray you will follow a path that will provide good to others and you will continue to work with our charities to substantially impact all peoples of all religious beliefs." He sobbed as he said, "Please don't forget about me."

Trying to compose himself, he continued. "All of that said ..." He paused and pulled back to look at her wistfully. He wanted what he was about to say in his heart of hearts. And it was the one thing he knew his father wanted that would save his marriage. "If it turns out, Sophia, that you are pregnant with my child, I plead with you to reconsider our vows. It would be a great honor to have a child by you."

She let the tears roll down her face. "Dullah, as I said, I will never"—the word came out fiercely—"never dishonor you. If perchance I am blessed enough to be carrying your child, I will do whatever it takes, move heaven and earth, to do whatever you wish, *mon amour roi.*"

With tears now freely flowing down his cheeks, he kissed her forehead like he had done so many times before. Then he turned and strode out her house and her life. She saw him turn and nod his head, and then he was gone.

Within thirty minutes the G5 flew overhead, wagging its wings one last time as it flew over her home. *He is the prince of thieves*, she mused. *But he didn't steal a building; he stole my heart.*

She closed the door to her room and lay down on the bed. Tears rolled down her cheeks as she contemplated the idea of being pregnant. She would know in two or three weeks. *I need time and space*, she thought. Looking out the window across the highlands at the home they had shared for the last few years, she knew she would stay in Scotland. It would give her time to recover and, if a miracle occurred, to let the child within her grow.

Slowly, she changed into riding clothes and went to saddle her beautiful white mare, a gift from Abdullah. She briefly wondered where he had found such a lovely horse. Little did she know that within the year, she would find out.

As she walked the mare along the ridge that they had often traversed together, she realized that in some ways, she was freer than she had ever been in her life.

She knew this was a chance to choose her destiny and do something different, something even better for the world. What was it he had said? That it was his sincere wish that she find her destiny, that she use her charities to have a substantial impact on all peoples of all religious beliefs. This, she realized, was the embodiment of the Quran.

When she had been in Arabia or with Abdullah, she had realized that parts of her life were spinning out of control. There had been days when she admitted that it was hard to live in Arabia. And yes, she had even wondered if she could always continue. Then of course, she would think of Abdullah and just move forward because of her abiding love.

This simple understanding gave her an amazing feeling of empowerment. When she arrived home from her ride, there was a note from Rima.

Dear Sophia,

I am so sorry we did not see each other. I can judge, however, that you are in pain. Do not fret or despair, Sophia. This is just another chapter in our mutual destinies. I will see you soon. Together we will get through this chapter.

I am grateful for the love and passion and strength you have given Abdullah. We, men, women, and all wives, are equal in the eyes of Allah. Although the time was far too brief, you have given him a joy he will hold within himself the rest of his natural-born days.

Please, never be concerned about my knowledge. That is a Western way that only brings guilt, whereas in the Eastern path, the love you and Abdullah have should have only brought pleasure and contentment. I tried to forewarn you about our cultural differences from the beginning. I fear I failed.

Despite our country's societal challenges, we firmly believe that the position of the female is to take care of the family. Yes, I hoped, but never discussed with Abdullah, that you two would produce a child. He has never been fulfilled in that the most sacred of experiences, knowing the joy of the moment of conception. Even his father wanted him to have another child with you.

More than children, I know he wanted you as his second wife forever. And truth be told, it was also my dream. You must understand that his decision to divorce you is only to protect you.

We are and always will be here for you in every way possible. I am torn. I dream for another child for Abdullah, one he has conceived with complete gratification. Yet I also wish you peace for a different life. I fear that you would have difficulty accepting all of our ways. I will accept, rejoice, and cherish either outcome.

Forever yours in the eyes of Allah. Go in peace, my sister.

Rima

Chapter 41

The King Comes to Scotland

*T*he king had recovered from his stroke. Abdullah spoke to Sophia every day, as did Rima. Yet not once had anyone again mentioned a divorce. No paperwork had arrived.

So it was a considerable shock to Sophia when Abdullah's Rover drove up to the front door of her cottage, and the king alighted. After they had exchanged pleasantries and he was seated in her cozy sitting room, she finally asked, "What brings you here, Your Highness?"

"To see you, Sophia. Why do you stay here—I mean in this cottage?"

"I like it. It's small and cozy, and I can see …" She looked out the window toward Abdullah's mansion.

"You grieve for my son, Sophia?"

"I do, but I understand."

"You know that soon Abdullah will become king."

She smiled ruefully. "My worst nightmare." Holding her hand up to forestall any other comment, she said, "We all knew it was coming."

"You know you are not yet divorced, Sophia."

"I do know that, Your Highness. It is something that I prayed would never happen. I even dreamed that I could be his wife, even if it meant only here, overseas. I assume you are here to give me bad news."

"It's still a fine day here in the Highlands," he said, artfully changing the subject. Then looking toward a nearby coatrack, he spied an old Barbour coat. Walking over to the coat, he slowly took it off the rack, looked at the label, and put it on. "Let's go for a ride."

On the walk to the stable, the king led the way. Their silence was comfortable. When they were riding toward the ridge above the loch, he said, "You have done great things for my son, Sophia, and for Rima. I know he is steadfast in his hope that you and he can be together again. But it has been a month, Sophia. Have you seen my son?"

"That depends on your definition of the word 'seen.' We have been to one Aratex board meeting together. We had a private lunch at that meeting. We have not been together as man and wife."

He stopped his horse to look at her. "Really, Sophia?" he said with an arched eyebrow.

"Really, Your Highness. I would not lie to you. The top floor of the Aratex building is not really convenient for a get-together!"

The king said with a deep sigh, "Well, I thought ..." He let the last of his sentence go unfinished.

"Well, what?" she snapped. "You think he is going to take me on the conference table?"

The king blushed. "Well, yes, maybe," he said, nodding.

"Oh, stop it! You know exactly when we have seen each other."

"I repeat, my son is steadfast in his hope that you and he can be together again. He would do anything to make that happen."

Sophia sighed. "Yes, as I said, so am I!"

They continued the rest of their ride quietly.

Upon their return to the stables, the king said, "If I were to let you and Abdullah stay married, then when he becomes king, what then? It isn't fair. However, it is the system we were born into."

"I would become a princess in hiding," she said sadly.

"Exactly," he said. "And if someone tries to overthrow him ..."

She bent her head to hide the tears she felt coming. "The consequences would be perilous, maybe even deadly," she said evenly, looking directly into his eyes. "I do understand that even though I am his wife, I also am a symbol and a signal to the world— one that in your country and region made me a target."

"So you do understand. You would be a princess hidden in a palace. You would not even be able to work, under laws that even Islam does not condone. My father cut a deal with the devil to form his kingdom. The radical clerics have a great deal of control. The only way to keep the country together is to work with them, even when they are morally wrong."

"Yes," she said. "I have thought of this."

"And what were your conclusions?"

Her shoulders slumped as she said, "That we should divorce. I can do more good for you and Abdullah from the outside than within. But that does not mean Abdullah and I cannot dream or wish or want. Knowing the right thing to do doesn't mean you don't wish for a different outcome. It means you live in the present, with maybe one last vestige of hope that it could be something different."

He smiled. "Sophia, you will soon have my foundation. I am gifting it to you so that you can expand your charity work worldwide."

"I am honored, Your Highness," she said. Holding his hand as they walked back from the stables to the cottage, she said, "It's becoming cold. Please come in for tea."

"Can I stay here tonight, Sophia? I like your cozy cottage."

Seeing the sad, faraway look in the old king's eyes, she said, "And you have been here before?" Then she added, "And that is your coat?"

He nodded finally, saying, "Yes. Would you indulge an old dying man a dream from long ago?"

"Of course, I would, Your Highness. Now it is time for prayer. Would you please lead so I can join you? We are, after all, still family."

After prayers and over dinner, they talked about Abdullah, his future, and how hard the king thought it would be.

"Your Highness, you know our last Aratex board meeting was over a month ago. I have not seen Abdullah since."

"I do, and I know the strain it has put on him."

She smiled. "His strain is his worry for his country, not just me," she said. Again holding up her hands to silence him, she continued, "I know he loves me. I don't think that will ever change. But as I said, I do with a heavy heart agree that I can do more for you, my kingdom, and my religion from outside than within."

"This house is still very restful and meditative. You have not changed it much, have you, Sophia?" Then changing the subject again, he said, "Do you still love him?"

"With my heart, my soul, and if necessary, my life, I do."

The king said quietly, "Sophia, do you love him enough to give him up?"

"I do! If it's what Abdullah wants, I will accept a divorce. Your Highness, please understand, intellectually I understand, but I am emotionally stricken. I know in time that will pass. I gave an oath to Abdullah that will not be broken no matter who divorces whom."

The next morning, as the king got ready to leave, Sophia said, "Your Highness, I do have an important question to ask you. And I hope you will consider giving me a truthful answer … Did you know I was the heir to Aratex before I did?"

The king sighed. "I guessed, but it was not confirmed until you knew. Clearly, I knew of Barbara's stake in Aratex. When I heard of Barbara's passing, I knew there would be a new owner. I even asked Sir Joshua, and he refused to tell me. Then when Abdullah offered for Number Eleven, I thought that Henry was in charge and was afraid that he would control Aratex. Then when I heard you were heir to two-thirds of the Devon estate, I knew you would somehow be involved."

"How did you learn of my Devon inheritance?" she asked. "From Abdullah?"

"Yes, I learned of your Devon inheritance from Abdullah."

"So," she sighed, "Abdullah did know about my Aratex holdings before he married me!" As she said this, she felt an overwhelming grief crushing her body. She felt as if she had been played as a little toy in a big game for the last five years.

"No, Sophia, he may have surmised, but he did not know." The king was emphatic. "Believe me, he truly loves you and only you. Just as I truly loved Barbara."

Chapter 42

Divorce, 1998

*S*ophia called her friend and trusted financial advisor Douglas in New York, pleading with him to come to Scotland and then fly to Arabia with her. She sounded so melancholy when she told him the news that he could not refuse her request. One of the king's 737s was dispatched to New York to pick him up.

In Scotland, through her tears, she explained what was happening. She and Abdullah must divorce in a traditional ceremony in front of the king in Arabia. Sophia and Douglas would fly in and fly out the next day. Both flights were scheduled to be under cover of darkness.

The next afternoon, they flew to Arabia. Rima met them at the airport and told Doug that the king wished to have an audience with him, and then Abdullah wished to see him also.

Sophia would stay in her villa until the ceremony the next day. Rima stayed with Sophia the entire night, often holding her friend as she cried.

Doug's meeting with the king was short. After greeting him warmly, the king, coming right to the point, said, "I do understand how distressed Sophia is at this turn of events. Rest assured, my son and I are also. I wanted you to know because you are the closest to a male relative that Sophia has. I insist she is to always be well taken care of."

Doug started to speak, but the king motioned him into silence. "Yes, I know about her wealth. And yes, I will expand that. What I really mean is she needs a friend. While the Grosvenors are also close friends, English society can be fickle. Please look after her as a favor for me."

"I will," Doug said quietly. And the meeting was over.

The next morning, Douglas's meeting with Abdullah was much harder. And then in a change of plan and protocol, Abdullah came to Sophia's room. His eyes were red, he had a strong five o'clock shadow, and he looked like he had not slept in days.

"Today will be the hardest day of my life, Sophia. I don't want to do this. I honestly believed that forever was forever. And I hope you can find it in your heart to still love me a little or at least forgive me." He started to walk out the door.

"Abdullah." He stopped and came back toward her. She put her hand on his cheek. "I tried with every ounce of my being I tried.l"

Pulling her close he whispered. "It is not you who failed. I know that Sophia. I failed and my country let you down. It is a burden I will carry for the rest of my life.

"I did mean I would love you forever. And I always will. Maybe what being one of two wives taught me was that love comes in many forms. While I will desperately miss our time together, just like you and Rima, we can still love in the manner available to us."

"And when you find someone else to spend your time with, I will be forgotten?" It hurt him to say it as much as it hurt Sophia to hear it.

"It will be hard to forget a man I still share so much with. Yes, that time may come. Please let us vow to cross that Rubicon when it arrives. Not today. Even then, I will love you. Now, *mon amour roi*, I have only one gift left for you.

"This envelope will explain. Would you please keep this a quiet truth? This is the access code to a safe in the Aratex medical laboratory. It is yours to do with as you please. This, my daily prayers, and my loyalty to our country are all I can give you now, my liege."

They were divorced in the ballroom of the king's palace—ironically, the same ballroom where she and Abdullah had danced to "Don't You Forget about Me." The shadows in the room added to the occupants' gloom.

She stood silently in the center of the room, dressed in a black abaya with a gold-encrusted veil, with only her eyes, glistening with unshed tears, showing.

Abdullah stomped into the room and took his place between the king and Douglas.

Sophia thought they were a strange trio, one frail and elderly king, an Arabian prince, and a Jewish merchant banker.

Abdullah's eyes, usually so vibrant, were dull. The look on his face was one of pure rage. Breaking tradition, he stepped forward and took Sophia's hand, squeezing it tightly. Quietly, he said, "Nothing can separate us forever. We will be together again in Paradise."

As he spoke, his look of anger turned to pain. Loudly enough for Doug and the king to hear, he said the words, "I divorce you, I divorce you, I divorce you," three times.

Sophia thought she was dying and was afraid she might faint. The tears just below the surface for both of them were not shed in public. Then Sophia bowed her head. In Arabic, very quietly, so only Abdullah could hear, she said, "I accept, *mon amour roi.*"

And it was done. Doug and a very quiet Sophia flew out that afternoon.

Doug pulled three envelopes from his jacket pocket as the plane left Arabian air space. "These are for you, Sophia. One is from Abdullah, the next is from the king, and the last includes papers for your divorce and settlement. I have been instructed to have you read them in reverse order—Abdullah's last. Before I do, I must confess to a secret that Abdullah kept from you."

Sophia almost stopped breathing. Did he have a girlfriend? A child somewhere? She was expecting the worst. "What is it, Doug?" she asked carefully.

"Whenever you two vacationed, Abdullah bought a house. He did so in your name. He has also given you the Lear and the G5. I hold all the deeds and funds to maintain them forever."

She sighed. "Great, I can fly around the world with my memories." Then she started to cry.

"Now," he said, "please read these."

Tears rolled down her cheeks, and her hands trembled as she accepted the envelopes. The first paper she pulled out was a stock certificate for 5 percent of Aratex Holdings. "I give you and Abdullah what Barbara gave to me in equal measure," said the accompanying note. The second was the paperwork for the Lawrence Foundation, and the final paper was the deed to her palace by the sea in Arabia.

The letter from the king was a loving yet simple explanation of his gifts. It closed with the words "Never will a woman be more missed." He had signed it with his first name only.

The final letter was from Abdullah. She was sobbing as she undid the seal on the envelope. It was handwritten on his letterhead.

Dearest Sophia,

Mon amour reine, I am as heartbroken as you are.

Sitting with our current sadness, it will take courage for us to believe we can bear the pain. We must for the sake of our love and our country. I will always carry your heart with me in my heart.

Unfortunately, now some business. First, I insist that I maintain your security at all times. Second, I have taken the liberty of having Sir Joshua file the necessary papers in Scotland ... I cannot say or write the word. Third, I look forward to seeing you at the next Aratex board meeting. Until then, I am your loving mon amour roi, as always and forever.

Nothing can separate us forever.

We will be together again in Paradise.

I will always love you.

Abdullah

311

Sophia turned to the east and silently mouthed her afternoon prayer from the Quran.

As the plane was descending into Heathrow to drop off Doug, Sophia said quite calmly, "Have I been willfully blind to everything for the last seven years? I wonder if he ever really loved me."

Douglas looked at her red, puffy face, saw more questions than answers and a whole lot of heartbreak, and finally answered. "Sophia, you may have been blinded by Abdullah's love for you. I believe it is still very real. Don't be so hard on yourself. You will heal in time." Putting his arm around her, trying to comfort her, he said, "Remember, I'll see you in two months in Australia. We're sailing the world championships, and I want to see Nockatunga."

She flew on to the Highlands in a daze. Captain Winston drove her from the airstrip to the cottage. When she arrived home to her cottage in Scotland, she found that Mrs. Kelly had arrived from London and had prepared a light meal. As soon as she finished her dinner, she said goodnight and went to her room. Numb with exhaustion, she finally fell into a deep sleep.

Two weeks later, the king of Arabia died of a massive stroke. As she watched the funeral and burial over her satellite TV feed from Arabia, she had mixed emotions. Abdullah bin Abbas, her now ex-husband, was now the king of Arabia. She was saddened by the old king's death, but her thoughts primarily went to the enormous responsibility her ex-husband now had, for the safety and well-being of thirty-four million people.

Slowly, she walked to her private prayer room, saying the words of Allah for the new king. Then she wandered back to the small study and wrote Abdullah an email.

Mon amour roi,

My prayers are with you for your grief and the hopes you have for the future of your kingdom.

Your amour reine

The next morning over coffee, Sophia was gazing out over the loch as a storm moved in across the Highlands. Finally, she began to grapple with her mixed and frequently turbulent emotions about her past. She had chosen this life yet was now uncertain how the events of the last few years had happened.

Sophia, she said to herself, *you are the author of your own life. We live with and in what we create. It was my choice to care enough to have heartbreak. It was my choice to ignore the bad parts. And now it is my choice to heal and move forward in peace.*

Made in United States
Orlando, FL
22 April 2023